U.S.S. SEAWOLF

ALSO BY PATRICK ROBINSON

One Hundred Days
(with Admiral Sir John "Sandy" Woodward)

True Blue

Nimitz Class

Kilo Class

H.M.S. Unseen

PATRICK ROBINSON

HarperCollins*Publishers*

U.S.S. SEAWOLF. Copyright © 2000 by Patrick Robinson. All rights reserved. Printed in the United States of America. No part of this book may be used or reproduced in any manner whatsoever without written permission except in the case of brief quotations embodied in critical articles and reviews. For information address HarperCollins Publishers Inc., 10 East 53rd Street, New York, NY 10022.

HarperCollins books may be purchased for educational, business, or sales promotional use. For information please write: Special Markets Department, HarperCollins Publishers Inc., 10 East 53rd Street, New York, NY 10022.

FIRST EDITION

Designed by Ruth Lee

Printed on acid-free paper

Library of Congress Cataloging-in-Publication Data has been applied for.

ISBN 0-06-019630-0

00 01 02 03 04 ❖/RRD 10 9 8 7 6 5 4 3 2 1

U.S.S. Seawolf is respectfully dedicated to the men of the U.S. Navy SEALs, the fighting troops who always operate in harm's way, and among whom valor is a common virtue.

CAST OF PRINCIPAL CHARACTERS

Senior Command

The President of the United States (Commander-in-Chief, U.S.
  Armed Forces)
Vice Admiral Arnold Morgan (National Security Adviser)
General Tim Scannell (Chairman of the Joint Chiefs of Staff)
General Cale Carter (U.S. Air Force Chief)
Harcourt Travis (Secretary of State)
Rear Admiral George R. Morris (Director, National Security
  Agency)

U.S. Navy Senior Command

Admiral Joseph Mulligan (Chief of Naval Operations)
Rear Admiral John Bergstrom (Commander, Special War
  Command [SPECWARCOM])

Admiral Archie Cameron (Commander-in-Chief, Pacific Fleet [CINCPAC])

Rear Admiral Freddie Curran (Commander, Submarine Force, Pacific Fleet [COMSUBPAC])

USS *Seawolf*

Captain Judd Crocker (Commanding Officer)
Lt. Commander Linus Clarke (Executive Officer)
Lt. Commander Cy Rothstein (Combat Systems Officer)
Lt. Commander Mike Schulz (Engineering Officer)
Lt. Commander Rich Thompson (Marine Engineering Officer)
Lt. Kyle Frank (Sonar Officer)
Lt. Shawn Pearson (Navigation Officer)
Lt. Andy Warren (Officer of the Deck)
Master Chief Petty Officer Brad Stockton (Chief of Boat)
Petty Officer Chase Utley (electronics)
Petty Officer Third Class Jason Colson (Captain's Writer)
Petty Officer Third Class Andy Cannizaro
Seaman Engineer Tony Fontana
Seaman Recruit Kirk Sarloos (torpedoes)

U.S. Navy Personnel

Commander Tom Wheaton (Commanding Officer, USS *Greenville*)
Captain Chuck Freeburg (Commanding Officer, USS *Vella Gulf*)
Lt. Commander Joe Farrell (Hornet bomber pilot)

U.S. Navy SEALs

Colonel Frank Hart (Senior SEAL Staff Officer, Mission Controller, USS *Ronald Reagan*)
Lt. Commander Rick Hunter (Assault Mission Leader)
Lt. Commander Russell "Rusty" Bennett (Team Leader Recon, Evacuation Beach, and Assault Team A)
Chief Petty Officer John McCarthy (2 I/C Assault Team A)

Lt. Dan Conway (Leader Assault Team B)
Lt. Paul Merloni (2 I/C Assault Team B)
Lt. Commander Olaf Davidson (Leader, Forward Landing Beach Group, and Assault Team C)
Lt. Ray Schaefer (2 I/C Assault Team C)
Lt. Bobby Allensworth (personal bodyguard to Lt. Commander Hunter)
Petty Officer Catfish Jones
Petty Officer Rocky Lamb
SEAL Riff "Rattlesnake" Davies
SEAL Buster Townsend (command radio operator)
Chief Petty Officer Steve Whipple (satchel bombs and machine gunner)

British SAS Personnel

Colonel Mike Andrews (Commander, Bradbury Lines)
Sergeant Fred Jones (Seconded SEAL Assault Team A)
Corporal Syd Thomas (Seconded SEAL Assault Team A)
Sergeant Charlie Murphy (Seconded SEAL Assault Team A)

CIA Command and Field Operatives

Jake Raeburn (Head of Far Eastern Desk)
Rick White (California Bank, Hong Kong)
Honghai Shan (Chinese International Travel Service)
Quinlei Dong (Canton Naval Base)
Quinlei Zhao (Pearl River trader)
Kexiong Gao (Pearl River trader)

People's Liberation Army/Navy

Admiral Zhang Yushu (Commander-in-Chief)
Vice Admiral Sang Ye (Chief of Naval Staff)
Admiral Zu Jicai (Commander, Southern Fleet)
Admiral Yibo Yunsheng (Commander, Eastern Fleet)

Colonel Lee Peng (Commanding Officer, *Xiangtan*)
Commander Li Zemin (Security Chief, Canton Naval Base)

White House Staff

Kathy O'Brien (private secretary to Admiral Morgan)

Court Martial Attorneys

Lt. Commander Edward Kirk (for the Pentagon)
Counsellor Philip Myerscough (for Lt. Commander Clarke)
Counsellor Art Mangone (for Captain Crocker)

U.S.S. SEAWOLF

1330. Wednesday, April 27, 2005.
Naval Air Tracking Station.
West of Hsinchu, North Taiwan.

SINCE FIRST LIGHT, THEY HAD BEEN OBSERVING the blue-water Fleet of the People's Liberation Army/Navy moving menacingly back and forth in a classic "racetrack" pattern, 50 miles offshore. Twenty-two warships in total, including the new 80,000-ton aircraft carrier from Russia, so new it did not yet have a name.

The Taiwanese had nervously tracked the destroyers of mainland China: the Luhus, the old Ludas and the new Luhai; they'd logged the surface-to-surface missiles unleashed in short fireballs by the Jiangwei frigates, just as they had done three times before in the previous 18 months.

They had watched the fleet move ever nearer, then finally cross the unseen dividing line down the middle of the Strait of Taiwan and continue into Taiwanese territorial waters. Instantly the supervisors signaled Tsoying, their main naval base, and the automatic alert to the U.S. Pacific Fleet in Pearl Harbor flashed onto the satellite.

Two hundred miles east of Taiwan, the American admiral on the giant U.S. Nimitz-class aircraft carrier *John C. Stennis* signaled his warships west. And the massively armed, 12-strong guided-missile fleet out of San Diego glowered, then turned their bows arrogantly back toward their friends on the independent island, which now felt the hot breath of the Chinese dragon.

But at 1357 on that clear, cool April day in the Taiwan Strait, every alert there had ever been in the tracking stations of Taiwan faded into obsolescence. Mainland China suddenly fired a big, short-range land-attack cruise missile straight at the capital city of Taipei.

The military tracking radars in Taiwan's coastal station west of Hsinchu picked it up 45 miles out, hurtling in over the Strait at 600 mph, low-level, no higher than 200 feet, on a varying course around zero-eight-zero, right out of Fujian Province. At first they thought it was an aircraft overflying the Chinese fleet, but it was too fast and too low, making 10 miles every minute.

There was no time to shoot it down, and decoys were useless against the kind of preprogammed inertial navigation system used in a Russian-designed M-11 cruise, which this most certainly was. The military barely had time to assess the danger before the missile came screaming in over the coastline, plainly visible to any local citizen who happened to look upward.

At the time there was heavy traffic all along the Taipei West Coast Freeway, and one military truck driver spotted it, couldn't believe his eyes, and drove straight into a tourist bus, ramming it right through the central guardrail into the path of oncoming traffic and causing a 59-vehicle pileup in which 14 people were killed.

Simultaneously, the emergency radio procedures desperately urged people to remain in their homes, if possible below ground, in the face of imminent missile attack. No one knew whether the cruise carried a nuclear-tipped warhead, but the danger of radiation was uppermost in the minds of the authorities.

Everyone in air traffic control at CKS International Airport, four miles from the traffic pileup, watched the missile streak across Taiwanese airspace, both onscreen and from the big viewing windows. It seemed to make a slight course adjustment and then rocketed across the city of Taoyuan. It was still making 600 mph and maintaining height as it cleared the railroad terminal, passing dead overhead the new McDonald's off Fuhsing Road.

Right now it was 120 seconds from Taiwan's capital and all the military could do was warn the populace to take cover. They informed the U.S. and United Nations Headquarters that they were under immediate missile attack from China, and at 1406 the cruise came in sight of Taipei.

But, to the astonishment of the military, the missile kept right on going, straight across the center of the city, over the Tanshui River and on to the second-largest container port in the country, Keelung up on the northeast coast. But it did not stop there, either, but headed right on out into the Pacific, where it crashed and blew up 30 miles off Taiwan's coast.

The Taiwan military protested in the strongest terms to Beijing, seeking assurances that there were no more missiles on the way. The Prime Minister himself contacted Beijing directly, to deliver an icy warning to China's Paramount Ruler that Taiwan's armed forces would fight to the last inch of their ground to preserve their independence. And, if they had to, Taiwan would hit back at China with U.S.-built guided missiles, which were far superior to anything the Chinese had in their current arsenal.

"We may go," the Prime Minister concluded. "But we'll take Beijing with us. That I promise."

The Chinese neither apologized nor gave any assurances that such a thing would not happen again.

0900 (local). Wednesday, April 27, 2005.
Office of the National Security Adviser.
The White House, Washington.

Admiral Arnold Morgan was listening with mounting fury to the reason why the Chinese ambassador to Washington was not able to report to the White House in the next 20 minutes.

"He's in a conference, Arnold," insisted his secretary. "They won't even put me through to his assistant. They say they'll get a message to him and he'll call you in a half-hour. He's actually speaking with the General Secretary of the Communist Party, who you know is in town dining with the President tonight."

"Kathy O'Brien, upon whose very footsteps I worship the immediate airspace," growled the NSA. "I want you to listen to me very carefully. I do not care if Comrade Ling Fucking Guofeng, Honorable Ambassador to our nation, is in direct spiritual contact with Chiang Kaishek, or speaking at this very moment to the deranged ghost of Mao Zedong or any of those other goddamned coolies who rose to power. I want him here in twenty minutes, otherwise he will be Ling Fucking Guofeng, *FORMER* ambassador to our country. I'LL HAVE HIM DEPORTED BY SEVENTEEN-HUNDRED TONIGHT."

"Arnold, I will pass on your wishes to the highest possible authority."

Seventeen minutes later, Ambassador Ling was escorted into Admiral Morgan's office.

"Siddown. This is serious. And listen." The admiral was not in a gracious mood.

The ambassador sat, and said with the utmost courtesy, "Would it be out of order, Admiral, for me to wish you good morning?"

"Yes, it would, since you mention it. I'm more concerned with the fact that a few hours ago, your goddamned pain-in-the-ass country almost caused a fucking war."

"Admiral, surely you are not referring to that insignificant incident in our Taiwan Strait?"

"Insignificant? You crazy sonsabitches threw an M-11 cruise missile straight over the city of Taipei. You call that insignificant?"

"Admiral, I have received a most reliable communiqué that it was a mere accident. The missile somehow became out of control . . . in any event it failed safe, and flew into the Pacific. Quite harmless."

"Ling, I don't believe you. I think you guys have taken up a new twenty-first-century sport called *Frightening the Taiwanese to Death*—I mean you had a battle fleet in their territorial waters at the precise time the missile came in. What the hell did you expect them to think?"

"Well, I can appreciate their anxiety."

"Ling, what would you have done if the Taiwanese had had a little more time, and our Carrier Battle Group had been a lot closer? How about if the Taiwanese had started throwing missiles back? And we decided to take out a couple of your navy bases, maybe knock out a few of your missile sites? What then?"

"Admiral, I do not think that would have been very wise, for either the Taiwanese or yourselves. We are no longer the backward, militarily unsophisticated nation you once considered us. These days we have missiles to match your own, in both power and range. Serious intercontinental ballistic missiles. ICBMs, Admiral. Made in China. You would do well to remember that."

"Ling, the most you guys have ever done is to employ a group of devious little spies and sneak thieves to try and steal from us. But when you get the stuff it's always too advanced for you to adapt. You've had more missile test failures than even I can count. You always *think* you can match us for military hardware and technology. But you never can. And you never will. Any more than we're any good at chicken chow mein."

Ambassador Ling ignored the insult. "Admiral," he said, "your assessment of our capabilities was probably accurate for many years. But no longer. We have effective long-range missiles now. We are as big a threat to you as you have always been to us."

"Maybe. But we don't go around launching cruise missiles to fly over the capital cities of other countries, terrifying the populace, edging nations into war. So I'm warning you and your government, right here and right now: You wanna play hardball with the US of A over the nation of Taiwan, you better take a damn close look at the rule book. Because when we decide to play, we play for keeps."

Ambassador Ling did not answer immediately. Instead he looked thoughtful, academic, like the professor he once was. And when he spoke it was quietly, and carefully considered.

"Nonetheless, Admiral," he said, "should it come to an ICBM contest between us, I wonder if you would really care to swap Taiwan for Los Angeles."

Friday, October 7, 2005.
Pacific Ocean. 120 miles west-southwest of
San Diego, California.

THE DARKNESS CREPT EVER WESTWARD THROUGH low, overcast skies, and the gusting northwest breeze whipped white crests onto the long wavetops. At this time of the evening, in the 20 minutes of no-man's time between sunset and nightfall streaming in over the immense ocean, the Pacific takes on a deeply malevolent mantle. Its awesome troughs and rising waves glisten darkly in the last of the light. There's no bright, friendly phosphorescence in the bottomless waters out here. To stare down at the black seascape, even from the safe reassuring deck of a warship, is to gaze into the abyss. *Oh Lord, your ocean is so vast, and my boat is so small.*

Eight hundred feet into the abyss, way beneath the twilight melancholy of the surface, USS *Seawolf* thundered forward, making almost 40 knots, somewhere south of the Murray Fracture Zone. The 9,000-ton United States Navy attack submarine was heavily into her months of sea trials, following a massive three-year overhaul. *Seawolf* was not at war, but a passing whale could have been forgiven for thinking she was. Forty knots is one hell of a speed for a 350-foot-long submarine. But *Seawolf* had been built for speed, constructed to lead the underwater cavalry of the Navy, anywhere, anytime. And right now she was in deep submergence trials, testing her systems, flexing her muscles in the desolate black wilderness of America's western ocean.

Powered by two 45,000-horsepower turbines and a state-of-the-art Westinghouse nuclear reactor, *Seawolf* was the most expensive submarine ever built. Too expensive. The Navy was permitted to build only three of her class—*Connecticut* and USS *Jimmy Carter* were the others—before budget restraints caused the cancellation of these jet-black emperors of the deep. Over a billion dollars had been spent on her research and development before *Seawolf* was commissioned in 1997.

Now, after her multimillion-dollar overhaul, the submarine was, without question, the finest underwater warship in the world, the fastest, quietest nuclear boat. At 20 knots there was nothing to be heard beyond the noise of the water parted by the bulk of her hull. She could pack a ferocious wallop, too. *Seawolf* was armed with a phalanx of Tomahawk land-attack missiles that could travel at almost 1,000 mph to a target 1,400 miles distant. She could unleash a missile with a 454-kilogram warhead and hit an enemy ship 250 miles away. She bristled with eight 26-inch torpedo tubes, launching bases for big wire-guided Gould Mark 48s, homing if necessary to 27 miles. Highly effective, these weapons offered a kill probability of 50 percent, second only to the British Spearfish.

Seawolf carried sonars estimated as three times more effective than even the most advanced Los Angeles–class boats. She used both TB16 and TB29 surveillance and towed arrays. For active close-range detection she used the BQS 24 system. Her electronic support measures (ESM) were nothing short of sensational. Any ship anywhere within 50 miles could not move, communicate, or even activate its sonar or radar without *Seawolf* hearing every last telltale sound. She was not a gatherer of clandestine information, she was an electronic vacuum cleaner, the last word in the U.S. Navy's most secretive, private, advanced research.

And Captain Judd Crocker was darned proud of her. "Never been a submarine to match this one," he would say. "And I doubt there ever will be. Not in my lifetime."

And that was worthwhile praise. The son of a surface ship admiral, grandson of another, he had been born into a family of Cape Cod yacht racers, and he had been around boats of all sizes since he could walk. He never inherited his father's unique talents as a helmsman, but he was good, better than most, though destined always to be outclassed by the beady-eyed Admiral Nathaniel Crocker.

Judd was 40 years old now. A lifelong submariner, he had served as *Seawolf*'s first Executive Officer back in 1997 and commanded her five years later. He received his promotion to Captain just before she came out of overhaul, and resumed command in the high summer of the year 2005.

That was the culmination of all his boyhood dreams, and the culmination of a plan he had made at the age of 15 when his father had taken him out to watch the annual race from Newport around Block Island and back. The admiral was not racing himself, but he and Judd were guests on board one of the New York Yacht Club committee boats. It was a day of intermittent fog out in the bay, and several competitors had trouble navigating.

Even Judd's committee boat was a little wayward in the early afternoon, straying too far southwest of the island, about a half-mile from the point of approach of a 7,000-ton Los Angeles–class submarine rolling past on the surface toward the Groton submarine base. The sun was out at the time, and Judd had watched through binoculars one of the great black warhorses of the U.S. Navy. He was transfixed by the sight of her, noting the number 690 painted on her sail. He almost died of excitement when a couple of the officers on the bridge waved across the water to the committee boat. And he had stared after the homeward-bound USS *Philadelphia* long after she became too small to identify on the horizon.

Submarines often have that effect on nonmilitary personnel. There is a quality about them, so profoundly sinister, so utterly chilling. And Judd had gazed upon the ultimate iron fist of U.S. sea power with barely contained awe. In his stomach there was a tight little knot of apprehension, except that he knew it was not really apprehension. It was fear, the kind of fear everyone feels when a 100 mph express train comes shrieking straight through a country railroad station, a shuddering, ear-splitting, howling display of monstrous power that could knock down the station and half the town if it ever got out of control. The difference was that the submarine achieved the same effect in menacing near-silence.

Judd Crocker was not afraid of the submarine. He was fascinated by a machine that could demolish the city of Boston, if it felt so inclined. And as he turned back to the infinitely lesser thrills of the yacht race, he was left with one thought in his mind. What he really wanted was to drive the USS *Philadelphia*, and that meant the United States Naval Academy at Annapolis three years hence. From that moment on, Judd never took his eye off the ball, which was why, a quarter of a century later, he commanded the most awesome submarine ever to leave a shipyard.

"Conn—Captain . . . reduce speed to twenty knots. Five up to five hundred feet . . . right standard rudder . . . steer course two-two-zero."

Judd's commands were always delivered in a calm voice, but there was pressure behind the words, betraying not anxiety, but the fact that he had given the matter careful thought before speaking.

"Conn, aye, sir."

Judd turned to his XO, Lt. Commander Linus Clarke, who had just returned from a short conference with the engineers.

"Everything straight down there, XO?"

"Minor problem with a jammed valve, sir. Chief Barrett freed it up. Says it can't happen again. We going deeper?"

"Just a little for the moment, but I want her at one thousand feet a couple of hours from now."

They were a hugely unlikely combination in command, these two. The captain was a barrel-chested man, a shade under six feet tall, with a shock of jet-black hair, inherited from his mother's Irish antecedents. Jane Kiernan had also bequeathed to him her deep hazel-colored eyes and the carthorse strength of the male members of her family, farmers and fishermen from the wild windswept outer reaches of Connaught on Ireland's western shores.

Judd was a rock-steady naval commander: experienced, cool under pressure, and self-trained in the art of avoiding panic in any of its forms. He was popular with his crew of 100-plus because his reputation and record demanded respect, and because his presence, a mixture of imperturbable confidence, professional approach, and great experience, all leavened with a quiet sense of humor, inspired total trust.

He knew as much as any of his expert crew, and often more. But he still took care to show that he valued their work and opinions. He would mildly set them straight only when strictly necessary—often with an apparently simple and innocuous question that would cause his adviser to think again, and work it out for himself. He was anyone's idea of the perfect commanding officer.

Judd had high qualifications in hydrodynamics, electronics, propulsion, and nuclear physics. His appointment to command *Seawolf* had come directly from the top, from Admiral Joe Mulligan, the Chief of Naval Operations, in person, himself a former nuclear submarine commander.

The reasons behind Linus Clarke's recent appointment as Captain Crocker's executive officer were less apparent. The lieutenant commander was only 34, and he was known to have served for several months with the CIA at Headquarters in Langley, Virginia. No one ever asked anyone precisely what he had been doing there. But serving naval officers with Intelligence backgrounds were rarely appointed second-in-command on big nuclear attack submarines.

Linus wore his mild celebrity with relish. He was a tall, slim Oklahoman with dead-straight floppy reddish hair. And he wore it rather longer than is customary among the disciplined officer corps of the U.S. Navy. But his rise had apparently been consistent, and he had graduated from Annapolis in the top quarter of his class. But no one was interested then, and he managed to disappear very successfully for a few years before emerging from the portals of the CIA with a rather mysterious reputation.

There was a total of 14 officers in the wardroom of USS *Seawolf*, and while it was obvious that each of them knew something about Lt. Commander Clarke, no one quite knew everything. Except for Captain Crocker. And, like the rest of them, he avoided the subject. Among the enlisted men there was a certain amount of chatter, principally emanating from a seaman in the ship's laundry who claimed that the name on the XO's dog tags was not Linus Clarke. But he could not remember what the name was, and he was thus only half-believed. Nonetheless, there was chatter.

Linus himself was naturally rather secretive, and he added to this by adopting a measure of irony to his conversation, a thin, knowing smile decorating his wide, freckled face. He also adopted the slightly self-serving attitude of one who is a bit too daring and adventurous to spend a long time in the company of the hard, realistic men who handle the front-line muscle of the U.S. Navy. He undoubtedly saw himself as Hornblower, as opposed to Rickover.

A typical Clarke entrance to the wardroom would be, "Okay men, has there been any truly serious screw-up you need me to sort out?" He always grinned when he said it, but most people thought he meant it anyway.

One week after his appointment to *Seawolf*, still moored in San Diego, there had been a small cocktail party ashore. After three quite strenuous glasses of bourbon on the rocks, Lt. Commander Clarke had ventured up to his new captain and confided, "Sir, do you actually know why I have been detailed to your ship?"

"No, can't say I do," replied Judd.

"Well, sir, we're going on a highly classified mission, and as you know, I've been on similar missions before. Basically, I'm here to make sure you don't screw it up. You know, for lack of experience."

Captain Judd Crocker gazed at him steadily, concealing his total disbelief that *any* jumped-up two-and-a-half, even this one, would dare to speak to him in such a way. But he rose above it, smiled sardonically, and declined to say what he really thought—*Oh, really? Well, I'm deeply comforted to have such a rare presence on board.*

At that moment, Linus Clarke made a mental note to be extra careful in all of his dealings with the commanding officer in the future. To himself, he thought, *This is one cool dude . . . I thought my little speech might throw him a little . . . but it sure didn't.*

He was correct there. Judd Crocker had been around ranking admirals all of his life, men of enormous intelligence. He had sailed the East Coast with the heavyweight financiers of the New York Yacht Club, crewing on the annual summer cruise up the New England coast, and sometimes navigating all the way up to the glorious archipelago of the Maine islands. Since he was a boy, and even when he was a midshipman, he'd sat in some of the most expensive staterooms in some of the biggest oceangoing yachts in the United States, and listened to conversations of great moment. It would take rather more than an insolent, smartass remark by a slightly drunk lieutenant commander to unnerve him. But he assumed, too, that young Clarke had also had his share of company with the great and the mighty.

Nonetheless, they did not form what the Navy traditionally hopes will become a natural trusting partnership in command of a ship that had cost something close to the national debt.

Beyond the Silent Service, Judd Crocker was married to the former Nicole Vanderwolk, 10 years his junior and the daughter of the redoubtable Harrison Vanderwolk, a big-hitting Florida-based financier with major holdings in three states. Like the Crockers, the Vanderwolks had a waterfront summer house on toney Sea View Avenue in Osterville, a couple of doors down from the former residence of the U.S. Army's youngest-ever general, "Jumping" Jim Gavin of the 82nd Airborne, legend of the Normandy landings.

The Vanderwolks, the Gavins, and the Crockers were lifelong friends, and when Judd married Nicole it was cause for a mass celebration in a yellow-and-white-striped tent, the size of the Pentagon on the sunlit shores of Nantucket Sound.

Unhappily, they were unable to have children, and in 1997, shortly after Judd was appointed to *Seawolf*, they adopted two little Vietnamese girls, ages three and four, renaming them Jane and Kate. By the turn of the century they were all ensconced in another waterfront property out on Point Loma in San Diego, both sets of parents having clubbed together to buy the $2 million home as an investment while Judd was stationed on the West Coast under the command of the Submarine Force U.S. Pacific Fleet (SUBPAC). The deal was simple: When it was time to sell, the admiral and Harrison would receive $1.1 million each. Judd and Nicole would keep the change. The way things were going in the California real estate market, Judd and Nicole were winning, hands down.

The private life of Linus Clarke was rather more obscure. He was unmarried, but there were rumors of a serious girlfriend back at his family home in Oklahoma, a place to which Linus retreated at every available opportunity. He made the journey by commercial jet to Amarillo, Texas, and then used the small Beechcraft single-engine private plane owned by his father for the last northerly leg of the journey.

And once on the family cattle ranch, deep in the Oklahoma panhandle, Linus, as usual, disappeared. Given his family connections, it was not much short of a miracle that no word ever appeared about him, even in local newspapers. But perhaps even more unlikely was that he had always avoided the media during his tenure in Washington and at the navy base in Norfolk, Virginia.

Judd Crocker thought it a major achievement by the young lieutenant commander, but of course, on a far grander scale the English royal family had been doing it for most of the century, effectively "hiding" sons Prince Charles and Prince Andrew for years while they served in the Royal Navy. It had been the same with King George V, of course, and Prince Philip. Indeed, Prince Andrew hardly had his photograph taken when he flew his helicopter off the deck of HMS *Invincible* during the Falklands War. It was the same with Linus Clarke. And he seemed determined to keep it that way.

And so the aura of mystique clung to him. On the lower decks the men knew who he was, and that he had CIA connections. But the subject was not aired publicly. In the wardroom he was watched carefully. It was an unspoken fact that no one wanted him to make a mistake.

"I guess," remarked Lt. Commander Cy Rothstein, the combat systems officer, "we always have to remember just who he is."

"That's probably the one thing we ought to forget," replied the captain. "And we better hope he can, too. Clarke has a major job on this ship, whoever the hell he is."

Right now, as *Seawolf* cruised through the pitch-black depths of the Pacific, still making 20 knots, Judd Crocker was preparing to go deeper, down to almost 1,000 feet, for the torpedo tube trials, another searching examination of the submarine's fitness for front-line duty.

Behind Judd Crocker's crew were weeks and weeks of meticulous checking in which every system in the ship had been tested at the primary, secondary and tertiary level. They'd completed their "Fast Cruise"—driving the systems hard while still moored alongside, still fast to the wall. They'd tested for "fire, famine and flood," Navyspeak for any forthcoming catastrophe. They'd done all the drills, all the tuning, all the routines, checking and changing the water, changing the air, running the reactor, checking the periscopes, checking the masts.

They'd found defects. Engineers from *Seawolf*'s original builders, General Dynamics of New London, had been aboard for weeks, fixing, replacing, and adjusting. The process was exhaustive and meticulous, because when calamity comes to a submarine, the kind of calamity perhaps easily dealt with on a surface ship, it can spell the end for the underwater warriors. Laborious and time-consuming as sea trials may be, every last man in a submarine's crew gives them 100 percent of their effort. Pages and pages of reports had been written, signed, and logged as they tested and retested.

Out here in the Pacific they were effectively going over all of the same ground again, the same stuff they had checked over and over on the Fast Cruise. But this time they were at sea, and that added a massive new dimension to the equation. Moreover, these tests would be conducted both dived and on the surface.

"*Conn—Captain. Bow down ten . . . one thousand feet . . . make your speed fifteen knots . . . right standard rudder . . . steer course three-six-zero . . .*"

Judd Crocker's commands were crisp and clear, and they all heard the slight change in the beat of the turbines as *Seawolf* slowed and slewed around to the north, heading down into the icy depths.

The captain turned to his XO and said, "I'm going to run those tube tests again. You might go up for'ard in a while and take a look. I still think those switches are awful close together."

Fifteen minutes later, Linus Clarke made his way to the forward compartment, which housed the launching mechanisms for *Seawolf*'s principal weapon. By the time he arrived, Chief Petty Officer Jeff Cardozo had already supervised the loading, easing the torpedoes through the massive, round hinged door. The identical door at the seaward end of the tube was of course sealed shut, not only hydraulically, but also by the gigantic pressure of the ocean 1,000 feet down.

The really tricky part occurs next, when the air is vented out of the tube, ready for the tube's flood valve to be opened to let seawater in. This will ultimately equalize the pressure inside the firing tube with that of the sea beyond the outer door. Chief Cardozo was on duty, eyeballing his tubes crew.

Nineteen-year-old Seaman Recruit Kirk Sarloos from Long Beach was at his post in front of the panel of switches that controls the torpedo systems. After flooding the tubes, equalizing the pressure inside with the sea pressure outside the hull, and opening the bow shutters, the brutally powerful pressurized air turbine system will blast the torpedoes out into the ocean without leaving as much as a bubble on the surface. When the missiles have warheads fitted—not today—that procedure will spell death. For someone.

"*Number one and number two tubes ready for flooding . . .*"

"*FLOOD NUMBER ONE TUBE. . . !*"

Kirk hit the two switches for number one tube, listening to the hiss of air forced out through the vent by the water rushing in through the flood valve. He shut both valves as he heard the hiss turn to a gurgling, crackling noise when the last of the air was displaced by seawater. He hit a third switch, equalizing the pressures in case she changed depth.

"*NUMBER ONE TUBE EQUALIZED,*" he called. "*FLOOD AND VENT VALVES SHUT.*"

"Open number one tube bow doors."

Again Kirk hit a switch. *"Number one bow door and shutter open."*

Number one tube was now ready to fire.

"FLOOD NUMBER TWO TUBE."

Kirk's eyes scanned the switchboard, and he flipped both switches. Except he hit the flood-and-vent switches for number one tube by mistake, and a steel bar of water blew clean through the open valve and caught him hard in the upper chest, the colossal force hurling him 10 feet back across the compartment into a bank of machinery. At this depth the pressure behind the water was equal to around 30 atmospheres.

A lethal inch-wide column of ocean was blasting straight into the casing of the torpedo-loading gear, breaking up into a fine dense mist of blinding water particles. Kirk lay motionless, facedown in the deafening thunder of the incoming ocean. It was like a roar from the core of the earth, a hiss that sounded like a shriek, as the single jet dissolved into a lashing white screen of spray, completely obscuring everything. In that hell-kissed compartment, the three men in the compartment couldn't see, couldn't hear, and couldn't be heard.

Chief Cardozo knew where Kirk was, and he covered his eyes from the sting of the spray. With his head down he struggled through the water. It was 15 feet but seemed like 15 miles, pushing forward in the disorienting blindness of the flood. He grabbed the young seaman and somehow dragged him clear of the blast of seawater. Kirk was groggy, but he hadn't drowned.

Lt. Commander Clarke, unfamiliar with the sheer force of the ocean at this depth, grabbed the nearest intercom and yelled, *"WE HAVE A MAJOR LEAK FOR'ARD. BLOW ALL MAIN BALLAST AND SURFACE, CAPTAIN. FOR CHRIST'S SAKE . . ."* He exited the torpedo room and raced up to the conn.

Captain Crocker, surprised at the unorthodox intervention of his XO, but aware now that there was a problem, overruled his number two. *"I HAVE THE CONN. PLANESMAN . . . BELAY THAT ORDER . . . TEN UP . . . MAKE YOUR DEPTH TWO HUNDRED FEET . . ."*

Now in the conn, Lt. Commander Clarke could not believe his ears. Agitated, his ears still ringing from the shattering blast of the leak, he turned to the chief of the boat, the senior enlisted man aboard the submarine, now in the control room, Master Chief Petty Officer Brad Stockton from Georgia.

"Is he crazy? This submarine is sinking. We've got an unbelievable leak in the torpedo room. Jesus Christ! We gotta get to the surface."

"Easy, sir," replied the veteran master chief. "The boss knows what he's doing."

Linus Clarke stared at Brad in disbelief. "That water's gonna sink us. He hasn't seen it. I have." And he turned as if to argue further with his captain. But the master chief grabbed his arm in a steel grip and hissed, "STEADY, SIR."

Judd Crocker turned to his XO and quietly asked, "Did you shut the bulkhead door behind you ?"

Linus Clarke hesitated, and then admitted, "Er . . . nosir."

"Good," said the CO. "Check it's still open."

Linus began to wonder if he could get anything right today, and moved off to check the door.

Judd Crocker turned to the combat systems officer now standing beside him, Lt. Commander Cy Rothstein, the smooth, composed intellect of the ship, known locally as "Einstein."

"This may be quite minor, Cy," he said. "I just want to cool it. I know a leak at depth is unnerving. But I can't feel the pressure increasing in my ears. And look at the barometer. No change. Even if we are taking on water, the flow rate is small, the leak is small. Right now I have to conclude it's not sinking us.

"I don't know how bad it is down there, Cy. But the trim's not altering significantly. I'm damn sure it's not going to sink us in the next twenty minutes. Go deal with the problem. Aside from a lot of noise and flooding, which we seem to be coping with, there's nothing disastrous happening . . . yet. So let's not act as if there is. Because that way we might make it worse."

"Aye, sir."

Both men knew that only the most thorough mental preparation by the CO for all imaginable eventualities will ultimately ensure the survival of the crew. Fear is the enemy when things go wrong, because panic follows fear, and inappropriate reaction follows panic. Confusion follows that, with disaster close behind them all. Judd Crocker knew the rules. Especially the unwritten ones.

At this point Master Chief Stockton and Linus Clarke reentered the control room.

"Hi, Brad. How do we look ?"

"It's only a tube vent valve, sir. We don't have a hole punched in the hull or anything. It's just a matter of shutting the damn thing and then getting the water pumped out."

"Someone make the wrong switch?"

"Guess so."

"Schulz got it in hand?"

"I wouldn't say that, sir. But he's on the case."

Meanwhile the water continued to blast through the valve and into the torpedo room, the water eventually collecting in the bilges. The engineers worked to close the valve. But the entire electric system in the torpedo room was blown, so it had to be done by hand. Which was incredibly difficult because it was so close to the steel bar of water, which was prone to knock men clean across the compartment.

However great, however small, a leak at depth in a submarine plants fear in the minds of the men who operate her. There was already, inevitably, only one word in the minds of some of them: *Thresher*, SSN 593, the Navy's most advanced and complex attack submarine, which sank with all hands 200 miles off Cape Cod on April 10, 1963.

Every submariner knew the story, and in several minds there were already alarming similarities. *Thresher* had gone to the bottom with her entire crew within 10 minutes of incurring a major unstoppable leak in her engine room. The men of *Seawolf* had now been working for seven minutes, and that span of time gave them room to think about one of the Navy's worst-ever disasters, the loss, 42 years earlier, of the top American nuclear submarine because of a leak during her sea trials in the deep submergence phase. *Jesus, was this creepy, or what?*

The U.S. Navy's final report on the loss was required reading among officers and irresistible to the men. It laid the likely and primary blame on a catastrophic failure of the casting of a big hull valve that effectively left tons of water bursting every second through a 12-inch-diameter hole in the pressure hull. There was no way to shut the valve off. There was no valve left.

On that fatal spring morning in 1963, the submarine hit the bottom and broke up minutes after it first reported a problem to its accompanying warship USS *Skylark*. Sixteen officers, 96 enlisted men, and 17 civilian engineers perished with her. And like *Seawolf*, she was, without doubt, the best submarine in the U.S. Navy.

The captain too had allowed the apparition of the sinking *Thresher* to flicker across his mind. But being Judd Crocker, he was able to discard it almost instantly. Not so Lt. Commander Linus Clarke. "My God, sir," he blurted. "I implore you to take this ship to the surface."

The CO stared at his number two. "XO, take the conn. Slow down to ten knots. Clear your baffles and come to periscope depth . . . then prepare to surface if I so order. I'm going for'ard to inspect the damage. You have the ship."

"Aye, sir, I have the ship."

Judd Crocker could see that the XO's mouth was dry, and there was a strange cast to Linus's voice as he ordered, *"Helmsman— XO. Make your speed ten . . . right standard rudder, come to course one-two-zero. Sonar-conn . . . clearing baffles prior to coming to periscope depth."*

Judd never even bothered to change into seaboots, just made his way for'ard, pondering, as all COs might do at times such as these, why *Thresher* had imploded and crashed to the bottom with such alarming speed: first indication of a problem 0913, slammed into the seabed 8,000 feet below at 0918.

Seawolf's CO had always had his own private theories as to why the disaster occurred with such terrifying swiftness. First, he believed that the old method of linking alarm systems was a truly lousy idea, because one instantly triggered the next, which triggered the next, which ended up with an automatic reactor scram when the power cut out.

But the key to *Thresher*, according to the studies of Judd Crocker, was that she was going too slowly, creeping along 1,000 feet below the surface at only around four knots. When the valve casing burst and the reactor shut down, she had power for just a very few minutes, but she had no momentum, and she used her power revving her turbines, building speed to drive her upward virtually from a standing start. That power, Judd believed, failed when she was only 150 feet below the surface. There just was not sufficient thrust to carry her upward all the way, and she simply slid back down, gathering speed before crashing into the bottom at some 80 knots.

When he arrived at the scene of the flood he was taken aback by the noise, the apparent amount of seawater entering the ship, and the stupefying roar of the leak. Lt. Commander Schulz appeared to have the situation in hand, and he had two burly engineers, wielding wrenches, shutting the valve, soaked through, working in the dark mist in a maze of pipes and valves, fighting their way to get at the bronze fitting.

And even as he stood there, already soaked by the freezing spray, unable to speak because of the noise, he felt Mike Schulz tap him on the shoulder and, grinning, offer a silent thumbs-up.

As the valve was finally shut and the noise stopped, Judd squelched his way back to the control room and announced that the torpedo tube trials would be delayed only as long as it took to pump out the water, repair the electronics and clean the place up. He didn't want to get too far behind the eight ball. This section of the tests was supposed to be completed by noon the following day.

And once more he ordered a speed change, back to 20 knots, running silent, steady, without further hysterics. The way he liked it.

"Carry on, XO," he said. "Go back down to eight hundred feet at twenty knots. I'm just going back to change my shoes. I'll be back in five. Get someone to bring me a cup of coffee, willya? I'll drink it while you're changing your underpants."

Linus Clarke had the sense to laugh.

Thursday evening. June 15, 2006.
The Pineapple Bar. Pearl City, Hawaii.

"Well, guys, we got our celebrity XO back, right?"

Chief Brad Stockton was referring to the one fact that had occurred on this day that *everyone* knew. Lt. Commander Linus Clarke, fresh from another six-month stint at CIA headquarters, had arrived by air from San Diego to resume his duties on *Seawolf.* The CO had been palpably noncommittal in his assessment of the merit of that appointment. In Chief Stockton's view, Judd had always known that Linus would be his number two on this particular mission.

They were leaving in a few days, *Seawolf* having finally completed her trials. But their destination remained wrapped in secrecy. In Brad's opinion they were heading southwest for a long way, bound for the Indian Ocean and then the Arabian Sea, where there was the usual unrest along the oil tanker routes, Iran still making veiled threats about her historical ownership of the Persian Gulf.

Among the rest of this cheerful gathering, on this warm tropical night just north of Pearl Harbor, opinion was divided. Petty Officer Chase Utley, the communications operator, thought they might be headed northwest, way up the Pacific toward the Kamchatka Peninsula, where the Russians were reportedly planning to conduct missile tests off their base at Petropavluvsk.

"Jesus, I hope the hell not," said veteran Seaman engineer Tony Fontana. "That place is the goddamned end of the world, coast of Siberia for Christ's sake. We'd be about ten thousand miles from the nearest bar."

"Well, how the hell could that matter?" said Chase. "We never get out of the ship on these patrols anyway."

"That's not the point," retorted Fontana. "It's just a feeling of being at least somewhere close to civilization."

"For civilization read Budweiser," said Stockton, grinning.

"I'm serious," added Fontana. "You guys don't understand. There's a terrible feeling . . . kinda desolate when you're operating at the absolute ass-end of the world off Siberia. You just know there's nothing there, nothing in the sea, or even on the land, 'cept for rocks and trees and shit. Something happens, you're a dead sonofabitch, thousands of miles from anywhere."

"You ever been up to the Kamchatka?"

"Well, no. But I used to know a guy whose cousin had been there!"

They all fell over laughing. Fontana was a funny guy who really should have gone for a career in standup comedy, or at least on television. He'd never quite advanced as he should have in the Navy, owing to a determination to be the last man to leave any party. He'd twice missed his ship, which had been regarded as a character flaw by the powers that be. But the tall, tough, Ohio-born engineer was outstanding at his job, and various COs had found a way to get him forgiven. Just as well, in the opinion of Brad Stockton. Tony Fontana had been the man who had shut the valve in the torpedo room the previous October.

At this point newly promoted Petty Officer Third Class Andy Cannizaro from Mandeville, Louisiana, arrived with an armful of beers, set them down on the table and expounded his own theory on where they might be headed two days hence.

"Shit, it's obvious to anyone except for a bunch of morons," he confided. "*Seawolf* is going to China."

"China? Fuck that," said Tony. "Crazy bastards will probably try to sink us. Fuck that."

"You ever been there?" asked Andy.

"Sure. My uncle used to run a laundry in Shanghai . . . went broke . . . guy by the name of Kash Mai Chek."

Seaman Fontana's endless store of magnificently awful one-liners was so vast that no one could ever quite remember whether they had heard them before or not. But they always got a major laugh, mainly because they were always funny, but also because everyone liked Tony.

"Jesus, this is unbelievable," said Andy. "Like trying to have a conversation in a nuthouse. Anyway, when we leave here I happen to know that our course is two-seven-zero, due west, and in case any of you guys are having trouble with that, it's a direct course to Taiwan . . . and I guess y'all know what that means."

"I'm not sure you're right, Andy," said the group's second petty officer third class, Jason Colson. "I'm not revealing any secrets, but I can say I've never once heard the word 'Taiwan' mentioned recently."

Jason, like Andy, was 24. But whereas Andy was actively involved in the pure movement of the submarine, watching the planes and the pressurized water systems, Jason was the captain's writer, which essentially made him a clerk. But he was privy to a lot of information, and at a major level of secrecy, as he formally recorded and logged the actions and plans of the commanding officer of *Seawolf.*

If anyone at this table had the remotest idea where this next mission was going, it would most certainly have been Petty Officer Jason Colson, and he most certainly did not know.

"Well," said Andy, "I did hear we were headed due west, not southwest. And if we hold that course we'll run straight up one of the eastern beaches of Taiwan."

"Christ, that's nearly four thousand miles away."

"Yeah, but we can knock off seven hundred miles in a day at two-thirds speed," said Fontana. "Pushed, we can make nearly a thousand miles. Jesus, we could be on the beach a week from now, surrounded by Taiwanese pussy . . . slit-eyed beauties fighting to get at me. Give me that beer, Andy. I'm trying to hold myself back."

Everyone laughed again. But then Chase Utley said quite seriously, "Do you guys really think we might be going to China? Because if we are, that really gives me the creeps. That place is damn scary. I mean, what was all that shit about in the papers last week?"

Brad Stockton, the Senior Petty Officer, the absolute focus for all interdepartmental discipline on board *Seawolf,* stepped into the conversation the moment it took an earnest, thoughtful tone.

"It was just the Chinese Fleet moving too close to the shores of Taiwan and firing missiles right across the landmass of the island. Just too close."

"Yeah, but didn't the *Ronald Reagan* show up and drive them off?"

"Well, it showed up. But it didn't actually drive them off. They left of their own accord. They usually do, steaming away up the Strait, northwest away from Taiwan toward their own coastline."

"You mean the carrier did not actually warn them off?"

"No. Not precisely. But the sight of that ship would give anyone pause for thought. Apparently the Chinese just backed right off before we got within two miles of them."

"I thought we used to be good friends with China, back in the late nineties."

"Well, I guess we were. But they're hard to be friends with. They just have a totally different mindset from us. Like the Japanese, they will take, take, take. Until you stop 'em."

"You think we might ever have to fight a war with 'em? I mean, a real shooting war?"

"I doubt it. They are damned self-interested, and they like money better than war. And they always back off if we even look like growling at 'em. But these days, you never know. They've been building up their goddamned navy for a lot of years now. Three hundred thousand personnel, new ships, Russian submarines, a new carrier and Christ knows what else."

"I'll tell you what," said Jason. "I was looking at a copy of the *Wall Street Journal* the other day and they had a front-page article on China. Some minister or other—had a name a bit like Kash Mai Chek—said something dead scary. He was talking about the appearance of the big American carrier, and he was quoted as saying, 'Do you really think the USA would trade Taiwan for Los Angeles?' I mean, that's bad shit."

"It sure would be if they really could throw a ballistic missile right across the Pacific."

"And can they?"

"Who knows," said Stockton. "Who the hell knows."

"I bet our XO knows," said Andy. "That's one mysterious guy. But he spends half his life in the CIA, and I'm told he's officially involved with Navy Intelligence."

"If you ask me, he ought to stay there," said Jason indiscreetly. "I mean, did you guys tune into that shit that broke out last October?"

"You mean when he ordered the ship to the surface against the CO's wishes when we had the leak in the torpedo room?"

"Yeah. That was one scared dude."

"Yeah, he was scared," said Chief Stockton. "But so was I."

"So was everyone."

"The CO wasn't."

"I bet he was. He just wasn't letting on."

"Well, if everyone was just as scared as everyone else, how come the CO pulled everyone together, took command, and refused to panic?"

"Because he's the goddamned CO, that's why. That's what he's trained for," said Brad. "In case you haven't noticed, they don't make many people commanding officers of nuclear submarines, not out of all the thousands of guys who want to join the Navy."

"They don't make many XOs, either. And ours was one scared dude."

"Right. But it was his first major incident on a deep submergence trial. You know, the guy had no idea what to expect. And he thought he might die in the next five minutes. And that tends to concentrate your head. People react differently. He'll learn . . . I think."

"Yeah, well he might. But I sure know who I'd rather have in command."

1625. Friday, June 16.
Office of the President's National Security Adviser.
The White House.

Vice Admiral Arnold Morgan was irritated, which was not a totally unusual situation. He sat behind his huge desk, glowering. On the wall opposite were three magnificently framed oil paintings, one of General Douglas MacArthur, one of General George Patton, one of Admiral Chester Nimitz. *Guys who had some semblance of an idea of what the hell was going on.*

The admiral, however, remained irritated, despite being gazed down upon, not disapprovingly, he thought, by three of the twentieth-century titans of the U.S. military.

"KATHY!" he yelled, bypassing the excellent state-of-the-art White House communications system. "COFFEE FOR ONE . . . NONE FOR THAT LATE BASTARD FROM THE PENTAGON . . . ANYWAY, WHERE THE HELL IS HE?"

The slim-line pastel green telephone on his desk tinkled discreetly like a little silver bell, which also irritated him—"*God-damned faggot phone*"—and he grabbed it like a wild boar with a truffle.

"MORGAN!" he rasped. "SPEAK."

"Oh, such a relief to find you in such rare good humor, Admiral," came the voice of his very private secretary and even more private girlfriend, Kathy O'Brien, the best-looking lady in the White House and possibly the best-looking redhead in Washington. "I do hope you don't object to my using the phone, rather than standing up in the hall out here and trying to bellow through a five-inch-thick oak door like a rutting moose . . . LIKE YOU."

The admiral dissolved into laughter, as he usually did at the sassy turn of phrase of the lady he loved. Recovering his natural poise, he continued, "WELL . . . where the hell is he?"

"You mean Admiral Mulligan, sir?"

"Who the hell do you think I mean? John the Baptist?"

"I didn't even know John the Baptist was working in the Pentagon."

"Jesus Christ, Kathy! Where the hell is he?"

Kathy's tone changed. "Arnold Morgan," she gritted, "I have told you five times that I have been in touch with the office of the Chief of Naval Operations and on each occasion I have been informed that Admiral Joseph Mulligan has left his office and was on his way here. Each time I have told you exactly that. I am not a traffic cop, I am not a chauffeur, I am not Admiral Mulligan's mistress. I have no idea where he is. When he arrives I will be sure to inform you."

Before she put down the phone, Kathy O'Brien whispered, "Good-bye, my darling, rude pig." Slam.

"*KATHY!!*"

Phone rings. "What?"

"WELL, WHERE THE HELL IS HE?"

"As a matter of fact he has just walked through the door . . . shall I send him in?"

"Jesus Christ."

Admiral Joseph Mulligan, the six-foot-four-inch former commanding officer of a Trident submarine, former C-in-C of the Submarine Force U.S. Atlantic Fleet (SUBLANT), and ex-Navy tight end in the 1966 Army-Navy game, came marching through the door.

"Hey, Arnie . . . sorry about the lateness . . . been sitting in the car on the phone to Norfolk for the last twenty minutes . . . that damned new cruiser . . . Jesus, it's more trouble than it could ever possibly be worth . . . got any coffee?"

"Yeah, but I'm not sure you're getting any. I'm not good at sitting around waiting for disorganized sailors."

"Heh, heh, heh." The big Boston Irishman who occupied the most senior position in the United States Navy chuckled. The two men had known each other for many years. Both of them had commanded Polaris submarines, and they had been through a few scrapes together. As long as Admiral Morgan was the President's right-hand man on military and national security matters, the Navy was not going to be looking for a new CNO any time soon.

Just then Kathy O'Brien came in with fresh coffee for them both. Admiral Mulligan thanked her graciously while the boss muttered, "'Bout time . . . I was better looked after when I was an ensign."

"He doesn't get a whole lot better, does he?" said Joe Mulligan. "No wonder all his wives left him."

"No wonder indeed," said Kathy, smiling as she swept out of the door.

"Christ, she's beautiful, Arnie. You better marry her while you've still got the chance."

"Can't. She's rejected me 'til I retire."

"Then you've both got a long wait."

"Guess so. But I'm hanging in there."

"Anyway, old pal, what's on your mind."

"China, what's on yours?"

"Cookies. Got any?"

"Jesus, don't they feed you at the hellhole you work in?"

"Only rarely."

"KATHY!! COOKIES FOR THE CHIEF."

"Okay, Arnie, tell me what's on your mind, as if I don't know. It's that Chinese missile, right?"

"That's the one, Joe. And whether anyone likes it or not, we are, in the end, gonna have to do something about it. We can't have a bunch of fucking coolies running around with a ballistic missile that could flatten L.A."

"Well, I agree. Not hardly. But you know, there really is no reason to think they could (a) build one that big, (b) aim the sonofabitch straight, and (c) make sure it goes off bang in Beverly Hills."

"Joe, I know that. But you know they've been building a brand-new Xia-class ICBM submarine. We've just picked it up on the overheads. Damn thing's conducting surface trials in the northern Yellow Sea right now. They got pictures at Fort Meade. Whatever else, you can bet they didn't build it for nothing. They built it to carry a missile that could, if required, threaten the USA."

"Can't argue with that, Arnie. But they're still a long way from firing a missile right across the Pacific Ocean."

"Are they? And might I ask how the hell you might know that?"

"Mainly, old buddy, because they've never tested anything like that, and because every shred of intelligence we have says they are simply not that advanced."

"If this new fucking Xia-class boat is any good, they won't have to be that advanced. They could drive the sonofabitch way across the ocean and let one rip a thousand miles off our west coast."

"Yeah, I suppose they could. If they owned such a missile."

Arnold Morgan stood up and pulled out a cigar from a snazzy-looking polished wooden box on his desk. He walked slowly around the room, nodding formally at the portrait of Admiral Nimitz. He clipped the end of his cigar, and ignited it with a gold Dunhill lighter, a gift from a Saudi Arabian prince who thought, wrongly, that he might study in the U.S. to become a submariner.

"Lemme lay a few facts on you, Joe. Get one of those cigars, if you want one, but listen. By the year 2000, we actually *knew* the Chinese had stolen top-secret design information for our most advanced thermonuclear weapons, and had transferred ballistic missile technology to Iran and Libya, among others. Beautiful, right?"

"Beautiful."

"They had also stolen our top missile guidance technology. They've got three thousand corporations in the US of A, probably half of 'em with lines to Chinese military intelligence, and you can't trust politicians one fucking inch to do the right thing. Jesus, Joe, Clinton's attorney general *denied* the FBI permission to wiretap the fucking Chinese spy's phone, and then the President himself went on television and told a barefaced lie, denying he even knew about the leaks when he plainly did. Then they hushed up half the Cox report in order to save his ass.

"Clinton made it possible for the goddamned Chinese to get their hands on American technology *no one should see*, and what's worse, they're still in here, stealing and lying.

"Joe, five years from now the People's Liberation Army/Navy is gonna consist of around three and a half million people. They are no longer especially concerned with a major ground war doctrine. They are, for the first time in five hundred years, becoming expansionist, and have formally recognized their massive navy as their Senior Service.

"Right now more than a third of the entire Chinese military budget is going into Navy research, development and production. They've finally managed to get four Russian-built Kilo-class submarines, despite my best efforts. They have this brand-new Xia-class SSBN, they have a production line of new Song-class SSKs, two new six-thousand-ton Luhai-class destroyers, they have a land-attack cruise missile program, they're aiming for two big aircraft carrier battle groups inside the next eight years—one for the Indian Ocean, one for the Pacific.

"And how about this Burma bullshit? The Chinese have piled nearly *two billion dollars' worth of military hardware* into that country, updating all the Burmese naval bases, which they of course will be utilizing. That adds up to a permanent Chinese presence in the Indian Ocean. Christ, Joe! These guys are on the move, I'm telling you. And I'm not proposing we make moves to stop 'em. Not yet, anyway. But I do seriously want to know if the little pricks can hit L.A. with a ballistic missile fired from the South China Sea. Is that too much to ask, for Christ's sake?"

The President's National Security Adviser faced the U.S. Navy Chief, and for the first time the two men were silent. Admiral Mulligan took a deep swig of coffee. Admiral Morgan drew deeply on his cigar, and then he spoke again, with equal care.

"Joe, China supports twenty-two percent of the world's population on only seven percent of its arable land. Because of their grotesque mismanagement of their farming areas, they're losing millions of acres a year. In the next fifteen years their population is going to one and a half billion, and sometime in the next five years they're gonna have an annual shortfall of two hundred and eighty-five million tons of grain, which is a lot of cookies."

"Yeah, I know the feeling . . . we're a bit short in here as well."

Admiral Morgan grinned but ignored him. "Joe, we're looking at a nation that sooner or later is going to have to raise a gigantic sum of money every year to buy grain and rice to feed its people. Either that, or they're gonna steal it. Or at least frighten someone into selling it to 'em cheap. And remember, they already require nearly six million barrels of oil a day. That's more than us, for Christ's sake. In my view they are a very grave danger, and we have to get a grip on the situation."

"Arnie, I agree. But are you proposing a new offensive of some kind?"

"No. But I'm proposing that we put the old one on a real fast track. Every day I'm getting reports that their Dong Feng–31 missile has been fitted with a nuclear warhead based on the designs stolen from the Los Alamos laboratories in New Mexico. Every report I get says they've done it, and that their new warhead is based on our ultra-compact W-88—which you know packs a punch ten times heavier than the goddamned bomb that hit Hiroshima—and the fucker's only three feet long. If the Chinese really have stolen the technology to manufacture that warhead, they could fit it into a missile in about ten minutes.

"And we both know they could deploy it in a submarine, specially a brand-new one, tailor-made for it. My guys think the DF-31 might have a range of five thousand miles, which would not get it across the Pacific, but launched from a submarine they could get it damned near anywhere."

"Well, we sure as hell can't measure it, since we don't know where they keep it, so we're not gonna find out its fuel capacity in a big hurry."

"No, Joe. But we could measure the submarine."

This time Admiral Mulligan stood up. And he walked over to the window and said slowly, "Arnie, we had a similar conversation at the end of last year, and I told you then that there is only one submarine in our fleet I'd risk going into Chinese waters to undertake such a mission. And that's *Seawolf*. She's fast, she's quiet, and she could make a getaway if she was detected . . . just as long as the water's not too shallow. She could, if necessary, also obliterate any enemy, but I know we don't wanna do that.

"I promised you before Christmas that I'd put this thing into action just as soon as *Seawolf* came out of overhaul and finished her trials. But since then we have another real problem—you know, it turned out the Chinese got ahold of the new sub detection technology from the Lawrence Livermore lab. That little prick Yung Lee, or whatever his fucking name was, stole it.

"According to the Livermore guys, it was just about the last word in that kind of technology—low-angle polarimetric and interferometric satellite radars to pick up very small pattern changes in the ocean's surface. The system works straight through clouds and will pick up the subtlest changes caused by a submarine's propeller. The Livermore guys say it will even identify the type of propeller."

"Shit. Did we throw that little Hung Ling guy in the slammer?"

"I think so . . . but anyway, I'm real reluctant to send the best submarine in the U.S. Navy deep inside Chinese territorial waters, because now I know they might find it, and then wipe it out, with all hands. Jesus, any submarine's nearly powerless if it gets detected in shallow waters with enemy surface warships in the area. And you can believe me, if the goddamned Chinks caught our top submarine prowling around their trial areas deep in the northern part of the Yellow Sea, shit, they'd become enemy real fast."

"Joe, I know the risks. Where's *Seawolf* right now?"

"She's at Pearl. On forty-eight hours' notice to head west, for the Yellow Sea . . . and I sure hate to send 'em."

"Joe, so do I. But they gotta go."

1200. Saturday, June 17.
Office of the CNO. The Pentagon.

Admiral Mulligan was on the phone to an old friend, Sam Langer, the recently retired chief nuclear systems engineer at General Dynamics, the corporation that had built *Seawolf* and carried out her major overhaul at the Electric Boat Yards in Groton, Connecticut.

"Sam, just a small point—you remember we talked about a little device to be fitted onto *Seawolf*'s emergency coolant system, about a year ago ?"

"Sure I do, Joe—small adjustment to the isolating valve on the 'cold leg'?"

"Yup, that's the one. I remember we talked about it, just couldn't remember whether you did it."

"Well, it was supposed to be, er, nonpublic, wasn't it?"

"Correct. That's why it doesn't figure in the plans and billing. Anyway, did you do it?"

"Yup, sure did."

"Remind me."

"It was nothing, really. Just a small adjustment to that valve. In the event of an electrical failure or a reactor scram, that valve will just drift open—and I guess that will deactivate the emergency cooling system. But it will give no indication of having done so."

"Would it kick in automatically? If, say, we had an unforeseen reactor scram or something?"

"Christ, no, Joe. The captain and his nuclear engineer would have to set it correctly. I believe the whole idea was in case the submarine should fall into enemy hands?"

"Yes, it was, Sam. Yes it was. Did you tell anyone about it?"

"Well, the guys who fitted it knew. Although they didn't know what it was for. And I took the captain over it very carefully, just a few months ago. When he came down to see the ship. Judd Crocker, right? He and his engineer, tall blond guy, Schulz, I think his name was."

"So Captain Crocker is thoroughly aware of it?"

"More than aware, sir. He spent about an hour in there looking at the emergency cooling system. By the time he left, he knew more about it than I did."

"Hey, Sam, thanks a lot. Come on down and have a drink next time I'm in New London."

Admiral Mulligan picked up his secure line and dialed Kathy O'Brien's number in Maryland. The admiral himself answered the way he always answered: "MORGAN, SPEAK."

"Christ, Arnie, it'd be great if I'd been Kathy's mother or someone. You call your daughter and some gorilla says, 'MORGAN, SPEAK.'"

"Heh, heh, heh. Hiya, Joe. I'm happy to say that Kathy's mother, like the President, has come to terms with most of my little ways. What's hot?"

"*Seawolf*'s reactor, since you mention it."

"Whaddya mean?"

"I just wanted to let you know . . . remember that conversation we had around a year ago, about fitting some device on the big nuclear boats that would cause them to self-destruct? I just wanted to let you know, there's one on *Seawolf*."

"That's the trip on the isolating valve in the emergency system?"

"That's it. Captain Crocker knows all about it . . . and you remember it won't kill the ship by itself, should it fall into enemy hands. But it would enable us to damage the ship, knowing it would self-destruct completely as soon as the reactor went down."

"It's a kinda gloomy subject, Joe. But it's important to know, and I'm grateful. I just hope to hell we never have to use it. By the way, how many of those goddamned political nuclear committees did you have to go through to get it done?"

"None."

"Howd'you fix that?"

"Simple. I never told anyone. But it's there."

"Heh, heh, heh. You're a great man, Joe Mulligan."

0100. Sunday, June 18.
Submarine Jetty. U.S. Navy Base, Pearl Harbor.

The night was stiflingly hot, windless above a calm sea, and USS *Seawolf* was ready. She lay moored alongside like a vast, black, captive undersea monster, which was precisely what she was. Except that she was bigger, faster, quieter, more aware, and more deadly than any other creature in all the world's oceans.

Since the late afternoon, deep in the reactor room, the marine engineering officer, Lt. Commander Rich Thompson, and his team had been pulling the rods, the slow, painstaking procedure of bringing the nuclear power plant up to the required temperature and pressure to provide every ounce of energy *Seawolf* might need on her long voyage. You could run the whole of Honolulu off Rich Thompson's nuclear reactor.

The signal to leave had arrived direct from SUBPAC shortly before lunch: *"CO USS Seawolf: Proceed immediately to Yellow Sea as authorized in orders of 170900JUN06. Observation only. Do not, repeat not, be detected."*

Junior Petty Officer Jason Colson, Judd Crocker's writer, had already transferred a full copy of the orders into the captain's private ledger, and now he, in company with the CO; the XO; Lt. Shawn Pearson, the Navigation Officer; Cy Rothstein; and Rich Thompson were the only personnel privy to the hair-raising nature of their mission. It was not classified as "Black," because that involved attack, possibly combat. But this was equally secret, equally highly classified, equally dangerous.

Down in the engineering area, outside the reactor room, Lt. Commander Schulz and Tony Fontana were busy, but still in the dark about the mission. Lt. Kyle Frank, the young sonar officer from New Hampshire, had not yet been briefed. Petty Officer Andy Cannizaro still thought they were going to Taiwan, but Master Chief

Brad Stockton had been at it too long to make second guesses. He was seeing the CO later that morning when he knew he would be informed.

For one o'clock in the morning, the jetty was relatively crowded. The departure of a nuclear submarine is always something of an event in any major naval base, and Pearl was no exception. Many of the engineers and even some of their wives had come down to watch *Seawolf* go. The squadron commander was there, the duty officer, and the line handlers. There was no reason for tension, but there always was a tautness in the atmosphere as deep inside the ship the men finalized their entries in the next-of-kin list, which detailed every member of the ship's company and whom the Navy should contact should the submarine fail to return. Nicole Crocker's name, and the address of the house on Point Loma, was right at the top of that list. There was little information about Lt. Commander Clarke, certainly nothing about his blood relatives.

At 0115, Captain Crocker came on the bridge, high above the dock. He was accompanied by the officer of the deck, Lt. Andy Warren, and the navigator, Pearson. All three men wore just summer shirts in the heat. The order to "Attend Bells" was issued at 0125, and a frisson of anticipation quivered through the ship. After all the months of preparation, those two words meant one thing: *We're going, right now.*

Linus Clarke ordered all lines cast off, and Andy Warren leaned into the intercom. "All back one third." Deep inside the ship, the massive turbines began to roll. The giant propeller, churning in reverse, caused a soft wash to roll up over the stern as *Seawolf* came off the jetty, moving quietly backward in the wide Pearl Harbor seaway. Fifteen seconds later she was stopped in the water, and then Judd Crocker called out, "Ahead one third." And his 9,000-ton nuclear boat moved forward over the opening few yards of her 4,600-mile journey to the forbidden waters of the Yellow Sea.

The spectators beneath the dock lights waved as *Seawolf* stood down the moonlit seascape, running fair down the main southerly channel.

"All ahead standard," called Lieutenant Warren, and everyone felt the sonorous increase in speed. A glance behind showed a white wake developing behind the stern.

"Course one-seven-five," advised Shawn Pearson.

And *Seawolf* slid into her surface rhythm, the flat water cascading up over her bow and parting at the great upward curve of the sail, to form the two strange vortexes of swirling water on either side, behind the bridge, a condition common to all big underwater nuclear boats.

"We should hold this southerly course for three more miles after we fetch the harbor light, sir," said the navigator. "Then we turn to the west, course two-seven-zero, for several thousand miles."

Judd Crocker smiled in the dark and said quietly, "Thank you, Shawn." Adding, "Around twenty-five miles on the surface?"

"Yessir. We got one hundred and twenty feet right after the light on Barbers Point off to starboard. But twenty miles after that it goes real deep. In this flat sea, I thought we may as well stay on the surface."

"You might find it's not so flat after Barbers Point, Lieutenant."

"I suppose so, sir. But I'm not trying to interfere. I'm basically here to protect the innocent."

Judd Crocker chuckled. He liked his young navigator, but on this ship he thought Shawn might be a bit short of customers to protect.

Seawolf eventually went deep in the area Pearson had suggested, and within 15 miles she had 12,000 feet of water beneath her keel. The CO increased her speed to 30 knots and she ran smoothly 800 feet below the surface, aiming at the steep undersea mountains of the Marcus-Necker Ridge, and then on toward the sloping Mid-Pacific Mountains, which rise up to bisect the Tropic of Cancer.

At this speed *Seawolf* would make 700 miles a day, which would put her at the gateway to the Yellow Sea in a little under a week. God knew how long it would take to locate her quarry.

The crew were, almost to a man, unaware of their destination. On a mission such as this it was strictly a need-to-know situation. And Tony Fontana had come around to Brad Stockton's way of thinking that this ship would turn southwest in the near future and run south of the old East Indies, avoiding the busy, shallow Strait of Malacca, and then run north up to the Arabian Gulf.

But the general consensus was that they were headed to a point somewhere on the far eastern seaboard of the continent of Asia, either China or Russia. Taiwan was the favorite, because most of the men knew there was constant trouble out there. But no one had written off the 1,500-mile-long stretch of the Kamchatka Peninsula because of the big Russian naval base on the edge of those freezing, lonely waters. One thing they all knew: *Seawolf* was headed due west right now. No arguments there.

But the mere fact that they had not been told their destination suggested that this was no ordinary mission. *Seawolf* was heading into very serious waters, of that there was no doubt.

1930. Sunday, June 18.
Home of Kathy O'Brien. Chevy Chase, Maryland.

Admiral Arnold Morgan was lighting the barbecue grill. He was using one of those "chimneys" that require only lighted paper to start the charcoal burning. However, he had used four times more paper than was required, *and* he had used Match Light charcoal, which did not even require any paper. The result was a kind of controlled blaze upon which Dante himself might have roasted a few sausages.

Inferno was the word, and the admiral gazed at it with some satisfaction. "Get some goddamned power in there, right?" he told Kathy's Labrador. "Get a little *real* heat going. You wanna cook lamb, you need power, right?"

Kathy, accustomed to Arnold's unique view of how to light a barbecue, emerged from the house carrying a large platter on which was placed a large, marinated butterflied lamb, cut from an entire leg bone. She took one look at the fire and cast her eyes heavenward. "In case you hadn't noticed, this is not a butterflied brontosaurus," she said. "Just a regular leg of lamb, which requires nice hot gray coals, under the lid for about an hour. It does not require flames three feet high, nor will it taste any better for having been roasted in your personal version of Hiroshima."

"I'm getting there," he muttered, grinning. "Just gotta let the heat subside a little."

"Oh, it should be just about perfect sometime on Tuesday evening. How about a drink while we wait?"

The admiral took the heavy plate from her and placed on it a small red table next to the inferno-grill. Then he placed his arm around her shoulder and told her he loved her as he did every evening before dinner. Then he asked her to marry him, and she said no, and he headed for the fridge to retrieve a bottle of her favorite 1997 Meursault and poured two glasses.

It was a ritual that amused them both, an affirmation that she would not become the third Mrs. Arnold Morgan until he retired from the White House, on the basis that she had no intention of sitting at home alone in Chevy Chase while he ran half the world.

The sun was setting now, somewhere out behind the Blue Ridge Mountains of Virginia. And they sat outside watching the dying flames—of the sun, not the grill—in the clear light blue of the evening sky.

The cool, pale gold taste of the perfect dry wine from the slopes of Burgundy relaxed them both, and they discussed the possibility of taking a break together, perhaps to go back to Europe and visit their old friend Admiral Sir Iain MacLean in Scotland.

But Kathy did not hold out much hope for that. "You're very preoccupied this past couple of weeks," she said. "Is it China?"

"Uh-huh," he said. "They're a goddamned PITA."

"A what?"

"A PITA."

"What's that? You always have initials for everything . . . SUBLANT, SUBPAC, SPECWARCOM . . . what's a PITA?"

"Pain in the ass, stupid," he said.

Kathy's laughter took her unawares, and she only just managed not to blow Meursault down her nose. When she recovered her poise, she said, "You are not only crude to the point of absurdity, but I feel like I'm in love with Mao Zedong. China this, China that . . . it's about a million miles away. Who cares?"

"My publishers, for a start. They're just beginning to prepare *The Thoughts of Chairman Arnold.*"

Kathy shook her head, smiling at the ex-submarine commander to whom she had lost her heart. She had loved him since the first time she ever saw him, three years earlier; ever since that first day he had come growling into the office as the President's National Security Adviser and told her to "get Rankov on the line and tell him he was, is, and always will be a sonofabitch. A lying sonof-abitch at that."

Stunned by the instruction, she had inquired lamely, "Who's Rankov?"

"Head of the Soviet navy. He's in the Kremlin. Oughta be in a salt mine."

Amazed that the admiral still had not looked up from his papers, she had said, "But, sir, I can't just call him in his office and call him a sonofabitch."

"A lying sonofabitch."

"Sorry, sir. I actually meant a lying sonofabitch."

Then Admiral Morgan had looked up, a faint smile on his craggy, hard face. "Oh, okay, if your goddamned nerve's gone before I've been here ten minutes, I'm sure as hell gonna have to whip you into shape. How about a cup of coffee, but get the Kremlin on the line first, willya? Ask for Admiral Vitaly Rankov. I'll talk to him."

Kathy had retired to order the Admiral's coffee, and when she returned, she heard him yell, "RANKOV, you bastard, YOU ARE A LYING SONOFABITCH."

She did not, of course, hear the great roar of laughter from Arnold's old friend and sparring partner in the Russian navy, and she could only stand there in astonishment. Kathy O'Brien had worked in the White House for several years, but never had she encountered a man such as this. She'd worked for confident men before. But not *this* confident.

The relationship between the twice-divorced admiral and the spectacularly beautiful private secretary had taken months to develop, mainly because it was beyond Arnold's imagination that any woman this pretty, this smart, with her own private money, could possibly have any interest in him.

In the end it was Kathy who made the running and invited him to dinner. Since that evening they had been inseparable, and everyone in the White House knew it, though no one ever mentioned it, mainly from fear of the admiral.

The President himself was very aware of the romance, and equally aware that the future Mrs. Arnold Morgan would not marry him until he retired. He had asked her personally about it once, and she told him flatly, "His other two marriages failed because he happens to be wedded to the United States of America. His other two wives did not, I believe, understand how important he is. All they knew was that he was in the office and not at home. I'm different. I know why he's in the office. But I'm not waiting at home for him. I'll marry him when he retires."

Which was why they lived almost all the time at Kathy's home in Chevy Chase, and found a way to have dinner together every night. And with every passing week, Kathy O'Brien loved him more, not so much for his power to terrorize global military leaders, but for his intellect, his knowledge, and always just below the surface, his humor.

Kathy O'Brien understood that even in his snarling, sarcastic White House mode, Arnold Morgan was amusing himself mightily, toying with the opposition, dazzling even himself with his brilliant nastiness.

Just then the phone rang, and Kathy, looking comfortable, said, "You better get it, darling. That's your secure line."

The admiral strode to the phone, and the voice at the end was deep and strident.

"Hey, Arnie. Joe. Real short. They're on their way, cleared Pearl early this morning, their time."

"Thanks, Joe. I'm grateful. Wish 'em well from me if you get a chance."

"I'm afraid they're gonna need all the good wishes we can get to 'em. That's a dangerous spot they're headed to."

"I know it. But they're in a hell of a ship . . . just so long as they don't get caught in shallow water. Chinese pricks."

2100. Monday, June 19.
USS *Seawolf.*

JUDD CROCKER WAS FROWNING. AND WHEN HE frowned, he resembled the Pirate King. His looks were classic Black Irish, the dark Mediterranean coloring of the Spaniard, descended, as he was, from one of the hundreds of Spanish sailors who washed up on Ireland's shores after the defeated Armada ran into a storm in 1588. You would not, however, have mistaken him for a matador. More likely the bull.

He was an enormously powerful man. In Newport, you'd take him for a winch-grinder on a major racing yacht, in Canada you'd wonder why he wasn't wearing a checkered shirt and swinging a double-bladed ax, and outside Madison Square Garden or Shea Stadium, someone would have offered him a contract.

Judd was a major presence in a submarine. He seemed all business, but he was quick with his lopsided smile, and quicker with a droll, often teasing remark. Some might think him sardonic, but that would be an exaggeration. It was just that he was extremely thoughtful, and tended to be a couple of jumps ahead of the opposition.

Right now, bent frowning over a big white, blue and yellow chart of the northern half of the Yellow Sea, he was trying to stay a couple of jumps ahead of the Chinese. But it was not proving easy. Sitting alone in his cabin, poring over the ocean depths of a distant sea in which he had never sailed, he was exercising his mind fully.

And the air in the little room was filled with mumbled phrases like, "Damn, can't go in there . . . too shallow . . . that's not a sea, it's a frigging mud flat . . . beats the hell out of me why they'd even want submarine bases up there . . . Christ, there's nowhere within five hundred miles of the shipyards where you could even dive without hitting the bottom . . . beats the hell out of me . . . no one even knows whether he'll run down the eastern shore or the western shore . . . least of all me."

The subject was China's new Xia-class submarine, the Type 094, 6,500-ton, superimproved version of old Number 406, the Great White Elephant of the Chinese fleet, so named because she was essentially slow and tired (20 knots flat-out, running downhill); carried largely useless missiles that mostly failed to work; was as noisy as a freight train; and spent much of her life in dry dock. The 406 made the Americans and the Brits laugh at the mere thought of her, the joke being that she was *so* noisy it wasn't worth her while going underwater anyway.

But that was before Mr. Lee and his cohorts stole all the new technology, from California and New Mexico, before President Clinton held out the red carpet for China to learn anything she damn pleased, to the obvious fury of the Joint Chiefs, not to mention a whole generation of U.S. Navy admirals.

Now, according to the Chinese, the new *Xia* was designed to be fast and silent, her ICBMs would work, and they would have a significantly longer range than the old ones. She also carried the very latest sonar. *Would the U.S. really trade Taiwan for Los Angeles?*

More important, so far as Judd was concerned, the new *Xia*

was ready to begin her trials. The American satellites had been watching her for months, nearing completion up in the remote Huludao Yards, way up the Yellow Sea on the desolate eastern shore of Liaodong Bay. The *Xia* was the reason *Seawolf* had made the journey to Pearl Harbor in the first place. And last Saturday afternoon through its probing lens, the satellite had spotted the telltale infrared "paint," the sign of heat inside the submarine. The Chinese had begun to take *Xia*'s reactor critical, which explained the Americans' hurry, leaving in the middle of the night.

So far only Captain Crocker was privy to all of the information, and every 12 hours he was ordering *Seawolf* to periscope depth, to suck a fast message off the satellite, telling him whether the *Xia* was still testing her systems moored alongside in Huludao or whether she was at last heading south, into deep waters.

Right now, with Judd Crocker and his team 1,300 miles out from Pearl, the *Xia* was still at her jetty, and Judd fervently hoped she would stay there until he had covered 3,000 more miles to reach the eastern waters of the Yellow Sea, where he hoped to pick her up as she steamed south, probably on the surface. The rest was going to be truly hazardous.

The CO planned to brief his senior officers as to the precise nature of the mission. But first he was trying to familiarize himself with the vast but somewhat shallow waters of China's submarine production area. The only available charts were Japanese, and their underwater surveys were, Judd thought, pretty unreliable. But the northern waters of the Yellow Sea have been for centuries almost bereft of foreign shipping, except by invitation of mainland China.

Because it is essentially a cul-de-sac, there is literally no reason to go there. Running north from Shanghai, the Yellow Sea quickly becomes 300 miles wide, but after less than 200 miles it becomes bounded by South Korea to the east. Three hundred northerly miles later it runs into a choke point, only 60 miles wide, at the entrance to a massive bay stretching almost 300 miles northeast-southwest. There is no escape from the bay except back through the choke point.

Way up to the north of that bay, on the borders of the old province of Manchuria, lies the great shipyard of Huludao, on the north side of a jutting peninsula, bounded by a gigantic sea wall. It is here that China builds her attack submarines. All five of the 4,500-ton Han-class (Type 091) guided missile boat, were constructed in Huludao. It was here that the original *Xia* itself was built.

But Liaodong Bay is not much deeper than 100 feet anywhere, bounded as it is by great salt flats, so when an SSN leaves here it must not only run to the choke point on the surface, it must proceed south on the surface for another 400 miles before reaching *any* deep water whatsoever. The northern Yellow Sea is a strange place to build underwater warships. The weather in winter is shocking, the border of the snowswept plains of Inner Mongolia being only 100 miles away. Huludao possesses only one advantage, that of privacy, indeed, secrecy.

Curiously, another of the major Chinese shipyards is also located up in those northern waters—the one at Dalian(Dawan), on the northern peninsula of the choke point, where they build most of the great workhorses of the Chinese Navy, the Luda-class destroyers.

Judd stared at the chart, trying to put himself in the Chinese captain's mind: *What would I do if I was in a brand-new ICBM submarine, and was almost certainly being watched by an American nuclear boat somewhere?*

Well, the Yellow Sea's deeper to the east along the Korean shore, so I'd come to the choke point and keep running southwest for maybe four hundred miles. I'd stay on the surface until I was down here . . . where am I? Thirty-four degrees north . . . then I'd run north of the island of Cheng Do . . . then I'd make a beeline for the deep water . . . over by these islands west of Nagasaki . . . then I'd dive, real quick as a matter of fact . . . that's what he'll do, I think. That's where I'll be waiting for him.

Judd Crocker called a conference of his key personnel in the control room: Lt. Commander Clark; Lt. Commander Rothstein; the navigator, Lt. Shawn Pearson; the sonar officer, Lt. Kyle Frank; the marine engineering officer, Lt. Commander Rich Thompson; the chief of the boat, Master PO Brad Stockton; and the officer of the deck, Lt. Andy Warren.

"Gentlemen," said the CO as he closed the door, "I have asked you to come in for a briefing on the nature of our mission. In short, we are going to China, to the eastern waters of the Yellow Sea, where we are trying to pick up their brand-new ICBM submarine, the new *Xia*, track it south, and then ascertain its precise measurements from keel to upper casing."

"How exactly do we do that, sir?" asked Rothstein. "They probably won't invite us over with a tape measure."

"Cy, we have to get under its keel, directly under, and then use an upward sonar to get a complete picture of the underwater shape and depth of the submarine, from surface to keel. Then we range her from surface to casing and that way we have a dead accurate measurement of her precise height."

"Yes, I see. But what exactly do you mean directly under its keel—you mean a couple of hundred feet below?"

"Cy, I actually mean a hell of a lot closer than that."

"Can you tell us why we're doing this, sir?"

"Yes, Brad, I guess so. Inside that submarine will be the very latest intercontinental ballistic missiles, the one they'll throw at L.A. should they ever decide on such a course of action. For obvious reasons, we *must* know the precise range of that missile, how far it will go and whether they really could hit our West Coast from the far side of the Pacific Ocean. Basic intelligence, really. We're on a top-classified spying mission, and *we must not get caught.*"

"Presumably, sir, we're discussing the technology they stole from the USA in the final years of the nineties?"

"And a bit before that, Cy. Anyway, you all know the theory. We can't measure the missile, but if we measure the submarine that carries it, we'll know its height. Which I'm guessing will be around forty-five to fifty feet. There's probably around nine feet of engine in there, and maybe four feet of warhead. The rest's fuel, and our guys can ascertain within about a hundred yards how far that baby will fly."

"How about the diameter, sir?"

"They have that. Picked up the hatch measurements from the satellite photographs."

"Sir, I've known you for a lot of years," said Brad Stockton. "And I can tell you're holding back the bad news . . ."

They all laughed, and the CO continued, "There's so much of that I'm not sure where to start!

"First of all we have to find the submarine, but we'll have plenty of assistance from the overheads so long as she's on the surface. Second, they'll guess the Americans are watching, so they'll be pretty vigilant watching for us. Third, Fort Meade is afraid they have stolen our most up-to-date ASW system, which will allow them to spot us underwater from space, from their own satellite. Which would make us pretty easy prey if the water's not deep and they send ship after ship to look for us."

"Jesus Christ. Do we know if they have this stuff operational?"

"No. We only know that they have it. We're not sure whether they know how to use it. Anyway, if we stay in deep water, we're fairly safe. They have nothing that will catch us, nothing remotely fast enough."

"And sir, if we had to, could we blow 'em out of the water?"

"Andy, that would be frowned upon. If they hit us, they'd probably get away with it—a marauding American nuclear boat creeping through Chinese waters, et cetera. But if we hit them, I'm afraid it would be regarded as an act of war, since we really have no reason to be there, four thousand miles from our home base."

"You mean you'd just let them destroy us?"

"No, Andy, if it came down to a straight us or them, well, there could be only one answer to that."

"Not us. Right, sir?"

"Not us. That's correct, Andy. But officially, we're not allowed to do that. Our orders are to stay undetected."

"But that, as we all know, may be easier said than done," said Cy Rothstein quietly.

"Correct. But we have to try. And we have to get our mindset straight. We are in a devastatingly powerful attack submarine. We could probably take out half the Chinese fleet if it came right down to it. But that's not our job. We will be thanked profoundly at home only if we come back quietly with information, photographic evidence of what the hell the goddamned Chinese are up to . . . and how much of our stuff they have stolen and utilized."

"Is that our only mission, sir?"

"Not quite. The Chinese have recently commissioned their third and newest Luhai-class destroyer, a big six-thousand-ton gas-turbine ship with an endurance of fourteen thousand miles, and guided missiles they can project to seventy miles. The Pentagon thinks the damn thing may have a ballistic trajectory ASW weapon. It's called a CY-1. They want us to locate the destroyer and take a look. But we'll need to be careful. CNO thinks it might be fitted with China's first decent towed-array, developed from the stuff they stole from us."

"Guess we better be careful," said Lt. Pearson. "Especially if they got the ole CY-1 into action."

230700JUN06.
North of the Ryukyu Islands. 29.10N 129.30E.
Speed 30. Depth 300. Course 305.

Seawolf ran swiftly underwater into the approaches to the East China Sea on Friday morning, five days after leaving Pearl. The journey through the great Pacific wilderness had been uneventful. They never even heard another ship. Nine times during the journey *Seawolf*'s periscope came jutting out of the water, but the one-second signal from the satellite was always the same: the new *Xia* was still moored securely alongside in Huludao, her reactor still running.

Judd Crocker slowed to 20 knots as they picked their way through the tiny Japanese islands, with 1,500 feet of water beneath their keel. Up ahead was the unseen line of the south-flowing Japanese current that forms the seaward frontier of the China Sea.

Seawolf was not going that far, and when Pearson called out their position at longitude 129 degrees, the CO ordered, "Right standard rudder . . . make your course three-six-zero . . . speed twenty knots . . . depth two hundred feet."

To Clarke he added, "We'll make our patrol area just south of the entrance to the Korean Strait—the water's deep and Japanese. We can hang around here until something shakes loose, then we can creep up

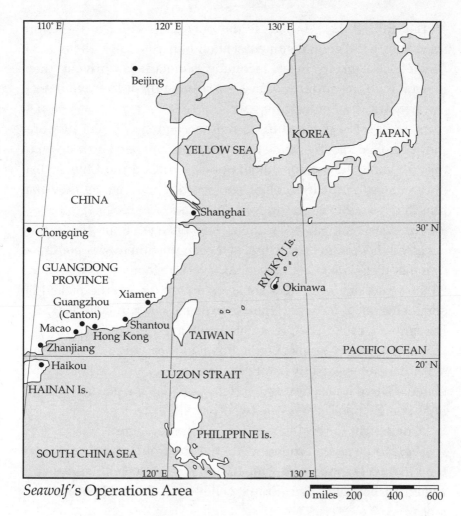

Seawolf's Operations Area

0 miles   200   400   600

to the one-hundred-meter line and wait for the Chinaman. That's if I'm right about the course he's bound to take over here to the east. If he's on the other side, we're in trouble, because we can't track him underwater. Alternately, if he's over there he'll be on the surface anyway, so the overheads can track him, and we'll catch up with him later."

And so they slid along the eastern side of the Yellow Sea, off the far southern coastline of Japan's 130-mile-long province of Kyushu. This is the last major land before the flag of the Rising Sun peters out into its lonely chain of remote Pacific islands, running southwest for 540 miles, almost to Taiwan.

But around these islands is the only deep water in the entire area, before the great continental shelf of the People's Republic of China rises up to meet incoming submarines, driving them inevitably to the surface, or at least forcing them to leave behind the giveaway trail of a swirling wake.

Seawolf's CO planned to do neither, and in 350 feet of water they patrolled silently below the surface, their speed now down to only 10 knots, the senior officers hoping to God the Chinese had not yet mastered the satellite sub-spotting techniques they had hijacked from the laboratories in California.

The weekend passed without any change. Four times they accessed the American satellite, and each time there was confirmation that the *Xia* had not moved. At 0900 on Monday morning, June 26, however, one of Frank's sonar operators thought he picked up something out to the west: "Hard to explain . . . just a slight rise in the background level . . . doesn't sound much like weather."

The CO joined Frank standing behind the operator's chair, and several minutes went by before they picked up any further sight or sound. "There it is again, sir . . . right there . . . we got faint engine lines coming up. Relative one-twenty-five . . . ."

"Come right to one-thirty-five to resolve ambiguity."

Seawolf swerved around while the sonar men tried to resolve the bearing. It took more than 10 minutes because the lines continued to be faint. Kyle Frank called it at 0922: "Bearing two-eight-zero."

By now the "waterfall" screen was showing a much more definite picture of the engine lines, and the computer was scanning and comparing at high speed, trying to pinpoint the exact ship they were locating.

"It's a submarine, sir, no doubt about that," said Frank as his eyes darted from one screen to another. For a few moments he was silent, and then he blurted out, "Jesus, sir, it's Russian . . . right here we got ourselves a real live Russky . . . look at that. It's a Kilo-class boat, I'd guess ten thousand yards off our starboard quarter . . . what the hell's that doing here?"

"Possibly the same as us—waiting for the *Xia*?" asked Rothstein.

"I doubt it," replied Judd. "The damn thing's stacked with Russian technology anyway. I'd be surprised if there was anything they don't know about it. They're all best friends these days. They don't need to spy. I'd say the Kilo was Chinese—I think they have about five of them now, and one of them is out here on some kind of exercise."

"Shall we go a little closer, sir . . . see if we can learn anything?"

"I think we might, Linus. But I don't want to go too close, maybe five thousand yards off track. Steer course two-five-zero . . . make your speed six knots . . ."

Seawolf edged in closer, and as she did Kyle Frank's man picked up a new sound, machinery noise only, bearing one-four-zero.

"This is possibly a surface ship, sir, moving left slow or stopped, with a diesel engine running . . . puts us right between the Kilo and him."

"I'll have a look down the bearing, Sonar." *Seawolf*'s CO kept the periscope up for a span of about seven seconds. He instantly identified the contact as a 5,000-ton Dazhi-class support ship. The computer told the sonar room it was 40 years old and carried four electrohydraulic cranes and a large stock of torpedoes.

"Know what I think?" said the captain.

But before anyone could answer, Kyle Frank's sonar operator had picked up another passive contact very close to the Kilo.

"*Jesus Christ!*" said the operator to himself. "*Bastards've opened fire on us.*" But he was all pro when he made his announcement.

"TORPEDOES . . . INCOMING . . . POSSIBLY TWO . . . BEARING TWO-EIGHT-THREE . . . BEARING STEADY . . ."

Lt. Commander Clarke said, "My God, sir . . . what if they have warheads . . . STAND BY FULL DECOY PATTERN . . . we ought to be firing back . . . these bastards are shooting at us . . . trying to sink us, sir."

"Negative, XO," replied Captain Crocker.

"WHAT DO YOU MEAN, NEGATIVE!" Linus Clarke's voice was almost out of control. "I'M LOOKING AT TWO TORPEDOES INCOMING FROM A CHINESE SUBMARINE!"

"Sure, Linus. Just shut up for a minute, willya? I'm gonna let 'em go right by. RIGHT STANDARD RUDDER . . . MAKE YOUR COURSE TWO-EIGHT-THREE."

"But how the hell do you know they're going right by, sir?"

"Well, first of all they haven't gone active. Second, it's gotta be about a hundred to one against the torpedoes being at the same depth as us. And five hundred to one against them being on the exact right course to hit us. That's an acceptable risk."

"POSITIVE TWO TORPEDOES BEARING TWO-EIGHT-THREE . . . BEARING STILL STEADY, SIR," called the sonar operator.

"'Course it is," replied the captain. "We've just wandered into a torpedo test-firing exercise. That old Dazhi support ship I saw is acting as a TRV, torpedo recovery vessel—and none of the Chinese on either ship has the remotest idea we're here. We'd sure know if they did."

Right now, not for the first time in this submarine, the CO and his XO had totally different mindsets.

Judd Crocker's thought process had told him with great clarity, *Up range from us is an obvious torpedo recovery vessel. The Kilo has loosed a couple off. Neither of them is aimed at me in this small patch of water. I assess it's at least 5,000 to 1 against either of the weapons hitting us, and even if one did, it plainly does not have a warhead, and it would not be in any way terminal.*

Linus Clarke's view was diametrically opposed: *We are virtually in enemy waters. These bastards are shooting. Jesus Christ! My captain has placed our submarine right in the path of the torpedoes. He refuses to put out decoys. HE ACTUALLY DOES NOT WANT TO DO ANYTHING . . . HE MUST BE OUT OF HIS MIND. It's a basic law of the universe . . . cover your ass. My God, a minute from now we could all be dead.*

And even as the tortured thoughts of the XO thudded through his brain, the big TEST 96 missiles came cleaving through the water, not increasing in speed from 30 knots, not going active, but nonetheless coming nerve-wrackingly close to USS *Seawolf*'s position.

"Bearing's still almost steady, sir . . . I now have two separate weapon tracks . . . but they'll pass either side of us . . . the first one out to starboard, the second a little further away to port . . . no danger, sir, unless they switch on active homing."

And everyone in the control room area heard the sonar reports.

"WEAPON ONE MOVING RIGHT TWO-NINE-FIVE . . . LOUDER . . . CLOSING . . . NO TRANSMISSIONS ON THE BEARING.

"WEAPON TWO MOVING LEFT TWO-SIX-ZERO . . . LOUDER . . . NO TRANSMISSIONS ON THE BEARING."

A minute later: "WEAPON ONE MOVING RIGHT FAST ZERO-ONE-FIVE . . ." The tension in his voice was dying. An air of calm was returning. "Weapon two moving left fast two-zero-five . . ."

Then, "Weapon one moving right, zero-six-five . . . slightly fainter . . . Doppler opening . . . weapon two moving left, one-six-three, fainter. Doppler opening."

"Guess you called that one, sir. They just went right by as if we were just a little old hole in the water," said Rothstein, smiling and, as he often did, contemplating the complexities of the human mind. *"Here we had a scenario, not four minutes long, not one minute ago, and we had two highly educated people simultaneously seeing that scenario from totally opposing perspectives. If they'd been in a courtroom giving evidence, the jury would have been in complete confusion. And rightly so."* "Almost all evidence," said Cy to no one in particular, "is colored by opinion. Therefore it should largely be ignored because it is unreliable in the extreme."

"Well, my reasoning wasn't that difficult," said the CO. "The Chinese obviously did not have a warhead fitted or the Dazhi wouldn't have been right in the path of the weapons. They were just testing tube functioning, or maybe something more complicated, maybe even some kind of a tactical trial. I don't think anyone's ever seen a full-functioning explosive trial. Certainly not with a TRV downrange.

"Also, there's no sign of a target. And if there was, there would be a lot of ships out here monitoring the whole event. My conclusion, therefore, was it was a non-warhead trial . . . but meanwhile I'm going a bit further off-track. I want to creep around behind that Kilo, hang around for a bit, ready for a second firing if there's gonna be one. I'd like to get a full recording of the noise of the tubes being prepared and the firing sequence.

"And Linus, old buddy, have faith, willya?"

270100JUN06.
32.10N 128.00E. Speed 9. Depth 150.
Bearing three-six-zero.

Judd Crocker was trying to catch three or four hours' sleep in his sparse, but private, cabin when someone knocked sharply on the door three times and then came straight in, the light from the companionway outside shining in on the sleeping CO.

"Sir, wake up," called Frank. "I think you should see this. The *Xia*'s moved . . . cleared Huludao at nine last night. She's making twenty-five knots through the Yellow Sea heading southwest on the surface straight for the choke point."

The captain's brain whirred. "What time is it, Kyle?"

"'Bout oh-one-twenty, sir."

"That means it's been running for, what? Six hours. That's one hundred and fifty miles. She'll be right off Dalian now. What's that . . . four hundred and fifty miles north of us . . . we wanna be looking for her around eighteen hours from now, right? Say around nineteen-thirty this evening."

"Yessir. That's what I have on this piece of paper, 'cept it took me ten minutes to work it out."

"Okay. Access the satellite again at oh-six-hundred, check her course and speed. Call me at oh-five-fifty-five.

"Yessir."

By midday it was apparent that the *Xia* was running toward the eastern reaches of the Yellow Sea, down the shores of South Korea, and on into the first reasonably deep water, where Judd Crocker and his men awaited her.

1400. Tuesday, June 27.
Chinese Eastern Fleet Naval Base, Shanghai.

Five hundred miles west of the lurking *Seawolf*, Admiral Zhang Yushu, Commander-in-Chief of the People's Liberation Army/Navy (PLAN), had placed the entire Eastern Fleet on high alert for a prowling American nuclear submarine. His own overheads had seen *Seawolf* clear Pearl, but they had not spotted her since, which was not a great testimony to their skill with the stolen American sub-spotting system from the satellites.

And now he sat in the office of the Eastern Fleet Commander, Admiral Yibo Yunsheng, himself a former commanding officer of the first, disastrous *Xia*. They were ruminating, over endless cups of fragrant China tea, on the problem of getting the gleaming new 13,000-ton *Xia III* safely under the water away from the prying eyes and, they hoped, the sonars of the U.S. Navy.

"You just know they're going to be out there somewhere," said Admiral Zhang, scowling, his dark eyes at the same time hard and irritated behind his heavy, horn-rimmed spectacles. At the age of 59 he was, without question, the most forward-thinking C-in-C the People's Liberation Navy had ever had. A tempestuous man of six feet, he was tall for that country, and he wore his thick black mop of hair longer than is customary in the Chinese military.

But he had the ear and the trust of the Paramount Ruler of China. Zhang was enormously powerful, and if he had a mind to mobilize the entire fleet, to seek out and destroy any American interlopers, then that command would be carried out to the letter.

A former commanding officer of a Luda-class guided missile destroyer, Zhang was a worthy opponent for Captain Judd Crocker, and indeed for Admirals Arnold Morgan and Joe Mulligan, half a world away, strangers at arms, their minds locked onto the precise same subject, China's new submarine, with its menacing cargo of intercontinental ballistic missiles.

"Where do you think they'll wait?" asked Admiral Yibo.

"We have to assume in the first available deep water, out east off the Japanese coast . . . but it's a vast area, and if they have sent the *Seawolf*, she'll be extremely hard to locate. That's a very, very quiet ship. They say she's virtually silent under twenty knots."

"Hmmmmm," replied Admiral Yibo. "Not good."

Just then a uniformed secretary came in with a single sheet of paper that she handed to the Eastern Fleet commander. "For you, sir, I think quite important, from Naval Intelligence, Ningbo. Captain Zhao."

The memorandum was brief: "*Received signal from Kilo 366 1700 yesterday June 26. 'Suspected transient 10-second contact from nuclear underwater boat while tracking torpedo test firings.' We have no data on Chinese submarine in area. No further contact. Alerted all surface ships in East China Sea.*"

He read it aloud to Admiral Zhang, whose scowl became, if anything, darker. "That's it," he said through gritted teeth. "It's *Seawolf*. The question is, where?"

"Why are you so sure about the ship?"

"Oh, I'm not that sure. But the coincidences are strong. We took the reactor critical in *Xia III* and within twenty-four hours we have America's top nuclear boat leaving Pearl in the middle of the night. According to our sources on the island, her destination was unknown. She's out there, Yibo. Trust me. She's out there."

"But what harm can she do us?"

"Aside from unlocking all of our systems, finding out the *Xia*'s capabilities in every respect, and gauging the power and effectiveness of her missiles, it is not beyond the bounds of possibility that the *Xia* could just disappear in deep water. You don't know those devils in the Pentagon like I do. They've done it to us before, and they'll stop at nothing to retain their position as the world's dominant power."

Zhang, a man known as the supreme pragmatist of the High Command of the Chinese military, actually changed physically at the very prospect of conflict with the Pentagon. His stern but passive expression grew immediately dark and vengeful, as if someone was threatening his immediate family.

It was not so much the advent of an obvious opponent, it was this particular opponent, the all-powerful United States of America. It seemed that whenever there was a standoff, China came off worse, especially in matters naval. The big American Carrier Battle Groups, forever prowling close to Taiwan, Japan and the Philippines, were literally the bane of his life, always too strong, too fast and too threatening.

And how could he ever forget the terrible weeks two years previously when the U.S. Navy decided to eliminate *seven* of his new-built Russian submarines, the elusive diesel-electric Kilo-class boats? The colossal cost of trying to protect them, the sheer helplessness he felt in the face of the pitiless underwater marauders from the Pentagon—no, Zhang would never forget those days.

He would never forget the ultimate humiliation, the ruthlessness of the U.S. Navy. And he would never forgive either; not for the gigantic cost in losses to China's military, nor for the loss of so many of the PLAN's leading submariners. Worse yet, he, Zhang, would *never* forgive the U.S. for the loss of face he had suffered, both before his peers and in his own warrior's soul.

"Zhang, would you sink *Seawolf*, if you could?"

"I might. I just might."

"But how?"

"I think two Kilos might do the job very satisfactorily. Should we ever locate her again."

271801JUN06.
33.00N 128.10E. Depth 150. Speed 5.
Course three-one-five.

"The satellites have her, sir. The Chinaman is steering zero-nine-zero, running north of Cheju Island . . . that's about seventy miles to our west-nor'west. Still heading straight toward. We just need to hang around right here, she's gonna come right on by."

Pearson spoke in the certain navigational tones of a man who was guiding the destiny of *Xia III*. But Judd Crocker understood that. They'd come a long way, and their quarry was about to fetch up over the horizon.

Personally, Judd was kind of impressed with himself that he had called her course out several days ago. All on his own, studying the chart. But he tempered that self-congratulatory mode by telling himself that any submariner on earth knows you head for the deepest water, whether you come from Massachusetts or Manchuria.

And now they could only wait, stay dived and silent, and keep a weather eye out for escort ships. His orders were rigid on that one point: Don't get detected. He just had to make sure the sonar room stayed on high alert, listening for a rise in the levels, listening for the throb of the *Xia*'s propeller, watching for her engine lines on the screen, staying well off track, and then falling in quietly behind, tracking her until she dived. And then sticking to her like a limpet.

If the *Xia* dived, they would have no more help from the overheads. The next satellite pass was not due for another couple of hours. By then *Xia III* would be long past. At least she should be. And Judd checked his watch again—1900 now—and, echoing the plaintive cry of his ultimate boss, he muttered, "Well—where the hell is she?"

The answer was, close. At 1900 *Xia III* was still on the surface, just clearing the northeast headland of Cheju Island, and setting a southeasterly course that would take her within five miles of the waiting *Seawolf* at around 2010. She had made an even more direct beeline for the deep water than Judd Crocker had expected, and he smiled quietly as his sonars picked her up, steaming toward him at 25 knots.

"Conn-Sonar. I'm getting something, sir . . . just a faint mark on the trace . . ."

"Hard left rudder . . . resolve ambiguity . . ."

Seawolf swung left, permitting her towed array to reveal whether the approaching ship was to port or starboard.

"Right off our port bow, sir. Bearing three-four-five. Designate track two-zero. Checking machinery profiles right now."

The control room was silent as everyone listened for the verdict from the sonar officer—almost the only sound in the entire ship was that of Frank's fingers punching the keyboard of his computer. Then he called it.

"Conn-Sonar. Right here we have a twin-shafted nuclear ship with shrouded props . . . the engine is Russian, big GT3A turbines . . . profile fits the engine lines of a Russian Typhoon ICBM."

"So that's how they did it," murmured Judd Crocker. "They doubled the size of the old *Xia* to cope with their new stolen missiles—but they used a Russian engine for propulsion. They sure are buddy-buddies these days. I know one Admiral Morgan who is not going to love this."

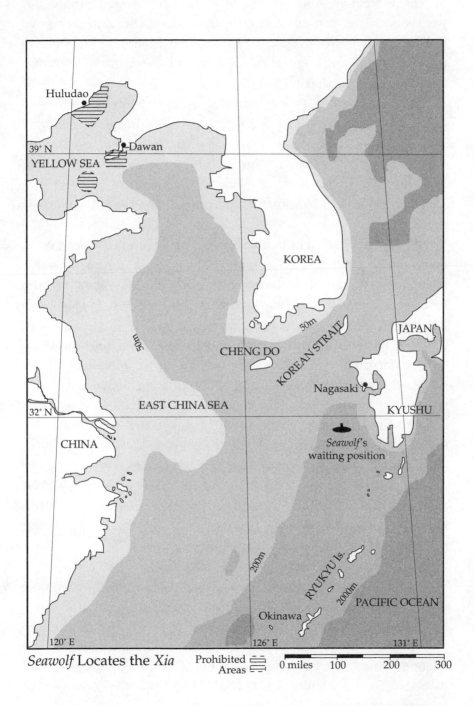

Huludao

39° N
YELLOW SEA

Dawan

KOREA

CHENG DO

50m

KOREAN STRAIT

JAPAN

Nagasaki

32° N   EAST CHINA SEA

50m

KYUSHU

CHINA

Seawolf's
waiting position

200m

RYUKYU Is.

2000m

PACIFIC OCEAN

Okinawa

120° E   126° E   131° E

Seawolf Locates the *Xia*   Prohibited
                                Areas   0 miles   100   200   300

The *Xia* came on toward them, passing to the east about 7,000 yards distant, still on the surface. *Seawolf* fell in behind, about two miles off the Chinese boat's stern, and together they proceeded through the deep trough of ocean that runs west of the Japanese archipelago of small islands.

Captain Crocker twice made a sharp 15-minute move to periscope depth for a visual check on the big missile submarine from Huludao. But his chances were limited. Right on the 32-degree line of latitude, 62 miles off the western coastline of Kyushu, *Xia III* dived, driving down to a depth of 200 feet, her speed dropping to 12 knots, the first time she had ever been below the surface.

Seawolf tracked her, adjusting her own depth and speed, very occasionally pinging the *Xia* with the very latest disguised active sonar, almost impossible to detect, even by the Americans and the Brits. The trouble was, no one on board the American spy ship knew whether the Chinese were using the same system, despite the fact that they had acquired it under the most suspicious circumstances.

The uncertainty concerning China's ability to actually use what they had hijacked was unsettling to the officers of *Seawolf*. Were they being located by a silent satellite probing the waters from space? Were they being unknowingly pinged with a disguised active sonar, as they were pinging the *Xia*?

"Generally speaking, Linus, my policy is that no news is good news. It's my belief that if the Chinese could locate us, they'd do it right away, and then act immediately to clear us right out of the area. Or at least try to. So far, no one's done anything. Which means we are almost certainly undetected."

"Can't argue with any of that, sir," said Clarke.

But at that moment, the peace of *Seawolf*'s control room was ruffled.

"Conn-Sonar. The *Xia*'s turning . . ."

Frank's operator was watching the turbo alternator, and on the 60-hertz frequency it had been showing for some while it had moved to 63 hertz, which meant the *Xia* had shifted the range rate from zero to some 18 knots closing.

"JESUS! She's coming almost straight at us . . . speed six knots . . ."

"LEFT FULL RUDDER," snapped Crocker. "Make your course zero-nine-zero. I'm going clear to the east of her . . . make your speed six knots."

Seawolf swung away, toward the Japanese coastline.

"Sir, have we been detected?"

"Does she know we're here, or what?"

"Christ, I bet it's that satellite system they stole. Are these guys watching our every move?"

"Easy, gentlemen," said Judd. "She's probably just clearing her baffles, checking her stern arcs, making sure no one *is* following her. Put yourself in her place . . . you're on the maiden voyage of the last word in Chinese missile submarine technology. You're running south down this lonely sea to find deep water to conduct your trials. On board you probably have, or at least you will have, intercontinentals powerful enough to knock down a major American city.

"You *know* the U.S. is more than just interested. You *know* they will at least try to take a look. You *know* the U.S. is light years ahead in all submarine technology. Would you take the occasional look over your shoulder? Sure you would, just to check."

"Conn-Sonar. Range rate now opening . . . the *Xia* has probably resumed her course, sir. She bears one-eight-zero . . . speed twelve knots like before . . . ."

"Excellent," said the CO. "She was just checking, and I expect she'll do it again before we're much older. Stand by, Kyle, it could happen any time."

They ran on south for another 100 miles before the *Xia* turned again, and again Captain Crocker evaded, moving east and waiting for the Chinese captain to return to his course.

But the pattern changed as they approached the 26-degree line. The *Xia*, now running south-southwest in line with the islands, made as if to turn, but then took an even more westerly route, heading quite suddenly for the northern waters of the Taiwan Strait.

Judd attempted to follow, at least up to the line of the Japanese current, where the water was still 3,000 feet deep in places. But beyond there it began to shelve right up to 150 feet. *Seawolf* could not go into the Strait without being immediately detected, because of the surface wake.

And to no one's surprise, *Xia III* came suddenly to the surface 30 miles off the northwest coast of Taiwan, before proceeding down the much-disputed stretch of seaway that separates mainland China from her wealthy independent neighbors.

Seawolf was stranded, and with mixed feelings Captain Crocker turned around and headed back into the deep water east of the island.

"Gentlemen," he said, "we're going to plan B. My guess is that the *Xia* is heading for one of their bases, maybe with a problem, or two, or ten. I expect she'll make for Xiamen. From there when she continues, I think she'll go south and exit the Strait at the far end. We, meanwhile, will make a fast run around the seaward side of Taiwan in deep water, and then creep up the south coast to wait for her."

Wednesday evening. June 28. Gulangyu Island, Xiamen.

Admiral Zhang's summer home, with its curved red roof and lush trees and flowers, was situated across the narrow Lujiang Channel, on the Isle of the Thundering Waves. Tonight, he and his wife, Lan, enjoying the soft sea breezes, sat quietly sipping white wine with their great friend Admiral Zu Jicai, Commander of the Southern Fleet.

Both men had flown into Xiamen by Navy aircraft that morning, Zhang from Shanghai, Admiral Zu from his Fleet HQ in Zhanjiang way down in the south.

"And so, my friend Yushu, you really believe there is an American submarine out there in the China Sea tracking the new *Xia*?"

"I do, and I dearly want to do something about it. But I don't know what I can do. I know they're out there, but heaven knows where."

"It's a big ocean, and we don't really know where to start, huh?"

"No. We don't. But I am wondering whether that slight valve

problem that has caused our submarine to put into Xiamen tonight might, in the end, be good for us."

"How do you mean?"

"Well, if you were the American Commander and you were quietly following the *Xia* down the Yellow Sea and she suddenly broke off and headed down the shallow Taiwan Strait on the surface, what would you do?"

"I don't know, really, but with a big ship like *Seawolf*, I obviously could not follow her."

"Correct. So what would you do? Wait . . . I'll tell you. First, you would guess there was a problem and that she was heading for one of our bases on the far shore, right? And you, my friend Jicai, driving that very fast American attack submarine, would race right around the outside of Taiwan and try to pick her up again when she exits the Strait at the south end."

"Well," said the Southern Commander thoughtfully, "you could send the *Xia* back to the north end, leaving the Americans stranded 300 miles away in the south."

"No point. The American satellites would pick the *Xia* up in an instant, and simply let *Seawolf* know where she was."

"You don't think the Americans would actually hit the *Xia*, do you?"

"Jicai, I really do not know. The trouble with submarines is they don't get hit. At least not publicly. They just vanish, usually in thousands of feet of water. If *Seawolf* did hit our new submarine we would have no idea where it was. It could take years to find. We don't have the technology—and even if we found it, we could certainly not bring it to the surface. It would just be another of those submarine mysteries. And there would be no point even asking the Pentagon. They'd just say they had no idea what we were talking about."

"That's why you are so anxious to get them out of our waters, eh?"

"Precisely. But I do know one thing. They are out there. I feel it. I am certain of it. I know them so well."

The following morning, Admiral Zhang went for a long walk very early, before the heat of the morning set in. Then he and

Admiral Zu had a light breakfast of tea and pastries before taking the short walk down to the shore, where the naval launch picked them up and ferried them over to the base.

Although Zhang was technically in charge of the entire Chinese navy, it was Admiral Zu, working now in one of his own Southern Fleet bases, who called a staff meeting of six commanding officers currently in residence with their ships' operational, destroyer and frigate captains.

He carefully explained the suspicions of the Commander-in-Chief, who sat impassively beside him. And he mentioned to them the possible detection by the Kilo, three days previously, of an American nuclear submarine.

He outlined an area off the southwest coast of Taiwan where he expected the American boat to be waiting tomorrow around midday. He pinpointed the position, 22.45N 119.50E, in the southern entrance to the Strait, 20 miles west of the Taiwan Banks, where the ocean shelves away from 300 feet to 1,000 feet. "That's submarine country, gentlemen," he said. "As you all well know.

"Tomorrow morning the *Xia* will leave Xiamen and head back out to deeper water to continue her trials," he told them. "The American satellite will undoubtedly observe this. We thus expect the Americans to be on station somewhere around the area I have just given you, and the wishes of our Commander-in-Chief are that you open up with a barrage of depth charges and mortars. We want you to make enough noise to suggest a war is starting.

"Essentially we want to frighten them off—send them back to Pearl Harbor. But if one or more of you happens to blow the American hull apart and sink her, then you will receive the unspoken but nonetheless heartfelt thanks of our country."

All six of the commanding officers smiled, and for the first time Admiral Zhang himself stood up and spoke to them. "Gentlemen, I am sure you understand. Such a terrible shame if the Americans brought their best submarine blundering into our waters, without telling us, right into the middle of one of our frequent fleet exercises in antisubmarine warfare. Such a pity for them to lose a great ship like that . . . but what can we say? We had no idea they were there. Most unfortunate. Most unfortunate."

That speech received a serious laugh, with much nodding of heads, as the captains left to rejoin their warships.

Their little fleet would comprise the two heavily gunned Luda-class guided missile destroyers, *Zhanjiang* and *Nanchang*, both equipped with two FQF antisubmarine mortars (range 1,200 meters) plus four BMB depth-charge projectors. The new updated Luda III-class destroyer *Zuhai*, the fastest of the three, would be the only one carrying the CY-1 antisubmarine weapon.

The three light frigates were all of the Jianghu-class (Type 053), *Shantou*, *Kangding*, and *Jishou*, 1,500-tonners, all with A/S mortars and racks of depth charges, plus the Echo Type 5 sonar system, hull-mounted, active search and attack, medium frequency.

"Thank you, gentlemen," said the C-in-C. "I know you will not let me down."

300700JUN06.
22.00N 120.10E. Depth 300 feet. Speed 12.
Bearing zero-two-zero.

USS *Seawolf* was creeping silently along southwestern Taiwan, heading nor'nor'east, staying in the deep water, 18 miles offshore. Lt. Shawn Pearson was hunched over his chart, plotting their course inch by inch up the coast. "We can continue along here for quite a way, sir," he said. "Seventy miles from now, still holding this course, we'll still be in almost five hundred feet of water . . . wanna leave two sandbanks to port twenty-five miles further on from here, but aside from that we're golden."

"Our biggest problem is knowing when the *Xia* leaves," replied the CO. "It's only about seventy miles from the Xiamen base to the choke point of the Strait. She's gonna be across here, on the surface, hopefully just south of us, in about three hours. If the satellite passes don't fit our program we just need to get inshore and watch for her to show up."

"She's big enough, sir," said Frank. "Half again as big as us. And she makes a noise. If she comes this way, we'll find her."

In fact *Seawolf* picked her up at 1130, 18 miles away. It was a sharp piece of work by the technicians, because they had been busy in the previous hour with a lot of surface ships, all Chinese, all navy, all growling their way out from Xiamen, probably on some kind of an exercise.

Right now Judd Crocker had his ship positioned at 23.25N 119.55E, facing the open sea, with Taiwan 20 miles astern. They patrolled slowly, just south of the lonely Peng-hu Islands, with their miles of breathtakingly perfect sandy beaches.

The ops room was still picking up a lot of activity 30 miles to the southwest, but that was not a priority. The priority, all 13,000 tons of her, was right now headed at 25 knots to a point 20 miles southwest, and Judd Crocker ordered, "Left standard rudder . . . make your course two-one-zero . . . make your speed fifteen knots."

That way he figured he'd run right in behind the *Xia* and finally track her out to the really deep water he craved. But one hour later, the picture changed rapidly. Sonar picked up a succession of thunderous explosions in the water, the unmistakable sound of antisubmarine depth charges.

What the hell's going on?

That was one unspoken question. But there was another more important one running through the assembled minds: *Have they spotted us?*

If they have, they're a bit off target, thought the CO. *They are moving toward us, but their depth charges are going off 10 miles south of us. Since one of 'em has to blast within 15 feet of the pressure hull to do any serious damage . . . well, right now it's not life-threatening.*

Typically, Judd said, "Well, XO, what do you make of all this?"

"Not a problem yet, sir," said Clarke. "But if they are advancing in line, and hammering away with all that hardware, they have us in some kind of a trap, right? We can't go north into the shallow water, and they are to the south of us. We have to go through them. Sir, they've got us bottled up."

"Not quite, Linus," replied the CO, not ordering a change in speed or direction. And now the explosions were growing louder, a situation Judd knew was going to get worse. At 3,000 yards a depth charge can sound like an atomic bomb, if you're scared.

"Conn-Sonar. Heavy ordnance out there right now, sir. Still depth charges and some lighter stuff as well."

"Scare charges, possibly hand grenades," muttered the CO. "They haven't the first idea whether we're here or not. Gimme a reading on the *Xia*."

"Still making at twenty-five knots on the surface, sir. Still on course one-three-five. She'll pass four thousand yards to our southwest. The way the Chinese Battle Group's moving, she'll be about three miles north of 'em when we pick her up."

"Thanks, Kyle."

Seawolf kept moving stealthily forward, slowing down to ensure her precise position astern of the *Xia* when the moment came. It was like maneuvering at the start of a yacht race, into the final countdown, burning off time, jockeying for position. Judd Crocker, personally at the conn, was good at that, not as good as his father, but certainly too good for the Chinese.

"I'm going in closer," he said, amid the thunder of the charges. "Right in tight behind the *Xia*, maybe less than a mile . . . watch it for me, Linus . . . check with Kyle and Shawn . . . this is pretty damned tricky . . . remember that right now we can't go real deep if we get caught . . . keep our speed as low as possible . . . but get right on the stern of that damned big submarine of theirs.

"Those frigates will sure as hell stop throwing depth charges and mortars when she closes them. I'm not sure how good a shot their lead mortar man is, but he doesn't want to slam one into China's newest submarine. They'd probably execute him . . . so they'll let up for sure while the *Xia* goes through.

"Then they'll probably start up again, but by that time we'll be through as well, so long as we get in real tight, right in her stern arcs. I'm coming to periscope depth for a quick look. How's your trim, Andy?"

Seawolf 's massive hull angled up and then leveled off right below the surface. The periscope slid smoothly up from the top of the sail, breaking the surface of the calm turquoise sea.

"She's right where she's supposed to be . . . I'd say she'll cross our bow in the next five minutes . . . . still heading southeast."

"DOWN PERISCOPE . . . FIVE DOWN . . . MAKE YOUR DEPTH THREE HUNDRED.

"Don't want to hang around near the surface too long," muttered the captain. "Even though we're far away from any shore radar, and those warships are causing such a commotion they probably wouldn't detect us if we ran up a flag. But we take no chances . . . not in this game. We just assume that every man's hand is turned against us."

Seawolf edged forward, running smoothly now at 10 knots, her sonar room softly tracking the oncoming *Xia* on passive. "Okay, sir . . . we should turn in right now . . ."

"Left standard rudder . . . course one-three-five . . . make your depth three hundred feet . . . increase speed . . . twenty-five knots . . . we're going in now . . ."

Clarke now had the conn, and he steered the American prowler almost into the wake of the *Xia*. There was less than 1,000 yards between them, but at this depth *Seawolf* left no telltale surface disturbance, and her superb acoustic cladding made her *almost* undetectable.

The thunder of the depth charges was growing louder now, inside the two-mile range. For the past few minutes it had seemed as if they were headed into a major war zone, as the mortars detonated with booming resonance deep in the sunlit summer waters of the Strait.

"Enough to wake the dead," observed Brad Stockton.

"Worse than that," added the CO. "It's enough to wake the Taiwanese Navy. They'll be wondering what the hell is going on. Dollars to doughnuts they're on the horn to the Pentagon right now, reporting that mainland China appears to have declared war."

At 25 knots, the *Xia* and her shadow were covering a mile every two and a half minutes. And suddenly the underwater bombardment stopped as the giant Chinese missile boat came within range. Up on the surface the three Luda-class destroyers formed up line astern to watch the great symbol of Chinese naval power come steaming by on the surface. Captains are called Colonels in the People's Liberation Army/Navy, and all three of them now stood with the ship's company, beneath the ensign of the PLAN, the scarlet flag with its single yellow star set above the distinctive black and white bars. The three Jianghu frigates formed up identically to the east, and the entire six-ship Fleet offered a salute as the *Xia* went by, officers and men alike cheering and clapping as she rolled past.

They were still cheering as she steamed away from them, for almost a mile—almost a mile too long for Judd Crocker and his men, who had also slid right by, literally under the Chinese noses. And now *Seawolf* was safely heading southeast, beyond the barrage. And when the depth charges began anew, blasting holes in the calm waters, in a northern direction, it was much too late to harm the American interloper. And soon the noises began to soften and then die away altogether, as Clarke gunned *Seawolf* onward out into the deep Pacific, away from Admiral Zhang's trap.

Now there was complete peace beyond the Americans' pressure hull as they proceeded along the lovely south coast of Taiwan, where the plains of lush farmlands rise up to meet the great range of the Chungyang Mountains sweeping southward, down to the sea.

"SHE DIVES, SIR! . . . THE *XIA*'S GOING DEEP . . . MAINTAINS HER SPEED AND BEARING . . . RANGE ONE MILE . . ."

"Let's drop a little further behind now . . . we can follow her easily at two miles," said the captain. "Just wanna be on the safe side, and we don't need to be so close. Make your speed fifteen for six minutes.. . . ..then return to twenty-five . . . so long as the Chinaman maintains . . . watch her, Kyle."

And now the two submarines moved in tandem. At the 22-degree line of latitude the *Xia* made a course change to the southwest, running fast down the coast of the mainland province of Guangdong, about 65 miles offshore in water 10,000 feet deep.

In Judd Crocker's view she was headed for an unknown ops area where she would conduct her sea trials. By 1830 they were

300 miles shy of the Canton Roads, forbidden waters for centuries to all but Chinese shipping. This rule, of course, excluded the British, who arrived regularly, assuming as ever their general ownership of the entire world, and ultimately not giving a bilge rat's ass whether they were invited or not.

Pearson estimated they would be right off Canton (Guangzhou in modern Chinese) by first light on July 1. Meanwhile, in company with *Xia III*, they charged through the night on a head of steam generated by Thompson's sweet-running pressurized water reactor (PWR).

The other major head of steam in Chinese waters that evening was generated by a fuming Admiral Zhang, who glowered across at the lazy, gaff-rigged junks while he made the short ferry journey home to Gulangyu. No wreckage had been found, no one had reported any kind of a hit or oil slick, and his captains had been driven to the conclusion that no American nuclear boat was tracking the new *Xia* at this time. Each of the surface warships had kept up the barrage around the new Chinese submarine for a total of two hours, and had blown upward of 200 depth charges and the same number of ASW mortars. Result: a big fat nothing.

Zhang did not believe them. At least, he did not believe their conclusion. But he did believe they had tried and missed. Which was a personal blow to him, because in his heart he had truly hoped one of those depth charges would have blown a big hole in the hull of USS *Seawolf*. The fact that they had not done so merely meant they had not fired one close enough. It did not mean *Seawolf* was not there. It meant that she was devilishly hard to find, and that she was being driven by a master, with a brilliantly competent crew.

0900. Friday, June 30.
Office of the National Security Adviser to the President.

At one minute past the hour Admiral Morgan let fly, ignoring as ever the state-of-the-art White House telephone system.

"*COFFEE!*" he bellowed.

At one minute and eight seconds past the hour, his door opened briskly and Kathy O'Brien walked in.

"Good. Nice and quick. The way I like it. Bit more practice and you'll be just fine."

The admiral did not look up.

"I am afraid that even I, even at my most devoted, cannot produce coffee the way you like it in under ten seconds."

"Right," he said, still not looking up. "Three buckshot and stir, *s'il vous plaît . . .*"

The admiral had taken to the use of occasional French phrases ever since their perfect weekend in Paris in April. Kathy hoped that one more visit would persuade him that the *t* in *plaît* was in fact silent.

"Oh, Great One," she said, "whose mind operates only on matters so huge the rest of us mortals can't quite get it . . . I bring messages from the military."

And she scuffed his papers all over the place and told him that she loved him, even though she had only just got to work, whereas he had been at his desk since 0600.

"Where's my coffee?" he wondered, grinning, faking absent-mindedness.

"Christ, you're impossible," she confirmed. "Listen do you want me to get Admiral Mulligan on the phone or do you not? His assistant called two minutes ago and asked you to get back to him secure."

"Of course, and hurry, will you? Goddamned women fussing about coffee when the country's far eastern fleet may be on the brink of destruction."

"It's you who stands on the brink of destruction," retorted Kathy as she marched out of the door. "Because I may of course kill you one day."

"Now what the hell have I done?" the admiral asked the portrait of General Patton. "And where's the goddamned CNO if it's that urgent?"

The pastel green telephone tinkled lightly, grotesquely out of character with its master. "Faggot phone. Faggot ring. I'd rather listen to a goddamned battleship's klaxon." He picked it up.

"Hey, Joe. What's hot?"

And then Arnold Morgan went very quiet as the Navy's top man in the Pentagon outlined the recent uproar in the Taiwan Strait.

"Taipei came in right away when it started, sometime before lunch today. They reported a small Chinese battle fleet about twenty miles off their southwestern naval base at Kaohsiung, hurling hardware every which way.

"The Taiwanese have a pretty big air base down there at P'ing-tung and they sent up a couple of those Grumman S2E turbo trackers . . . worked the place over from twenty-five thousand feet, reported a lot of action, ordnance flying around, mortars and depth charges. They reported no missiles over their land, and they were not fired on.

"The only thing that surprised them was a big ICBM submarine, heading southeast, probably out of Xiamen, on the surface, flying the pennant of the People's Liberation Army/Navy. They didn't report any other submarine in the area, either on or below the surface. Which I thought was surprising, because the Taiwanese have turned those Grummans into real specialist ASW aircraft—new sensors, new APS 504 search radar, sonobuoys, Mark 24 torpedoes, depth charges, depth bombs, the lot. If there was another big sub in the Chinese ops area, they'da surely found it. Hell, we've sold 'em all our latest stuff. They have, legally, nearly as much as the Chinese stole . . ."

"And your conclusion, CNO?"

"I don't know where our man is."

"Well, they plainly haven't hit him, or half the world would know by now."

"Right. According to Taipei, the bombardment was over by fourteen-thirty."

"So I guess he's still there, lurking."

"Well, he could hardly have followed them into the Taiwan Strait, Arnie. Not without a big risk. Too shallow. Maybe he hung around to the south, then picked up the *Xia* on her way to her ops area. I presume she's conducting sea trials."

"And our people believe she's going to be based at the Southern

Fleet headquarters at Zhanjiang, Joe . . . so she's plainly on her way south, probably right off that base."

"I guess we oughtta be grateful we're undetected. Anyway, I'm just checking in. Thought you'd wanna be kept up to speed."

"I'm grateful, Joe. By the way, you know my conclusion? The Chinese *believe* we're out there watching. And if they get half a chance, I think they may actually hit our ship. And then say how goddamned sorry they were, but we really should have told them if we wanted to go creeping around their coastline."

"Wouldn't that be just like them? Devious Orientals."

"Chinese pricks. 'Bye, Joe."

Admiral Mulligan was oblivious to the compliment. The National Security Adviser never said good-bye to anyone except the CNO. He was too busy, too preoccupied to bother with that. Even the President was occasionally left holding a dead phone while his military adviser charged forward with zero thought for the niceties of high office.

"He just don't pay no one no never mind," was the verdict of Arnold's permanently cowed chauffeur, Charlie. "Ain't got time, man . . . ain't got no-o-o-o time."

020130JULY06.
20.50N 116.40E South China Sea. Speed 25. Depth 200. Course 250.

Lt. Commander Clarke had the conn as they ran through deep water more than 100 miles south of the Chinese Naval Base at Shantou. The *Xia* was showing no signs of stopping, turning, or slowing down, just heading resolutely southwest down the coast.

Judd Crocker's team assessed that her ops area would be somewhere out around 20.25N 111.46E, east-southeast of Zhanjiang, Southern Fleet HQ. And there she would doubtless dive, before heading out to begin her deep submergence trials. But there she would also probably come up occasionally, access her satellite, report defects if anything urgent popped up, and perhaps rendezvous with a surface escort.

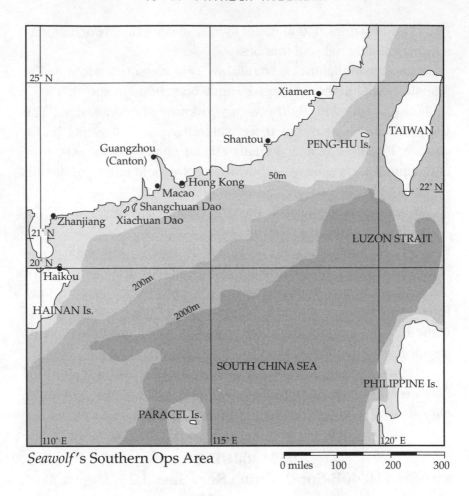

Seawolf's Southern Ops Area

The first time she did that, night or day, Judd Crocker would personally take *Seawolf* deeper and slide with the utmost stealth under her keel. Dead under. Accurate to a few inches, unseen, undetected, pinging sonar all along the hull, drawing an automatic picture on the fathometer trace; the one that would tell the U.S. Navy scientists back in Washington whether or not China had the capacity to hurl a big missile at Los Angeles and hit it.

By any standards, Captain Crocker had been charged with the most stupendous task. Spying on a foreign submarine, listening and watching, recording and tracking, was one thing. Trying to get a real close look, straight up her skirt, as it were, was entirely another, even more so without being caught doing it. But it had been done before, notably by the Brits in the Barents Sea at the height of the Cold War in the late 1960s and early 1970s.

One of their COs got very close underneath a 10,000-ton Soviet Delta-class nuclear boat designed to carry submarine launched ballistic missiles (SLBM), and took soundings upward along the entire submerged part of the hull. He got away with it, too . . . but to complete the measurements he had to raise his periscope 100 yards off her port quarter for the photographs that would reveal the above-water height of the missile tubes.

He eased the periscope up, the tip of it only 18 inches above the flat, calm surface. His aim was a seven-second, three-exposure snatch. But an oil smear wrecked all that. To his horror, he saw an image too badly blurred for camera work. And that meant at least a 30-second delay while it hung out to dry in the hostile Russian air.

To his further horror, as the image cleared he saw a small crowd gathering on the Delta's bridge. And they were pointing straight at his periscope, and his recording camera, the eyes of the West, the ultimate intruder.

A massive three-day ASW hunt ensued, conducted by most of the Russian Northern Fleet, but the British commanding officer essentially ran rings around the Soviets and got away with the required measurements scot-free.

Very few American commanders knew that story, and none of them knew the man who did it. But not many COs had been tasked with repeating the maneuver, as Judd Crocker now was.

Happily he was sound asleep as Linus Clarke sped southwest, astern of the *Xia*, covering 25 nautical miles every hour.

The watch changed at 0400. Captain Crocker came back into the control room, and Clarke handed over formally.

"You have the conn, sir."

"I have the conn."

Both men were surprised at the noise the new Chinese boat was making. At 25 knots you could hear her for a long way, but then she was traveling fast for her, whereas *Seawolf* was merely cruising, just a little over half-speed, right in her quarry's deaf stern arcs.

*   *   *

As Admiral Zhang had remarked that morning, "If only we could find a way to adapt that American satellite technology we acquired from them. But alas, we seem doomed to failure on that one. As I seem doomed to failure to find and 'accidentally' sink the American prowler. They cannot fool me, however. I know they're out there, still tracking my very beautiful new *Xia*."

It was 4:00 A.M. now and the C-in-C could not sleep. He remained alone in his study, overlooking the water. He was still in uniform, but he wore no shoes. Outside it was raining hard, with the onset of the South China monsoon season. Tomorrow there would be heavy mist out over the water.

But for now he just pored over his chart. The one that gave him all the depths after the 100-meter line south of Zhanjiang, the one that marked out clearly the operations area of *Xia III*.

At 0430 he tapped in a message to Zu Jicai, the Southern Commander, instructing him to place all 14 of his operational destroyers and frigates on one hour's notice to leave for the *Xia*'s ops area. He instructed each ship to be on full ASW alert, laden to the gunwales with depth charges, depth bombs, torpedoes and, for those equipped with launchers, ASW mortars.

He ordered a satellite message to be delivered to the *Xia*'s CO that he was to surface immediately if he detected even the slightest suggestion of an American nuclear boat, and to report instantly to HQ. That way he could get his ASW fleet out there fast. That way the *Xia* would be safe. Even the American gangsters would not dare to hit her while she was on the surface in full view of the satellites.

He paced the room, slapping his left palm with his big ruler, running his fingers through his hair. "The trouble is, I have to rely on the American CO making a mistake. And since he is driving the top submarine in the American Navy, he probably makes very few.

"But if he does, I'll get him. And what a moment that would be." And in his mind he imagined the moment when he would speak to the C-in-C of the American military, sympathizing with the terrible loss of *Seawolf*.

But Mr. President, we are so sorry. However, if you send a big nuclear boat into any part of the South China Sea, especially so

*close to our coastline, to spy on our perfectly legal naval opera-
tions . . . then accidents can sometimes happen. What more can I
say? If only you had told us you were coming, we would have
been so much more careful.*

*Perhaps you will in the future. Again, our profound apologies,
and deepest sympathies to the families of the brave men who died.*

And for the first time in this longest of nights, a thin smile flickered across the broad face of the Commander-in-Chief of the People's Liberation Navy.

Even though there was no reality; it was only in his mind.

030800JUL06.
20.00N 112.46E. South China Sea. West of Hainan
Island. Speed 6. Depth 300. Course: racetrack pattern.

SEAWOLF'S QUARRY HAD SLOWED RIGHT DOWN
and gone deeper, and Linus Clarke seized the opportunity to
take a fast look at the surface picture. He ordered the American
submarine to periscope depth, but he didn't see much. A tallow-
colored mist hung low over the South China Sea, and visibility
was down to a matter of perhaps 40 yards. He activated the lens
into its all-seeing nighttime mode, but still there seemed to be
nothing around. The seas were deserted, except for *Seawolf* and
Admiral Zhang's ballistic missile ship *Xia*, and she was two miles
away, 500 feet below the surface.

These heavy mists are commonplace in July, around the 180-
mile-long, tropical island of Hainan, home of yet another sprawling
Chinese naval base in the northern town of Haikou. With the onset

of the monsoon from the southwest, this was the heavy rain season, and the heat along Hainan's spectacular beaches was ghastly, the humidity in the high nineties.

The operations area of the *Xia* was more or less where the brains onboard *Seawolf* had expected, 60 miles east of the Haikou base, 170 miles south-southeast of Fleet Headquarters, within easy reach of assistance and rescue, a process not entirely new to the Chinese navy, given their track record of trying to run nuclear submarines.

Linus Clarke ordered *Seawolf* back into the depths. The sonar was quiet, and on the lower decks the men played poker between watches and ate steaks for lunch in the time-honored tradition of serving the best food in the U.S. military to the men who serve underwater, in the crowded, windowless ships, constantly in harm's way during the course of their duties. Tonight being Monday, they were showing a rerun of an old football game between the Giants and the Redskins from the ship's sizeable library of sports videos. A sweepstakes was being run, five dollars a chance for the nearest guess at the date of the game, winner take all. The competitive nature of *Monday Night Football* dies hard, even 300 feet below the surface of the South China Sea.

The evening was full of promise, except for one piece of potentially bad news. "Einstein" reckoned he had the sweepstakes buttoned up. He'd recognized the picture of the Washington running back on the videocassette cover, and claimed he'd used to go to the Redskins games with his father on his birthday. If he could just get the year right, he was home and hosed. *Trust Einstein. Golden sonofabitch.*

Still, if they ever had to fight, Lt. Commander Rothstein, the combat systems officer, would be their man at the sharp end, and in a sense they would be in his hands. The best hands, they all knew. No one could outthink the tall, cool intellect of the missiles. That was why Captain Crocker had specially requested him for the officer complement. Nonetheless, it was still a bitch that he'd probably wrapped up the football sweepstakes before the game even started. *Let's all hope he gets the year wrong . . . . Fat chance. That running back only played two seasons . . . and fucking Einstein has been a Redskins fan since he was born.*

Despite the fact that he was built like a running back himself, Judd Crocker would miss the game tonight; he hoped to get some sleep. Linus Clarke wanted to see the game and volunteered for the midnight watch afterward, assisted by Brad Stockton and Kyle Frank, who would both be on duty.

And the night passed predictably. They stayed in contact at three miles distance with the *Xia;* the Redskins mowed down the Giants; and Einstein won the sweepstakes with the date of his birthday. Tony Fontana, who was next closest by only three weeks, came grumbling down the companionway muttering, "Sonofabitch . . . he even remembered it was an afternoon game played in bright sunshine . . . if we'd both got the date right, he'da done me on the fucking time of day. Sonofabitch. I mean, Jesus, how could we have picked a game played on Einstein's sixteenth fucking birthday?"

Everyone in earshot fell over laughing at the indignation of the engineer from Ohio, and Rothstein graciously offered Tony his five bucks back, admitting he had been on a strong inside track right from the start. Fontana took it, too. Quickly.

Meanwhile, the track of *Xia III* appeared to be southwestward, along the coast of China. She was still deep, and relatively silent, for her, and at 2300 still seemed to be in no hurry, moving forward at only around seven knots. The CO came wide off track to 7,000 yards, and swung onto course two-seven-zero to follow her, slowly and carefully, at the same speed.

By the time Linus came back to the conn, Judd Crocker had *Seawolf* running silently in the *Xia*'s stern arcs again, three miles back, moving easily through the warm calm waters. Up on the surface there was steady rain sweeping across the seascape, the warmth of the air causing the sea fret to gather into a pale, luminous haze right above the water, lit by the moonlight. It would have been quite ghostly had anyone been up there sightseeing. But all around the two steel predators in the deep, there was nothing, hardly a sound, and no one was looking.

Seawolf's XO had an uneventful watch, but he'd been awake

for 12 hours straight, and he was tired out by 0400 on this July Fourth holiday morning, except, of course, that neither he nor any of the crew was entitled to holidays out here. Judd came back to the conn for the watch change, wished Linus a happy Fourth, and told him to go get some sleep.

And once more the new watch took over the ship two hours before dawn would break over the South China Sea. Frank had been aware of no other ships in the area. And *Xia III* still ran slowly west-sou'west, three miles out in front. The navigator reckoned she'd covered only about 28 miles all night.

It was difficult to maintain a mental state of urgency as he rested through the stillness of the uncluttered night, but Judd Crocker was trying to get himself up for this. His mission was clear, the prime part of his mission, that is: to establish the length of the vertical missile tubes on the Chinese ICBM submarine. And his opportunity could come at any time, maybe at dawn, if she surfaced. That would be the time to conduct the most dangerous project he had ever known. If he screwed it up and the Chinese ship heard him, they would plainly get on his track and send for their cavalry, China's aircraft, fast-attack ships, destroyers, frigates, helos, and God knows what, and try to sink him. And they were within 200 miles of two substantial PLAN bases—less than an hour's flying time for a good patrol aircraft, and helicopters loaded with Russian sonobuoys.

Judd Crocker was playing for higher stakes than Einstein and Fontana. It was no wonder that he had been unable to raise any enthusiasm for *Monday Night Football.*

Dawn came flooding across the misty water from out of the eastern reaches of the Pacific shortly after 0540. The rain had stopped. The sonar room still had strong tabs on the *Xia*, and *Seawolf* was working her way along at periscope depth, making a long covert approach, waiting in case the Chinese submarine should surface. Judd thought this could happen at any time, and kept himself ready for urgent action. After all, she was only on workup and might not stay dived for extended periods.

The CO had all of *Seawolf*'s intelligence-gathering equipment on the top line, and the Electrical Intercept (ELINT) and the Communications Intercept (COMINT) were on high alert, the ESM Mast jutting up out of the water with the periscope. Judd was observing a beautiful calm morning on the surface, but with very poor visibility, as they made their way quietly through the known operations area of the *Xia*.

Sonar called that the *Xia* was making unusual noises and could be preparing to surface, but Judd could not see very far through the sunlit mist. His sonar chief thought the *Xia* had gone quiet as she waited between trials, whatever it was they were testing. And suddenly *Seawolf*'s comms picked him up again on the ESM mast.

"Captain-ESM. Racket two-seven-zero . . . STRENGTH FOUR-TWO . . . X-Band . . . approach danger level."

"Captain, AYE . . . DOWN ALL MASTS!"

Still at periscope depth, the Americans ran on for 4,000 more yards, the CO occasionally raising the periscope, straining for a fleeting glimpse. And quite suddenly, lo and behold, there she was, a dim shape in the haze, right up ahead.

"My God!" breathed Judd Crocker. "There she is, our top priority. Is this some kind of a break or what?"

"Captain-Comms. We have an extremely loud signal on your periscope warner."

"Captain, aye."

But *Seawolf* had her target in the cross-hairs. Linus Clarke returned to the conn, drawn by the bush telegraph of a submarine when something big is about to happen.

"We got her, sir . . . ?"

"We got her, Linus. She's just lying there, doing zilch, surfaced, making about five knots, on two-seven-zero.

"I don't think they have the remotest idea we're around. They reckon if that barrage back off Taiwan hit nothing, nothing was there."

"Well, it is oh-six-hundred, sir. They probably think the entire United States Navy is on vacation for the Fourth—and they're dead safe to sit down for a nice breakfast. Sweet and sour corn-flakes. Chopsticks drawn!"

"Heh, heh, heh." Despite their obvious differences, the CO liked the company of Linus Clarke, and he said quietly, "I'm going right in under his stern for the underhull fathometer run."

"Aye, sir."

Seawolf hurried on, into water already shelving up as they closed on the distant mainland. It was not an easy patrol. This being their first day in the area, they had no feel for local inhabitants, no idea who might be scouting around, no place to hide if they should get caught.

Clarke was plainly excited by the prospect of the next hour. He was mercurial in his thoughts: "Should we move under quickly . . . get right in and do our business . . . or should we take it slow and quiet? . . . Personally I'm in favor of speed . . . let's go for it . . . . I mean, we don't want to get caught out here off her stern with our pants down."

And for once he got it roughly right.

The captain said, "I just wish we had more time for a thorough recon of the whole area over here, but time we don't have. Linus, I'm going straight in."

Seawolf came forward at six knots, leaving no wake on the surface. At 350 yards the CO took a last look to confirm the exact bearing and distance of the *Xia*.

"FIVE DOWN . . . MAKE YOUR DEPTH 110 FEET . . . make your speed eight."

"Conn me in on sonar, XO."

"Passing eighty feet, sir."

"UP PERISCOPE."

At this close range, every yard counted. And for the first time, *Seawolf* seemed sluggish, not getting down quickly enough, as if hanging in the water, still going straight, with momentum that appeared to be lasting forever.

"CHRIST! Sir, she's real close," called Linus.

"Okay, okay. I got you. Keep talking me in . . . come on, *Seawolf*, for Christ's sake, fast down and level . . ."

"There's her screws. Bearing. MARK."

"Bearing right ahead, sir. True. Two-seven-zero."

"Read off the sky-search angle, someone."

"Three degrees below horizontal, Captain!"

Linus's voice was rising.

"Good."

"Bubble amidships, sir. Depth one hundred ten feet . . . course two-seven-zero." Andy Cannizaro's voice betrayed tension, but it was firm and clear.

"Captain, aye . . . that angle's not so bad as you think . . . it's the refraction, Linus . . . the periscope's gonna pass underneath her, believe me . . . start the fathometers."

"Upward fathometer recording, sir. Steady trace from the surface, fifty-six feet from the top of our sail, sir."

"Captain, that's nice."

Judd Crocker was now performing the most delicate balancing act of his life, as *Seawolf* matched speed with the bigger Chinese boat, which now rumbled along the surface directly overhead, casting a mammoth black shadow over them, its massive screws thrashing water right above them, threatening instant decapitation of the sail if the American submarine rose more than about 15 feet in the water. But the burly yachtsman from Cape Cod knew all too well what happened when the propellers of a big nuclear ship smash into the hull of another: a lot of steel and sometimes a lot of people end up littering the ocean floor.

Judd held her steady, at six knots, keeping his ship exactly under the center of the *Xia*'s keel, with no time now for even a thought about the Chinese sonar room right above them.

"The *Xia* maintains speed and course, sir . . ."

And then the operator called it: "MARK! Upward sounder showing twenty feet above our sail, sir. I'm looking up right now, right on her center line."

"Beautiful," whispered Judd, trying to be quiet, like the rest of his men, afraid that somehow their own heartbeats would give them away.

Still at the periscope, he had the picture right in focus. "MARK! Large grating on her keel line . . . very slightly to starboard. Helm . . . come right one. I repeat, one degree."

And now the CO ordered a fractional increase in speed for *Sea-*

wolf to complete a long run straight underneath the *Xia*, moving slowly from stern to bow.

CO: "MARK! Intakes right above, port and starboard . . . MARK! Second grating . . ."

And all the while the racing pens of *Seawolf*'s upward fathometers flew across the moving-paper recorders, making a pinpoint-accurate picture of the *Xia*'s keel, her precise shape and measurements from her waterline downward. With agonizing slowness they edged forward, and now no one was speaking, and the only sound came from the sonar room as the moving pen kept writing, and, as Lt. Commander Omar Khayyám might have added, "and, having writ,/Moves on."

It was the fathometer man who broke the silence. "MARK! We've lost the hull trace, Captain. We've gone right by . . . we're back looking at the surface."

Seawolf's team had done it. The first half of the critical picture was in the bag, but now the CO would have to attempt another desperately dangerous maneuver, coming right around the stern of the *Xia*, and risking everything for a second crucial set of pictures, to be taken through the periscope camera, right off her stern, up close and personal. This would complete the picture, giving the measurement of the missile tubes above the waterline.

"RIGHT FULL RUDDER . . . MAKE YOUR DEPTH SIXTY-TWO FEET . . . THREE UP . . . MAKE YOUR COURSE ONE-EIGHT-ZERO"

Seawolf swung away, making a hard turn to starboard, right off the *Xia*'s bow, from just below her keel, the beginning of a wide, fast three-quarter circle that would take her right around the Chinese submarine, and across her stern as it ploughed slowly along the surface.

"MAKE YOUR SPEED FIVE KNOTS . . ."

"UP PERISCOPE!"

And now they were directly in the photography-run procedure, with a view less than 100 yards away.

Judd Crocker stared out at the Chinese submarine while *Seawolf*'s photographic system snapped off the shots. It seemed to take forever. And suddenly Judd saw men appearing on the bridge of the *Xia*. At least he thought they were just appearing. He was certain they had not been there when he first looked, it seemed moments ago.

And then his fears were dramatically confirmed. One of them pointed straight between Judd Crocker's eyes, directly at *Seawolf*'s periscope.

Nonetheless he held his nerve, waiting for the camera crew's report. By the time it came, eight seconds later, there were three Chinamen, all pointing at *Seawolf*'s periscope.

Strangely Judd said nothing, but kept the mast up for another whole minute, providing the Chinese on the bridge with a spectacular view of the American periscope heading south.

Linus thought that as camera runs go, this one had been a disaster. The periscope had been clear of the water for a minute and a half, God knows how long after the report of completion. Linus Clarke, not for the first time, thought his captain had completely lost his grip.

"Captain, sir . . . your periscope's been up for ninety seconds . . . they'll surely see us," he added anxiously. But late.

"You're surely right, Linus. Why do you suppose I don't give a rat's ass?"

"Jesus, Captain, beats the shit out of me."

"Down periscope." Judd Crocker made that last order at the very final moment, giving the Chinese on the bridge just a few seconds more to watch him vanish, directly to the south.

But now the CO's escape options were closing. IF they had been spotted, and he must now assume they had, since it would have been a minor miracle if they hadn't, he should clear the datum. To the west made little sense, because that way led to the shallow water surrounding the island of Hainan and the Chinese navy base. To the north were the busy operational waters of Admiral Zu Jicai's Southern Fleet headquarters, and it seemed quite likely that the *Xia* might be heading home, since her exercise area contained a plain and obvious intruder.

For the moment he had to get away from her, because if that ship was about to summon half the Chinese navy to locate *Seawolf* and hunt them down, well, he had to know that, which meant listening to her enemy report to base. This might not happen for at least 20 minutes: drafting, formatting, command approval, encryption, and radio tuning. All this preceded the transmission of a highly classified military signal.

And he thanked God for his two Chinese-speaking "spooks" from Naval Intelligence, who would pick that signal apart a lot faster than it had been put together. And now he was ready for the course change to three-six-zero.

"Right standard rudder . . . make your course north . . . speed ten."

And for 15 minutes they ran on, from two miles off the *Xia*'s port quarter and crossing her stern, heading inshore. The navigational plot confirmed she was still heading west.

So far as Linus could see, the situation was precarious enough already without heading straight for the Chinese southern naval headquarters.

Clarke was now seeking reassurance from the captain, not directly, of course, but there was anxiety in his voice as he ventured, "Probably lost 'em now, right, sir? Guess we got away with it? Time to head for deep water?"

But Judd Crocker was deep in thought, and he believed they had most definitely been located. "Make your speed eight knots . . . up periscope. Comms-Captain . . . be alert for a contact report from *Xia* . . . any second now . . . lemme know when it's in."

"Comms, AYE."

Another five minutes went by, and *Seawolf* continued northward.

"Captain-Comms . . . contact report coming in . . . translating."

"Captain, aye."

"Captain-Comms . . . reception completed."

"Captain . . . roger. Down periscope."

"Send it right up to the conn."

"Aye, sir."

Petty Officer Chase Utley brought it up in person and handed it to the captain, who scanned it quickly.

"Good. They have us headed south at twelve knots from datum position 20.00N 111.30E.

"Rig for silent running. Make your speed seven knots."

"But, captain," said Linus Clarke, "you givin' up? That's steering straight for the Chinese blowhole, straight for the Southern Fleet's biggest base. That's crazy."

"Not at all, Linus. That's strategy. Because the last place they'd ever dream of looking for us is straight up their own ass."

0705. Tuesday, July 4.
Office of Southern Fleet Commander. Zhanjiang.

Admiral Zu Jicai stared at an amplifying signal from the *Xia III*: "*0655. July 4. 20N 112.46E. Positive periscope contact visual close aboard. Assessed POSIDENT U.S. nuclear submarine. Last known course south. Speed 12. Clearing area to west.*"

Admiral Zu hit the buttons ordering his operational fleet into action: "*Execute ASW contingency Plan Seven . . . search datum 20N 111.30E . . . search orientation one-eight-zero. Speed of advance 12.*"

The Southern Fleet had been on high alert for this for the past 24 hours, and the ships detailed for this mission prepared to leave, seek out, and if possible blow apart the American marauder.

Four destroyers were casting their lines by 0742—three of them, *Changsha*, *Nanning* and *Guilin*, were almost identical to the *Nanchang*, which had taken part in the underwater barrage off Taiwan. They were all 3,500-ton heavily gunned guided-missile warships with antisubmarine mortars and depth charges, a bit slow but dangerous when they arrived. The fastest of the four was the updated Luda III, *Zuhai*, with its very advanced sonars and specialist CY-1 antisubmarine weapon.

Admiral Zhang himself had personally ordered the *Zuhai* straight to Zhanjiang from the failed Taiwan trap, in readiness for the task Admiral Zu's fleet now had to tackle.

Five Jangjui-class frigates were also on their way. These were small antisubmarine specialists, similar to the *Shantou*, which had been in action off Taiwan the previous day. *Zigong, Dongguan, Anshun, Yibin* and *Maoming*, their sonar Echo Type 5s ready, were preparing to load their depth-charge launchers before they'd cleared the harbor wall.

Two fast-attack craft were also dispatched, 500-ton Haiqing Type 037s, which carried China's biggest ASW mortars, and were currently being built at the fastest rate of any patrol boat in the Chinese Navy. The Haiqings had very hot sonars, hull-mounted, active search and attack only at slow speed.

From the naval airstrip, two frontline attack aircraft, Harbin SH-5s, were preparing for takeoff, engines screaming as they waited for clearance, their big powerful depth bombs and state-of-the-art Russian sonobuoys loaded.

Two French-built Aerospatiale Super Frelon ASW helicopters were already in the air heading south. And these were really dangerous. They ran above the water at a steady 140 knots, and they carried HS 12 dipping sonar, with superb French-built search radar. Their specialist weapon was antisubmarine torpedoes, and they had the capacity to find their quarry. They'd be out in the ASW search area well inside the hour.

Two Haitun helicopters were also dispatched. These refined Dauphin 2s, locally built, would travel at 140 knots all the way, with a range of almost 500 miles. Once out there, they could do a lot of searching, and they carried medium-range, radar-guided anti-ship missiles, should *Seawolf* be forced to surface.

Admiral Zu picked up the telephone and reported his actions to the Commander-in-Chief, who listened carefully. "I told you so, Jicai. They're out there. They've been out there for days."

"But how did they avoid the underwater barrage yesterday?"

"Because the American commanding officer knows precisely what he's doing, that's why. Remember, he's faster than us, he's quieter than us, and he's a lot cleverer than us, because he's had a lot more practice driving state-of-the-art submarines. Remember, too, *Seawolf* is lethal. Her combat systems officer is probably the smartest man in the U.S. Navy, next to her CO. I don't know what weapons she's carrying, but if she decided to sink one or all of our ships, she could probably do it.

"Of course, I doubt she would. The Americans don't really want a hot war any more than we do . . . but she mustn't be provoked. We just want to blow a big hunk off her hull while she's under the water, and then let her sink gracefully to the bottom . . . such a pity, Jicai, to lose such a fine ship under such unfortunate, accidental circumstances . . . if only we had known she was there."

040845JUL06.
20.20N 111.30E. Speed 6. Periscope depth.
Course three-six-zero.

Seawolf crept north, toward Zhanjiang. She made no sound, and she left no wake. At 10 minutes before 10:00 A.M. Judd Crocker ordered her periscope up for a few seconds only, and instantly comms reported, "Multiple danger level X-Band rackets. CHAOS . . . no other word for it."

Though Judd could not know it, the sky was already alive with clattering naval helicopters a few miles to the south of them, and two patrol planes were making long circles around the central operations area. He risked a quick all-around look, and spotted the *Xia* four miles over to the west, heading north in the now-improving visibility.

Putting the periscope down, he risked a 45-second exposure of the ESM mast. And they picked up signals nineteen to the dozen. In the communications room the spooks were translating from the Chinese at their fastest possible rate. There was no doubt, the PLAN's Southern Fleet was conducting a major search for an UNIDENT submarine, last seen three hours ago.

Perhaps even more important, less than eight miles off *Seawolf*'s bow, traveling fast on a southerly course, was a fleet of at least six Chinese warships, maybe more. Kyle Frank had detected certainly one destroyer, five frigates, and maybe a fast-attack patrol craft. *Seawolf*'s comms room was working overtime.

So was the sonar room. Exit routes from the base sounded like an angry hornets' nest. As the minutes ticked anxiously by, the plot showed eleven different surface contacts heading south toward *Seawolf*.

Fifteen minutes later, the destroyers, frigates and patrol ships came thundering past, fanning out, one by one, powering south out to the datum and their search positions. Efficient Russian-made sonobuoys had already been dropped into the water, forming a silent acoustic barrier for anyone trying to escape south without detection.

"I'm kinda glad we're not in the middle of all that shit," said Judd Crocker. "Mighta been pretty damn tricky getting out of there."

The CO was on top of his game right now. As soon as they were detected, he had set his escape course to the north, and retired to the wardroom for breakfast. And there, over a sumptuous plate of eggs, bacon, sausage and hash browns, he had committed the entire contents of the photographs to memory. He learned every dimension of the *Xia*, every line of her contours, just in case they should be caught, in case they should lose the ship, and the photographs. In case he should be one of the survivors.

Later in the day he would ask Einstein to commit the details to memory as well, and possibly Linus Clarke. That way they had a fair chance of bringing home the other bacon, even if things went bad for them. He realized that capture might mean a highly unpleasant interrogation by Admiral Zhang's men, but he doubted the Chinese would execute them.

He thought that the Chinese government might be prepared to infuriate the Pentagon by "accidentally" whacking the colossally expensive American submarine. But they would probably not wish to take the American Chiefs of Staff to the brink by putting a hundred men to death, in what might be construed by the world community as cold-blooded murder.

Anyway, if he, Judd Crocker, lived, the Pentagon would have intricate details of the precise size of the *Xia III*, and the ICBMs she carried. And that's what mattered. "Meanwhile, the Chinks are still conducting their search resolutely to the south, the wrong way," Judd chuckled. "Fuck 'em."

As far as he was concerned, the photographic mission on the *Xia* was over, and he considered it a job well done. He now intended to ease *Seawolf* slowly away from the ensuing uproar to the south and quietly access the satellite for signals. He turned the ship back toward Taiwan and selected a southeasterly course toward water his charts told him was about 360 feet deep. Then he could run 200 feet below the surface, carefully making around 15 knots away from Admiral Zu Jicai's large search party. By midafternoon they'd be more than 60 miles away, in lonely deep water. All they had to do was to stay dived and be careful, and trust the satellites to find the big new Luhai-class destroyer for the second half of their mission. Meanwhile, they'd just prowl, softly.

As it turned out, the new satellite message from the U.S. was rather more detailed than Judd had anticipated. The 6,000-ton gas turbine Luhai had been spotted, moored alongside at the naval base in Guangzhou, the old south China trading city of Canton. This made her nearly impregnable, because the port of Canton lies 70 miles up the wide and furiously busy Pearl River Delta, which in turn is protected by a myriad of islands, including Hong Kong and Macao.

There was no possibility of going up there to spy on a heavily guarded destroyer, so Judd Crocker decided to go to bed for a couple of hours and allow Linus to steer the ship clear of the local manhunt, the failure of which was currently driving Admiral Zhang Yushu almost mad with frustration. He kept telephoning Admiral Zu and saying the same thing: "That submarine must be out there . . . . Only a madman could have gone back inshore . . . . It has to be there . . . and it must be found."

But as the day had worn on and their efforts came to nothing, even Zhang was changing his tune. "A madman or a submarine genius," was his latest verdict.

Seawolf's course was adjusted easterly, because this would take them closer to the Canton Roads, north of which, on the left-hand side of the river, south of the People's Bridge, was moored the Luhai. She'd plainly have to leave sometime.

Clarke took over the conn shortly after midday, hit the sack for three hours at 1600, then came back at 2000, thinking that this was, one way and another, a hell of a way to spend a national holiday.

Judd Crocker had dinner that night with Lt. Commander Roth-stein, but before they were able to tackle some serious plates of apple pie and ice cream, there was a call from the conn for the cap-tain, and when he arrived in the control room, he found Linus Clarke, who sounded concerned.

"We've had some pretty decent cover for the past hour and a half," said the lieutenant commander. "There was a fleet of about eight local junks, fishing, right off our starboard quarter. They moved away a while ago, and it was all quiet. But I suddenly got this light . . . .I've been watching it for about twenty minutes, sir. I think it could be coming out from Canton. It's a single red light on a steady bearing . . . sonars have been tracking him, classified as a Luda DDG. We have his signature, and right now he's making about twenty-five knots. Looks like he'll pass close west of us. He might just be going along the coast . . . but he has no other contact, just his port running light. Thought you might want to take a look."

"Yes, I would. Thanks, Linus . . . here, lemme have a peep." And for a few moments, Captain Crocker stared through the periscope.

"Hmmmm. Kinda weird. Known warship. High speed. Middle of the night. No radars on . . . better watch him . . . okay, Officer of the Deck . . . I'm gonna open the range a bit. If he has no radar at that speed, he's blind."

Judd pondered. "ELINT-Captain—you got any radars active out there?"

"No, Captain. Nothing. Certainly no threat radars. Only that old Russian shore-based system which can pick up our masts in calm water at twenty miles. Anyway, even if there was, it's no threat to us . . . we're more than thirty miles out even from the offshore islands."

Captain: "You sure this Luda's characteristics are identical in all respects to the one in our books?"

"Yessir. But I can check again . . . checking right now, sir . . ."

The red light kept coming, and Judd kept watching, until even-tually ELINT returned.

"Sir, now that we look more closely, that radar signature is a bit different. There's a degree of fuzziness on the PRF. It's either off-line, or they've modified. But I'm still certain it's the land-based one we know about."

The captain kept checking through the glass, watching for the red light, when suddenly, to his horror, it turned to green *and* red, which meant he was now seeing *both* running lights. The Chinese warship was, incredibly, steaming straight toward him in the pitch dark, from about 1,000 yards, on the calm ocean.

"Captain-Sonar. Contact has reduced speed. He now has turns for twelve knots. Active short-range sonar transmissions on the bearing. Transmission interval fifteen hundred yards."

Judd Crocker knew what the damned thing looked like. And he knew that the 3,500-tonner, with its sharp, rising steel bow, could put *Seawolf* on the bottom if it was determined to ram. He had no idea how the Luda knew they were there, but he knew how quickly he had to move . . . he had roughly 60 seconds to get deep to avoid collision.

"THIS GUY'S CLOSE ABOARD," he snapped to Linus. "HEAD-ING STRAIGHT TOWARD . . . WE'RE GOING DEEP . . . TEN DOWN!! ALL AHEAD TWO-THIRDS TWO HUNDRED FEET . . . CHECK ALL MASTS RIGHT DOWN . . . RIG FOR COUNTER-ATTACK."

The American submarine, now angling fast through the water, 10 degrees down from the horizontal, her mammoth turbines accelerating, was 100 feet below the surface in 30 seconds, 150 feet in 45 seconds.

"TWO HUNDRED FEET, SIR . . ."

"Captain-Sonar. We passed through a layer at ninety feet, sir, his old sonar will be virtually useless beyond a thousand yards . . . "

But Sonar's words were almost drowned out by the outrageous roar of twin screws overhead, as the Luda came thundering past, right above, and started to fade astern. A few tightly held breaths were released.

But Judd Crocker's main concern was the dreaded click-and-bang of a depth-charge attack. Naturally he kept these fears to himself.

But now the sonar room had detected a change, and Lieutenant

Frank called: "She's turning, sir . . . the Luda's turning . . . I think she may be coming back. Transmission interval still fifteen hundred yards, sweeping. Not in contact."

"Hope you're right, Kyle. I'm staying deep and quiet . . . what's your prediction for her sonar range in these conditions?"

"Captain-Sonar . . . range prediction above layer seventeen hundred plus yards to first surface reflection. Below layer twelve hundred at optimum evasion depth . . . that is one-forty feet."

"Captain, aye. Make your depth one-forty."

Seawolf slipped quietly up and away, the engineers deep in the ship watching the computer screens, the planesmen holding her level, steady at 140 feet below the surface. Sonar heard the sound of the Luda's obsolete sonar gradually grow fainter as the Americans continued their stealthy way east, riding the deep waters on Lt. Commander Mike Schultz's 90,000-horsepower turbines. *Seawolf* could go nearly twice as fast underwater as the 30-year-old Luda could on the surface, but not in these shallow waters.

Twenty minutes later, the Luda's transmissions had faded away completely to the southeast. Forty minutes later, Judd risked coming above the layer to hear better. But there was nothing. And once more *Seawolf* was prowling in lonely waters. For the first time the captain had a moment to gather his thoughts, and he asked Kyle Frank, Linus Clarke, Andy Warren, Shawn Pearson, and Cy Rothstein to come into the control room.

"Gentlemen," he said, "something real strange just happened. I am getting a distinct impression that someone out there doesn't like us!"

"Funny you should mention that, sir . . ."

"Yeah, I was just thinking the same . . ."

The tone was light. But the subject was deadly serious . . . how did that damned Luda find them, miles from anywhere at periscope depth, in the middle of the night? *Not using any of its own sensors?* Why had it changed direction so suddenly, while the captain was looking through the periscope, watching the starboard green running light turn to *green and red*? Who the hell had vectored it onto the precise correct course to ram them?

They all knew the Luda's sonar was hopeless at 25 knots, even in a calm sea in the layer. There was no way she could have navigated herself onto *Seawolf.*

"No, sir. She was being vectored from outside her own ops room. Someone must have picked up our mast in this flat water . . . must have been from the shore . . ." Cy Rothstein looked concerned.

"It has to do with the curve of the earth," said Frank. "No one can operate shore radar from a range of more than twenty-two miles."

"We can."

"Yes, but no one else has technology even approaching that."

"They didn't used to have. But the Chinese plainly have it now," said the CO.

"How far?"

"I don't know exactly," said Shawn, the navigation officer. "But I think the nearest of the islands outside Zhoujiang Ku would be around forty miles north of here, and that's where they must have been scanning from."

"Then I am drawn to the conclusion that the Chinese have stolen our most advanced radar secrets as well as everything else," said the captain.

"Jesus Christ. It would be just our luck to have them use it personally against us."

"Hey . . . forty miles . . . that's one hell of a way for shore radar . . . they into some satellite hookup or what?"

"Who knows? But we're gonna have to be damned careful, that's for sure."

"I'm too young to die," said Shawn, his voice rising to a little girl's squeak. "And I hate the Chinese, and I can't find my way home."

Judd Crocker laughed as always at his young navigator, but a shadow quickly crossed his face when he spoke. "We have to face it, there is a certain Chinaman in that damned navy who is determined to get us. He's been trying to do it for three days.

"He's twice mobilized half the fleet trying to blow us apart with charges and mortars, he's had navy fliers circling around trying to hit us with torpedoes from the air, he's had sonobuoys in the water, and a half-hour ago he ordered one of his elderly destroyers to run flat out through the night and try to sink us by ramming.

"Gentlemen, we have to take this fucker seriously or he's going to whip our asses . . . and we have to remember that every time we raise the periscope anywhere near the shore, he's gonna be watching. Remember, a half-hour ago, he wasn't guessing . . . he *knew* where we were, and as far as I'm concerned, that's a first."

0100. Wednesday, July 5.
The home of Admiral Zhang Yushu.

Again the C-in-C could not sleep. He'd been walking alone on the beach, staring out to sea, his thoughts cascading through the deep waters. Where was the American submarine? *What kind of a devil was driving it, and how did he manage to evade capture, and why did he not just leave?* Admiral Zhang was completely bewildered. *That man has somehow avoided contact with an entire battle fleet, destroyers, frigates, fast attack craft, ASW helicopters, and aircraft. He's dodged depth charges, depth bombs, sonobuoys, and mortars. And last night, he showed up again, not so far off Guangzhou. We actually had his mast on the radar, but we never got near him.*

WHAT DOES HE WANT? That was the final question. And Zhang Yushu could not answer that, either.

He walked disconsolately back to the house, listening to the sounds of the midsummer night. But to him the clockwork chirp of the cicadas was the pinging of a distant sonar. The whisper of the wind through the palm trees was the swish of a submarine's blades through the water. And the sound of the waves breaking on the shore was the sound of his barefoot youth in the nearby city of Xiamen, living on his father's boat, moored right off the beach.

He'd come a long way in a relatively short time. But he had to find that submarine. And the longer the chase, the more determined he was to blow a hole in Captain Judd Crocker's *Seawolf.* Or, better yet, sink it.

The admiral crossed the wide porch and softly entered his study through the French windows. He poured himself some iced tea and sipped it slowly. Then he had an idea, he picked up the telephone and dialed his secure line to Admiral Zu, who would not complain at being awakened. Not this week, with tensions running so high in the People's Navy.

Jicai picked up on the third ring, and with good grace accepted his Commander-in-Chief's apology for the hour.

"I called because we must not be beaten by this submarine," he said. "And because I know you want it removed as deeply as I do."

"Probably deeper, sir. How about a thousand fathoms?"

Admiral Zhang chuckled. "Jicai," he said, "we have tried every conventional sonar and radar system we own. We have been close but never close enough, fast but never fast enough. I am drawn to the conclusion that we have access to only one system that may detect the American ship in time for us to strike."

"Sir, it is entirely untried. We don't even know if it will work."

"The Americans plainly think it does. They have it fitted to all of their most advanced warships."

"Yessir. But they have the original. Ours is . . . well, in the nature of a copy."

"Yes. But it's only a towed array. And we know how to make towed arrays that work very well."

"Yessir. But we've never made one this long. And we've never even tested it yet."

"That may be so. But our scientists have been very thorough, and the report says it will work better than any towed array we have ever had. The report says it will work as well for us as it does for the Americans."

"Well, sir, it is one thousand yards long, which seems to me phenomenal . . . they say it will pick up every sound in the ocean for miles and miles."

"If it will really do what our people say it will do, Jicai, it might find the American submarine for us. It is currently fitted to the new destroyer."

"Yessir. It's in a special housing on the stern. Under guard at the jetty in the Pearl River."

"Can it be deployed right away?"

"Yessir. It's completely ready for its final trials. Scheduled to start in two days."

"Send it to sea, Jicai. Send it out to the area where the Luda picked up their mast, then have it start an area search pattern based on that position. The American probably thinks we're hopeless at ASW, and he may not have cleared that datum. If he runs, we cannot catch him; but if he underrates us and stays, we might. The only ship we have that could catch them is the one with the new enlightened towed array."

"When do I send it, sir? First light?"

"No, Jicai. Not first light. Send it now. And tell Colonel Lee to find the *Seawolf.* Personal orders of the Commander-in-Chief."

0200.
Canton Naval Base.

They cast off all lines at 2355, and two tugs hauled the 500-foot-long Luhai-class warship out into the wide south-flowing stream of the Pearl River. Her new name, *Xiangtan,* could be seen, freshly painted in black, high on her light gray hull. A sweeping, blood-red stripe at the waterline was reflected in the dock lights that glistened in the dark shadows of Canton's ancient river. Colonel Lee ordered, "All-ahead half speed."

The Navy tugs escorted her downstream for 15 miles to the great delta, even though she ran on her own enormous power, two Ukrainian-built turbines. The tugs positioned themselves on either side of her bow, acting more as pilots than extra engines and brakes. And they steered her through the tricky shallow waters of the southern fork of the river.

Xiangtan was a warship in the old-fashioned sense, armed to the teeth with antiaircraft guns, torpedoes, and missiles, surface-to-air, and surface-to-surface, the latter a phalanx of sea skimmers with a range of 70 miles. She was the most modern frontline fighting ship in the Chinese Navy, and she could make 30 knots through the water, a crew of 250 manning her, two heavily armed Harbin helicopters on her stern, to increase the speed and reach of her ASW capability.

Her radars and sonars were the finest that PLAN could purchase, but tonight they were overshadowed by the giant towed array, an ultrasensitive underwater acoustic cable that would soon be strung out behind her, trailing deep astern of China's finest warship, listening to the strange acoustic caverns of the ocean, distilling the noises, filtering the fleeting contacts, but listening hardest of all for the least suggestion of *Seawolf*'s machinery.

Xiangtan's crew had answered the call of their commander, many of them racing in from their homes around the dockyard, to take up what amounted to "action stations" in the middle of the night. No one knew what was happening, except they were going downriver to the open ocean, two days ahead of schedule. Whatever it was, it must be big. *"They're saying Admiral Zhang Yushu ordered it personally."*

Through the darkness they swept southward, the tugs with big probing spotlights above their bridges, in addition to regular running lights. As the Delta grew ever wider, the escorts peeled away, leaving the destroyer to run down the strictly marked channel to the west of Lan Tau Island. She then steamed past Guishan Dao and Dhazizhou Dao, leaving Macao seven miles to starboard, heading straight into the defined navigational routes that lead all ships from Canton out to the China Sea.

By 0500, in the pearly predawn light of Wednesday, July 5, Colonel Lee had his ship running fast through the still-calm waters, in light rain, almost 100 miles south of the Pearl River Delta. He could not of course know it, but Lt. Commander Linus Clarke was conning USS *Seawolf* slowly back toward the east, some 15 miles off his starboard bow.

Colonel Lee was pleased at his progress so far. They'd made good time into the search area, and his crew had deployed the towed array perfectly, and now it hung off the stern, riding back in the water for 1,000 yards, a grotesque electronic tail, five inches in diameter, black in color, its core the most advanced acoustic electronics in all the oceans.

If there was an element of doubt, it was only in the Chinese scientists' ability to hook it up to the onboard computers, to process the array's astonishing acoustic capability. The technique they had yet to master was that processing, because the Americans had improved it by a factor of 100. Nothing in all the history of modern naval warfare had ever been so good at identifying specific target frequencies from the monstrous background noise of the ocean. Admiral Zu Jicai knew its capability, knew it could hear a clockwork mouse scampering under the Tower of Babel—from 20 miles away.

050500JUL06.
20.30N 113.45E. Speed 10. Depth 150.
Course zero-eight-five.

Seawolf was at peace. Nothing was coming up on sonar, Captain Crocker had finally gone to bed, and Linus Clarke had the conn. It was not until 0525 that Frank's operator began to pick up faint engine lines, faint but getting stronger as the hard-charging *Xiangtan* ran toward the Americans' chosen course.

Normally, the approach of any warship—never mind a big Chinese destroyer—would have necessitated an immediate call to the captain to return to the control room. But Linus Clarke did not think he was personally having a good patrol. There had been three times when he had betrayed nerves of a kind no XO who hopes one day to have a command should ever display.

In his mind, he had only betrayed natural human reactions to extreme danger: the flooding of the torpedo room, deep beneath the surface; straying right into the path of incoming underwater missiles; being spotted by the big Chinese ICBM submarine. Linus knew that Captain Crocker was a top-class commanding officer, but he also knew their orders forbade them from getting detected. And so far they had been detected three times, once off Taiwan, obviously, once by the *Xia*, and again last night by shore radar. Judd might be tough, experienced and gifted, but he wasn't

Superman, and Linus thought it was about time he showed some of his own mettle, demonstrating that he too was capable of commanding an American nuclear boat on a highly classified mission.

He had a lot of CIA background now, and a lot of important contacts. He really wanted to take a look at this oncoming Chinese warship, and he ordered *Seawolf*'s team to reduce speed and slide up to periscope depth as the contact came within two miles. They might as well take a good look. If push came to shove, they could always go deep and outrun her, just as Judd had done to the much smaller Luda.

In the ops room of the Luhai destroyer there was a ripple of activity. One of the sonar operators, new to the screen that reflected the findings of the giant 1,000-yard-long American-designed towed array, thought he was getting something, but he could not tell what.

It was, however, a sufficient change in the levels for him to call out engine lines. And Colonel Lee, the very senior captain of the ship, instantly ordered a reduction in speed, as if silencing the water beyond the hull would make their contact more easy to identify. *Xiangtan* slowed almost to a halt while the Chinese technicians worked the computer keys, trying to tap into the new electronic system.

Meanwhile, now at periscope depth, *Seawolf* was 2,400 yards off the Luhai's starboard beam. Clarke had his night-sight camera up and snapping, and he was visually able to see a large modification to the destroyer's stern, an unusual housing, bigger than normal for foreign ships, though not entirely unusual in the U.S.

Linus's mind raced. He knew what he was seeing. Everyone in the Silent Service knew that China had gotten its hands on that high-tech modern towed array, along with its processing computers. And right here was the evidence, a major Chinese warship with a big winch housing for a long towed array, the design and technology of which had been flagrantly stolen from the U.S.

"I'm going in closer," he said. "Officer of the Deck, keep her straight and level, PD . . . I want to pass in across her stern and get some closeups of that housing. Might even catch a glimpse of the actual array in the water."

"Steady, sir . . ." Andy Warren was issuing a veiled warning. "We don't know how long that array is."

"Don't worry, Andy. I'm not going in closer than a mile. It won't be that long, will it? And this is a destroyer . . . the array will be angled down in the water, not straight out behind like a submarine deploys."

"Sir." Master Chief Brad Stockton had arrived in the control room. "You want me to let the CO know we're groping around the ass of a six-thousand-ton Chinese destroyer? It's the kind of thing he takes a big interest in."

"I don't think there's a need, Brad. Just taking a look. She's not even transmitting on anything. I thought we'd cross her wake about a mile astern, get our pictures, than retreat a couple of miles and keep the ESM mast up, see if we can vacuum up a few details of her new radar and communications systems. Ex-USA, I believe."

"Well, okay, sir. If you say so. But I do think the CO should know roughly what we're up to. We're awful close to a critical part of our mission. And remember, sir, we don't know how long that towed array is, and we don't know what angle they have it down in the water."

"My judgment says we're fine," replied Linus. "And since they seem to have stolen everything from us short of the Washington Monument, we've got a lot of rights, and I'm about to exercise those rights. Turning in now . . . right standard rudder . . . steer course zero-nine-zero . . . make your speed eight . . ."

And USS *Seawolf* turned across the wake, sliding through the water astern of the destroyer, her periscope jutting out as she made the crossing.

Except she never got there. Almost, but not quite. Her giant propeller snagged on the tough towed array, 75 feet below the surface, wrapping the thick black rubberized tail hard around, twisting it into an impenetrable ball 15 feet across, and then winding it on and on, with the array trapped between the blades, until finally the shaft could fight it no more, and *Seawolf*'s entire propulsion mechanism came to a halt, the propeller jammed rigid.

No one knew it, but the very first tug on the array by the vast inertia of the submarine had yanked it clean off the stern of the Chinese destroyer. And now its weight was slowly dragging the submarine's stern down.

There was no semblance of uproar, just a heavy slow-motion quiet at a strange angle. And it was, even to a *sleeping* submarine commander, tantamount to a shriek for help that would have pierced the deafness of Beethoven. In two and a half seconds flat, Captain Judd Crocker was wide awake, fighting his way out of his cabin door. Five seconds later he reached the conn.

"What's going on, XO?" he snapped, seizing the periscope, which was still up and trained on the stern of the *Xiangtan*. There were only three seconds left before the periscope dipped below the surface, but for Judd Crocker that was plenty. *Xiangtan*'s stern was only 500 yards away, *not* the mile young Linus had believed.

"Depth ninety feet, sir . . . increasing. Speed zero. Bow up angle seven degrees. INCREASING," reported the planesman, an edge entering his voice as the great submarine wallowed backwards in the water.

"It may not be that bad, sir," offered Linus. "Just temporary. I think we may have snagged something, sir."

"SNAGGED!" exclaimed Judd. "We're in the middle of the South China Sea. Or at least we were when I was last in the conn forty minutes ago. There's nothing out here to snag. Barring a Chinese destroyer close aboard."

"I went across her stern to get pictures," said Linus Clarke. "I stood at least a mile off. But I still seem to have been too close."

"Jesus, Linus! What d'you mean a mile, for Christ's sake. It's only five hundred yards. I've just looked. Oh, Jesus Christ! Linus, you had the fucking periscope in low power. It looked like a mile to you, but it was five hundred yards for real. And you just drove straight into his towed array."

"LOW POWER, SIR. OH MY GOD! OH MY GOD! I can't believe this. I'm extremely sorry . . ."

"So am I, Linus. So am I," said the CO resignedly, hardly believing it himself. Judd had seen this once before when a student of his had made the same mistake. And now one twist the wrong way on the periscope handle had pushed the Chinese destroyer almost four times farther away to Linus's eye than it actually was.

"Conn maneuvering . . . unable to answer bells. Main propulsion shaft jammed. Investigating . . . emergency propulsion is available."

"Captain, roger. We may have something wrapped around the screw . . . so propel maximum on emergency . . . and try main propulsion in astern . . . we might just be able to unwind it."

"One hundred feet, sir . . . ten degrees bow up."

Judd shouldered the XO to one side and ordered a short blast of high-pressure air into the after-main ballast group, in a desperate attempt to stop the stern-down trend.

Somehow he remained outwardly calm. But inwardly, he was seething. *FUCKING FUCKING FUCKING XO . . . what a total prick . . . we'll be real lucky to get out of this one.*

Judd's mind raced, scanning the options. *What do I do? Dive? Surface? Declare war? Scuttle the ship? Surrender? Call the cavalry? FUCK ME!*

And then, *Steady, Judd. For Christ's sake, steady. Think it through, from best to worst.*

Best was easy. *If we're very lucky the destroyer's CO will think his array snagged the bottom—maybe won't even notice it's off for a few minutes—if he's real stupid.*

But from there, the entire scenario went south. *Because he's still not going away, is he? He'll want to mark the position to get the fucking thing back.*

Judd's mind raced on. *Since he's going no place fast, it's me who must make the move. But I'm stuck with three knots max on emergency propulsion . . . and I've got 50 fucking tons of deadweight on my stern. And not much chance at all of restoring the main shaft. Holy shit!*

This was the real loneliness of command. There was no one he could turn to, least of all his XO. And all around him his team was coping, rock steady, with a crisis beyond the realm of their worst nightmares.

"Conn maneuvering . . . shaft will not move in astern, sir . . . EPM running ahead full."

"Planes are answering. . . . One hundred and ten feet steady . . . trim's good, sir . . . that is with five degrees bow up."

"Conn-Sonar . . . all contacts drowned out by EPM, sir."

Judd knew he was running out of options. If he stopped the emergency propulsion motor, *Seawolf* would also stop. And the weight aft, too heavy to be compensated for, would drag her down, stern first.

The only chance of stopping that was to blow the main ballast tanks. And holding even an approximate trim that way was unbelievably noisy anyhow and unlikely for more than 30 minutes before the sheer physics of the game overtook him.

Lack of air, a depth surge up, or, even worse, down, or an excessively steep angle—any of those could routinely "scram" the reactor, crippling the beleaguered *Seawolf* totally.

If, alternatively, he left the noisy emergency motor running, he was deaf to the outside world, but could probably maintain depth, give or take 30 feet.

But he couldn't maintain a steady periscope depth under those circumstances, which meant he'd be blind as well as deaf. At PD, on the little emergency motor, he'd end up showing the whole sail occasionally, which would nicely advertise his presence to the entire South China Sea. The EPM was only a get-you-home kit for peacetime use. It was about as stealthy as a buzzsaw.

Judd fought off a feeling of helplessness. There was only one conclusion. He had to get back to the surface and check out the propeller. But that meant surfacing right beside the Chinese destroyer, though at least they were in international waters.

And so he issued the command, and *Seawolf* wallowed her way clumsily up, her motion slow and ungainly, barely under control, a wounded whale with a harpoon jutting out of her backside. Judd Crocker took the periscope in the dawn light. The rain had stopped and the sea was very beautiful, but the sight that greeted him was not good.

Through the glass he could actually see the ghastly tangle of thick black wire wrapped hard around his propeller, locking it rigid.

Worse yet, he could see now, 200 yards off his port beam, one

6,000-ton Chinese destroyer, with a gun turret pointed straight at *Seawolf*'s bridge. From where Judd was looking it seemed to be pointing straight between his eyes.

"*Jesus, Mary and Joseph!*" he breathed.

The CO's mind flew. The situation was dire, but not unique. Submarines had wrapped their propellers around towed arrays before, most spectacularly when a Royal Navy nuclear boat did it in the Barents Sea back in the early 1980s, surfaced, cut it free, and made her way home safely.

And of course everyone knew of the incident somewhere off the Carolinas in the late 1970s when a cruising Soviet submarine wound the towed array of an American frigate into its prop. Navy folklore says the submarine had to surface, much like *Seawolf* had done now, while the crew tried to cut their way free with inadequate equipment. The American crew apparently sat on the stern of the frigate, eating hot dogs for lunch, howling with laughter and loudly cheering every failed attempt by the Russians to clear their huge propeller.

Judd knew also that one of the giant Soviet ICBM Typhoons had wrapped one of its two propellers around the array of another of the Royal Navy's nuclear spy ships in the Barents Sea, HMS *Splendid*, on Christmas Eve 1986. The Typhoon ripped it off the much smaller British submarine, and the Soviets retreated with the array still entwined.

But right now Judd had to decide what to do himself. Until they unlocked the prop shaft they were trapped, so the decision essentially made itself. There was no point submerging again, with no propulsion. They could not get away, and in the end they'd have to return to the surface.

So the CO ordered a diving team to prepare for immediate action. Master Chief Brad Stockton selected eight men, four for the initial dive, with four more for backup on the casing behind the prop. Within minutes, the men were being suited up in wetsuits and flippers. Brad ordered scuba gear to be brought out, along with oxyacetylene cutting equipment, big double-handed wire cutters, even axes, anything to hack the array off *Seawolf*'s prop.

The team made its way to the sail door, starboard side, hidden from the *Xiangtan*, and one by one they moved along the casing toward the stern, where they would begin the work. However, the first man around the aft end of the sail instantly came into the view of the Chinese gunnery team, and in a hail of small-arms fire the entire diving team was driven back, bullets slamming against the one-inch-thick steel of the sail, and ricocheting in all directions. It was a miracle no one was killed. But no one was, and they retreated safely back into the submarine.

So the first guideline was laid down: The Chinese were not about to let the American submarine break free, or even allow its crew out of the hull.

Judd Crocker appreciated the situation, and reconsidered his narrowing options. If he had any mobility, he could have considered taking out the destroyer with torpedoes, but more Chinese ships and aircraft were surely on their way.

The captain of that goddamned destroyer won't be keeping this little epic to himself, he thought. *Unlike my fucking XO.*

Since he could not get to the screw and then get away, they were, by any standards, already prisoners of the Chinese. But the *Xiangtan* was not trying to sink them, and they were in international waters with several miles to spare.

It seemed for a few moments that no one on either ship knew quite what to do, but suddenly the Chinese made the first move, launching one of their Haitun helicopters off the stern. Judd watched it through the periscope, clattering low over the sea and hovering right above *Seawolf*'s bow. Then its door opened, and four men were lowered onto the submarine, each of them carrying what looked like heavy-duty gear on his back.

"What do you make of that, Brad?" asked the CO, handing over the periscope.

"I don't know what they're doing, but that's not a diving cylinder he's using . . . it's metal welding gear . . . you know what I think? These guys are planning to weld a couple of big iron hooks on our bow so they can tow us into shore."

"Are you kidding?"

"No . . . that's what they're doing."

"Well, why don't we drown 'em . . . just submerge again?" offered Shawn Pearson.

"Good call," replied the CO. "Open main vents . . . Officer of the Deck, take her down."

Seawolf's ballast tanks flooded up again and she commenced her rolling motion, wallowing down into the sea rather than sliding into it with full propulsion. Judd kept the periscope up and watched the Chinese helicopter come in fast and low and take the men off. But he could not go on doing this indefinitely without running out of air. So he ordered the submarine back to the surface, back to the standoff, which in a world of bad options was probably his best.

He drafted an immediate signal to Pearl Harbor: "Seawolf *surfaced in position 20.30N 113.35E. Immobilized by towed array around propeller. Chinese destroyer* Xiangtan *in company. Small-arms fire prevents work on propeller. For'ard gun mounting continues trained on my sail. Surface and air assistance required soonest.*"

The satellite signal from SUBPAC was back in 15 minutes: "*LRMP arrives 1200. CVBG arrives within air range 24 hours. Surface support 48 hours. Diplomatics in hand.*"

"Well, that all sounds a bit slow. Six hours for a long-range maritime air patrol to get here, a day for a carrier group, two days for surface ships. I suppose we can just about stop the Chinks doing anything major to our bow for that long. But it's not likely to be easy."

Meanwhile, on the stern of the destroyer there was a lot of activity. And at a little after 0600, both Haitun helicopters got into the air, carrying between them a heavy steel hawser in a huge U-shape beneath them. Judd watched them lower it deep into the water right behind the stern of the submarine. Then they towed it forward of the propeller, then even farther forward, still deep-submerged below the ship, until it was right in front of the rudders and the after-planes.

Then the two Haituns went back to a height of around 100 feet, and slowly began to fly in a tight circle, almost overlapping each other, though staying well clear of each other's blades. This had the effect of twisting the hawser into a steel knot around the narrow stern of the submarine. It could not slide forward because of the massive bulk of *Seawolf*'s hull. And it certainly could not slide aft, past the huge bottom rudder and twin after-planes.

The Luhai quickly began to reverse, and the two ends of the hawser were lowered onto the aft deck where the helicopters landed, and it seemed to Judd that about 10,000 Chinamen took over. He guessed what was coming next, and he was right. The ends of the hawser were made fast on the deck. And at 0730 on the morning of July 5, 2006, in the South China Sea, USS *Seawolf*, the pride of the U.S. Navy's Silent Service, began a long tow, backward, into captivity. For how long, no one knew; for what purpose, Judd Crocker had a very fair idea, particularly since there was now a Chinese escort of two aircraft overhead and a fast patrol boat close aboard on either side.

Cy Rothstein assessed that the Chinese would tow them into Canton and try to strip-search the entire ship, copying every one of *Seawolf*'s secrets, the sonar, the radar, the computers, the propulsion machinery, the nuclear reactor, the combat weapons, the cladding on the hull. Never had China been so lucky. Never had she had such a supreme opportunity to create an underwater fleet in the absolute image of that of the USA.

The only question left, in Cy Rothstein's opinion, was the fate of the crew. Would they release them? Or would they subject the principal officers and crewmen to a searching interrogation, enlisting the help of the best submariners in the U.S. Navy to assist them in their quest to match the West in terms of modern sea power?

Cy did not, obviously, know the answer to that one. Nor did anyone else. But at this point Judd Crocker was forced to reconsider his scuttling options—i.e., getting the crew off and into the water with life jackets, then sinking the boat.

He realized the catastrophic potential of his boat falling into the hands of the Chinese. Now, only scuttling could prevent this, sinking her in international waters where the U.S. Navy could protect their secrets. But such a drastic course of action carried too high a price. The Chinese had opened fire on his men once, and for all

Judd knew they would probably do it again. The cost of scuttling *Seawolf* might be killing the entire American crew.

Judd Crocker realized they were effectively prisoners of the Chinese, and that they might be subject to interrogation. However, he did hold out reasonable hopes that the diplomats might sort something out, and that some horse-trading on behalf of the U.S. government might gain their release. In the meantime, they could do nothing except wait for the next move from their new hosts.

And an uncomfortable wait it would be, already close to Chinese waters. *Xiangtan* was dragging them toward Canton at four knots, which meant a journey of 20 hours. And with no propulsion, they rolled back and forth all the way, despite the calm seas. All other power systems were working, so they had light and air conditioning from the reactor. They also had plenty of food and water, and they had their communications, so the CO was able to keep SUBPAC up to speed with each development.

But there was little to report. They could either seal themselves in the mighty steel capsule of *Seawolf*, defy the Chinese to the end, and keep the hatches tightly battened down in the hope of release. Or they could surrender to the Chinese and feign outrage at being arrested in international waters during the perfectly peaceful conduct of their business.

Surrender or not, he ordered all evidence of the photographs, including the camera and the film-developing material, destroyed and then jettisoned out through the torpedo tubes. The passport of his XO was shredded and went with them.

Judd more or less rejected the possibility of a policy of sealed-in defiance, on the basis that the Chinese at some point would try to smash their way into the submarine, and that would entail a significant battle in which a lot of people would most certainly die, both Americans and Chinese.

One way or another, it was deeply frustrating to be sitting in one of the most powerful combat systems on earth, a nuclear boat with the capability of sinking not only *Xiangtan* but many of her seaborne colleagues, too. She carried the ADCAP Mk 48 torpedoes for just this sort of task, in case the U.S. went to war during one of her tours of duty.

She also carried the long-range Hughes Tomahawk land-attack missiles with nuclear warheads. One of these things could probably knock down Beijing, never mind Canton. Under pressure they could take out a sizeable chunk of southwest China.

And yet Captain Crocker was powerless, since he was not permitted to start World War III off his own bat.

Nor was he in any position to fight it out with the destroyer, because if *Xiangtan* was sunk, there were plenty more warships to replace her. And in the end *Seawolf* would surely go down fighting.

But the last signal from Pearl Harbor had forbidden him to open fire. SUBPAC was playing this one down for the moment, trying to reason with the Chinese Navy, expressing alarm that an American ship should have been apprehended in this way in international waters.

The Chinese were, predictably, stonewalling: *"So very sorry about this unfortunate incident. Extremely upset that you should have your ship carrying big thermonuclear weapons of war crashing into our peaceful destroyer, which was testing new engines in the South China Sea. . . . We have merely answered a request from your Commanding Officer for assistance. . . . We mean no one harm. . . . We will help to get your submarine going soon, then we will talk. Very, very sorry."*

Midnight. July 5, 2006.
Office of Southern Fleet Commander.

It had been without question the happiest day of Admiral Zhang Yushu's eventful life, more joyful than the magical day when he had married Lan, more hopeful than the day they had purchased their lovely summer home on the water, more exciting than the day he had been appointed to the highest possible command in the People's Liberation Army/Navy.

And now he strode around Admiral Zu Jicai's large private office, banging his right fist into the palm of his left hand, throwing back his head and laughing, congratulating himself heartily on the great prize he had secured for China: *Seawolf* and her crew.

Maybe one day the Paramount Ruler would feel obliged to return it to the Americans, but not before Chinese Navy scientists had wrung her dry for every last piece of technology the ship possessed.

"Oh, my friend Jicai," he exclaimed, "this is a wonderful day for us. A few hours from now, they'll be here. Is everything ready, the biggest submarine jetty? We have a detention center for half the crew? Put the rest in civilian jail with military guards. Then we go to work on that ship, hah? This is beautiful, just beautiful."

Zhang was ecstatic, but he appreciated the strong element of luck that had put the submarine into his hands.

However, he was a supreme pragmatist who knew what he knew. And right now he knew he had captive, perhaps for only one month, the last word in world submarine technology. He knew he would have among his prisoners men whose expertise in the field of sonar, radar, computers and weapons was the envy of the world.

There would be, in his power, American engineers and technicians who could demonstrate every working part down to the last, the subtlest detail. He would have nuclear experts, electronics experts, missile experts, modern United States warlords who knew how to hurl a big ICBM farther than anyone in China had ever dreamed. And above all he *knew* he would have captive the top submarine commanding officer in the U.S. Navy.

What he did not know was that among the captured officers of *Seawolf* was the only son of the President of the United States of America.

0300. Friday, July 7.

PEARL RIVER DELTA. NINE MILES SOUTHEAST OF THE port of Macao.

They changed course from zero-one-three to a more westerly three-three-four two miles off the headland of Zhu Zhou Island at the gateway to the delta, *Xiangtan* dragging her giant black steel prisoner backwards through the navigation lanes.

Signals from SUBPAC during the past six hours confirmed to Judd Crocker only that the American cavalry would arrive too late. There could be no rescue now. And no one knew what their fate would be after this miserable, slow journey to the port of Canton.

It was raining again outside the hull, and two Chinese Navy tugs came out of the darkness to meet the destroyer they had escorted outward the previous morning. The captains conferred briefly and the tugs took up positions on either side of *Seawolf* for the long push back up the river to the base.

They could go more quickly now in the dead, flat, near-deserted water, and the Chinese destroyer pushed on immediately, increasing speed to seven knots all along the wide expanse of the Delta, which is 15 miles across in some places west of Hong Kong.

Inside the submarine, Judd Crocker handed over to Linus Clarke a brand-new identity: an American passport, bearing his photograph, issued under the name of Bruce Lucas, born in Houston, Texas, in 1972, son of oil company executive John Lucas and his wife Marie. Bruce's service papers showed entry to the Naval Academy in 1990, promoted to Lieutenant Commander in 2004. Second tour of duty in *Seawolf* as Executive Officer. Torpedo specialist. The next-of-kin register listed his parents in the Houston suburb of Beaumont Place as those to be contacted in the event of accident.

Bruce Lucas was also the name that had always been on his U.S. Navy dog tags. The laundryman had been correct.

Well aware that the submarine was in the Delta, Judd Crocker broadcast to the ship's company, outlining the predicament they were in and assuring them that SUBPAC had the matter well in hand. He explained that both navy and government policy, under these circumstances, was to negotiate through diplomatic channels.

For obvious reasons they did not want a really hot battle to develop, nor did they want any heroics. The Chinese had no right to the submarine, no right to arrest the crew. However, since the submarine was unable to move, and it did contain weapons of mass destruction, nuclear, not germ, well . . . the Chinese probably had a case for taking it into custody in their waters while the diplomats argued.

"And that brings me to an extremely important point," he added. "As many of you probably already know, Lieutenant Commander Linus Clarke, my Executive Officer, is the son of the President of the United States. He has been a career naval officer for all of his college and working life, and it sure was not his fault his dad decided to run for office and won. When that happened, Linus was already on his way up the ladder, a lieutenant on the carrier *John C. Stennis*. There was never any reason for him to give up his career just because his father was in the White House for five years.

"But nonetheless, the Navy has a procedure for such matters, particularly if we find ourselves in an awkward spot like now, with Lieutenant Commander Clarke in a vulnerable position, and his father somewhat compromised. He thus has a brand-new identity that I would like you all to memorize.

"He is no longer Linus Clarke. He is Lieutenant Commander Bruce Lucas of Houston, Texas. Please commit that to memory. Should we be interrogated, remember not to let either Linus or me or your President down. Our executive officer is Lieutenant Commander Bruce Lucas as of right now. His dog tags say it. His passport says it. His Navy papers say it. And our next-of-kin records confirm it. He's never even met anyone who lives in the White House. He's Lieutenant Commander Bruce Lucas. Understood? That's all."

There really was little for anyone to do while *Seawolf* was under tow. Communications accessed the satellite every half-hour seeking new orders from SUBPAC, and the cooks were providing a very few meals for those who felt sufficiently well. But generally, the submarine had turned into a ghost ship. Officers sat in the wardroom drinking black coffee. Most of the engineers and electronics teams sat around belowdecks, playing cards or dozing, and the turbines were not driving anything.

The systems that provided air conditioning and fresh water were working normally, and of course Lt. Commander Rich Thompson had the nuclear reactor, from which all power stemmed, running correctly. Master Chief Brad Stockton patrolled the boat ceaselessly, checking and encouraging the younger members of the crew.

The key to the immediate future rested in the reception the Chinese Navy gave the Americans when finally they arrived in Canton. If they were treated reasonably and permitted to remain on board their ship while the diplomats argued, that would be perfect, because it would mean no damaging announcements admitting that the finest submarine in the U.S. Navy had been hijacked by the People's Liberation Army and all the crew were held captive in Canton.

That would cause outrage in the United States. There would be demands that the President act. It would be the 1980 Tehran hostage crisis all over again. And if the Clarke administration failed to frighten China into releasing the ship and its company, they too would be finished.

As potential crises go, this one was well on its way, but SUB-PAC and its masters in the Pentagon were not announcing anything until *Seawolf* arrived in Canton and the Joint Chiefs could see precisely how the cards fell.

Meanwhile, Captain Crocker summoned Lt. Commander Mike Schulz, and the two of them went alone into the reactor compartment.

"Mike," said the CO, "I don't know what's going to happen when we get to Canton. But there must be a chance the Chinese are going to try and get complete details of this submarine. I have some unwritten orders from the CNO in the event we fall into enemy hands. And it involves that isolating valve on the emergency cooling system. The one we both looked at in New London. I want you to activate it right now, so there will be no indications of failure when it fails."

"Aye, aye, sir," replied Lt. Commander Schulz.

And so the Americans lurched on up the channel, the big steel hawser taking the strain as it had done for almost 150 miles now. They cleared the more agricultural reaches of the Delta, still moving north as fast as the destroyer and the tugs could drag and push them.

But it was three o'clock in the sweltering afternoon when they eased into the narrowing river and made their way into the submarine jetty. Judd Crocker decided there was no point in sealing themselves inside, and he and Master Chief Stockton opened the hatch and went up onto the bridge.

They blinked in the fitful sunbeams that now penetrated the rain clouds, and they blinked at the chilling sight that awaited them. A 200-strong armed naval guard was in formation on the jetty as they pulled alongside. The tugs edged *Seawolf* in, her 350-foot-long portside against the dock.

The Chinese used their own gangway to board the American ship. Immediately 20 of the guards crossed onto the casing and took up positions, still with their arms at the ready, in groups of five, covering the four main hatches. There was no way off the submarine, and in a matter of moments, the brutal reality of the situation was rammed home to both men staring down from the bridge.

A Chinese naval officer walked across the gangway carrying a bullhorn and he aimed it high, straight at them. Then in immaculate English he read out a written statement to Captain Crocker and his men:

"My name is Commander Li Zemin. I am in charge of all security at the Canton Naval Base of the People's Republic of China. We believe your submarine to be carrying formal weapons of war, including a nuclear capability. These foreign weapons are strictly banned in the waters of the South China Sea. They are banned by the Paramount Ruler of the Republic, and here in China we insist that our laws and customs are obeyed.

"The crew of this ship is thus under arrest under the laws of the People's Republic and you will begin disembarking, enlisted men first, then your petty officers and junior officers, with the high command of the ship disembarking last.

"We are in touch with your government, which denies you ever had orders to come so close to our shores. We thus hold you responsible, each man personally, for this most unfortunate breach of the peaceful trade routes of China. In due course you will face trial, and this may mean a long term of imprisonment.

"Meanwhile, you will begin vacating the ship. But you will leave the nuclear plant running, and you will permit your chief nuclear engineering officer to remain in the reactor room in order to confer with our Chinese naval scientists.

"Needless to say, should anyone offer any armed or physical resistance whatsoever, he will be shot instantly, plus a minimum of two of his colleagues. Now open the doors and begin filing out with your hands above your heads. You will be unarmed. Any man found carrying any weapon will be instantly executed."

It had taken Admiral Zhang Yushu all morning to write that speech, and he was immensely proud of it. "Show those arrogant bastards who's boss now, right, Jicai?"

Up on the bridge, Judd Crocker felt the wintry realization of their plight. There was no way around this. Unbelievably, but irrevocably, he and his crew were prisoners of the Chinese, and the way Commander Li was talking, that was liable to be so for a long time. Thoughts surged through his mind. What would the Pentagon do? What about the government? What about the President? How long would this nightmare last?

Whichever way he sliced up the problem, the Chinese were in the saddle right now. And at 17 minutes after 3:00 on that Friday afternoon, the commanding officer of USS *Seawolf* ordered the ship's company to vacate the submarine and to surrender to Commander Li's men in the precise manner he had ordered.

Beyond the jetty, he could see a line of 10 open Navy trucks, each one surrounded by more armed guards and drivers. Admiral Zhang had been flying them in all day, in small military aircraft from both Zhanjiang and Xiamen.

And now the door was opened and the CO saw the young Californian seaman recruit, Kirk Sarloos, lead the men out, his hands high behind the back of his head. There was something almost surreal about this, almost as if it could not be happening. But it was happening, and it was happening badly. A guard stepped forward and slammed the butt of his rifle into the small of Kirk's back, knocking him hard toward the gangway. It was a long time since any of the Americans had witnessed gratuitous violence, some of them never. But there was no doubt that they were about to discover the realities of captivity in a country with a human rights record bordering on the plain barbaric.

The Chinese marched the Americans off the ship in groups of 10, herding them toward the trucks, throwing the occasional kick, the occasional punch, the occasional slam of a rifle butt. Not many of the crew made the trucks without some painful reminders, and the towering engineer from Ohio, Tony Fontana, received a massive blow to the head with a pistol for calling the Commander a "slit-eyed, fourth-rate Chinese motherfucker who ought to be working in a goddamned laundry."

Then one of the deck crew laughed and was knocked unconscious for his trouble. Things were looking very bad from where Captain Crocker stood.

The evacuation took an hour before Commander Li, in the company of eight guards, entered the ship and ordered the two Americans off the bridge. He instructed them to stand unarmed in the control room while his men took down details of their names and ranks.

He formally told the CO that *Seawolf* was now confiscated by the Navy of the People's Republic. The American crew had been taken to a civilian jail within the boundaries of the City of Canton, but the "High Command" of the ship, which would include the senior engineering officers, would be detained in the naval compound, while the "extraordinary engineers of China become familiar with the submarine."

It was five o'clock in the afternoon before Judd Crocker, Bruce Lucas, Cy Rothstein, Shawn Pearson, Andy Warren, and Brad Stockton were individually marched out at gunpoint and driven to a cell block designed for Navy discipline but currently unoccupied. It was a low gray single-story building with small, high windows that had probably not been cleaned since the Revolution. A smiling portrait of Mao Zedong was painted on the end wall.

Each cell was tiny, filthy, eight feet wide by nine feet long, with a full-length steel-barred door, like something from an old Western movie. There was a stark wooden bench, a bucket, and no water. And one by one the guards pushed the men inside and slammed the doors shut and locked. The six cells were adjoining and faced a dirt-floored outside corridor that went right around. There were four empty cells at the end of the corridor now occupied by Judd and his men, which probably meant that there were 10 more cells in the back. Judging by the silence, they were empty.

As the last door slammed on Brad Stockton, Commander Li came briskly through the outside door and walked slowly past all six of the Americans.

"These are temporary quarters," he said. "You will be moved tomorrow with the rest of your men. But first you will meet the most distinguished Commander-in-Chief of the People's Navy, who will discuss with you the terms of your stay here . . . and the degree of technical cooperation we expect from you."

At this point Captain Crocker spoke for the first time. "Commander, we are obliged to provide you with our names, ranks, and serial numbers, under the terms of the Geneva Convention of 1949. We are not obliged to provide you with anything further. Those are the rules of war, and are generally adhered to by all countries. *Civilized countries*, that is."

"Two things, Captain Crocker," snapped Commander Li. "First, my country had been a very substantial civilization for four thousand years when your people were still eating tree roots. Second, we are not at war, which I suggest makes the Geneva Convention irrelevant."

"You are treating my men as if we were at war."

"Perhaps a different kind of war, Captain Crocker. Be ready to meet our exalted Commander-in-Cheif, Admiral Zhang Yushu, in one hour. I think you will find him . . . persuasive. In terms of pure science, of course."

1800.
Office of the Southern Fleet Commander.
Canton Navy Base.

Admiral Zhang Yushu occupied the big chair and desk normally reserved for the Southern Commander, Admiral Zu Jicai. Gathered around him in this great carpeted military office, seated on huge, carved wooden antique "thrones," was the very backbone of the navy of China. To his right sat his friend Jicai, under whose command *Seawolf* now fell.

Admiral Yibo Yunsheng, the Eastern Fleet Commander, had just flown in from Shanghai. A former commanding officer of the old strategic missile submarine *Xia*, Yibo was a wise and tested warhorse of the Chinese Navy, and Zhang put great trust in his words.

The Chief of Naval Staff, Vice Admiral Sang Ye, had arrived from Beijing. He and Zhang had known each other for many years, and neither would tolerate a wrong word about the other. Sang Ye held great influence over the purse strings of the Chinese Navy, and this was an operation that might require the spending of big money.

The Chief of the General Staff himself, Qiao Jiyun, had flown to Canton on the same private jet that had brought Sang Ye, because it was plainly not merely a matter for the Navy. This was a national military matter that might, if improperly handled, suck China into a headlong confrontation with the USA.

To stress the strong political ramifications of the situation, the Paramount Ruler had insisted that the newly promoted Political Commissar of the People's Liberation Army/Navy, Admiral Xue Qing, attend this strategy meeting in company with a full staff of deputies, who now waited in an outside room.

The main office, in which now sat the most senior figures in the Chinese Navy, was not really an office at all, but much more of a room of state, as if transplanted from the Great Hall of the People. It seemed to be a thousand years old with its massive 100-foot-long antique Persian rug, which had once been transported with Marco Polo all the way along the old Silk Road.

But the room was only four years old, constructed especially for great meetings such as these in one of the buildings of China's new Senior Service. Only since the turn of the twentieth century had the colossal importance of the Navy been recognized. It had plainly superseded the Army as the front line of China's military ambitions, and indeed defense.

For several years, visiting politicians and commanders had sat in plain functional Navy-base rooms until, one morning back in 1999, the Paramount Ruler himself expressed disgust that the most exalted and trusted people in the entire country were somehow sitting in a military slum attempting to solve the destiny of one and a quarter billion people.

"I like coming to Ghuangzhou," he had said, using as ever the modern Chinese name. "And I am always honored to talk to my commanders here, and to see our great ships. But please, will someone provide us with a comfortable room in which we may speak—something commensurate perhaps with the expectations of those who occupy high offices of state, and from whom much is expected."

Thus the great room was constructed, with four towering round columns decorated with deeply patterned red silk. Exquisite ornamental lacquer ware, inlaid with gold, from the Ming dynasty of the mid-fifteenth century, was placed upon the most spectacular carved tables from the same period. Upon the wall, behind Admiral Zhang, was a giant painting of the procession of the Ming Emperor Wuzong, his ornate carriage of state pulled forward by a team of elephants.

Two paintings of similar size, each 10 feet in height, were set above the door, one of the former Paramount Ruler Mao Zedong, the other of the Great Reformer Deng Xiaoping, who had once occupied the chairmanship of the Military Affairs Commission. It was he who had promoted Zhang Yushu to C-in-C of the Navy.

And now Deng's protégé sat at the enormous 12-foot-square carved desk, flanked on either side by two traditional high blue-and-white Ming vases, placed strategically, port and starboard, upon the scarlet leather. They were there as a testimony not only to the grandeur of Chinese culture, but also as a reminder to visiting foreign commanders and dignitaries that China invented fine porcelain in the seventh century, or, as the Paramount Ruler preferred to state it, *"One thousand years before Europe, porcelain that has never been equaled."*

Staring happily out from between the vases, Zhang looked like an emperor himself. He called the meeting to order and quickly outlined the story of the captured American submarine.

"Frankly," he said, "the submarine is an embarrassment. Its presence here will infuriate the Americans, who will, first, want it back, second, invent ways to punish us economically and third, may even carry out military action against us, which would be unfortunate in the extreme.

"The USA is very powerful and very vicious when it has a mind to be. And they would have a case against us. Whatever we may say diplomatically, their submarine was in international waters, where they had a perfect right to be . . . and we have effectively stolen it.

"However, that will not of course be our argument. We will concentrate on how shocked we are that the U.S.A. should have brought such a weapon of mass destruction that close to our coastline—as close as the Cuban missiles were to theirs in 1962 when President Kennedy was happy to risk starting a world war.

"Gentlemen, I should like to clarify our purpose. In our great quest to create a modern, blue-water Navy, we lack one thing—the knowledge to build world-class submarines, which is the one boat that will always keep us safe from attack, allow us to blockade and retake Taiwan, and provide us with control over the world's shipping routes to the east. But despite all of our careful acquisition of the secret computer formulas and discoveries of Western nations, we have not been able to copy them adequately. There are subtleties in the systems that we do not understand. . . ."

Admiral Zhang quite suddenly stood up. And he paced behind his chair in front of Emperor Wuzong's parade, and then he stated very simply, "Gentlemen, the answer to all of our prayers is currently parked on submarine jetty zero-five."

He paused to allow the full effect of his words to settle on his colleagues. And he added, "Working from plans and documents is one thing, but it is not nearly so effective as working from the real thing, which you can touch, and dismantle and restart, and strip down and examine with the finest available minds in China, and even beyond. I have already sent for a team of twelve senior submarine engineers and scientists from the Russian Central Design Bureau of Marine Engineering in Saint Petersburg.

"They were of course reluctant to come at such short notice, but we are, as you know, their biggest customers these days, by a very long way. And they felt they had to oblige us. I sent a military aircraft to bring them in, in the hope that my friend and colleague Vice Admiral Sang Ye will not object to the expenditure."

"I am honored to write the check in this instance," said the Navy Chief of Staff, smiling.

"I am also flying in two other Russian sonar engineers in another plane from Gorky leaving tomorrow . . . and I hope that will be agreeable as well?"

"So long as it's not a Boeing 747 for two people," replied Admiral Sang, smiling again.

"Oh, no. Most certainly not. It's just a military aircraft of ours, based out on our far western border. It will refuel there, on the way back to us."

"And the fee to Central Design for the technicians?"

"Er . . . two million American dollars."

"Expensive people."

"Yes, Admiral. But for this we must have the best. Can you believe our good fortune? We stand today on the brink of building underwater ships that can compete with the Americans. In my view, *Seawolf* has saved us twenty-five years of research, by which time we would still be behind."

"How long, Admiral Zhang, do we need the submarine?" asked the Political Commissar, Admiral Xue Qing.

"We could make limited progress in two months. We'd need years to make a complete examination and copy."

"And what do you propose to tell the Americans during that time?"

"Oh, that the submarine sustained very bad damage in the crash, and our wish is to repair it to the point where it can safely leave for California. We'll tell them we have a major problem with the reactor and have no wish to release it if there is any form of danger."

"What if the Americans say they'll come and pick it up, and repair it with their own technicians?"

"Oh, that would not be acceptable to us. That ship has been quarantined because of suspected nuclear activity, and may not leave the jetty until it is safe. I am afraid we would never allow a foreign warship into the Pearl River Delta."

"In fact, you just wish to fence with them until you are good and ready to release it?"

"Correct. Of course, it will hurry things along if we get some cooperation from the crew."

"They will tell us nothing."

"Oh, they might, with some persuasion."

"And where will you keep the crew during all of this?"

"I have already instigated the reopening of the old jail on

Xiachuan Dao, about eighty miles along the coast from Macao. It will hold, if necessary, three hundred people including staff and guards, and I'm hoping to have it functional by Sunday. There's electricity and water on the island—originally installed by the Japanese, but still working."

"Do you regard this as a place to *hide* the Americans?" Admiral Zu Jicai was asking the question.

"Yes, in a sense I do. Because I believe the advantage is with us, so long as Washington does not know where these men are."

"How long do you think it will take the Americans to find out?"

"With luck, two to three weeks. They'll organize satellite searches, heat-seeking infrared, and they may finally notice some unusual activity on an island that is virtually deserted, as it has been for centuries. Also, the CIA has a very effective spy system."

"What will the Americans do if and when they find out where their crew is being detained?"

"Nothing, because they will be too late. I intend to move all the prisoners away from the coast within sixteen days to a new jail deep in the interior, which even the Americans will never find. That buys us another twenty-one days with *Seawolf* . . . and then with profound sympathy we will tell them there has been a major nuclear accident on board, such that the whole area has had to be sealed off."

"And the crew?"

"I am afraid they cannot be permitted to return, either, because by then they will know a great deal too much. We are going to interrogate them, vigorously, under the pressure of time.

"All of their senior operatives will know we are planning to copy *Seawolf*, and it will not take the Pentagon long to work out that we intend to achieve total domination of our own coastal waters, plus the oil routes of the Middle East to the Far East."

"But Zhang," protested Admiral Xue. "We cannot just execute them. There would be a world outcry."

"We also cannot let them return, because then there would be an even bigger world outcry, perhaps at some of the methods we may be obliged to use in order to re-create that submarine and secure their . . . cooperation."

"Then what do you propose to do with them?"

"There will be a military trial, held behind locked doors. Each member of *Seawolf*'s crew will be charged with treason against the Chinese people, and with bringing illegal nuclear weapons within striking distance of the peace-loving people of this Republic. They will be charged with endangering life on the high seas, and with the reckless operation of a nuclear submarine containing weapons of mass destruction, entirely against the spirit of the Nuclear Non-Proliferation Treaty of 1991."

"But we did not even sign that treaty," interjected Xue Qing.

"That does not preclude us from understanding it," replied Zhang, uncharacteristically haughty. "And there may be further charges leveled at the Americans, involving lying to the Chinese military authorities while we struggled to make safe their lethal weapons, in order that the good people of Guangzhou may continue to lead their lives without fear of nuclear radiation in our ancient and historic city. Furthermore, we will charge them with sabotaging the reactor and deliberately causing a major nuclear accident in our port.

"Gentlemen, I would suggest that a prison term of perhaps thirty-five years per man would not be unreasonable for such crimes. And during those years, they will of course quietly disappear. But none of them will ever leave China alive. It is already too late for that."

Each of the six men in the great room nodded assent to the master plan of the Navy's Commander-in-Chief. This was unusual for China, because civilized talk and discussion is an art form in that country. But the men involved today were wise and experienced. And each of them was aware that the moment Colonel Lee had conferred on the satellite with Admiral Zhang and taken the American ship prisoner, the die was cast. They had done it. And there could be no going back now.

In 10 minutes, the C-in-C would be in the cell block, informing the Americans of precisely what was expected of them as military prisoners of the Chinese government.

1930.
Cell Block Mao. Canton Navy Base.

Admiral Zhang Yushu kicked open the door and strode into the dirt corridor in front of the six occupied cells. He wore full dark blue uniform, with sidearms and high black boots. In his right hand he carried a slim wooden officer's baton. He was accompanied by Commander Li and four guards, all of whom saluted the Navy Guard lieutenant, with three stars on his shoulder, already on duty inside the door.

As Zhang made his entry, the lieutenant stood to attention rigidly, all five feet two inches of him, and literally screamed, in English, "STAND UP NOW! EVERYONE . . . STAND UP IN THE PRESENCE OF THE MOST EXALTED COMMANDER-IN-CHIEF OF THE PEOPLE'S NAVY!"

The weary Americans dragged themselves up, and the guard screamed again, "YOU WILL SALUTE THE COMMANDER-IN-CHIEF! YOU WILL SHOW THE UTMOST RESPECT WHILE YOU ARE HERE! STAND UP AND SALUTE! YOU ARE CRIMINALS IN A PEACEFUL COUNTRY!"

"Captain Crocker," said Admiral Zhang in fluent English. "Remember, there is no one in this world who can help you. You have been caught red-handed, apparently preparing for an act of war in our Chinese waters. There is nothing your country can do for you. Oh, I realize that mighty Uncle Sam could hurl a nuclear missile at the city of Canton and probably obliterate it, killing two million of my innocent countrymen. But it would not concern us overly. We would still have almost one and a quarter billion people left. War has always meant attrition to us. We can stand losses per-haps as no nation has ever done."

He walked to the end of the line, glaring at each man. And then he walked back, and as he did so he intoned, "In any event, the U.S.A. is not going to hit Canton, because they most certainly want their submarine back, and they probably do not want to kill all of you, so they are not going to start bombing us.

"Neither are they going to launch some kind of an invasion against a country as big as ours. Which brings me back to my original point. In the end the U.S. government will do nothing for you. You are entirely in our power, and I advise you most strongly to cooperate to the full."

The American captain stared at him, and said firmly, "Under the terms of the Geneva Convention, neither I nor any of my men are obliged to tell you one thing."

This had the effect of infuriating the lieutenant beyond reasonable control. Either that or he was going for the Chinese equivalent of an Oscar.

"YOU!" he yelled. "YOU! YOU WILL NOT ADDRESS THE COMMANDER-IN-CHIEF UNLESS YOU ARE GIVEN PERMISSION."

"Why don't you fucking zip it, asshole," growled the unshaven Brad Stockton, whose hard-muscled athletic build had been known to strike terror in the lower decks of various submarines.

"Yeah, why don't you," added Shawn Pearson. "Anyway, I've met you before . . . didn't you used to work in Wing Fat's Chop Suey House down by the docks in Norfolk?"

"Yeah, I've seen you in there," said Master Chief Stockton. "Cheap little joint run by cheap little Chinese assholes."

"SILENCE!" roared Admiral Zhang. And then, his voice instantly softening, "Captain Crocker, you will now inform your fellow officers that they will speak only when they are spoken to . . . perhaps you would do that before we continue our little talk."

"Admiral Zhang, might I suggest," said Judd politely, "in an ancient and honorable American tradition, that you take that stupid little stick you're carrying and go fuck yourself, and possibly your mad sidekick at the same time."

The C-in-C, who spoke excellent but formal English learned strictly from textbooks, looked faintly bewildered at this outburst of colloquialism. But his lieutenant, who had lived for a few months as a student in California, understood perfectly, and once more went into a frenzy.

"YOU ARE PRISONERS OF THE PEOPLE'S REPUBLIC OF

CHINA!" he screamed. "YOU WILL NOT BE INSUBORDINATE OR I WILL HAVE YOU PUNISHED IN A WAY YOU WILL NOT FORGET! NOW SILENCE!"

"Hey, Zhang, who is this fucking little creep you hang out with?" asked Shawn. "Remember ancient Amellican proverb, you judge a man by his friends, and right now I'm seeing twin assholes."

The admiral's face was thunderous. He had come into this corridor to intimidate, to frighten his prisoners. And right now he was considering having at least two of them shot. But he was a man of clear purpose, and he snatched from the lieutenant a document that listed the names, ranks and serial numbers of the Americans.

Angry though he was at their insolence, he saw no advantage in putting to death the Master Chief of the entire boat, plus the tall young Navigation Officer, who probably knew more about certain electronic systems than anyone in the entire Chinese Navy.

"Your attitudes," he said gently, "will get you precisely nowhere. At the same time, my well-meaning requests are being rejected. I will thus leave you now until the morning. You will be given a bowl of plain rice and water . . . and Captain Crocker, try to bear in mind, there is NO ONE on this earth who is going to do one thing for you. Your government is in the process of abandoning you completely, which leaves the field of submarine research open for me to conduct as I wish."

Judd Crocker, with a sidelong glance through the grill to the next cell, which contained Lt. Commander Bruce Lucas, just nodded and murmured, "I'm not sure I'd count on that, Zhang old buddy, not if I were you . . ."

0140. Friday, July 7.
Office of the National Security Adviser.
The White House.

"I mean, Jesus Christ, Joe, this has been going on for thirty-six hours. How come it's taken so long to get me informed? What the hell's the matter with you guys?"

"Arnie," said Admiral Joe Mulligan, "the Chinese have been playing this down right from the start. Look at it from our point of view . . . SUBPAC gets a signal that *Seawolf* is immobile on the surface one hundred miles offshore in the South China Sea. That's not good, but it sure ain't life-threatening. We open up the lines to the Chinese Navy, which tells us they've had a request from the American captain for assistance, which they are providing . . . now NONE of that is life-threatening."

"I wouldn't believe those little pricks in a thousand years, Joe. Neither should you."

"I understand. But all parties, including SUBPAC, have been playing it down, trying to work out a way to get the submarine free, and subsequently part on good terms with the Chinese. Arnie, it's called diplomacy, and sometimes you gotta have it."

"And some other times it's called bullshit."

Admiral Mulligan smiled despite himself. "Arnie," he said, "can someone get me a cup of coffee?"

Admiral Morgan ignored him, and continued griping and moaning. "And then, having been given a total fucking runaround by Beijing for the biggest part of a day and a half, you phone me at midnight and tell me to get my ass into the office because you have something big to impart. Christ, Joe! You've had all day."

"Arnie, how long have you known me?"

"Too long, asshole. I'm supposed to be asleep."

"You're not going soft on me, are you? Where's the steely submarine CO I once knew?"

"Joe, you have raised me from my bed. We are the only two people in the West Wing of the White House in the small hours of the morning, and I am in deep shock at the general failure of the U.S. Navy to get this situation onto a fast track."

"Arnie, I haven't finished."

"Oh . . . well, go on. It can't get much worse, can it?"

"Yes, it can. *Seawolf*'s XO was Linus Clarke."

The blood drained from the craggy face of Arnold Morgan. His mouth went dry, and deep within him he felt a slow trembling sensation. He walked to his desk and sat down, folding his hands together in front of him. For a moment he was literally speechless, struck dumb by the enormity of the CNO's words.

After what seemed five minutes, he just said, "Does the President know "

"No."

"Do we yet know if they are off the ship?"

"Our information is that the ship is alongside in Canton, and that the crew has been taken off and incarcerated."

"Holy shit," breathed the President's principal military adviser.

For a few more moments, neither man spoke. And then Admiral Morgan asked, "Do the Chinese know the identity of Linus?"

"No. We've always had procedures about what to do in this kind of emergency. Like get rid of all evidence, his papers, passport, etc. And provide him with new stuff that was kept sealed away throughout the voyage. I have checked, and the procedures have gone into effect. Linus has become Lieutenant Commander Bruce Lucas of Houston, Texas. The Chinese have no idea."

"Well, I guess that's something. . . . Okay, Joe. Let me just walk through the situation with you once again. I want to take a few notes."

"No problem. Take your time."

"Right. Now *Seawolf* is on patrol in the South China Sea, where she's been for the best part of a couple of weeks. Out of Pearl, right? Under the command of the very capable Captain Judd Crocker, whose father served with me."

"Correct."

"We do not yet know the result of the mission, but knowing that particular CO it was probably going well."

"Right."

"Then, in the middle of the goddamned night, *Seawolf* apparently runs across the stern of China's new guided-missile destroyer, and gets wound up in its towed array."

"That's what we're seeing on the satellite pictures."

"Right. Now why did Judd Crocker not just send a team over the side and cut the sonofabitch free? He would háve had all the right gear on board."

"Small-arms fire, sir."

"You mean the slit-eyed Orientals opened fire on the team and stopped them?"

"Looks like it. Judd's signal did not make clear whether there were bullets flying, or merely threats."

"No reason to think Judd Crocker's gone soft?"

"Negative. He's probably the best submarine CO in the U.S. Navy."

"I know he is. Which means there must have been bullets . . . but anyway. We now have *Seawolf* wallowing around with no propulsion, attached to the Chinese destroyer. So they make her fast, and we get a signal in from Judd that the submarine is being towed into the port of Canton. He did not clarify whether at that stage he considered his crew were prisoners."

"Probably because he was uncertain himself."

"Right. Now anyway, you guys open up the lines to the Chinese Navy, which informs you they have had a request from the American captain for assistance, and they are now giving that assistance, correct?"

"That's what they said."

"So the situation is now slightly confused. Crocker's not protesting strenuously that he has been arrested in international waters, and the Chinks are just saying they are doing their best to help."

"That's it."

"Well, then what?"

"Arnie, it gets a bit hazy from here. We alerted Langley immediately and they came in with a signal that a big company of navy guards has been flown into Canton. Then Fort Meade adjusts the satellite and comes up with a picture of huge activity on the submarine jetty. It looks as if the crew has been taken off . . . then a coupla hours later the CIA hear from one of their field officers that almost a hundred American crewmen have been transported in Navy trucks to a civilian jail up in the northeast of the city, near that famous Canton landmark . . . what's it called? The Mausoleum of the Seventy-two Martyrs."

"Better make sure they don't have to rename it for the One Hundred and Seventy-two Martyrs."

"Anyway, that's where we are. China is saying how peaceful they are and they will try to get our submarine working and back to sea. The crew are guests of the People's Republic, and everyone hopes this incident will soon be over and forgotten."

"Do you believe them, Joe?"

"Some. How about you?"

"None."

"Hmmm. Okay, Arnie. I hear you. But let's not lose sight of one thing: It's not really in their interests to move to the brink of a serious confrontation with the U.S. And neither will they want to receive worldwide condemnation for rubbing out an entire American submarine crew. I am thus drawn to the conclusion that they may make some propaganda out of this. You know, poor peaceful Chinese with mad-dog American gangsters in their backyard. But in the end they will wish to stay friends, and they will probably hand back our ship and her company. Perhaps with some kind of trade sweetener."

"And a contribution to the Democratic Party's election campaign."

"Arnie, I am just trying to show you our mindset for the past twenty-four hours."

"You want my advice?"

"Sure."

"Shove your goddamned mindset straight down the tubes. And get a new one."

"Huh?"

"Joe, seriously, lemme say this to you. The job of Chief of Naval Operations is very time-consuming. You have overall responsibility for running the biggest, most advanced operational fleet in the entire history of the world. You have an enormous day-to-day, hour-to-hour responsibility.

"My task in this world is different. I am here to *think*. To sit right here, in this room, and ponder the military activities currently happening on planet Earth. I spend all day reading, discussing, assessing and planning, trying to seek out weak spots, trying to second-guess our goddamned enemies. Which is why I am about to pontificate to you, right here in the West Wing at damned near two o'clock in the goddamned morning, what I consider the precise mind-set of the Chinese."

"Okay, old pal, I'm ready . . . by the way, can anyone around here bring us some coffee?"

"Joe, you can get anything around here if you want it badly enough. 'Cept for goddamned peace and quiet."

He picked up the telephone and was instantly connected to the 40,000-calls-a-day White House switchboard. And Joe heard the outlaw-sweet tones of the most feared man in international military relations.

"Hello, this is Admiral Arnold Morgan. To whom do I have the pleasure of speaking this evening? Maryanne? Perfect. Nice name. Now, Maryanne, I am sitting here in company with Admiral Joseph Mulligan, the professional head of the entire United States Navy. And what we seek is not too complicated . . . one pot of coffee, and one plate of cookies. . . . Now I realize this is not in your job description . . . but I want you to find someone to achieve those two objectives . . . coffee and cookies. You may use my name, quote my wishes shamelessly to any underling you may find . . . you may cajole and threaten.

"I know, Maryanne, that the hour is late, but my problems are many, and my needs are simple . . . and it is because of these particularly stressful tasks that very clever young ladies such as yourself are employed . . . thank you for your indulgence . . . 'bye."

"Jesus, you old smoothie."

"Even I can't yell at people at this late hour and expect 'em to function . . . but I have faith in Miss Maryanne."

Six minutes later, a well-groomed young man in a starched white jacket knocked and entered with a large pot of coffee, bone china cups and saucers, a large plate of Pepperidge Farm cookies, and a sizeable plate of chicken sandwiches. . . . "Thought you might be hungry, sir."

"You see, Joe, charm and diplomacy are sometimes necessary."

Admiral Mulligan shook his head at the sheer blinding insincerity of the man. Even Admiral Morgan chuckled, but quickly added, "But not when you're dealing with devious Orientals."

"Okay, Arnie," said Admiral Mulligan, munching cheerfully. "Lay it on me."

The NSA walked across the room to his conference table and poured them coffee, firing a couple of rounds of "buckshot" into each cup—he never could remember the name Hermesetas, but he would have had it been that of a submarine. Then he walked over to a huge computer screen on his wall, the hard drive of which contained the up-to-date charts of all the world's oceans. He switched on the system, punched in CHINA, then YELLOW SEA, then pulled up the northernmost point of that cul-de-sac ocean, the Bay of Liaodong.

"Right. Now here is where they built the new Chinese ICBM submarine, at this port up here, Huludao. Now we know how shallow the Yellow Sea is and we know the submarines, even newly built, leave there on the surface, running south down the coast of Korea towards the deeper water.

"Now we wanna assume two things. One, Judd and his boys are on the case, following the new *Xia III*. Two, the Chinese suspect he might be around somewhere, which I have no doubt pisses them off royally.

"Anyhow, over the next few days there was quite a serious game of cat-and-mouse going on. We get some stuff on the satellite about a big depth charge and ASW mortar exercise off Taiwan. That was no exercise. Trust me. They thought they'd caught Judd, and they might've, but he got away.

"Now I'm guessing we have right here an even-more-pissed-off Chinese Navy. Look at the stuff from Fort Meade, look at these pictures from the South China Sea. Suddenly, up to the surface comes the new *Xia*. We photograph it from the satellite, right here on this chart. Three hours later we get a Fort Meade report of another big Chinese exercise, planes, choppers, ships everywhere, ten miles from where we saw the *Xia*. Again that was no exercise. Again that was Judd. Again he got away. By Christ, he's hard to catch.

"Now, let's assume he's got what he came for, the photographs and measurements. But the Chinese still can't find him. But they don't give up. They actually send out their big new destroyer, *Xiangtan*, from Canton, into the area where Chinese Naval Intelligence is now guessing *Seawolf* might be. The main area search failed, right? So they decide to sniff out the inshore areas where a really cunning American CO like Judd might go. Where he would be least expected."

Joe Mulligan stared at the chart of the southern coast of China and nodded thoughtfully.

"Then there's a bit of a fluke," said Arnold Morgan. "The fuckers trip over each other. And, lo and behold, the Chinese have the devil that's been haunting them for several days. . . . Wily little bastards try to put us off the scent with a succession of hurt but helpful messages. Meanwhile they steal *Seawolf*—along with every god-damned thing they've already stolen—and now plan to torture our crew into revealing every last high-tech secret of the greatest attack submarine the world has ever known. What the hell else are they gonna do with it? Turn it into a fucking ferry to Kowloon?

"And that, Admiral, IS WHY I HAVE TO BE KEPT INFORMED OF EVERY LAST DUMBASS DEVELOPMENT THAT GOES ON IN YOUR DUMBASS NAVY CONCERNING CHINA . . . BECAUSE NOBODY ELSE GETS IT . . . EXCEPT ME."

Admiral Mulligan took his life in his hands. "Is their even a remote possibility that you may be wrong, Arnie?"

"Fuck off, Joe. And don't sound retarded even if you are."

The big CNO almost choked with laughter on his tenth cookie, because the truth was, Morgan was right. "*You think you know something, talk to Arnie, then you'll know much, much more.*" And he thanked God for him, and for their long, unbreakable friendship.

"Just think about it, Joe. Here we have one hugely pissed-off Chinese Navy, being given the runaround by the Americans. Finally, they get lucky. They have in their possession the submarine that will save 'em the trouble of this type of espionage for years and years.

"Joe, they are planning to copy that ship down to the last detail. If necessary they will torture key men in the crew to get the know-how, and it's my guess we'll never see either the men or *Seawolf* again.

"They'll either jail 'em, after some trumped-up trial, or they'll just go missing. It's such a vast country, so fucking mysterious, we'd never be able to find 'em."

"Well, if that's your take on it, I'll just get up and go, and you can give the President a quick call and announce the impending death of his only son. Good luck."

Admiral Morgan laughed, nervously for him. "Siddown, Joe. I'm not saying we acquiesce to any of this. I'm just trying to lay down the Chinese mindset. A worst-case scenario, I admit. But if we're gonna tackle it, we may as well face up to it. Of course, if I am wrong, then it'll sort itself out and no one will be hurt. But I've got a real creepy feeling about the Chinese, and I do not like *anything* I'm hearing over the past few days.

"Anyway, there's going to be just one outcome today, as far as we're concerned. The President's gonna tell us to get Linus back. Somehow. I hope."

0900. Saturday, July 8.
Cell Block Mao. Canton Naval Base.

The commotion outside attracted the attention of all six of the American prisoners. And each man stood at the bars of his cell as the main door was kicked forcibly in, swinging back hard against the stone wall to allow Commander Li to make his entry. He was followed by four more American prisoners, apparently transferred in the past hour from the civilian jail out by the mausoleum.

Judd Crocker watched them come in, handcuffed in a line, all very junior members of the crew—Seaman Recruits—led by Kirk Sarloos from the torpedo room. Behind him came young Nathan Dunn from Alabama; followed by the black engineer from Georgia, Carlton Fleming; then one of the cooks, Skip Laxton, 19, from Vermont.

Each man nodded to the officers as they passed and were then roughly shoved into the last four cells at the end of the line. At which point Admiral Zhang Yushu marched through the still-open door, turned to Captain Crocker and said icily, "Tell your men they will cooperate with my technicians in a tour of the ship later this morning . . . and do it NOW, Captain Crocker. RIGHT NOW!"

"Fuck off, Zhang. You're wasting your time and mine. I'm not obliged to do anything. And when we finally get out of here, you might find yourself a pariah in the international community for breaches of the Convention."

"Do not tempt me, Captain Crocker, to ensure that you never get out of here."

"SCREW YOU—you fat Chinese bastard."

"GUARD! Remove that man from cell number nine . . . now have him kneel on the floor right in front of his most insolent captain . . ."

They brought Skip Laxton out, and the tiny lieutenant knocked him to the floor with a rifle butt. "NOW KNEEL DOWN WITH YOUR FOREHEAD ON THE FLOOR, HANDS BEHIND YOUR BACK!"

The groggy American did as he was told, and once more, the Commander-in-Chief turned to Judd Crocker and told him to command his men to cooperate with the Chinese authorities in a scientific tour of the ship later that morning.

"YOU WILL ORDER IT NOW!!" he roared.

"The hell I will," replied the CO.

At which point Admiral Zhang Yushu nodded imperceptibly to the guard lieutenant, who aimed his service revolver and shot Skip Laxton dead, clean through the back of the head. In stunned silence the American officers watched the slumped body, the dirt spreading red beneath young Skip's forehead.

"You cheap-shit barbaric little murderer," shouted Brad Stockton. "When this gets out, you'll face a world courtroom as a war criminal. That was MURDER!"

"And it's not the end, either," said Admiral Zhang. "I am proposing to kill one of your men every time your captain denies my request. Because of your importance, and some of your other officer colleagues, you will all be spared for the time being. But I do not care if I have fifty of your more junior men killed. I'll do it . . . until you see reason. I am, you see, playing for extremely high stakes, the entire future of my country. The death of a few American pirates does not interest me one way or the other.

"Now bring out the next man . . . the one with the black face . . . and have him kneel just in front of Captain Crocker . . . now, sir . . . will you inform your men that they must cooperate."

"Very well," said Judd. "Since I am from a higher civilization than you, I have no choice . . . Men, you will accompany Admiral Zhang's technicians back to our ship with me, and you will tell him truthfully what he wants to know. And Li, you little asshole, I hope you enjoy your fucking tree roots for lunch."

They all stood silently and watched the Commander-in-Chief and his security chief march out of the cell block. And they heard the door bang shut behind them.

They did not, however, hear Zhang's icy verdict on the exercise. "I told you, Li," he said. "The West is ultimately soft, and the words of our great leader Mao Zedong must always be recalled . . . 'Real power comes from the barrel of a gun.'

"And you saw it for yourself. One bullet. That was all it took. One small bullet, and they caved in. One insignificant life in return for the greater glory of China, and all of our people. The future belongs to us, Li. And all these years later we must remember the most pure thoughts of the Chairman."

"And, sir, one question?"

"Certainly, my faithful Li."

"Would you really have ordered the execution of fifty men, had it been necessary?"

"Yes, Li. I think I might have. There are few moments in a commander's life when the end undoubtedly justifies the means. And, regrettably for the Americans, this was, and indeed is, one of them."

0800. Friday, July 7.
West Wing, the White House.

The 13-hour time difference between the South China Sea and the East Coast of the United States was a source of annoyance to Admiral Morgan. He constantly felt that he was a day behind, "trying to play catchup ball." As he usually put it, "Whatever they do in the normal light hours of a working day, it's nearly always the middle of the previous goddamned night here. That gives 'em an advantage. Chinese pricks."

And now he walked particularly briskly down the corridor

toward the Oval Office, his gleaming black shoes pounding along the carpet, his jaw set forward, arms swinging, eyes straight ahead. The towering figure of Admiral Joe Mulligan, moving on a longer stride than his five-foot-eight-inch colleague, had to increase his pace just to stay level.

The two Marine guards outside the President's office scarcely had time to move as the National Security Adviser walked straight between then, rapped twice on the polished wooden door, and went right in, followed by the head of the United States Navy.

The President rose from behind his desk and offered his hand to Admiral Mulligan. "Hello, Joe. Nice to see you again . . . Arnie and I have given up shaking hands since we see each other about five times a day . . . but there's some coffee here . . . which I'll pour for you . . . and I asked 'em to bring in some hot toast . . . I believe you've been here all night?"

"Yessir. We have," replied Admiral Morgan. "And I'm afraid the news we bring is not good . . . the Chinese Navy has somehow picked up *Seawolf* after some kind of a collision in the South China Sea. She's moored alongside in Canton right now. We think the crew has been incarcerated. And it is with the deepest regret that I must tell you, Linus is her executive officer."

The President sucked in his breath through his front teeth as the monstrous ramifications of the admiral's words slammed into his mind. He shook his head erratically, as if to say, "No, please, no. Tell me that's not true." And then he cast his hands outward, and he had to steel himself to say quietly, "Are they in danger? Will we get them back okay?"

"Sir, I think it may be most helpful if Joe ran through the whole incident very quickly. It'll give you a quick and accurate surface picture . . . then we can start to work out how we're gonna wring their fucking necks. Politically speaking, of course."

Despite himself, the President managed a meager smile, and then he nodded them to begin. He listened closely as Morgan and Mulligan gave their perspectives on the tragic events.

When they finished, the President turned to Morgan and asked, "You don't believe they'll return the men and the ship?"

"They might return the ship when they've finished with it, sir. But I doubt it. I think they'll find a way to say it's somehow nuclear-contaminated, and they are going to confiscate it to ensure the safety of honorable Chinese assholes, sorry, people."

"And the crew?"

"Sir, I think we have to assume they are going to try to wring them out for every last scrap of knowledge about the systems in the submarine. That may be hugely unpleasant. And then I think they may stage some kind of public military trial and put them all in the slammer for years and years, for endangering the lives of the peace-loving Chinese people with nuclear weapons. They'll try to turn it into treason against the Republic, and thus justify world opinion in their favor."

Just then a waiter came in with three plates of hot buttered toast and the President rose and thanked him, but Arnold noticed he did not eat anything.

Neither did he speak; he just sat and listened to his National Security Adviser outlining the gravity of the situation, reminding him of the zeal with which China had been pursuing the creation of a blue-water navy and especially a top-class submarine service, using any and every method to bring their technology up to speed.

Eventually the three men fell silent. And when the President finally spoke there was an air of terrible resignation in his voice. "Arnold, I accept your version of the Chinese intentions. There is no other reasonable way of looking at it."

The President stood up and walked across the room, standing by the portrait of General Washington. "Gentlemen," he said, "I know you both well. And I do not believe you came here to prepare me for the imminent death of my only son. Do we have a plan?"

"Sir, we do not. The implications here are so vast, the options so varied, that we're going to need a lot of advice. But I have taken the first step by telling the Chinese ambassador and his naval attaché to get their asses in here in the next half-hour."

"Good. That's a first step we always have to take, even though the ambassador's going to stand here and feign ignorance, and express his shock that we should think ill of the People's Liberation Navy . . ."

"You got that right. Slippery little bastard, whatsisname? Yung Pung Hi or something . . . but I'll send him away with a letter expressing our anger at their action of arresting a disabled American warship on the high seas in international waters. We have to let 'em know we expect them to come right back into line . . . or else."

"Yes, Arnie. I know you're especially gifted at that type of letter . . . but I must say, I have always dreaded the possibility of this day."

"You mean Linus, sir."

"I do. Don't get me wrong. The Navy has done a superb job for him, bringing him up to the brink of a command of his own. And they've done a wonderful job keeping the press off his back, allowing him to work away at his chosen career without outside interference, keeping his postings and tours of duty secret, even from me . . . but, oh my God, I have long dreaded something like this . . ."

He hesitated for a moment and then said, quite suddenly, "Joe, may I assume the Chinese have no idea who Linus is at this stage?"

"You may, sir. His entire identity has been very professionally altered."

"Thank God."

The President was thoughtful, and he returned to his desk as if succumbing to his fate. "Okay, we'll meet at nine-thirty in the situation room downstairs. I'll want a full political team with me. I think we should have the Chairman of the Joint Chiefs, plus Joe, plus you, maybe plus someone from SUBLANT if there's anyone senior and close to Washington. We better get the CIA Far Eastern Chief in here as well . . . then we can go to work."

Admiral Mulligan led the way to the door, followed by Arnold Morgan and the President, but when the CNO stepped out into the corridor, he found himself alone. Back inside, standing to the left of the half-opened door, the President had his arm around the wide shoulders of his military adviser, and Arnold could see that he was struggling for control.

"Get him back for me, Arnold. Please promise me you will . . . since his mother died . . . he's . . . he's all I've got . . ."

"We'll get him back, sir. I promise you that." But as he marched out to join Admiral Mulligan, Arnold Morgan had no idea how he would ever keep that promise.

The moment was not made easier by the fact that Arnold Morgan knew so much about the President's close relationship with his son. Naturally the entire nation, indeed most of the world, knew about the awful riding accident that had killed the First Lady out on the Oklahoma ranch after only a year in the White House.

But only the senior Navy personnel understood the full depth of the President's loss. He had pleaded for Linus to be airlifted from the submarine he was serving on, and the Navy had been happy to comply, to bring Linus home on compassionate leave to support his heartbroken father.

For six months, Linus had lived between the White House and the ranch. And those close to the Oval Office were in no doubt that the President could not have continued without his naval officer son at his side.

The result was excellent future relations between the Executive Branch and the U.S. Navy. But it caused the Commander-in-Chief of the U.S. Armed Forces to form a slightly unnatural dependency on the young and inexperienced Linus Clarke, sufficient to concern several service chiefs. And it explained much about the unmistakable arrogance in Linus's personality.

This was no ordinary parental devotion. This bordered on an obsessive paternal love, perhaps a substitute for the wife he had lost. It was common knowledge that the hugely eligible President Clarke had never so much as looked at another woman since his beloved Betsy had died.

No trauma would ever devastate any father more than that with which President Clarke was now trying to cope. And his words reflected his anguish.

**0930. Friday, July 7.
West Wing. The White House.**

T HE MEN SELECTED TO ATTEND THIS HIGHLY
classified meeting, in President Reagan's old Situation Room
in the West Wing basement, were all there before the Chief Executive made his entry. Each of them was standing around the table in
the center of the room awaiting seating instructions. At the end of
the room, a four-foot-wide computer screen was showing a navigational chart of a section of the South China Sea, homing in on the
forbidden waters of the Canton Roads.

"Gentlemen, good morning." The tall southwestern Republican
President was all business today. His usual smile was missing, and
there was no light banter in his greetings to colleagues. Immediately, he laid out his game plan for the meeting.

"I have already decided that we will form a small select committee here, and that my National Security Adviser, Admiral Mor-

gan here, is to take overall charge of the entire operation. I have cleared that with the Chairman of the Joint Chiefs and the Chief of Naval Operations.

"My reasons are obvious. The situation in which we find ourselves has such inordinately strong political overtones that it ceases to be an entirely military matter. Therefore Admiral Morgan is the natural choice, being the acknowledged expert on the subject, and having a foot firmly in both camps.

"I know Arnie commands the respect of us all; certainly he has mine. And as my National Security Adviser, I have decided he will replace me in the Chair at this and all future meetings that deal with the China situation. I shall sit here, to his right, because, as you all know, I have a strong emotional involvement, and I would not wish to prejudice the intentions and actions of this committee. Decisions made here must be cold-blooded in nature, and I cannot risk placing others in danger because of my determination to save my own son. I thus will accept the plan of action recommended by this Committee. But I do stress the word *action*. The remainder of the seating will be decided by the Chairman."

Admiral Morgan moved briskly to the big chair at the head in which the President usually sat. He spoke sharply. "Lemme have Admiral Mulligan to my left. Next to him I would like the Secretary of State . . ."

Harcourt Travis, a tall, steel-haired ex-Harvard professor, like the President, moved forward into his allotted place.

"I think the Defense Secretary should come next . . . yup, Bob MacPherson . . . right there next to Harcourt . . . that way I have two political heavies opposite the President, and then I can place the Chairman of the Joint Chiefs, General Tim Scannell, to the President's right. Then, still on that side, lemme have the silken pen of Dick Stafford . . . then the head of Navy Intelligence, Admiral Schnider. Opposite them I want to place the White House Chief of Staff, Louis Fallon, with any CIA men at the same end, in company with the COMSUBLANT if he can get here in time.

"Okay, now let me call this meeting to order, and in so doing I am assuming you have all read the military brief . . . just outlining the whereabouts of the submarine and how the hell it got there. Thus far, we do know the crew has been taken off and imprisoned, and we know approximately one hundred of them are in a civilian jail in Canton. We do not know yet what has happened to the senior command of the ship, but we're on the case. And as you all know, President Clarke's son, Linus, is among that team. The Chinese naturally do not know who he is, and plainly we intend to keep it that way."

The President nodded and then asked Admiral Morgan to report on his half-hour meeting with the Chinese ambassador, which had concluded only 15 minutes previously, with the Beijing-born diplomat very nearly being sent out of the White House on the wrong end of Arnold Morgan's shiny black right shoe.

"That's easy, sir. He said he hadn't been briefed, was not in a position to discuss the matter, had total faith in the integrity of the People's Liberation Army/Navy. He promised to get back to us in the next two days. And I told the lying little sonofabitch that would be precisely two days too late. And he was to be back inside three hours with some real answers about Chinese intentions.

"Otherwise, I told him, we may consider a preemptive strike against Chinese naval hardware, in retaliation. I concluded the meeting by warning him that he could find himself personally with a very special place in the modern history of Who Flung Dung or whatever's the name of that asshole who writes their political memoirs."

The admiral glared around the table. "Damned difficult to deal with an out-and-out liar, right? The little bastard knows every last move being made in Canton right now. They have to keep him right up to speed because they know we'll keep wheeling him in here. Of course he knows what's happening. But he's just going to keep stalling.

"And that, gentlemen, is what I believe lies at the heart of the entire Chinese strategy . . . keeping us at arm's length with a succession of hollow promises while they wring out the crew and then copy the ship, every electronic system, every computer, every valve, every missile. In my view, we do not have that much time."

"Arnie," interjected the President. "Are you about to recommend we consider such a course of action—I mean, a strike against the warships of the People's Republic?"

"Sir, my answer has to be no. Because to be very frank, I haven't the first idea *what* we ought to do. Though I do not think we should risk starting World War Three. I said what I said to the ambassador because I was trying to frighten him into telling his political masters that we really mean business, and they should think carefully about keeping the submarine. It's no use being soft with 'em. They'll just construe that as weakness."

"Well, maybe Joe Mulligan could lay out a few naval strategies for us," said the President slowly. "Just possibilities, stuff we could mull over."

"Sir," replied the CNO, "the Navy could essentially hit anything you want it to hit. Towns, buildings, dockyards, warships, you name it. Give me forty-eight hours and anything you want to specify in this world is strictly past tense. And there's not a damn thing *anyone* could do about it . . . however, my happy task is just to carry out your bidding as a loyal servant of the President and the people. I do not have to live, professionally, with the consequences."

The President smiled an inward smile and nodded. "What would it require to storm Canton, besiege the dockyard, take the jail, put the town to the torch, rescue the prisoners, and, well, grab back the submarine, then leave?"

"Careful, sir," said Admiral Morgan. "Your priorities are showing."

The President grinned, a little ruefully. "I know, Arnie, I know. And I also know I sounded like a strategist from ancient Rome. But I would like to hear if there is any hope of just going in and taking back what's ours?"

"Tim?" said Admiral Morgan, nodding at the Chairman of the Joint Chiefs.

"Sir, to land a ground force sufficiently powerful to seal off Canton and effectively take the city would take us a month minimum to prepare. If we went in from the ocean, we'd have to fight a battle in the South China Sea, and while we'd certainly win it, you'd be talking serious death. We'd probably have to hit four of their major dockyards preemptive. And I guess we'd need a force of one hundred thousand to go in, and probably fight the Chinese for every yard of ground. You'd be into World War Three in days."

"Meanwhile the goddamned Chinks would kill all the prisoners," growled Arnold Morgan. "And probably sink *Seawolf*, if they could not get her safely away."

"I guess we just nixed the full frontal assault," said the President. "No way we can just send in the Marines."

"Not if we want to achieve our objective, sir," said General Scannell.

"We could, I suppose, issue some kind of ultimatum," said the Defense Secretary. "Let them understand that if they do not comply with our wishes by, say, five o'clock this afternoon our time, we'll start sinking their warships. Even they know they couldn't stop us."

"I already gave 'em that ultimatum," muttered Admiral Morgan. "Except I only gave 'em till midday."

Harcourt Travis, the Secretary of State and not an unqualified fan of Arnold Morgan's, spoke next. "It is unlikely in the extreme that they will submit to threats. You know the Chinese . . . they will bow low and say how deeply regrettable this whole incident is. We were very naughty boys to be prowling about in Chinese waters, but they understand . . . soon forgive and forget. Meanwhile they do all they can to make big American boat safe for homeward journey, and could they please have many more high-tech secrets in return for their cooperation. Business better than fight, eh? Make money! Ha-ha-ha!"

Everyone laughed at the elegant Harcourt's superb imitation of Chinese diplomacy. But his words were heeded.

"You got it, Harcourt. Right on the button," said Arnold Morgan. "That's what they are going to do. Keep stalling, politely, until they have what they want. Then they play some more hardball, put the crew on trial, jail them for years and years somewhere too remote for us to find, and then announce that the submarine is in no shape to leave their waters, and that they intend to hold on to it until it is."

"Fuck," said the President, inelegantly.

"The truth is that in the field of negotiations, we can't win," said Harcourt. "Because time is not on our side, it's on theirs. They want slowness while they copy the submarine. We want action this day."

"So whatever we do, we better do it quick," said General Scannell.

"That's the trouble, Tim," added Admiral Morgan. "We don't know what to do. Because if we make any kind of an attack, they may just start killing *Seawolf*'s crew."

"I cannot believe we are powerless," said the President.

"Nor can I," said Admirals Morgan and Mulligan in unison.

"Well, how about a systematic, controlled cruise missile attack on their navy bases, right down the coast from Xiamen, then Ningbo, Canton, Zhanjiang and Haikou? Tell 'em we'll stop when they hand back the submarine and the ship's company?" Defense Secretary MacPherson looked thoughtful.

"Two reasons," said Arnold Morgan. "First, they'll start killing the prisoners, and second, we do not know how far they can throw an ICBM from the *Xia III*. I suspect only Judd and Linus know that, and they're not available."

For a moment there was silence around the table. And then the chairman of the Committee, Admiral Morgan, began to roll his gold pen between his thumb and forefinger, a sure sign that something was formulating in his mind.

"I just want to clear up one thing," he said. "Because it's too easy to take your eye off the ball when you are watching a very great President, and a very dear friend to some of us, agonizing over a dreadful personal tragedy. Well, it's not a personal tragedy yet, but it seems like one from where he sits.

"What I wish to clarify is this. The issue is about one submarine, an attack submarine that cost us a billion dollars in research, a submarine that if it became a production model for Beijing would give us one hell of a headache. Because in their hands it could virtually lock Western shipping out of Chinese offshore waters. They could also dominate the narrow Strait into the Gulf of Iran, through which passes one-third of all the world's oil, and it would enable them to blockade and then retake Taiwan.

"*Seawolf* is the best stealth/attack underwater ship ever built. You can't hear it if stays under twenty knots, it packs a terrific wallop, and it escapes at over forty knots if necessary.

"Gentlemen, they must not have it."

"Arnie, I thought they'd already got it," said the President.

"Right. But they can't keep it. I'm afraid we're going to have to obliterate it, right there in Canton Harbor, before they finish their work on her."

"You mean send in a team and blow it up. We'd never get 'em out," said Joe Mulligan.

"No. That's not going to work. We'll have to hit it with a smart bomb, bang in the middle of her reactor room."

"Jesus, Arnie, that would turn the Canton dockyard area into a no-go radioactive nuclear zone for two hundred years," said the President.

"Yes. I suppose it would."

"And that's World War Three."

"It would be if they knew who did it. But how about we hit it from a great height, maybe sixty thousand feet, within hours of the time when they take the reactor critical? According to Fort Meade, it's shut off right now."

"Well, how do you know they plan to fire it up again?"

"They'll fire it. You wanna get right into a submarine, find out how it works, you want its power supply running. My guess is that *Seawolf* will be running hot sometime in the next week. We catch it chock full of Chinese technicians and blow it off the face of the earth from a Stealth bomber way up in the stratosphere. No one will even see our bomb, which will come in vertically after dark.

"And all anyone will ever know is that stupid Chink technicians blew up the submarine while they were working on it. Crazy pricks had no idea what they were doing. No Americans around for miles."

"Neat," said the President. "Pretty damned good waste of a great boat, though."

"That boat's already wasted as far as we are concerned. We're never going to see it again. But by hitting it, we ensure her secrets remain safe."

"At least until we get a new Democratic administration," said Harcourt.

"Don't make me shudder," said Arnold Morgan. "I'm already under severe stress."

"Okay if I conclude this meeting, Mr. Chairman?" said the President. "I understand what you have outlined. And I think it would be better if we reconvened this afternoon, say at fifteen hundred. Meantime you could get a quick feasibility study done about such a bombing raid. Then we could talk more about the crew, and maybe we'll have a few updates from the overheads, and possibly a reply from the ambassador. Let's plan on working through dinner. Let's face it, there's nothing else matters like this matters."

"Okay, sir. Just as you say. I'll get all the stuff together and we'll meet right here at fifteen hundred." Admiral Morgan motioned for Joe Mulligan to join him, and the two men stood up and left immediately.

They walked in silence for a few paces before the CNO muttered, "You know, Arnie, I hate to go around in circles, but aren't we always returning to the same problem . . . like any attack, they start killing the prisoners? I'm not sure it's much different if the submarine blows up, however it happens. Might they not just start getting rid of the prisoners since they don't really need them?"

"They might, Joe. And worse yet, they might start torturing them, trying to force information out of them about the systems. And that might be terrible. But I did not especially want to mention that in front of the President."

"No sense doing that. You can see how upset he is."

"Right . . . but Joe, we gotta think. We gotta get into my office and come up with something. And we gotta have it in the next four hours. Meanwhile, we'll bounce their ambassador around some more. And their naval attaché . . . but my God, Joe, this is a real bastard of a problem. Because we're dealing with a hostage situation, whatever the Chinese say. And that's always trouble."

"Especially one particular hostage."

"You got that right."

*   *   *

For the next four hours the two admirals went around and around the puzzle. And every time they were blocked by the same threat— that of the Chinese starting to kill the captive crew of USS *Seawolf*. Every hour Admiral Morgan called and threatened the ambassador, assuring him that American revenge would be swift and devastating. And every time, the reply was the same: "No problem here, Admiral. My government has no problem. Submarine being fixed. You have it back very soon. Crew honored guests of my government. No problem."

Admiral Morgan could have throttled him.

And all the while, a new plan was circulating through his subconscious. It was a plan driven by his natural flair for the subversive, the stealthy, and the downright underhanded. In his heart, Arnold Morgan loathed the idea of crash forward, kick down the unlocked door, and blast your enemy to pieces.

Admiral Morgan was an ex-nuclear submarine commander and his natural kingdom was the kingdom of the devil, the kingdom of deceit, stealth and cunning. Never in a thousand years would he have bombed Libya, Iraq, nor the Sudan nor Afghanistan, nor even Belgrade. He might have sanctioned a small, devastating sneak attack that left no trace. But more likely he would have sent in a Special Forces team to move quietly around, stalking the enemy, and then pouncing, grabbing and executing the leader and all of his cabinet. Good-bye Muammar, Saddam, Bin Laden, and Slobodan. Arnold Morgan loved Special Forces and the mass confusion they left in their wake.

And now, faced with an apparently insurmountable conundrum, complicated by a priceless American hostage, his thoughts returned to the kingdom of the night, in which brilliantly skilled American operators moved swiftly, silently and to brutal effect. He was not quite ready to articulate it. Yet. But Arnold Morgan, in the deepest canyons of his soul, was planning to spring the American captives right out of that Chinese jail. Every ounce of common sense told him it was probably impossible. But every instinct he had about the capabilities of Special Forces told him there was a chance. Not much of a chance. But one which, in this instance, he would have to take.

He dismissed the possibility of any strategy that would involve direct attack, any attack that would involve direct confrontation, indeed any confrontation whatsoever. Arnold Morgan's military brain was telling him to isolate the jail in which the prisoners were held. *Then have the guys go in, take out the guards and release the American crew.*

"Two things, Arnie," said Joe for the umpteenth time that day. "How do we get a dozen guys in there? How do we get more'n a hundred of 'em out of there?"

"Skip the details, Joe. Right here I'm talking principle." And without missing a beat, he picked up the phone and growled, "Kathy, get me SPECWARCOM in Coronado on the line . . . I want to talk to Vice Admiral Bergstrom. Right away. Wherever he is. Whatever he's doing."

By now, it was 2:00 P.M. on the East Coast, which put Admiral Bergstrom in his office talking to two of his top Basic Underwater Demolition/SEAL (BUD/S) instructors, the hardest men in the world's hardest regiment, the standard-setters of the U.S. Navy SEALs.

"Hey, Arnold, how are you, sir? Haven't talked for a few weeks."

"John, quite frankly I'm desperate. I must talk to you."

"Fine. Shoot."

"No, here."

"Where?"

"Washington."

"When?"

"Now."

"What, right now?"

"Right now."

"How do I get there?"

"Any aircraft you have."

"Alone?"

"Alone."

"Andrews?"

"Right."

"Six hours."

"I'll have a chopper waiting."

"See ya."

One thing, Admirals Bergstrom and Morgan knew each other well.

"He, of course, being our great Special Forces pragmatist, will be even more pessimistic than I am," suggested Joe Mulligan.

"Yeah. But he'll say, Okay, let's do it, but how? You're saying, Let's not do it, because it's impossible."

"Well, Arnie, it is."

"I know."

"It would be as if we had a hundred important Chinese prisoners in a state penitentiary in, say, the middle of Atlanta. And a dozen armed Chinese insurgents tried to get 'em out. We'd wrap those guys up in a matter of hours."

"Not if they made their move in the dead of night. And not if they'd been trained by Bergstrom's guys out in Coronado. And they brought with them all the right gear. Because that might prove very tough indeed."

"Okay, Arnie. I guess it might."

"And that's our chance, Joe. And we gotta try. Did you see the President this morning? The poor guy was close to tears. We have to do something. I'm just not prepared to tell him we won't even try."

1900. Friday, July 7.
The Situation Room. The West Wing. The White House.

The meeting had been running for four hours now. And the arguments swayed back and forth. Every time the military members of the committee suggested any form of attack, Harcourt Travis pointed out the appalling consequences of war with China. He stressed the Asian fixation with "loss of face." And he made no concessions whatsoever—"If the USA begins killing Chinese citizens in order to free the submarine and the prisoners, the Chinese will hit back, no question in my mind."

"But surely that would apply to any nation we considered had to be punished?" said General Scannell.

"Maybe," replied Harcourt. "But the Chinese are different. They have so many people. If we hit them a devastating blow and took ten million of their citizens off the face of the earth, their mindset would not alter. They would shrug and say, Irrelevant, we still have twelve hundred and forty million people left."

"Kinda scary, when you think about it," said Bob MacPherson. "But unless we are able to do *something*, I guess they'll soon be able to rampage about the world doing anything they please, just because no one feels big enough to fight them."

"I don't really think that's so," said Arnold Morgan. "The real issue is, who is prepared to risk a Chinese nuclear missile coming screaming out of the skies, aimed at the US of A?"

"Well," said the President, "who is?"

"I am," said his National Security Adviser.

"You are?"

"Sure I am," growled Morgan. "Remember a few other things about them. Not just their gigantic population of goddamned rice-growing peasants, slopping around in fucking paddy fields. Remember their lack of sophistication. Last time they tried launching an ICBM it nearly blew up their own ship. Every time they launch one of these programs they screw it up. So what could they hit? Pearl Harbor with a big missile, nuclear-headed? No, they couldn't hit something that small. And would they want to? I don't think so. They'd be having a discussion like this one. Guided by their political commissars, backing off, backing off, running scared.

"They'd make old Pung Yang Travis here look like Alexander the Great!"

"Thank you, Arnold," said Harcourt urbanely. "Inside every conservative Secretary of State there's always a noble savage trying to get free."

They all laughed at the light relief. And just then Admiral Brett Stewart, COMSUBLANT, arrived, apologizing for his lateness, explaining that he had been at sea when the signal had come through summoning him to Washington.

"I for one am delighted to see you, Brett," said Harcourt. "As the current commander of our Atlantic submarine strike force, you might be able to prevent our esteemed chairman from declaring war on China in order to get one of our submarines back."

"I already heard," said the admiral. "And I don't think we're going to get it back. Not even if we took out half the Chinese Navy. They want that submarine. They probably want it more than they've ever wanted anything. My guess is that right now they're in the process of moving in their engineers and scientists, probably with reinforcements from Russia, all getting ready to take *Seawolf* apart. Judging from the signals I'd say they'd opened fire on Judd Crocker's repair crew on the stern of the submarine. I expect you've gone over all that, and I'm sure you agree, they *really* want that submarine. Opening fire on an American Navy crew isn't something *anyone* does lightly."

"My thoughts entirely," said Admiral Morgan.

"Fact is, we cannot get the ship out of Canton," said Admiral Stewart. "Anyone know if they've shut down the reactor?"

"We think so," said the CNO. "Next satellite pass will show us."

"It would make sense if they had shut it down," said Stewart. "Then when they get their team in place, they'll take it critical, moving everyone through the process, step by step . . . telling us, no doubt, that there's some kind of a radiation leak and it's not safe yet to return it to us."

"Admiral Morgan thinks if we want to preserve the high technology in *Seawolf*, we have to blow it up."

"Correct," replied Admiral Stewart instantly. "Otherwise there's gonna be a dozen of 'em, flying the flag of the People's Republic, dominating all of the Far Eastern oil routes, and some in the Middle East. China's become expansionist in the past five years. If you want my opinion, they must not have a fleet of *Seawolf* submarines. And that means we gotta take out the original."

"Who agrees?" said Admiral Morgan. "If you do, raise your right hand, like I'm now doing."

Admiral Mulligan raised his, General Scannell also. So did the Defense Secretary, Bob MacPherson. Admiral Stewart raised his. The two CIA men raised theirs. Harcourt Travis said that such a military operation was so far out of his realm, he would abstain, but would not vote against.

The President himself stood up and asked if he might be excused for five minutes, but he too would abstain because his thoughts were too personal for objective thought. Everyone in the room could see he was on the verge of tears, and everyone knew that the apparition of the Chinese torturing his terrified only son had taken him to the brink.

He left the room, and as he did so Arnold Morgan stood up and followed him out, hurrying after him. "Sir, wait . . . there's something I want to tell you."

The President turned around, and the admiral could see the tears streaming down his face.

"Listen, sir. I want you to know this . . . and you have my promise. If we hit that submarine, we'll have Linus out of that fucking rathole inside three hours of the big bang. I got a plan. Stay with me, sir . . . I'll get him out of there . . . that's a promise."

The President nodded, tried to smile, and patted his NSA on the shoulder. "Thank you, Arnold. . . . give me a few minutes. I'll be right back."

Admiral Morgan walked back into the Situation Room.

"How was he, Arnie?" asked Harcourt Travis.

"'Bout like any of us would be if some fucking Chinaman was getting ready to pull our son's fingernails out."

"This President is just about the best friend the military ever had," said General Scannell. "We have to do our best for him, no matter what, even if the risks are high."

Arnold Morgan was now back in the chair. "I believe, gentlemen, we just voted overwhelmingly to obliterate *Seawolf* before they get a handle on her technology . . ."

Everyone nodded. And the chairman continued, "Okay, now let's try to formulate a rough plan, because we don't have that much time. From that plan we'll get some timing. As a point of principle, I think we should try to spring the crew, amid the mass confusion that there's going to be in Canton when we split *Seawolf*'s nuclear reactor in half."

"But how are we going to get a team in there?" asked Admiral Mulligan.

"With great difficulty, probably," said Arnold Morgan. "But let's stay with step one, how to destroy the submarine while she's moored alongside in Canton. "We got a bomb expert in here?"

"Not really," said the CNO.

"I'll get one," interjected General Scannell, and he took from his pocket a slimline mobile phone and hit one button that patched him straight into his office, and everyone heard him say, "Get ahold of General Cale Carter, and have him send in the Air Force's number one bombing expert . . . Situation Room, White House, inside the hour . . . tell him I'd prefer he came in person if he could . . . yup . . . right . . . bye."

They adjourned to a small private dining room at 2030, just as Vice Admiral Bergstrom landed on the White House lawn in a Navy helicopter from Andrews. Fifteen minutes later General Carter, a Southerner from Alabama, arrived and joined them for an excellent dinner organized by Admiral Morgan. In a sense it reflected his precise instructions to the chef: "Sirloin steak, medium rare . . . roast potatoes and whatever green vegetables you like . . . salad, but no rice, for Christ's sake no rice, and nothing stir-fried."

There were bottles of sparkling mineral water on the table, plus an ice-cold bottle of California sauvignon blanc—the admiral had growled that he never touched Chardonnay until after Labor Day.

No one tasted the wine, except for the President, who needed it, and Admiral Morgan, who wanted it. Between them they polished off the bottle while they brought General Carter up to date on the proposed bombing raid. The only opinion Admiral Morgan offered was that he favored a high-level bomb, from say 50,000 feet above the Pearl River, rather than a missile or a sea-skimmer.

General Carter nodded thoughtfully and said he'd like to make a few notes and then offer his opinion back in the Situation Room, where he could pull up a chart of the Pearl River Delta and "go professional on y'all."

It was after 10:00 P.M. when Admiral Morgan finally had the meeting rearranged to watch General Carter make his recommendations in front of the large computer screen at the end of the Situation Room.

"Mr. President, Admiral Morgan, gentlemen, I'd like to start by saying we can most certainly hit and destroy USS *Seawolf*. The challenge, as I understand it, is that you don't want anyone to know we did it?"

Admiral Morgan nodded.

"Well, that means we need to be real careful about how we deliver the bomb. The common misconception, however, is that the higher you are, the further away from the target, as it were, the less chance you have of being detected. And that ain't true. 'Specially near a naval or military base where there's likely to be a lot of radar.

"Fact is, you're more likely to be detected if you fly high than if you fly really low. Now, using the terrain of the land surrounding the Delta, I'd say you'd be better with a low-level flight. Because if you stay at two hundred and fifty feet above the water, straight up the middle here, you will *not* be detected. You'll be below the radars, which *cannot* find you, and you have the added cover of the land, which makes detection unlikely.

"Judging from where the navy base is, I'd say it was almost certain you would be detected flying at fifty thousand feet. Whatever stealth bomber we send, I think they'd catch it on the screen. I'm only guessing, but Chinese surveillance is probably on high alert while that submarine's parked right there in the dockyards.

"So, gentlemen, I'm recommending we deliver the bomb in a regular Navy F/A-18 Hornet. I like the aircraft. It's fast, makes well over one thousand mph, you can fly it off a carrier, and it's capable of carrying a bomb underneath weighing almost eight tons. The weapon I have in mind is the laser-guided Paveway Three, type GBU-24, made by Raytheon. It's about fourteen feet long and weighs only a ton, very nearly half of which is high explosives. That thing'll rip right through the casing of a submarine and straight into the reactor room like spearing an ole crawfish.

"Your pilot should use the old technique of toss-bombing. By that I mean he wants to come on in up the Delta with his throttles open wide, two hundred and fifty feet above the surface, making one thousand knots plus. 'Bout five miles before the target I wanna see him raise the nose on that Hornet to about forty-five degrees, climbing like a bullet, then release that bomb at the highest possible speed. That'll have the effect of throwing it high, maybe another three thousand feet. Right then it'll turn over and start dropping quietly toward its target.

"Its guidance system's gonna be seeking the reflected light from the laser, looking for the marker, adjusting its trajectory to hit the middle of it, adjusting its fins as it flies, making its corrections.

"Long before the bomb hits, the attacking aircraft will be out and away—past Hong Kong seventy miles to the south in a little over four minutes. And by the time he hits the open water of the South China Sea, the submarine and everything anywhere near it will be radioactive history."

"Thank you, General," said Admiral Morgan. "I really appreciate that."

"However, there is one further problem you may or may not have considered," said the Air Force chief.

"Lay it on us," replied the admiral.

"You will have to illuminate the target. We can program the bomb's strike zone accurate to fifty feet. But that's no good to you, is it? You want it accurate to five feet, so it hits the reactor room. If it misses by, say, ten feet, you'll just punch a big hole in the submarine and blow some of it up. But you won't blast the reactor room. To do that you gotta penetrate it with the bomb. That means you have to light up your target. And I'm not sure if you have anyone to do that."

"I'm not sure, either," said Arnold Morgan. "Jake, how're we placed in Canton?"

Jake Raeburn, head of the CIA's Far Eastern Desk, spoke up for the first time. "Admiral, we have several field operators in the area, three in Canton, one of 'em in the base. He's the best of them. He's Chinese, hates the regime, had a cousin killed in Tiananmen Square in 1989."

"Not in the Navy, is he?"

"No, he's a civilian electrician, been very valuable for several years. But he wants to bring his wife and son to America, which he's been promised. If he could pull this off, it'd be his last mission. I don't want him to die of radiation sickness."

"What kind of gear do we need in there, Cale?" asked General Scannell.

"The device is small, electronic, with its own power pack. Trouble is, it doesn't last that long. Once it's aimed and switched on, we got about six hours before it dies on us."

"You mean we're not talking about a hand-held device that a man would aim at the correct spot on the submarine?" asked the President.

"Nossir. Someone's gotta get this little contraption hidden and fixed in place beforehand, then switch it on when we're all set, then get the hell out before the bomb arrives."

"Can we do it, Jake . . . I mean, illuminate the target?" asked Admiral Morgan.

"Yessir."

The chairman was inclined to adjourn the meeting at 2300, because he wanted to spend a couple of hours with Admiral Bergstrom. But just as he began his summing up, there was a sharp knock on the door, and a uniformed guard entered with an envelope for the National Security Adviser.

He read the message swiftly, direct from Langley: "All prisoners observed leaving Canton jail by military trucks. Moved back to heavily guarded Navy dockyard—app. midday Saturday. Impossible to observe future movements in there. Our usual surveillance in place Pearl River."

"Might be good, might be bad," growled Morgan. "They've moved the prisoners out of that Canton jail, taken 'em back to the dockyard. And that's not all bad. The Canton jail was just about the worst possible place for us to get 'em out, bang in the middle of a well-organized city with a lot of military personnel in residence. In my view they're taking them somewhere else. And the only reason they've gone back to the dockyard is because they're traveling by sea, otherwise they'da gone to an airport or straight on by truck, right?"

"Guess they could be keeping them incarcerated in the navy base," suggested the President.

"If they'd had that facility, sir, they never would have moved 'em in the first place," replied the admiral. "My judgment is they're on the move to a military jail that's been specially prepared for them.

"Jake, we have to find them. Fast."

With that, the chairman called the meeting off for the night, and suggested they reconvene right there at 1100 tomorrow. "I want to get a few things done before we start," he added. Then he stood, thanked everyone individually, and motioned for the exhausted Admiral Bergstrom to follow him down to his West Wing lair. "We got some serious talking to do. Same subject."

Admiral Bergstrom rolled his eyes heavenward. And trudged after Arnold Morgan, who was now heading toward his second successive night without sleep. He sent for coffee and a couple of glasses of brandy to keep them awake. And then he spoke quietly to the SEALs boss. "John, you know my views about your guys. I'd rather have a couple of dozen SEALs than four thousand bombs."

He referred of course to the elite warrior troops of the U.S. Armed Forces. SEAL stands for Sea Air and Land, and the U.S. Navy runs six teams, each comprising 225 men. Three of them work out of Little Creek, Virginia, numbered two, four, and six. Numbers one, three, and five operate out of the island of Coronado, San Diego, home of the U.S. Navy's Special War Command—SPECWARCOM in the trade—which oversees all SEAL missions everywhere in the world.

The SEALs have had a short but valorous history, never once having left any man dead or wounded on the battlefield, not even in Vietnam. Their brutal training is comparable only to Great Britain's SAS regiment, and military men always point out that it's harder to become a SEAL than to graduate from Harvard Law School. John Bergstrom had earned his present command after serving with the SEALs as a team leader for several years. Now 61, he had retained his hard-trained physique. He stood six feet two inches tall, and his sleek dark hair was in the process of turning gun-gray.

His wife had died six years earlier, and he had never quite gotten over it. But he was a hugely popular man, both in the military and beyond. His personality was frequently lit up by a deep, amused chuckle, the kind of wry look at the world that comes essentially to those who have faced huge dangers and nowadays regard the rest of it as child's play. He was probably the best Special Forces Commander the Navy ever had, which was why he had occupied the Big Chair at SPECWARCOM longer than anyone else ever had. He and Arnold Morgan had a profound mutual respect.

They sipped their coffee slowly, both men pondering the mammoth task that lay ahead. "Since you don't want me to drive the Hornet up the Delta, Arnie, I guess you want me to get the guys out, right?"

Arnold Morgan smiled. "I expect you guessed from the conversation you just heard that the President's son Linus is the XO on *Seawolf*?"

"I knew that a month ago. And now he's in a Chinese slammer. That, Arnie, is not good."

"Not good. Much worse. He's between Chinese slammers, and we don't know where the hell the second one is gonna be."

"First time I've ever been asked to attack a place that ain't yet on the map," Vice Admiral Bergstrom chuckled, somewhat mirthlessly. "But I'll tell you one thing, if they keep them in the Navy dockyard at Canton, there's no way I'm sending my guys in, because that would be a suicide mission. And my SEALs don't do suicide. They're too expensive."

"John, there's no way I'd ask that, mainly because an attack like that would damn nearly amount to a declaration of war on China. Anyway, I agree, SEALs are not intended for that kind of frontal assault. That's the Marine Corps. Also, I would not want American troops going into a radiation zone, which that dockyard is going to become."

"Then you're telling me that we may have to sacrifice the crew of *Seawolf* in order to destroy the submarine?"

"Yes, John. I suppose I am. But I'm also telling you that if it's humanly possible to get them out, we're going to do it."

"Once we find them."

"Correct. But in the meantime I want to get ready, and right here we're looking at a project you and I have discussed many times."

"You mean the formation of our treasured elite SEALs Strike Force, a big team of fifty guys, ready to enter a foreign country at a moment's notice, stay undercover and then take out the enemy government, or leader, like Saddam, or Milosevic, or that fucking Saudi, whatsisname Bin Laden?"

"That's the one, John. The elite of the elite. The finest team we can put together. Remember, we always said it would operate from an aircraft carrier, where the team's commanding officer would form the mission headquarters. That's what I have in mind."

"You suggesting I start forming that team? And its first mission is to get the crew of *Seawolf* out of China?"

"Yes, John. That's what I'm suggesting."

"Jesus. This sounds big."

"It's the biggest. Our President, who's without doubt the best friend the military ever had, is close to the breaking point . . . it's the threat of the Chinese torturing his son for information."

"You think they might?"

"Yes, I do . . . don't you?"

"Yes, they might."

"John, I also think the Chinese are never going to free them. When they begin the process of interrogation it will quickly move up to torture. And once that happens, they will make sure no one ever gets out to talk about it."

"Will they put 'em on trial?"

"I would think so, then sentence them to long years of imprisonment, during which time they'll all disappear. No one will live to talk about their experience."

"Then we have to get 'em out."

"Exactly. Which is why I want you to assemble the best team of guys you have ever assembled. Bring 'em in from Virginia Beach and Coronado, supplement them with two or three SAS guys from England, if you like. I wouldn't mind a more international aspect to the team. But just make sure they're the best we can get.

"If the Chinese move the crew to a military jail within striking range of the water, we're going in, and we're going to get the Sea-wolves out. And I do not give a sacred Chinese monkey's ass if we have to kill every goddamned guard in the jail, we're going in. And if we can't find a leader with the balls for the job, I'll lead 'em myself."

"I didn't realize you were still a serving officer, sir?" said Admiral Bergstrom, grinning.

"Recruit me, asshole," replied Arnold Morgan. "I'm getting them out, and that's final."

"Two questions, Arnie. How do we get our guys in? And how do we get everyone out? We'll probably need fifty SEALs in order to ransack a Chinese military jail. And there's, what, a hundred, minimum, in the crew?"

"SUBMARINES, Johnny, SUBMARINES. Plus Zodiacs, using them as landing craft. CVBG parked a couple of hundred miles off."

"Jesus, Arnie. You trying to start a war?"

"John, I'm not planning to get caught by the Chinese . . . at least not until we're well clear with all the prisoners. Then they can do and think what they wish. And if they give us any trouble, we'll sink 'em. Chinese pricks."

"Arnold, what's the time frame? Bearing in mind we don't even know where they are right now?"

"The time frame is that we send in a recon team the first moment we locate the new jail. Then, three hours before the SEALs hit the beach, we bomb *Seawolf* in Canton, causing maximum panic and confusion. Under the cover of that uproar, the boys go in. Which means that right now you get back in your helicopter, go to Andrews, get back in your plane, and go to San Diego. You put together your hit team, no expense or effort spared. And you fly them all out to Okinawa forty-eight hours from now. They board the carrier instantly, and prepare to go in."

"You gottit. I guess. Assuming we can find the prisoners." The SEALs boss rose, drained his brandy glass, picked up his briefcase, and walked to the door. He turned back once and grinned. "By the way, it is the considered opinion of SPECWARCOM that you, Admiral, are a piece of work. Thank Christ you're on our side."

1800 (local). Saturday, July 8.
Chinese Naval Base. Canton.

They had canceled the evening trip along the Pearl River on the big ferry that leaves from No. 1 Pier off the Yanjiang Road, east of the People's Bridge, which left 170 mostly foreign passengers grumbling as loudly as it is wise to grumble in China. Softly, that is.

However, it was as well that they were not still on board, because this ferry was about to undertake a straight run to the ex-Japanese military jail on the northeast point of Xiachuan Dao, a six-mile-long island set four miles offshore, eighty miles west-sou'west of the port of Macao.

Admiral Zhang had not only commandeered the ferry, "in the name of the Navy of the People's Republic." He had also made ready the derelict jail in record time, sending in a military crew of 200 men to install the most modern communications systems, an up-to-date electric lighting grid, brand-new plumbing, albeit with surface pipes, a water-heating system, desks, phones and an intercom for the command headquarters. There were also major repairs made to the cement walls and the two tall guard towers. The cells remained as they had been since the prisoners of the Revolution had been removed, shot, and buried in a mass grave in the late 1940s. The cells were not anything you'd care to recommend to a rat.

"But," as Admiral Zhang was apt to point out, "these are very temporary quarters. We'll have the Americans in a new jail in the interior within a couple of weeks."

He was not of course making these observations out of any humanitarian considerations. In his heart he was afraid the American armed forces might attempt to free the prisoners. And he regarded Americans as freewheeling bullies who would stop at nothing, especially when they were superbly armed and trained. He did think they were a genuine soft touch when they were at a disadvantage and put under pressure . . . strangers to the sacrifice and hardships of revolution . . . but lethal, and utterly ruthless, when they were on top, as they usually were. Admiral Zhang hated America, as he hated the British for their long history of acutely arrogant behavior toward the ancient civilization of China.

And now the ferry was moored alongside in the navy yard. And through the bars of the end cell, Captain Judd Crocker could see between two buildings the lines of his men, each of them handcuffed behind their backs, moving slowly forward beneath the dock lights, embarking onto the ferry. He watched for almost an hour, and then the main door to the detention block burst open and four guards began unlocking the cell doors and placing handcuffs on the six senior men from *Seawolf*. The three junior seamen who also occupied the Mao cell block had left an hour previously, and Judd felt more certain than ever that he was about to join his full ship's company for the first time since they arrived in Canton.

And so Captain Crocker, Lt. Commander Bruce Lucas, Lt. Commander Cy Rothstein, Lt. Shawn Pearson, Lt. Andy Warren, and Master Chief Brad Stockton were marched down to the submarine jetty where Admiral Zhang and Commander Li stood at the end of the gangway. The guards marched them straight aboard and ordered them to sit down on the long shiny upper-deck benches, which were usually filled with tourists. Exactly opposite Judd was the ship's engineering officer, Lt. Commander Rich Thompson, master of the nuclear reactor, his face puffy beneath both eyes where Zhang's guards had beaten him.

The two colleagues nodded to each other before noticing the tiny guard lieutenant who had cold-bloodedly murdered young Skip Laxton. "YOU WILL REFRAIN FROM SPEAKING!" he screamed. "And remember, there are twelve armed guards in each section here, that's one for every three of you. You are no match for them. Do not try to escape or you will be shot instantly."

Deep inside the ferry they could hear the engines beginning to rumble to life, and on the dock they could hear the shouts of the shore crew as the lines were cast off. Through the tall square windows of the upper deck they could all see the lights begin to slip away as the ferry pushed out into the darkness of the Pearl River, heading south toward Hong Kong and God knew where after that.

Back on the jetty Admiral Zhang and Commander Li were still

deep in conversation, the commander having confessed himself bewildered at the C-in-C's insistence that all of the prisoners should be transferred to Xiachuan Dao, rather than keeping the key men in jail at the base where the submarine was moored.

"My reasons are many," he said. "But the principal one is that I do prefer to have the entire crew isolated in one place. Because in that place I now have interrogation facilities, and when I require a key member of the American crew to work with us on the submarine, I can fly him back here in a helicopter for one or two days, depending on his cooperation.

"Remember also, Li, I have my team of inquisitors making their observations at Xiachuan Dao, and that is important teamwork. As you know, in the field of interrogation it is vital to find the weak links—the men who will crack first. That way you can get a lot done very quickly. You don't want to spend time interrogating the hard men in the crew, because they will tell you nothing, and if they do, it will be lies. You can waste a lot of hours doing that, and we do not have much time to spare."

"Yessir. I see. And there is of course the question of security here at Canton. As you know, we have suspected but never proved leaks of information. You are right, as always, my commander. Better to keep all the prisoners together, isolated individually, but under the constant attention of our interrogation team. Much better, sir. Very, very good."

"And you begin at first light tomorrow, Li. I shall miss you here for two weeks, but you will be doing very important work for our great nation. I would like you to dine with me, in the Great Room, before you leave. That will make a more pleasant final briefing before the helicopter ride to Xiachuan."

"Thank you, sir. I would, as always, be honored."

0500 (local). Saturday, July 8.
Office of Admiral Morgan. The White House.

He sat alone, on the telephone for the fourth successive hour, unsurprisingly without a secretary, waiting for some word from the American Embassy in Grosvenor Square, London, trying to locate the private secure number of the American naval attaché. First they did not believe it was him, then they had to call him back in Washington, then they were cut off. Then he called back and spoke to a new operator who did not believe who he was, and also had to call back.

The latest development was two requests for him, Arnold Morgan, "to bear with me." Right now the line was silent, and the President's National Security Adviser was fuming. Three minutes later a voice came through and said, "You'll get Colonel Hart on the following number . . ."

Admiral Morgan scribbled it down and punched in the numbers on his secure line. It rang twice in London, where it was now 1010, and a voice said, "Colonel Hart's office."

"Will you put me through to him? This is Arnold Morgan in the White House."

The call was, in a sense, a breakthrough. The former Marine Colonel Frank Hart, known in the Corps as "Fagin," had been in a backwater for some years. Once a stalwart of Naval Intelligence and a two-year lieutenant in the SEALs, he became embroiled in some of the well-meant, in some ways brilliant, exploits of the Reagan Administration in foreign policy.

When some of these activities came to light, the left in both the press and Congress, in a grotesque exhibition of false righteousness, went after everyone involved. The main accusations were of lying, playing fast and loose with the Constitution.

There was a tirade of "Did the President know? . . . Did the Secretary of State know? . . . How dare these people act as if they were above the law. . . . Hang 'em . . . Shoot 'em . . . Jail 'em . . . Drive 'em from office . . ." It was like the Wild West with statute books. Careers were ruined, lives and families blighted.

But very rarely, perhaps never, did anyone ask the other questions, such as, Were these people acting in the supreme interests of the United States of America? Were they carrying out policies that the massively elected President believed were essential for the security of the nation in the darkest days of the Cold War? Was the entire exercise underpinned by a strata of goodness, of honorable men doing their level best for America and its citizens, against the threat of advancing Soviet communism?

The answer to all of those questions was undoubtedly yes. The only question to which the answer would have been no was, "Did any one of them commit one single act that could have been ascribed to a desire for personal gain?" No. Nothing more was proven except that they that they acted out of a sense of patriotism. Perhaps highly developed, maybe even overdeveloped patriotism. But nonetheless patriotism. Which was more than could have been said for some of their accusers.

Colonel Hart, a slim, hard-eyed, handsome man, a graduate of Annapolis, had been swept up in the maelstrom of all this. They never put him on trial, like some of the others, but his military and possibly his political career were essentially over when President Reagan left the White House.

However, there was an incident during a televised congressional inquiry that almost made him immortal. Colonel Hart, in full uniform, faced one of his accusers and said, almost menacingly, "Sir, I don't know what you do when you see the flag of the United States of America. But if you like, I'll show you what I do." And he placed his cap upon his head and executed a ramrod-straight Marine Corps salute. Men who had fought in three global wars found themselves shedding a tear for the colonel.

An awful lot of people never forgot that moment, and two of those people were Arnold Morgan and the current President, who both considered that the colonel had been dealt a very unfair hand.

Afterward Colonel Hart was quietly seconded into the diplomatic branch of the Senior Service. He worked first as a deputy naval attaché in the embassy in Buenos Aires. There followed tours of duty in both the Middle East and Europe before, in October 2004, he was appointed naval attaché in London.

There were many who thought he had the right credentials for a major ambassadorship in the not-too-distant future. But this fateful phone call from Admiral Morgan signified a sudden, unexpected swing in the career of Colonel Hart.

"Hello, sir," he said firmly. "It's been a long time."

"Too long, Frank," replied the admiral. "How they treating you?"

"Better than you, sir. No one's made me get into the office at five in the morning."

"Happens all the time when you're close to the seat of power."

"Ah, hell, I thought it was unique. Thought this might be a major call, a real address-changer."

"It is. You're probably going to hate it."

"Well, sir, since I am trying to work out the intricate military problem of which of us here attends a dinner being given by the First Sea Lord on July fifteenth, you'd better get right to it . . ."

Arnold Morgan laughed at a former brother officer wrestling with the kind of minutiae that routinely drive military men crazy. "Frank," he said, "would you consider taking up an active command, being seconded to the SEALs?"

"Who, me?" said the colonel lamely.

"Have I got a wrong number here?"

"Christ, Arnold. I'm sixty years old."

"What do you want? A birthday present?"

"Sir, I'm trying to be serious. I don't think I'm fit enough to get involved with those guys."

"Frank, I'm after your brain, not your goddamned muscles."

"Oh, that's rather different. What is it?"

"I have a major SEAL team being assembled. Maybe as many as fifty guys. They're going to be operating out of a carrier way out in the Far East. John Bergstrom is putting the team together personally right now in Coronado. But we need a hard, experienced commander who will have a grip on the somewhat volatile political situation. We're looking for a supreme staff officer who will hold this thing together. There's probably going to be some heavy decision-making with little or no time for consultation."

"Time frame?"

"Now. You'd have to leave for Washington now."

"I'd have to clear it with the ambassador."

"That's done. Presidential level."

"And with the CNO, Admiral Mulligan. He's still my boss."

"Done. Chairman of the Joint Chiefs level."

"And with the office of the secretary of state, like all diplomatic appointments or terminations."

"Done. Presidential level."

"Jesus, sir. You're not joking, are you?"

"Not this time, Frank."

"I don't have much choice, do I, sir?"

"Not much. Because if you funk it, no one will think that much of you. Worse yet, no one will think that much of me. Because you happen to be my idea."

"What do I do?"

"Gather up your gear and have a driver take you straight to the Royal Air Force base at Lyneham. There's a military aircraft there right now. It'll bring you straight into Andrews. Then a helicopter to the White House. Come to my office. Soon as you can."

"Sir, what about my wife and family?"

"Whatever she wants. I'll put six men on the move right now. I'll talk to her myself as soon as you're in the air."

"Yessir. My answer is affirmative."

"As I knew it would be. Thank you, Frank."

And the admiral replaced the telephone, muttering to himself, "I wonder how many of those goddamned little lawyers who tried to disgrace him would have stepped up at the age of sixty to command a SEAL operation in what has to be a theater of war."

2330. Saturday, July 8.
Pearl River Delta.

Lt. Shawn Pearson, *Seawolf*'s navigator, was trying to memorize their route. The ferry had been running south through the hot, muggy night for four hours now, and they ought to be somewhere down at the mouth of the Delta. Through the big starboard windows he could see shore lights, possibly four miles away, and he guessed correctly the port of Macao, but he did not discern a change in course.

The ferry ran on south through calm seas. Shawn guessed she was making around 17 knots. There was barely a swell, but he could hear the distinctive slash of the spray from the bow wave hitting the still, flat water. It always sounds slightly louder when there is no chop, and he knew they had not yet reached the open ocean.

It was another hour before he sensed a gradual swing to starboard, possibly to a course of two-three-zero, and there was a noticeable increase in the motion of the ship. So far as Shawn could tell, they must be running down the coast toward either the huge tropical island of Hainan, where he knew there was a big Navy base, or towards China's Southern Fleet headquarters, just to the north at Zhanjiang. So far as his excellent memory could recall, there was nothing significant between there and Canton.

Outside, peering through the windows, Shawn could see no land beyond the black expanse of moonlit water. No one had spoken a word since they had left the navy yard, and the guards patrolled tirelessly, walking between the long benches, glaring at any member of the American crew who was still awake.

The captain and the chief of the boat were both sleeping, but Lt. Commanders Bruce Lucas and Cy Rothstein were wide awake. Indeed, it was "Einstein" who asked permission to speak and requested water for the men. Surprisingly, Shawn thought, the guard nodded curtly and spoke in rapid Chinese to a younger man who yelled more incomprehensible Chinese out to the viewing deck.

Ten minutes later, two of the ferry's original stewards returned carrying four white buckets of water and some big plastic beakers. Since all the prisoners were manacled behind their backs, two Chinese guards walked down the length of each bench, one carrying the bucket, the other offering water to each American, holding the beaker to his mouth, tipping it, spilling it, almost choking the recipient, but allowing plenty of time for a few good gulps.

It wasn't the most elegant drink they had ever had, nor the most hygienic. But it was wet and cold, and all they would get for many more hours.

And all through the small of hours of Sunday morning, July 9, they pushed on southwest in moderate seas. Most of the crew slept, but Lieutenant Pearson considered it his duty to keep awake to try and get some kind of a handle on their position. So far the Chinese security had been red hot. There had not been a moment in time when even a two-word conversation had been possible without incurring the wrath of the guards. But Shawn thought and hoped things might ultimately become a little more slack in the following days, and it was his job to know approximately where they were.

His watch had been taken, along with everyone else's, on their first day of captivity, but through the windows on the port quarter of the ferry he could just see a rose-colored hue to the sky, and he guessed it must be around 0600, maybe a half-hour before sunrise. He had detected a slight decrease in speed and he had guessed at Macao around midnight. Six hours running at possibly 13 knots average would put them more than 70 miles along the South China coast from the mouth of the Delta. Shawn grappled for clarity, trying to remember the charts he had studied so often as *Seawolf* had made her way through the waters just south of here. But he could remember just two islands, one of them quite big, the other to the west, much smaller. The names escaped him. All he could think of was Sichuan Dao, in memory of his favorite Chinese restaurant back home in San Diego. Hell, it was something like that, anyway.

A half-hour later, the sun had fought its way out of the Pacific Ocean and was firing already warm, bright beams straight through the upper deck. And as it did so, the beat of the engines changed, and the ship began to make a hard turn to starboard. Shawn could see a sharp navigational light flashing every five seconds on a distant headland. He was not of course to know it was positioned on the offshore island of Weijia, 400 yards south of Shangchuan Dao, which he had mistaken for a Chinese restaurant.

He could now see land all along the starboard side of the ship, but they seemed to be heading away from it at an oblique angle. Judging by the sun, Shawn guessed a northerly course of three-four-zero, but he was not able to see out of the port side because of a bulkhead.

And now the engines had slowed right down, possibly to a speed of only seven knots. Shawn guessed the captain was creeping through some badly charted shallows. He could see land up ahead through the open deck area, and it looked like a long flat shoreline, with a mountain range rising out of the jungle, possibly a half-mile from the beach. He tried to get his bearings, confused by the fact that there was more open sea to the right of the land.

His best guess was that they were between islands, one to the right and one to the left, with the Chinese mainland a few miles to the north. He assessed that they were 80 to 90 miles along the coast from Macao, and that these must be the islands he had in his memory. The restaurant to starboard, the little one to port. But it was the little one to which they were slowly moving, through the sandy shallows.

Xiachuan Dao, virtually uninhabited for several hundred years, guardian of a military jail in which unspeakable cruelties had been enacted, lay dead ahead, its brightly lit torture chambers still intact after all these years.

0930. Saturday, July 8.
Office of Admiral Morgan. The White House.

KATHY O'BRIEN GAZED AT THE UNSHAVEN, dishevelled figure of the man she loved. The admiral was sound asleep at his desk, leaning back in the big leather Navy captain's chair, breathing deeply. It was a wonder he hadn't frozen to death, since the air conditioner had been turned up and running flat out since midnight. The admiral liked it cold.

Kathy put down the dark-blue sailor's duffel bag and kissed him lightly on the forehead, which had the effect of someone firing a cannon in the room. Arnold Morgan came hurtling back to consciousness after four hours' sleep, like all ex-submarine commanders, in about one-tenth of a second. He jolted upright, focused on Kathy, and smiled.

"Hey, you found me," he said superfluously.

"Arnold, my darling, this is not good for you. You have to get proper sleep."

"I've just had proper sleep, crashed right here at around oh-five-hundred."

"When I say proper sleep, I mean something a bit more relaxed, with clean pyjamas, clean sheets, and a bed, hopefully next to me. Traditional stuff."

"Oh, yeah, right," he said, not really listening. "Quick, get the Chinese ambassador on the phone and tell him to get his ass in here right now."

"Arnold, I'm not doing one single thing on this Saturday morning until you rejoin the human race. I want you to get showered, shaved, and changed. You've been in the same clothes for more than two days."

The admiral shook his head. "There's a crew of very frightened guys on the other side of the world who've been in the same clothes for more than two weeks. Anyway, I haven't got any stuff here, and I can't leave."

Kathy pointed at the Navy duffel bag. "In there, *sir*," she said with heavy emphasis, "you will find one shirt, one tie, one pair of shorts, one pair of dark socks, a pair of shoes, a dark gray suit, cuff links, your favorite soap, razor, green shaving gel, deodorant, shampoo, toothbrush, toothpaste, and aftershave. You will now report to that grandiose bathroom down near the pool and sharpen yourself up. When you return, in twenty minutes, you will find coffee and toast here. Who Flung Dung, as you insist on calling him, will be approximately ten minutes from his ETA. Is that more or less understood?"

"Christ," said Arnold Morgan, "you're more bossy than all of my wives put together."

"I'm also dancing attendance on a very silly person who has no idea how to look after himself and thinks he's still in a ridiculous submarine."

The admiral grinned, picked up the duffel bag, and retreated aft, toward the bathroom, moving fast, with the unmistakable upright gait of one whose working life had been spent in military uniform.

When he returned he looked immaculate. And he kissed Kathy, told her that he loved her beyond redemption, and steamed into the toast and coffee, preparing himself to treat his incoming Chinese guest with the utmost politeness—a trait that came approximately as naturally to him as to an Andalusian fighting bull.

At 10:00 sharp, the ambassador arrived, looking, as ever, pensive and worried, but still smiling and ingratiating.

"Hello, Ling, old buddy," said the admiral. "How are you today? . . . Good . . . good . . . siddown . . . want some coffee or would you rather have tea? Tea? Excellent, excellent . . . *KATHY!!*"

Even Mr. Ling looked mildly surprised that the admiral had apparently dispensed with the telephone system and preferred to stand in the middle of the room and unleash a kind of roar.

"China tea for my old friend Ling," he said, smiling when Kathy moved smartly back into the room.

"It's on its way, sir." She smiled back, a little too sweetly.

"Perfect," he replied, offering the ambassador from Beijing an armchair in front of his desk.

"Now, sir, I did ask you for a formal statement from your government, and I forgive you for its lateness. I presume you have it with you?"

"Yes, Admiral, I do. Would you like to read it?"

"Absolutely," replied the admiral as he took the offered piece of paper, which plainly had been prepared in Beijing and been transported to Washington in the diplomatic bag. The words were predictable.

It was with much regret that we discovered the destroyer *Xiangtan* was in a minor collision in the South China Sea with a nuclear submarine owned by the United States Navy. And we do of course regret that you did not see fit to inform us of a patrol in our waters by such a warship. However, accidents can happen, and it has been our pleasure to answer a call for help from your Captain Judd Crocker.

We have thus towed your *Seawolf* into the Navy yard at Canton and have been engaged in making her seaworthy again. We do think there has been some problem with the nuclear reactor and we are making tests to ensure it is running correctly, without radiation leaks, before the submarine leaves Chinese waters, sometime later this month.

Meanwhile, the crew are guests of the Chinese Navy, and we send this note of friendship to you in the hope that you would extend the same courtesies to our people, should the occasion ever arise.

The statement was designated as coming from the High Command of the People's Liberation Army/Navy, and it bore the personal signature of the Commander-in-Chief of the Navy, Admiral Zhang Yushu.

"Very nice," said Admiral Morgan, nodding. "Extremely cooperative. That's the secret of good international relations. Never look for trouble when there is no malice intended."

The ambassador was dumbfounded. He sat staring at the Lion of the White House unable to believe his ears.

"We are trying, sir . . ." he began, but words almost failed him. "My government admires you very much here in America. Soon you will have your ship back. And I assure you your men are all very happy now."

He sipped his tea, moistening his dry mouth. He was simply not able to comprehend the depth of the admiral's change in attitude.

"That's it for you, Ling, old pal. Now you pop off back to the embassy and keep me posted on the progress of repairs to *Seawolf*, there's a good guy. . . . KATHY!!! . . . see the ambassador out, will you?"

A half-hour later, the admiral was back in the Situation Room for the 1100 meeting. All the key men, both political and military, were there. And they were quite startled when the chairman announced that he had been working on a press statement to be issued from the Navy Office.

"You don't think this merits a presidential broadcast?" asked Dick Stafford, the President's speechwriter.

"It merits whatever we say it merits, Dick," replied the admiral.

"However, there are a couple of ground rules we have to stick with. The first is that any sign of panic, fear, weakness or worry betrayed by any of us will cause the press to go fucking berserk. We'll get scare stories . . . *U.S. Navy fears Chinese have kidnapped* Seawolf *and crew.*

"Any such reports will convey our total disbelief in the Chinese statement, put them on full alert for a possible United States attack or rescue attempt, and cause them to put whatever they are doing on an even faster track than it is now. Any such reports, from our standpoint, would be counterproductive in the extreme."

"And . . . ?" said Dick Stafford.

"I want the entire thing played right down. Today we are going to make a press statement before someone makes it for us—I mean the Russians know about this, probably someone in Taiwan, there's news correspondents in China, probably in Canton. Something's gonna leak real soon . . . that the biggest nuclear attack submarine in the U.S. Navy is somehow tied up in a Chinese dockyard, and no one knows where the crew is, and no one's talking. That's the biggest newspaper story in the world this year, trust me."

"What kind of announcement, Arnold?" asked the President.

"A small general press release from the Navy Department in the Pentagon. Nothing fancy. Nothing scary. Here, I just wrote it, lemme read it out:

"'*The U.S. Navy submarine* Seawolf *experienced minor mechanical difficulties during a patrol more than 100 miles off the coast of mainland China. The Navy of the People's Liberation Army responded to a call for help from the American captain and assisted the 9,000-ton ship to a dockyard, where routine repairs are being carried out.*

"'*All of the American crew are safe, and are currently guests of the Chinese Navy until they complete the work.* Seawolf *is expected to resume her patrol in the Far East, visiting Taiwan, in the next 10 days.*

"'*The U.S. Navy Department is grateful for the Chinese cooperation, a direct result of the strong military and commercial ties forged by President Clinton. And a personal message of thanks has been sent by Admiral Joseph Mulligan, the U.S. Chief of Naval Operations, to Admiral Zhang Yushu, the Commander-in-Chief of the Chinese Navy.'"*

The President smiled. Admiral Morgan shook his head and added, "I never told that many lies in that few words in my life. Here, Dick . . . get ahold of this before someone strikes me dead."

"Damned clever, that," said General Scannell. "If the newspapers don't smell a rat and they print that story as is, the Chinese will merely believe their subterfuge has worked."

"Precisely," said Admiral Morgan. "And that may buy us three or four extra days. With so many lives on the line we *ought* to be able to command them to print it. But under the Constitution we do not have that right. As usual, democracy favors the assholes."

This caused a burst of laughter to break out from all around this right-wing table of right-wing thinkers. And it was the President himself who restored the grim reality of the situation.

"Arnold, can we know what the military plan is right now? I agree, by the way, with your media strategy . . . my own involvement would only heighten the chances of the press whipping up a frenzy we don't need."

"Sir, I should perhaps inform everyone that you and I burned a little midnight oil last night after John Bergstrom had left. As a result of that, I appointed a rather controversial figure to command our rescue operation . . . Colonel Frank Hart, who will serve as the SEALs staff officer and mission controller on board the aircraft carrier."

A few eyebrows were raised at this, although the admiral had run it by Harcourt Travis and Bob MacPherson in the early hours of the morning.

"My reasons were obvious. Colonel Hart, an ex-SEAL team leader and former Marine Corps officer, has a lot of experience in dealing with foreign governments on military matters. He is a born decisionmaker, he is used to working alone, and he understands this type of operation better than any one of us. He may have to think very fast once we get moving. He may even have to abort the mission in a split second before a lot of people get killed. We must have someone of his caliber. And he's my choice. He ought to be here by now . . . where the hell is he?"

"And the actual operation . . . can we know?" asked Harcourt.

"Yes. John Bergstrom is putting together a team of approximately fifty of his combat-ready SEAL troops, taking men from several different active platoons. They leave for our base on the island of Okinawa midday Tuesday. The first minute we locate the jail where the guys are being held, we send in a twelve-man recon team, using a submarine and an SDV. In thirty-six hours they'll have that jail well documented.

"As soon as they're safe aboard, we check that *Seawolf*'s reactor is running. Then we launch the Hornet to take out the submarine. When that mission is achieved, under the cover of the mass panic in Canton, we send the SEALs into the jail. They overpower the guards, smash up the comms, blow up the helicopter and get the guys out, by Zodiac, SDV and submarines."

"You think we can actually pull this off? Seriously, Arnold?" asked Harcourt.

"Well, we need three things for success. First, we gotta find the goddamned jail. Second, we must have the nuclear reactor running. Third, we must have commanding officers who will get the three submarines close in, possibly making the last three miles on the surface."

"And what if they are discovered by a Chinese Navy patrol?"

"We're hoping the disaster in Canton will totally overwhelm the entire Chinese Navy. If we get detected long-range, it'll still take them more than two hours to get anywhere near us, because Canton will be right out of action and it's a long way to Zhanjiang. It will still take 'em a damn long time to get to us . . . just means the SEALs will have to fucking hurry."

"What are the odds against success?"

"The odds are not against. Ten bucks gets you twenty we'll make it. It's the surprise element. That and the fact that the navy dockyard in Canton is going to be a nuclear wipeout."

"What does Admiral Bergstrom think?" asked the President.

"He thinks we can pull it off. Otherwise he would refuse to send his precious SEALs in."

"Joe?" said the President, looking directly at Admiral Mulligan.

"We'll make it, sir. We're sending in the best we got."

The President arose. "Thank you, gentlemen," he said. "Please don't think I am unaware that most of you are doing this for me. And please tell the guys my personal thoughts and prayers will accompany them every yard of the way . . . may God go with them."

And everyone heard his voice break when he added, "If they could just bring him back safe . . ."

And they all saw the great man brush his right sleeve across his eyes as he walked with immense dignity from the room.

Midday (local). Saturday, July 8.
CO's Office. SPECWARCOM. Coronado, San Diego.

Admiral John Bergstrom arrived back in California at 0700, showered and changed at the base, having slept all the way on the military flight from Washington.

And now he was in overdrive, surrounded by three assistants, operating on the phone lines to Little Creek, Virginia, and to his own platoons right here on the Pacific Coast. He also had a phone open to Bradbury Lines, Herefordshire, England, headquarters of the British Army's fabled SAS regiment, which worked in tandem with the SEALs more often than most people realized.

The SAS commander, Colonel Mike Andrews, was sympathetic to the idea of three of his troopers playing a part in this highly classified American mission. He liked it for the camaraderie it would build between the regiments, and he thought it would be a tremendous shared experience in terms of strategy and operational methods. Also, he knew the politicians would love it, because the Conservative Prime Minister of the day had a relationship with President Clarke much like that between Margaret Thatcher and Ronald Reagan. Spiritually close. Philosophically unbreakable.

But most of all, he thought his men could really help Admiral Bergstrom, whom he knew, liked and respected. He had men who had fought and killed in Northern Ireland, Iraq and Kosovo, among other places. Iron men who had moved through rough terrain like panthers, experts with knife, gun and explosive. Men who had operated under the harsh SAS Rule OO1—kill or be killed, with only a split second to decide. Mike Andrews's boys would be priceless in the Chinese tropical jungle. And both he and Admiral Bergstrom knew it.

"Only one minor hurdle, Admiral," he said. "They would have to volunteer. I could not order them in to fight on behalf of a foreign power—not even you. And if they did volunteer, I'd have to clear it with the Ministry of Defense, probably as high as the Chief of Defense Staff. However, I do not anticipate a problem. I'll be back inside three hours. Same phone number? Excellent. 'Bye."

Admiral Bergstrom had already made up his mind who would lead the team in for the assault on the jail, wherever it was: Lt. Commander Rick Hunter, a former team leader from Little Creek, six feet three inches tall, not one ounce of fat on his steel-muscled 215-pound frame. Rick was a native of Kentucky, a big, hard farm boy from the Bluegrass State, son of Bart Hunter, a well-known breeder of thoroughbred racehorses out along the Versailles Pike near Lexington.

Bart naturally thought his son was insane to select a career that might bring him face to face with death on a regular basis when he should have been home on the farm, raising the yearlings, preparing them for the Keeneland sales. However, watching baby racehorses slowly grow up, studying pedigrees, talking to vets and spending a lifetime with other local "hardboots," all talking about the same subject, simply did not do it for Rick.

He dropped out of Vanderbilt University in Tennessee, where he was a collegiate swimming champion, and a year later he enrolled at the United States Naval Academy in Annapolis. From there he had never looked back, climbing the ladder of command and finally being accepted as a Navy SEAL, a job to which he brought outstanding talents. As a third-generation farmer, he was naturally a brilliant marksman with the strength of a full-grown polar bear. He was also a tireless swimmer and an expert in demolition, unarmed combat, and landing craft. As Bart Hunter's oldest son, he was used to exercising authority on the 2,000-acre horse farm. Men sensed that and turned to him as a natural leader.

A couple of years earlier he had led a sensational SEAL mission deep inside Russia. The operation had been "black," nonattributable, and few people knew anything about it. But John Bergstrom knew, and he was also aware that after such a mission it was customary not to use the same personnel again, but rather to use the men to train up the next generation.

However, in this case, the rules were somewhat different. This one *must* succeed. And direct from the presidential level, he had been told he *must* use the very best men. Lt. Commander Hunter was the best he had ever had. He was going to end up an admiral . . . maybe sitting in this very chair.

And Admiral Bergstrom had no hesitation in calling his commander at Little Creek and requesting that he dispatch Rick Hunter immediately to Coronado, in company with 20 more hand-picked SEALs, preferably veterans, possibly BUD/S instructors with special skills in jungle warfare, surprise attacks, explosives, "and jail breaks, if there's anyone around."

The BUD/S instructors were, of course, the toughest men in all the SEAL platoons. They were the granite-hard regulars who ran the training "Grinder," whose job it was to drive men physically and mentally into the dark uplands of total sacrifice, to take them to a place where unbearable pain becomes bearable, where fear vanishes, and where achievement is all. The BUD/S instructors drove men into a place they did not know existed, a place where, having given their all, they came back from the dead, from total exhaustion, and found more.

Of course, they did not all find more. Some collapsed, some hit a mental brick wall and just sat slumped on the ground, some just gave up, others did not really see the point. But when the dust cleared, there were a few men who still stood tall, chins out, shoulders back, eyes forward. Still defiant. Upon these few, these precious few, would be pinned the golden Trident badge of the U.S. Navy SEALs, the badge that sets them apart from all other combat troops in the United States Armed Forces.

The 21 SEALs who made the flight west from Little Creek to San Diego were a diverse and eclectic group, mostly veterans from every walk of life. Some had started in big-city tenements, others in wealthy suburban households. They were from the North and from the South, and they were black and they were white. And some were secretly scared, and others weren't. But they were united in spirit, prepared if necessary to die for one another. They were SEALs. And that is unlike any other calling.

Lieutenant Commander Hunter sat up front next to a younger officer, 30-year-old Lt. Ray Schaeffer, a native of the Massachusetts seaport of Marblehead who had gone straight from high school to Annapolis. Ray was a real seaman, a superb swimmer, expert navigator, yachtsman, fisherman, and the platoon middleweight boxing champion. His family had lived in Marblehead for generations. His father, a local sea captain, lived in a medium-sized white colonial house down near the docks. In one corner of the living room was an ancient illustrated family tree that showed that a Schaeffer had pulled one of the oars when the men from Marblehead had rowed General Washington to safety after the lost Battle of Long Island.

Ray had served with Rick Hunter on the mission in Russia. They had been detailed to that operation as complete strangers, but they returned as lifelong friends, and everyone noticed. Plainly they had faced immense dangers together, and whatever had happened, it now bound them in mutual respect. When Lieutenant Commander Hunter had been asked to begin naming the SEALs he would take with him to Coronado, the first name he uttered was Lt. Ray Schaeffer.

Behind them sat Lt. Dan Conway from Connecticut, another graduate of the Naval Academy. The son of a Navy frigate captain, grandson of a World War II submariner, Dan understood the folklore of the underwater warriors, having lived in the old family home in New London all his life. A tall, dark-haired man of 29, he had risen rapidly through the ranks as a SEAL, and was within months of becoming a team leader.

A former high school all-star baseball catcher, he juggled his career options between Fenway Park and Annapolis. The Navy won in a tight finish, and his father approved the choice of a long-term profession in dark blue. His mother, however, almost had a heart attack when he announced he was going to join the SEALs.

Dan Conway was a born athlete, with wide shoulders and a right arm that could hurl a baseball to second base like a howitzer. In unarmed combat he learned to be a master. In armed combat exercises, well . . . stay well clear of his right hand if it happens to be holding one of the SEALs big fighting knives. In the relentless training of "Hell Week," the physical endurance tests that break 50 percent of all applicants, Dan finished first.

He had been on the verge of collapse that day, sobbing for breath after the seven-mile beach run and the long swim in the Pacific. And he did not believe he could keep going for another five seconds, and one of the instructors ordered the remaining group to start running back to base. Two men went down, and returned on stretchers. Dan Conway drove himself forward, praying not to pass out. He threw up before they reached the gates, and when he got inside he fell onto the concrete. And another instructor stood over him and roared at him to get up, and go one more time through "the tunnel"—the huge flooded rowing boat, which required an underwater crawl *under* the seats.

Dan was gasping for air, his lungs throbbing, and the thought of going under the water for more than a minute was too much. And he shook his head, and he knew it was over . . . and then he got up, and drove himself through the tunnel, under the water, wriggling his way under the seats, tearing the skin on his knees, but still going forward. When he finally climbed over the gunwales, he blacked out and two instructors caught him as he fell. The last words he heard were, "Right here we got a real live Navy SEAL . . ."

Next to him sat Lt. Junior Grade Garrett Atkins from California. Garrett was two years younger than Dan, and had started his Navy career training to be a combat systems officer in a Los Angeles–class nuclear submarine. He was good at it, too, but Garrett was an outdoorsman, loved the beach, loved the mountains, drove all over the place in his Jeep Grand Cherokee, and grew to dislike the terrible confines of a big attack submarine.

Garrett was a tall, rather shy sportsman, an outstanding high school football player, and a baseball player. He wanted to leave the submarine service, but he did not want a soft option, and he decided to try something even tougher. They presented him with his golden Trident one year later, and he lived for the day when he would go into action with a SEAL combat platoon. It was a day not so very far off. Both he and his pal Conway sat in silence as they flew over the flat farmland of the Midwest, guessing that something big was about to break out.

Back in the main group were two outstanding petty officers, both experts at fighting in the mountains, both veterans of the Kosovo campaign seven years previously. From North Carolina came Catfish Jones—no one ever found out if he had a more formal name. Catfish came from a family that had lived in or around Morehead City for nine generations, right out there on the last mainland before the Outer Banks.

Catfish's aunt owned a bookstore right opposite the marina, but he had never taken to that line of commerce. Instead he tried a career as a deck hand on a big fishing trawler, working the rough Atlantic waters out beyond the Shackleford Banks, which guard the shores of Carteret County. Just southeast of here, the banks abruptly turn northeast and rename themselves the Core Banks, sweeping narrowly for 80 miles past Ocracoke Island on up to the storm-tossed waters around the Cape Hatteras Lighthouse.

These are tough seas in which to make a living, and men drown out there every year. They were not, however, apparently rough enough for Catfish, a 28-year-old, fair-haired, blue-eyed bull of a man. He stood five feet ten inches tall, with a 19-inch neck, and he had the strength to have once lifted the rear of a sports car clean off the ground with his bare hands while his buddies changed the wheel, in the pouring rain, in the middle of the night.

Catfish had a group of friends at the Camp Lejeune Marine Corps base a few miles down the coast from Morehead, and before he was 19, he had retired from fishing and enrolled in the Corps. Eighteen months later he applied to join the SEALs and finished second in his intake group.

It was said he had a harrowing time fighting in the Kosovo mountains north of Pristina, alongside the man who now sat next to him, 30-year-old SEAL veteran Rocky Lamb, a black career serviceman from the Bronx who had joined the Navy immediately after leaving high school.

Catfish and Rocky had worked together in those mountains for three weeks. And shortly after the American aircraft went down, they had pulled off two impressive rescues involving both American and British Special Forces, all of whom were surrounded by nearly overwhelming numbers. No one knew how many Yugoslav troops they had taken out in order to cleave a safe route out through the heavily patrolled wooded hillsides. But a lot of soldiers had a lot of gratitude for the two American SEALs. Both of their names were on Rick Hunter's list of top 10 choices for the mission in the South China Sea.

Also in that group were two young SEALs, both age 24, both country boys from way down in the bayous in St. James Parish, west of New Orleans. Riff Davies and Buster Townsend joined the Navy right out of high school rather than go to college. Riff ended up on an aircraft carrier, and Buster on a guided missile cruiser.

But these were a couple of guys who craved real adventure, and three years after they made their pact to join the Navy, they made another one, to try to gain entry into the SEALs. They were both from tough Louisiana families that for generations had ground out a living raising sugar beets in the hot swampy lands around the Mississippi Delta. From first grade they had been rivals as well as friends, playing football and basketball for their high school.

That rivalry drove them on through the rigors of the SEALs Hell Week, drove them through the BUD/S course, drove them to find reserves of strength and determination they never knew they had. In the months after they won their golden Tridents, they went on SEAL courses in various tropical locations, which caused them to rise to great heights in the estimations of their instructors. Riff and Buster could operate in the kind of oppressive, steamy heat they had known since birth, and both men were tireless on land and in the water. Everyone knew the strapping, powerfully built Buster had killed an alligator with a hunting knife at the age of 15, mainly because Riff told them all about it: "Big ole sonofabitch it was, too . . . ole Buster just rammed that long knife o' his straight into its eye and through its brain . . . just as well. I thought that sucker was gonna eat him right up."

But the legend of the two combat troops from the bayous really took root when young Davies, on an overseas exercise, stepped right into the range of a large, angry spitting cobra. Two other SEALs with him literally froze at the sight of it, swaying not eight feet in front of them. They stayed frozen, too, until Riff slammed it into a tree with a bamboo stick and blew its head off with his Sig Sauer pistol. According to one SEAL colleague, "It was like watching John Wayne nail a rattlesnake." The description earned Riff the memorable nickname of "Rattlesnake" Davies.

"Gotta watch out for them goddamned things," he said in his slow Louisiana drawl. "But they ain't near so quick as you think . . . just need a long stick and a good sideswipe . . . that way they take their eye off you . . . been killing snakes all my life, matter of fact."

Lt. Commander Rick Hunter as yet had no idea where they were headed after Coronado, but he was happy with the men he had chosen to fight with. So far as he could remember, there had never been this much haste, expenditure and urgency about any mission. In his mind that meant only one thing. They were either going to blow something very big to smithereens, or they were going to take out some form of enemy of the United States. Possibly both. But either way Rick smelled combat. He doubted it would be easy, and he wondered if some of them might be killed. Still, he was confident in the guys. And he took comfort in one of the old SEAL maxims: "There are very few of life's problems that cannot be solved with high explosives."

Nonetheless, he knew they were not invincible. SEALs bled and agonized like everyone else. It was just that it took about seven opponents to make this happen to one SEAL. *"Still,"* pondered the lieutenant commander, *"we haven't gone in for a while, and we must remember all our lessons—if there's an attack, we gotta be in first before our enemy knows what's happening, we gotta be well prepared, we gotta know the precise plan, we gotta know our enemy's strengths and his weaknesses, we gotta be 100 percent ruthless, and we gotta watch out for each other at all times. Above all, we gotta be quiet and quick."*

0730. Sunday, July 9.
Xiachuan Island.

The ferry eased its way next to the old stone jetty, which was set into sloping rocks on the south side of the wide northeastern peninsula. Behind them the prisoners could see a long, flat, sandy beach, washed today by warm, gentle seas. Up ahead the terrain was different, steeper, and Pearson noted the twin mountain peaks, one, the higher of the two, around a mile and a half west of the ferry. The other was more than a mile to the north.

It was hard to imagine where they were going, since the place seemed uninhabited by civilians. There was not so much as a fishing boat along the water, not even those long narrow bamboo rafts favored by the ancient people of this part of China. There was no sign of life save for a few seabirds, many of which had followed the ferry in. There was, however, already moored on the long jetty, a newly arrived 200-ton Huangfen fast-attack patrol craft, a Chinese-built Type Osa 1, capable of 39 knots, armed with four Russian 25mm guns, plus twin surface-to-surface missile launchers. Its diesel engines, with drive three shafts, were still running.

Everyone heard the ferry bump against the dock. The Chinese guards were out on the port side, yelling at a shore crew that emerged mysteriously from the wooded foreshore. The lines were thrown and made fast to old iron rings embedded in the concrete of the jetty. It was a drop of maybe six feet to dry land, but the guards had brought with them the big gangway from Canton. They secured it, and Commander Li materialized from nowhere. He stood on the concrete, barking orders.

Up on the viewing deck, the guard lieutenant who had been with them literally since they first arrived in Canton was now screaming at the Americans, ordering them to stand up and begin filing off the ship. They were of course still handcuffed behind their backs, and they walked forward to the gangway in lines, one long bench at a time, all under the leveled guns of the Chinese navy jailers.

It took a half-hour to disembark, and they were instructed to form a long double line, Captain Crocker and Lt. Commander Lucas in the lead. Finally, with six guards out in front, they set off, marching into the jungle down an old track, wide enough for an army jeep, but obviously recently cleared. It was dark, hot and shady beneath the tall trees. There were a lot of mosquitoes and other insects, and the air seemed to have a permanent hum to it. The guards marched beside them at 15-foot intervals. Pearson, the resident navigator, calculator and observer, thought there were more guards now than there had been on the ship. He also thought that no one would ever find them here on this godforsaken island in this godforsaken corner of the South China Sea, and for the first time he began to despair of ever seeing his family again.

They marched through the hot sweaty terrain for a half-mile, and now the ground began to rise. The men were tired and beginning to weaken from lack of food, not to mention water. The guards were yelling at them to keep up, and it was with some relief that they noticed the track was suddenly swinging right-handed, and they were headed down a long hill, at the bottom of which they could see sunlight, but nothing else.

Shawn Pearson calculated it had been about one mile from the jetty to the clearing, but as they marched out of the jungle onto flat open ground, everyone in the lead group was shocked at the sight that lay before them, because it was the unmistakable exterior of a military jail, complete with two tall bamboo watchtowers containing searchlights, rising starkly above gray stone walls 15 feet high.

The double doors to the main complex were set into the southern wall, which faced them. They were 12 feet high, made of jagged bamboo, and plainly brand new. To the left, dead ahead, were two other buildings, both stone with sloping roofs, the nearest one approximately three times the size of the other. Every window was barred, and there were two armed sentries outside the door to the biggest.

The Americans could not yet see the entrance to the smaller building, but they could see radio masts jutting from its roof.

On the right, there was a concrete helicopter pad on which was parked a Russian-built Kamov Ka-28 Helix, an ASW helicopter capable of firing three torpedoes or depth bombs. Right in front of it, nearer to the main complex, opposite the biggest of the two outside buildings, was a major fuel dump containing two 5,000-gallon cylinders that looked new, as if they had been brought in overland by helicopters. There was no other way to have gotten them there, so far as Judd Crocker could see.

And so the little captive army of American prisoners marched towards a Chinese jail shortly before 0900 on the sunlit Sunday morning of July 9. The doors were opened inwards as they approached, and the guards ordered them to keep going straight into a wide courtyard. Dead ahead was the main prisoners' block, a single-story building that stretched the entire length of the prison. Above it, on each outside corner, were the two watchtowers. To the left and right, abutting the main block, were two other buildings.

Directly inside the gates there were also buildings to the left and right. Sentries stood on duty outside the one on the right, which seemed busy, occupied by many navy personnel. The bigger building on the left appeared deserted. Indeed, the door was open and no guards were anywhere near it.

The main courtyard itself, in full view of the searchlights on the watchtowers, had once been concrete, but over the years it had cracked. Now there was grass growing on it, and because this was rainy July, the surface was wet, with long puddles reflecting the drab, morbid heartlessness of the surrounding buildings.

Commander Li's guard lieutenant called the American crewmen to order and told them to halt and stand at attention in the presence of the most honored Head of Security for the China's Southern Fleet. Then Commander Li himself stepped forward and informed everyone they would be kept here in the jail on this island for a period of perhaps three weeks; then, depending on their degree of cooperation, they would be sent home in their submarine. Meanwhile there was much to do, and cells were being allocated temporarily. They would be given permanent quarters later in the afternoon, "pending reports."

Commander Li then left the jail complex, marching out through the still-open gates, accompanied by an escort of four guards. Once clear of the main south wall they swung into the smaller of the two buildings the Americans had seen, the one with the radio aerials, the one designated Camp HQ and Commandant's Quarters, Commander Li's own little kingdom until further notice. The much bigger building was the main administration center, including stores and accommodations for the guard force.

Meanwhile, Commander Li was in conference with his four accompanying guards, all of whom were professional PLAN interrogators who had been silently studying the Americans for two days, including the sea voyage. And the first thing Li wanted to know was which of the senior officers might be vulnerable.

He was told that the captain was probably out of the question. They all assessed Judd Crocker as a hard and dangerous opponent, who not only would never tell them anything, but would probably take great joy in telling them a pack of lies about *Seawolf* and its workings. They felt the same about Brad Stockton, whom they assessed as "very dangerous" and the kind of man who might lead a breakout if he had the chance. They thought he was a man who would think nothing of killing for his freedom, and they recommended he be kept as far away from the captain as possible.

Commander Li was thoughtful. "A breakout would of course be childish," he said. "There is no escape from this island. At the slightest hint of trouble we would helicopter in reinforcements from Canton, if necessary move warships and patrol craft into the area. From the air, we could wipe them all out if we felt like it, or leave them to starve in the jungle. Remember, they only get off Xiachuan Dao if we say so."

The interrogators compared notes. They were agreed on two things: Lt. Commander Cy Rothstein might not stand up to physical abuse, and Lt. Commander Bruce Lucas was very, very frightened. The sonar officer, Frank, was very young and might be intimidated if he thought there was no way out except to reveal the intricate details of his electronic systems.

"How about the officer in charge of the reactor?"

"Well, you remember the captain ordered him to tell us what we wanted to know after we executed the American seaman in Canton? He was very difficult, and it was necessary to punish him before he would even assist us in shutting down the reactor."

"Do you think he learned a lesson, or will he continue to try to block our questions?"

"I think we have to work on the theory that he cracked last time and did what we asked."

"Yes. But, of course, he was also under orders from his own captain to comply with our wishes."

"Yessir. And we had to put someone to death to get Captain Crocker to agree to issue that order."

"Then we will put someone else to death . . . and then someone else . . . and then someone else . . . *until they obey.*"

1300 (local). Sunday, July 9.
Zhanjiang Naval Base.

Admiral Zhang Yushu occupied the main desk in Zu Jicai's office, as he always did on his visits, the Southern Commander deferring to his C-in-C. And now the two men sat together pondering the latest communication from the Chinese ambassador to Washington, His Excellency Ling Guofeng, a.k.a. Who Flung Dung, in a corner of President Clarke's White House.

The official communiqué revealed that the first editions of the American Sunday newspapers were carrying a small inside-page story about the crippled *Seawolf.* There had, apparently, been a press release from the Navy Department at the Pentagon quite late on Saturday evening.

The three newspapers studied by the ambassador had carried only four or five paragraphs, all under headlines along the lines of, "U.S. SUB GETS CHINESE HELP." Only the *New York Times* carried the paragraph that stated that the U.S. Navy's CNO had personally thanked Admiral Zhang Yushu. But the *Washington Post* had cross-referenced the story on the front page: "U.S. SUB STALLED IN CHINA."

Admiral Zu thought it was all extremely good news. "Well, sir, they believe us, at least for the moment. There's no sign there of any hostility, no sign even of American unrest. It is my view that our ambassador is doing a most excellent job."

Admiral Zhang was not so sure. "I don't trust them, my friend Jicai. I do not trust those men in the Pentagon one inch. And there are several things bothering me at this time.

"First, why did they take so long to issue a press statement— they could have done something last Wednesday. And why Saturday night, so late? That's unusual. There are few people in the Pentagon on Saturday night at nine-thirty, and even fewer in the newspaper offices. Why not issue it on Friday afternoon, when there are people everywhere? Or even save it until Monday morning? No, Jicai. This was deliberate. Very curious.

"Second, the New York paper mentions a personal word of thanks to me from the Chief of U.S. Naval Operations. Remember, this press release was written on Friday. It is now Sunday, and I have received no word of thanks from anybody. That makes it a lie.

"Third, I notice they do not mention Canton, as they would call the city. Why not? It's almost as if they do not want their own newspapers to be aware of the whole truth. Why not say where *Seawolf* is? Maybe they do not want American journalists snooping around the navy base in Guangzhou and finding out there is high security. If this press release were true, if they really believed there was cooperation, they would surely encourage their own reporters to come to Canton and see our two great nations working together to repair the submarine. Excellent public relations, excellent for them and for us. Excellent for future trade.

"I smell a very large rat, my Jicai. And he's not even due here for two years."

Admiral Zu smiled. "Are you sure you are not being a little too suspicious, Yushu? Perhaps they really do believe us, and are just wishing to remain our friends."

"I wish that were so, Jicai. And I agree there is much for the Americans and the Chinese to share. Unfortunately, I must quote one of our oldest proverbs to you: *tongchuang yimeng . . . to sleep in the same bed, but to have different dreams.*"

1100 (local). Sunday, July 9.
The White House.

Admiral Morgan and Colonel Frank Hart were deep in conference, and had been since 0800. Three times the admiral had called his old office at the ultrasecret National Security Agency at Fort Meade, Maryland, to inquire if there was any news on the whereabouts of the crew of *Seawolf.* But the agency had little to add. All anyone knew was that the prisoners had all been removed from the Canton jail and been taken to the naval base. Since no warship had been observed anywhere on the Pearl River, nor even moving across the Delta, the conclusion was that the men were still on the base, though precisely where was a mystery. The satellites were transmitting many excellent images, but the area seemed quiet and there did not appear to be a building that would hide more than 100 newly arrived prisoners.

It was the CIA that received the first break. Jake Raeburn from the Far Eastern Desk came through at 1105. He'd just heard from his field officer in Canton. Their man inside the dockyard had reported the prisoners had left, sometime on Saturday evening. No one knew their destination, but their information was they had headed downstream toward the Delta, under heavy guard, in a civilian ferryboat. So far as the local CIA man could ascertain, there were no American personnel left at the base. "He does have a report the evening ferry trip down the river for tourists had been canceled, so it sounds as if the Navy may have commandeered it."

Admiral Morgan was grateful and asked Jake to keep Fort Meade posted, and to "tell 'em to beef up overhead surveillance along that stretch of the Chinese coast."

To Colonel Hart he said, "We have to find them, Frank. We have to locate these guys in the next forty-eight hours, and right now I'm doing everything I can to throw the Chinese off the scent, make 'em think we believe their goodwill messages and have no intention of making any kind of an aggressive move."

"Yessir. I read the stuff thoroughly. And so far only one thing bothers me . . . you know, where the press release says there was a personal message sent from Joe Mulligan direct to Zhang Yushu . . . did you actually send that message?"

"Hell, no."

"I think you should."

"Why?"

"Because that statement of courtesy, one senior naval commander to another, falls into the category of politeness and respect. The Chinese specialize in offering compliments, polite, restrained and sometimes obsequious. And they have no problem with insincerity. In fact, that's a national pastime. But I sense that to mention a courtesy, and then deliberately not make it, might be seen as an insult or loss of face. They are very tricky about that, and I'd bet you anything Admiral Zhang will want to know if that courteous message from the White House actually arrived.

"If he's a very suspicious type, he'll be mystified at its nonarrival, and may even begin to doubt the validity of the whole thing. Send it and hopefully he'll continue to think we're all soft."

Arnold Morgan knew sense when he heard it, and he said instantly, "Good call, Frank. I'll jump right on it . . . KATHY!! NOTEBOOK!"

Ms. O'Brien appeared in a major hurry.

"Okay . . . take this down, will you? 'Admiral Joseph Mulligan, Chief of United States Naval Operations, presents his compliments to the High Command of the People's Liberation Army/Navy, and wishes to thank Admiral Zhang Yushu, Commander-in-Chief of PLAN, for his generosity in assisting the U.S. submarine *Seawolf* in her time of need. Please be assured that the U.S. Navy will pay for all costs incurred in the repairs, and be assured that if we are ever called upon to offer similar help to one of your ships, we will not hesitate to do so. Again, my thanks and best wishes. Admiral Joseph Mulligan, the Pentagon, Washington, D.C., USA.'

"Right, Kathy, call Joe's office and have them dispatch that electronically directly to the PLAN Headquarters in Beijing . . . tell 'em they don't need to bother Joe. It's my orders, direct from the President. Tell 'em to do it NOW. If not sooner."

"Yessir." Kathy left.

"Okay, Frank . . . now, where do we stand?"

Just then the phone rang, the admiral's secure line from Fort Meade, and the conversation was brief.

"You did? Uh-huh . . . uh-huh . . . gotta be right. We don't know when it sailed, right? No . . . guess not. Okay . . . keep me posted."

The admiral banged down the phone. No good-byes today. No courtesies, except to Yushu.

"They think they picked up the ferry, Frank. Caught it on the overheads making its way back up the Pearl River around twenty-one hundred local."

"Might be significant, might not," replied the ex-London naval attaché. "Because right here, in these Canton guidebooks you gave me, I'm showing an evening ferry trip downriver and back by twenty-two hundred. That could be just the regular tourist voyage."

"Hell, Frank. I forgot to mention it. That ferryboat trip was canceled at short notice."

"Then we just located the transport at least for our guys, right?"

"Right. And now we can get some kind of a handle on the distance—like the ferry probably took off at around twenty hundred. They plainly wanted it before twenty-two hundred and took possession around eighteen hundred . . . here's the ferry terminal . . . here's the Navy yard . . . it's only a couple of miles."

"And if the damn thing got back by twenty-two hundred Sunday, that means its journey took twenty-six hours," added Admiral Morgan. "Give 'em a couple of hours on station, to disembark the crew and refuel, and we're looking possibly at twelve hours out and twelve hours back . . . how fast do ferryboats travel?"

"On reasonably flat water, probably better than twelve, slower than twenty . . ."

"Well, if we settle for say fourteen . . . because they probably got as far as the ocean where they run into a bit of chop . . . that means they took the guys somewhere fourteen times twelve away . . . what's that . . . one hundred and sixty-eight miles?"

"The merit of that number is not its accuracy, sir," said Colonel Hart. "It's the knowledge that they could not have gone a whole lot farther than that. The weakness of the number is that the ferry may have stayed on station a lot longer, maybe allowing the Chinese officers to dine aboard, maybe using it as an office. And of course we don't know which way it went when it reached the bottom of the Delta. It could've gone east, right around Hong Kong, and then up the coast or even to an island. Alternatively, it could have gone west . . . maybe as far as these two little islands right here. What are they called? . . . Shangchuan Dao and Xiachuan Dao . . . that's about the limit of the ferry's range, given the twenty-six-hour envelope for the whole journey."

"Fact is, they could have pulled in anywhere along that coastline . . ."

"Yessir. But I'd say they at least reached the mouth of the Delta and went out into the sea, one way or another . . . otherwise they'd have gone by road."

"Good point. I'd better tell Fort Meade to concentrate the overheads on this stretch of Chinese coast right here . . . from Macao to these fucking little chop-suey islands . . . and then along here from Hong Kong east to . . . what's this place called? . . . right here . . . Humen . . . hey, that's familiar. I think there's a navy base there . . . check that big book over there, Frank . . ."

The colonel flicked expertly through the pages of *Jane's Fighting Ships*, and located the Southern Fleet Naval Base at Humen. "You're right, sir," he said, heading back toward the computerized charts on the admiral's big screen.

"How far's Humen from the ferry route just south of Hong Kong?"

"Around eighty-five miles . . . maybe a little more. But it looks like deeper water, and the coastline is desolate . . ."

"Well, I guess the Chinese could have some kind of jail facility along there to keep prisoners . . . but they might have a real facility in Humen, in the base itself . . . and that's the worst possible news for us."

"Right, sir. You mean we can't just storm a Chinese naval base?"

"Not with SEALS . . . and if we used Marines we'd need thousands of them, and it would be like a declaration of war on China. Hell, we can't do that."

"Well, right now, sir, we cannot do anything, because we don't know where they are."

"No, Frank. But we have to find them . . ." And he broke off, picked up his secure line and growled, "Get me Fort Meade in a big hurry."

Midnight. Sunday, July 9.
The Jail on Xiachuan Dao.

The Americans were now divided into groups of six, and each group was trying to sleep on the concrete floor of a cell that measured twelve feet by ten feet. The walls were stone. There was no window, but the door contained a large barred area two feet wide by three feet long, beyond which in the gloomy passage sat two armed Chinese guards on four-hour watches. Their instructions were explicit: "If anyone speaks, we are ordered to shoot the first man inside the bars."

The Americans believed him. And no one spoke. But, quite suddenly, the door to the main cell block opened, and the main lights were switched on and flooded in on the American crew members.

The guard lieutenant who had shot Skip Laxton stood halfway down the passage and announced, "We are now beginning the process of separation and interrogation," and he walked back to the first cell, ordered one of his men to open it, and shouted, "Lieutenant Commander Bruce Lucas and Lieutenant Commander Cy Rothstein . . . step outside IMMEDIATELY!"

Instantly Judd Crocker was on his feet pushing his way forward and screaming at the guard lieutenant, "Where are you taking these men? Don't think I've forgotten about you, you murdering little bastard . . ."

He half-expected to be beaten to the ground for his trouble, but Judd thought it was important to let his men know he was still in fighting order. He was, however, quite surprised at the Chinese officer's calm, smiling reply.

"Captain Crocker, I admire your spirit as the leader of these men. But it would do you well to remember, you are not on board *Seawolf* at the moment. Here you are just another criminal, and you may face trial a long time before I do."

Then he walked slowly to the next cell and demanded the immediate presence of Lt. Kyle Frank, who was dragged out protesting. But like everyone else he was still handcuffed, essentially powerless in the face of six armed guards.

The three Americans were then marched along the passage and out the door, the roars of Judd Crocker bellowing out behind them: "WHERE THE HELL ARE YOU TAKING THOSE MEN, YOU LITTLE FUCKER? YOU'LL ANSWER FOR THIS, I SWEAR TO GOD, IF ANYTHING HAPPENS TO THEM . . ."

Before he closed the door behind him, the guard lieutenant looked back inside and said with a wide smile, "Captain Crocker, please be quiet. You have been completely abandoned by your government. They, too, understand your criminal, unauthorized acts. They have given us permission to treat you as we would any other criminal. Good night."

And the captain felt upon him the melancholy chill of loneliness such as he had never experienced before. He could not believe what the lieutenant had said, but in his weakened state, starving, parched with thirst, his wrists throbbing from the chafing of the handcuffs, he had, for the first time, doubts. What if the Chinese were telling the truth? What if the U.S. Navy was furious with him for being detected? What if they believed it was he who had wrapped the prop around the towed array? Maybe the sacrifice of him and his crew was the only way out for the American government, save for some kind of war with China? *"That little bastard sounded pretty damn sure of himself . . . Jesus Christ!"*

Bruce Lucas, Cy Rothstein and Kyle Frank were marched across the courtyard through the warm rain and into the big, deserted building in the southwest corner of the jail complex. Inside there was one room to the right-hand side through which they could see a half-dozen Chinese guards. To the right was a long, brightly lit corridor down which they were directed. At the end were three or four rooms, each brightly lit, each containing two or three chairs. Each of them was disgustingly filthy, the walls and floor stained a deep ocher brown, the unmistakable marks of blood.

And now the Americans were separated, each of them ordered into one of the rooms and told to sit until further notice. Thirty minutes later the door to Cy Rothstein's room opened and through it came Commander Li, in company with two guards, carrying only their machine guns and dressed just in dark blue uniform shorts and shirts, with white socks and black shoes. A fourth man wore a white laboratory coat, and he carried with him a large sheaf of papers.

He and the commander occupied the two chairs, while the guards took up station in the corners of the room in full sight of Cy Rothstein.

"Now, Lieutenant Commander," said Li. "You are the combat systems officer of the submarine *Seawolf*, I believe?"

Cy said nothing.

"Silence is futile. We have plainly examined all of the ship's documents. We *know* you are the combat systems officer . . . please, do not be foolish."

Cy still said nothing, at which point Li ordered one of the guards to remove the American officer's handcuffs.

"Now listen to me, Lieutenant Commander. We are both adult officers of great national navies. You and your colleagues have transgressed all the normal rules of behavior on the high seas. Your own government has accepted this, and they have given us permission to put you on trial like any other international terrorist. Because, you see, that is what you are. Disowned by Washington, reviled by the peace-seeking Chinese people . . . you are entirely at our mercy.

"Lieutenant Commander . . . I am offering you a reasonable compromise. Help us, we help you. If you and your senior colleagues are prepared to give us the information we need concerning the working and running of *Seawolf*, there will be no trial. You and all of your colleagues will be set free and returned to the United States . . . probably in your own ship. No one will ever know what you have told us . . . certainly not from our side. No one admits anything, no one will ever know what you said in this private room."

For the first time, Cy Rothstein spoke. "I'll know," he said.

And so the two men sat on either side of an unseen line, Cy Rothstein wondering if he had the courage to take the physical beating he knew must be inevitable in this torture chamber, Li wondering about the wisdom of actually torturing a helpless American naval officer.

Commander Li decided to try one more time. "Lieutenant Commander," he said, "let me give you an example of the very simple questions we need to ask . . . for instance, the Hughes Tomahawk missile . . . the TLAM-N . . . we know the range is about fifteen hundred miles, but we have questions about the inertial navigation system. . . . Also, we are uncertain of its speed through the air. We want you to tell us the circular error probability. Our scientists think *Seawolf* carried two versions, one of them the TLAM-C/D. . . . Does this missile have added GPS backup or can it work just on its own inbuilt system? . . . Come, Lieutenant Commander, think how much easier it will be for all of us if we just sit here and have a talk . . . Why not tell me now a little about that high-explosive warhead . . . What is it? Four hundred kilograms? Maybe five hundred . . . why not tell me and make it easy on all of us?"

Cy Rothstein said nothing. He stared directly ahead, at which point, Commander Li stepped over the unseen line, and nodded to one of the guards.

Cy Rothstein saw him coming, slowly, a half-smile on his face, just to his left side. They say a soldier never sees the bullet that kills him, and the lieutenant commander never saw the vicious punch that slammed into his mouth, splitting open his lower lip and dislodging his two upper front teeth.

Stunned, unprepared for the pain, he briefly closed his eyes and gasped for air through his bleeding lips. He thus did not see the butt of the guard's gun come slashing into his ribs, fracturing two of them with one blow.

He fell sideways off the chair, crashing to the floor, feeling the crunch of the guard's boot raining kicks into his righthand ribs, feeling the staggering blow to the back of the head, which mercifully robbed him of consciousness. The lights went out in his mind, as well as the cell, as Commander Li left, in company with his two henchmen and the visiting scientist.

Out in the corridor there were now loud recordings being played of men screaming in agony. Linus Clarke had never been so afraid. And now his door crashed open, and Commander Li, with the two guards, made a swashbuckling entrance, all business. They siezed ropes from one of the three chairs and bound his legs to the legs of the chair. Then they bound his manacled hands to the bar across the backrest of the chair.

Commander Li stood in front of him and said, "Lieutenant Commander Lucas. You will answer each of my questions accurately and immediately, otherwise I am going to have you killed, not by summary execution, in the way I believe you witnessed with one of your colleagues, but in a more slow and deliberate way, which you will not enjoy . . ."

Linus was unable to stop trembling. Relentlessly Li continued, "Bruce Lucas, I understand you are the executive officer of the ship . . . correct? The second-in-command?"

Linus was too petrified to answer. He sat there unable to believe what was happening to him, an American naval officer in the opening years of the twenty-first century. He debated just telling the truth, answering the damn questions, then revealing who he really was in an attempt to save his life. Surely they'd never dare harm him if they knew who his father was?

But Li was becoming impatient. "BRING THE TOWEL!" he snapped. And the guard fetched a large white bath towel from the other chair, walked forward and draped it carefully over the head of *Seawolf*'s XO. For an insane moment Linus felt like a member of the Ku Klux Klan, without the eye slits.

He knew there was a large water barrel in the corner of the room, from which he had not been able to steal even a mouthful. And now he sat here under the towel, parched, hot and afraid, and he heard the tread of the guard's shoes as he walked across the room and dipped something into the water.

He heard the slow walk of the man back toward him and then

he felt the cool splash of water on the towel, right at the top of his head. Generally speaking it was not unpleasant. And then he heard the ladle dip in again, and again the water poured onto the towel. Then again, and then again.

By now the towel was becoming waterlogged, and it started sticking to his face, and he was trying to jerk it off his mouth and nose in order to suck in air from below. The more water, the heavier the towel became. And the heavier it became the harder it was to get it away from his mouth. Every time he sucked in, the towel sealed off his mouth and nostrils.

Linus began to panic. He understood he was in danger of either choking or suffocating, because by now the towel was so wet that the water was getting into his mouth and nose. Desperate now, he tried to stand, but that was impossible. He managed to get the towel off his mouth for a split second and gulped air, but the towel instantly smacked back across his face.

He had barely any air in his lungs, not sufficient even to blow the towel off his face. He flung his head forward and gasped air into his lungs. But it took all of his strength, and there was not enough air to exhale with any force.

"Jesus Christ!" he thought. *"They're trying to choke me, and they're doing it . . . they're just going to watch me die."*

He used the last of his energy to jolt forward and get the towel briefly off his face, enough for some air. But it came back, sealing his mouth and nose, and he somehow was pulling water out of the fabric and into his lungs. He tried to cough, but he had no air. And the towel was rammed against his face, and they were pouring more water.

Linus could not cry out. He could not breathe, and he could not fight the iron-hard clinging of the sopping wet bath towel. He lolled his head back and hurled it forward, but the towel was too wet now and it stayed right where it was, over his entire face. Suffocating him, very fast.

At which point Linus blacked out, toppling sideways, cracking his forehead on the floor, still tied to the chair. Only then did Commander Li stoop down and pull the towel off the bleeding head of *Seawolf*'s XO, in a truly grotesque sense saving his life.

1600. Monday, July 10.
Zhanjiang Naval Base.

ADMIRAL ZHANG YUSHU NOW HAD HIS MESSAGE of thanks and courtesies from the U.S. Navy's CNO. But he remained in a state of general disquiet. It was all so utterly uncharacteristic of the arrogant men who ran America's armed services. In his mind he believed it impossible that the admirals who had so imperiously removed his very own Kilo-class submarines from the face of the earth a couple of years earlier were now going to stand up for the plain and obvious kidnapping of a big United States attack submarine and its entire crew.

Zhang was nobody's fool. He knew the American satellites were photographing *Seawolf* every few hours, and he knew the American admirals must be absolutely seething with anger. And yet they were now treating Ambassador Ling Guofeng like an old friend, believing messages from the People's Liberation Army/Navy that no one in their right mind would take seriously.

But there was a ring of authenticity to the American communiqués. Almost as if they were *willing* the Chinese explanations to be true, as if trying to avoid the possibility of confrontation, as if trying to avoid at all costs any harm coming to their precious crew. *The West,* he thought, *so childishly preoccupied with the one disposable asset they too have by the millions and millions.*

It was a bewildering situation, but the senior crew members were proving to be stubborn. Except for one. And he had insufficient technical data in his mind. Time was of the utmost importance. Zhang could only go on lying to the Americans for maybe another 10 days. Either that . . . or the Americans might attack, storming the Canton dockyard, with world opinion on their side. Admiral Zhang knew he could mount some kind of defense, but in the end the Americans would smash their way in using vastly superior weaponry.

Zhang never removed the thought from his mind of the war 15 years earlier in the Gulf of Iran. After all the precombat talk of the strength and battle-hardened skills of the Iraqi elite commandos, the Americans made them look like children, obliterating their forces, their land, their bridges, their armaments, and anything else that got in the way. He was struck with fear at the prospect of the Pentagon turning serious attention to the naval base at Canton, and then possibly Zhanjiang, Haikou, Humen and perhaps even Xiamen. But he wanted a fleet of Seawolves, and he had the wherewithal, right now, to achieve that aim. But he had to be very, very careful and take no chances. Especially with American prisoners. They must never be allowed to get out of China alive. *And, above all, the Americans must not find them.*

Zhang paced the office of Admiral Zu. "Are you still sure, my Jicai? Still certain the Pentagon believes us?"

"Yushu, I have said it many times before. You have in your hand the personal message from Admiral Mulligan, conveying to you his compliments, thanking you for your assistance, assuring you of his friendship. It's like the old days when President Clinton was in power. They seem to value our friendship, they want our support and trade. And will do anything to avoid offending us."

"Zu, I cannot explain to you strongly enough the vast gulf there is between this Clarke administration and the one led by President Clinton. It's two different worlds. One friendly, appeasing, cooperative, and soft. This one hard, suspicious, protective, and cynical in the extreme. This man in the White House listens to his military commanders, and as we all know, military commanders, at least the best of them, are the only people in either country who are truly worth listening to in international politics. Unless the politicians happen to be ex-revolutionaries, like the great men who shaped the Republic of China. There haven't been proper revolutionaries in the United States for two hundred and thirty years."

"Then, Yushu, I do not think my advice and instincts are of any value to you. Because I believe you are deeply troubled by the situation. I see in you the ancient Chinese saying, *reguoshang demayl* . . . like ants on top of a hot stove . . . you are full of worries. And I have known you for many years. When you are so worried, you have to make your own actions. And I understand you. If the chances of a sudden American reprisal are, in my estimation, ninety-nine to one against, you are simply not concerned with the ninety-nine, only with the one."

Zhang smiled. "Jicai, I cannot leave the prisoners in the jail on Xiachuan Dao. It is vulnerable to the sea. To an attack from the sea."

"But we have an entire navy an hour or so away to fight them off. We have many troops. Land-based attack aircraft. What can they do that we cannot rebuff? The most they could do, thousands of miles from their own shores, would be to bring in a carrier battle group. But we now have four Kilo-class submarines. We could sink the damn thing. It's been done before. We would surely overwhelm them."

"Perhaps. But that CVBG has the fire power to wipe out half of China."

"But Yushu, they aren't going to do that. They will not bring the world to the brink of a world war for the sake of one submarine and a few sailors."

"Maybe, maybe not. But I have to move those prisoners fast, somewhere deep in the interior . . . *where no one will ever find them.* Because if the Americans can't find them, they won't attack. Because they are soft, and they value each human life in a way we would regard as absurd. So long as we have that crew, and they have our word no harm will come to them, I think they will keep their distance. But if they find them somehow . . . that's what I'm afraid of. I cannot think we have more than ten days' use of Xiachuan Dao. By then we must have another alternative prison camp. Away from the sea."

Admiral Zhang had been in the office since 0500 pondering his problem, a jail in the interior, so far from anywhere that its inhabitants would simply cease to exist, and over the years they could be silently removed without anyone ever knowing their fate. It was strange, but all day long he had drawn a complete blank. But now, stimulated by his own thoughts about the possibility of an American attack, he came up with a plan.

Zhang did not know the word "Eureka!" but if he had he would have exclaimed it right here in the office of the Southern Fleet commander. Because Zhang was presently so utterly absorbed with the chance to copy the *Seawolf*, he had entered an ancient Chinese condition known as *zuojing guantian*, which means, *looking at the sky from the bottom of a well*, not seeing the whole picture.

And now he moved into a higher gear, focusing his mind on a place he had only once visited—Chongqing, the great gray Chinese city that clings to the mountains above the confluence of the wide Yangtze and Jialing rivers, more than 650 miles northwest of Zhanjiang where he now stood. This was the deepest interior, a city of 15 million people in the innermost province of Sichuan, 700 miles from Shanghai, 800 from Beijing, bordered to the west by the massive 1,000-mile-long range of mountains that separate China from much of the Asian world.

Chongqing was for centuries almost inaccessible except for those who could navigate the Yangtze for 1,000 miles. Blisteringly hot in the summer, the city spends almost the entire winter under a deep blanket of fog. Its airport, set between mountains, is unsuitable for international flights, and even now it takes an excellent domestic airline pilot to make a landing there. The train takes 12 hours running south down the Tuo River and through the mountains from Sichuan's capital, Chengdu, a distance of 180 miles. From Kunming, 400 miles to the south, it takes 36 hours by train, because you have to go all the way north to change at Chengdu.

Chongqing was the capital of China during World War II, headquarters of Chiang Kaishek's Kuomintang military, and what those ruthless anticommunist twentieth-century tartars needed was jails in which to incarcerate hundreds of political prisoners. They built them well outside the city, mostly to the west, and Admiral Zhang Yushu knew precisely where they were.

He knew also they were a sprawling archipelago of prisons, some more remote than others. Tourists were admitted to see some of them on bus trips from the city, but it would take the C-in-C of the Navy one phone call to isolate an entire complex.

"Chongqing, Jicai," he said. "That's the answer, the remotest jail, in the remotest city, almost unapproachable by air, a nightmare by road, and no ocean. Not even the Americans could storm that place. And anyway, they would never, never find their prisoners. No one ever has, not in the old jails of Chongqing. Ten weeks from now the place goes under a blanket of fog. The American satellites would find that nearly impossible, even if they knew where to look."

"But, Yushu, those jails have not been used for a half-century—they will be in disrepair . . . what about water and electricity?"

"Jicai, let me ask you a general knowledge question: What lies three hundred and fifty miles downstream along the Yangtze from Chongqing?"

"At Yichang? Well, the Three Gorges Dam, of course. I don't quite see what that has to do with it."

"Because, Jicai, on that massive project there are a half-million of our workers, many of them skilled. There are billions of tons of cement and steel and machinery. Technicians working on one of the biggest hydroelectric projects on earth . . . one good shipload of men and material, and I'll have one of those jails up and running inside one week. Off limits to all tourists for a hundred years."

"I'll say one thing, my great leader," replied Admiral Zu. "It has never been a problem for you to think big. Really big. And I agree.

If you could make those arrangements, I don't think the Americans would ever find their submarine crew."

1200. Tuesday, July 11.
SPECWARCOM HQ. Coronado, San Diego.

Admiral John Bergstrom was putting together his SEAL strike force as if the mission was taking place tomorrow. Which it most definitely was not, because no one knew where the crew of *Seawolf* was located.

Nonetheless, he was operating on two assumptions: One, that the location would be somewhere near the sea, in accordance with the intelligence theories being advanced by Admiral Morgan and Colonel Hart. Two, there would have to be a detailed reconnaissance, probably sending in a dozen SEALs to wherever the hell the crew were discovered.

All day he and Admiral Morgan had conferred, and the President's security adviser was growing more and more irritated at the intelligence community in Fort Meade, which had been working flat-out six-hour shifts all through the night. Right now the situation was approaching dire. Admiral Bergstrom had his team in order, under the driving force of Lt. Commander Rick Hunter. But they were operating in a vacuum. Detailed plans for the assault were being drawn up, involving the best men among the 2,300 SEALs, but no one knew what they were supposed to assault. It was hugely frustrating.

Four hours from now, at 1600 (local), the now 64-strong SEAL attack force would fly from the U.S. Naval Air Station at North Island, San Diego, to the air facility the U.S. has maintained at Okinawa, one of the remote Japanese islands that stretch for 540 miles southwesterly from the final mainland of Kyushu down to within 100 miles of the northeast coast of Taiwan. Okinawa is situated about halfway down the island chain, 950 miles east-nor'east of the Pearl River Delta.

From Okinawa, the SEALs were scheduled to be ferried by one of the Navy's giant Sikorsky CH–53D Sea Stallion assault helicopters to the flight deck of the 100,000-ton Nimitz-class aircraft carrier *Ronald*

Reagan. The Sea Stallion helicopter carries 38 troops and would make three journeys between the airfield and the carrier, bringing in the 64 SEALs and all of their gear, plus Colonel Frank Hart, who was expected momentarily in Admiral Bergstrom's office.

In fact, he arrived at 1300, and John Bergstrom was glad to see him. The colonel's reputation had not been sullied among the military, only among certain left-wing politicians and their followers, usually referred to, affectionately, by Arnold Morgan as "the god-damned know-nothings."

"Glad to see you, Frank. How you been?"

"You ever done a couple of days solid with Admiral Morgan in his lair?"

John Bergstrom chuckled. "Coupla times. He's something, isn't he?"

"Well, aside from the fact that he misses nothing, outthinks everyone, doesn't need sleep, forgets to eat, forgets to go home, yells at people, and is probably the rudest man ever to work in the White House, except for Lyndon Johnson forty years ago . . . well, it was a breeze."

"Did you learn anything?"

"Everything."

"Frank, I am glad to have you aboard. If the admiral hadn't recruited you, I'd have gone myself. It's gotta be one hell of a dangerous mission, especially if the guys have to fight their way out and we have to get 'em off the beaches. That's likely to be one helluva job."

"I know it. What time are we leaving?"

"Takeoff at sixteen hundred from North Island. Using a big Galaxy on its way to DG. There's a few things you and I should go over right now: the list of gear, lines of communication, procedures if we have to abort, details of your principal commanders, makeup of the reconnaissance team, all of which I'll spell out for you. We've done our preparations on that. I have a file on it."

"Okay, John. All we need now is to find out what we're attacking, and where the recon goes in. . . . I just hope the water's not too shallow. The new ASDVs have a good long range, but I doubt SUB-PAC wants its ships on the surface if it can be avoided."

"They sure don't, Frank. But as you know, this mission carries with it some spectacular baggage. And if it's humanly possible, we have to get it done. Meantime, I've asked your recon team leader to come in and meet you in the next few minutes."

"Great, John. Who is he?"

Too late. The door opened and through it walked a legendary SEAL, Lt. Commander Russell Bennett, senior BUD/S instructor at Coronado, veteran team leader of a diabolical attack on the Iranian submarines in Bandar Abbas four years previously, veteran of the Gulf War, veteran member of the SEAL team that memorably blew the engine of General Noriega's presidential yacht 100 feet into the air above Balboa Harbor. "Mark one-thirty-eight demo charges, right on the shaft," reported SEAL Bennett.

He was 38 now, but still harder and fitter than the iron men he trained. A graduate of the Naval Academy, leading classman in the BUD/S course when he first came to Coronado, Rusty Bennett was the son of a Maine lobsterman, and as such brought certain skills to his chosen profession. He was a superb navigator, he could swim through ice-cold seas, and he could operate as efficiently underwater as he could on land. He was a man of medium height with dark red hair, dark blue eyes, a big well-trimmed mustache, and forearms and wrists made of cast steel. He was an expert on explosives, and one of the best climbers ever to wear the golden Trident. Mountains, trees, the smooth steel plates of any ship, Rusty could find a way to ascend. Any enemy who happened to spot him making an attack was probably looking at the last few seconds of his life.

He was precisely the kind of man the high command of the SEALs selects for the job of platoon leader. And this was the man John Bergstrom had chosen to take the SEALs in to recon the place where the American crew were held captive. Like Rick Hunter, Rusty had been off active operational duty since his last mission, but Admiral Morgan had stressed that he wanted the best, and no one would dispute the best was Lt. Commander Rusty Bennett.

And now Rusty stuck out his right hand in greeting to Colonel Frank Hart. "Good to meet you, sir. I've heard a lot about you."

"Most people have," replied the colonel, smiling wryly. "But not all of it good."

"I got better sources than most people, sir," replied the SEAL. "What I heard was good."

Each man had a handshake like a mechanical digger, and John Bergstrom swore that the floor shuddered as Bennett and Hart grinned and made a silent, white-knuckled military bond, which announced, one to the other, that they were partners in an exercise each of them knew was fraught with danger. There are no civilian handshakes quite like that.

"As you know, Lieutenant Commander," said Admiral Bergstrom, "Colonel Hart has been appointed at the highest level to take command of this operation. He has recently arrived here from the White House, where he has been working with Admiral Arnold Morgan, trying to get this thing on a fast track. However, we are working under the minor handicap of not yet knowing what our target is."

"Sir, I have not yet been briefed at all. I was told you were going to speak to me personally, which I think is why I'm here."

"Yes, of course. However, you do have a long plane ride with Colonel Hart in front of you, which will give everyone time to fill in the gaps. Meanwhile, I must stress the high degree of classification this operation has. And if you would both be seated, I will inform you where we stand."

"Yessir," replied the SEAL.

"You may have read in the newspapers last weekend a story about our attack submarine *Seawolf*?"

"Yessir, I did. The one that broke down or something. They're fixing it up somewhere in China, right?"

"Absolutely. Except it didn't break down. It got tangled up in a Chinese destroyer's towed array, and the bastards grabbed it and towed it back to Canton."

"Jesus."

"They incarcerated the crew, put 'em in jail in Canton, and have now moved them to an unknown jail. Admiral Morgan and I both believe they will torture the crew, in search of high-tech information."

"Are you kidding me?" Rusty Bennett was incredulous.

"Rusty, we know how anxious they are to steal every secret they can from us, involving both ICBM and attack submarines. They've spent millions of dollars and dozens of years doing it. And now they actually have America's top attack submarine captive in Canton, and more than a hundred American experts to help them finalize their blueprints. Admiral Morgan and I think they will stop at nothing to force that information out of them . . . and it gets worse."

"Not much, I hope."

"A lot . . . the Executive Officer of *Seawolf* is Linus Clarke, the President's only son."

Rusty Bennett hissed his inward breath through his front teeth. "Holy shit!" he said. "You mean Linus is in a Chinese slammer?"

"I do."

"What are the colonel and I supposed to do about it?"

"In short, get him, and all the others, out."

"Who, me?" said Lt. Commander Bennett hopelessly, in an exact parody of the phrase Colonel Hart himself had used three days previously.

"Well, not all on your own. You will undertake this operation in partnership with Colonel Hart and the overall team leader, Lieutenant Commander Rick Hunter, backed up by the most massive resources the U.S. Armed Forces have ever brought to bear on any peacetime mission in the entire history of Special Forces. There will be a total of sixty-four SEALs involved. You have been designated team leader of the recon force, the first men in from one of our nuclear submarines. Try to be quiet and not to kill too many Chinese guards, because if you get caught, it's all over."

The lieutenant commander smiled, raised his eyes heavenwards, and shook his head. "Are we up to this, Colonel?" he asked.

Frank laughed and replied, "I doubt it. But we better give it our best shot, otherwise the President of the United States is gonna be very, very disappointed in us. And that's not good."

All three men laughed. "Specially as we apparently don't know where the goddamned slammer is," said Rusty. "Anyway, I forgot to mention. I'm no good at jailbreaks . . . can't you get ahold of Al Capone or Machine Gun Kelly or someone?"

For the next hour, the three men continued to talk, Admiral Bergstrom half-waiting, as ever, for the line to ring from the White House and to hear the rasping voice of Arnold Morgan telling him, *We've found 'em.*

But that call did not come, and at 1500 the colonel and the SEAL left to collect their gear and join Rick Hunter in the car headed for the North Island airfield. They were the only three men who had been briefed on the full horror of the mission. John Bergstrom had long decided not to risk the dangers of the entire San Diego base finding out the shocking truth about *Seawolf.*

And now he stood outside his office and shook hands with the departing officers. "Okay, Rusty, Frank . . . go round up Rick Hunter and let's move on this one . . . and guys . . . I'll be thinking of you, every step of the way . . . anything you need . . . *anything* . . . you got it. Remember that. . . . God go with you."

The plan was for other officers and petty officers on the team to be briefed during the flight. The remainder of the SEALs would be given full details of the mission by Colonel Hart and Lt. Commander Hunter at a briefing to be called as soon as they boarded the carrier.

"Jesus Christ," muttered Admiral Bergstrom as he walked back into his office. "This could turn out to be a fucking nightmare."

2200 (local). Tuesday, July 11.
The Jail on Xiachuan Dao.

They had freed Linus Clarke from the chair to which he had been tied in the small hours of Monday morning. Since then he had been left entirely alone, save for one guard who brought him water and a bowl of rice at midday, and then again at 2200.

Tuesday had been silent, save for the guard bringing him the same meager offering sometime in the middle of the day. There was a bucket in the corner, which Linus was supposed to use as a head.

He was losing weight now, and his clothes were becoming disgusting. He had a dirty beard and was unrecognizable from the crisp XO who had reported for duty at Pearl Harbor only three weeks previously.

It was a little after 10:00 at night when the bright lights went on in his cell and a guard walked over and kicked him awake. Two of them walked him back to the torture chamber and sat him down, once more binding his legs and arms to the chair.

The guard lieutenant himself came in and looked at Linus, smiling. He walked around the chair, but asked no questions. Then he said very softly, "Just a little more persuasion, I think. And then you will tell us whatever we want to know, Lieutenant Commander Lucas?"

Linus summoned all of his remaining resolve and said nothing.

"You understand that everyone else has told us everything . . . only you are being foolishly stubborn."

Linus did not believe him. Judd Crocker and Brad Stockton would never crack. But had Einstein caved in? And what about the younger officers? Had they wilted before the interrogation? Linus no longer knew what to think.

The guard lieutenant said nothing directly. But he continued to walk and ponder the problem aloud, as if speaking of someone, rather than to them: "If you could just be sensible . . . so much easier for you . . . we only want to know routine matters . . . operational depths . . . the trim of the ship dived . . . various angles . . . ballasting procedures . . . the areas in which you are expert, Bruce Lucas . . . the operation of the periscope and the masts . . . all we ask is that you ensure we are able to operate such a submarine as well as you and your colleagues."

Linus said nothing. Stared straight ahead. At which point the guard lieutenant walked over to the doorway and returned carrying a bath towel, which he spread, and lifted and dropped gently over the head of Linus Clarke.

If the American XO had been afraid before, he now began to fall apart, trembling uncontrollably, trying not to scream out as the first water was poured onto the towel. Two nights ago he had thought he was dying. Tonight he had no further doubts. He could not withstand the terror of suffocation again. Perhaps he could lie. Tell them a load of rubbish. But what if they found out? His thoughts were rambling as the cold water splashed on the towel, always on top of his head.

And now breathing was becoming difficult again. The soaking wet cloth was sticking to his face. He was battling to suck air into his mouth and nose. And it was now a battle he was losing. The only air he could grab was through the towel, and the wetter it became, the more impossible the task. Linus was choking, and there was a special private terror in that.

He tried to make a noise, a noise of surrender, but he was only able to grunt, and he thought he was going to black out again. But suddenly the towel was lifted off his face, and he found himself staring into the dark, almond-shaped eyes of the diminutive guard lieutenant.

"Now, Lieutenant Commander, do you feel more like having a little talk now?"

The air rushed into the throbbing lungs of Linus Clarke and he sat there gasping, with the lieutenant holding the towel at forehead level, prepared in an instant to drop it back over the XO's face.

"YES! YES! WHATEVER THE HELL YOU WANT—BUT GET THAT FUCKING TOWEL AWAY FROM ME . . ."

"Of course," replied the tiny lieutenant. "I would regard that as a small courtesy among brother naval officers.

"Now, I propose we get you cleaned up and into some fresh clothes, and then you and Commander Li will take a little helicopter ride to Canton first thing in the morning . . . you can have a nice day talking to our technicians. Of course, if you do not tell the truth, we will bring you back here and you will spend the final moments of your life under this wet towel . . . but you understand that, Mr. Lucas, I am sure."

Linus Clarke nodded, grateful to be breathing, no longer interested in protecting the secrets of *Seawolf,* prepared to talk to them all day, if that was what it took to stop them from choking him to death.

Meanwhile, in the next cell, there was something approaching mayhem. It had begun in the middle of the evening when a guard had entered the cell that contained Captain Judd Crocker, the much younger Shawn Pearson, Chase Utley, and Jason Colson. For no discernible reason he had clubbed the navigator to the ground with the butt of his rifle, misjudging the fact that while the captain was still handcuffed behind his back, his legs were free, and he slammed his right foot right into the guard's groin.

Down went the guard, doubled over, writhing in agony. Judd, the full fury of his situation washing over him, almost kicked the guard to death. Three minutes later, when reinforcements arrived, he took out the first man into the cell with another stupendous kick to the groin. If his hands had been free, he probably could have flattened all six of them with the superhuman strength of the temporarily insane.

But his hands were not free, and now they had him alone, tied to a chair in one of the torture chambers, systematically beating him up. Only one of the Chinese guards had misjudged this situation, and he was on his way to hospital. The massively strong Judd Crocker had suddenly stood up straight and split the back of the chair from the seat. He spun around and carried the guard back with him, toppling the man over on his back. Then Judd too crashed backward, and the broken seat smacked right across the guard's face, breaking his nose and fracturing his skull.

It took six men to subdue the enraged submarine commander, but now they had him where they wanted him, his hands tied above his head to iron rings, embedded for years in the ceiling. His feet were spread apart, lashed to rings in the floor, and blood seeped from cuts around his eyes and face. His body was battered, his face unrecognizable. And every time they went at him he still roared insults . . . "FUCK OFF, YOU SLIT-EYED LITTLE PRICK !! FUCK YOU AND FUCK CHAIRMAN MAO . . . . YOU HAVEN'T GOT A DECENT PUNCH BETWEEN YOU . . . FUCK YOOOOOOOOU!"

At which point the mighty Judd Crocker passed out, and they cut him down, leaving him to bleed alone for the rest of the night.

In the next cell Cy Rothstein was equally battered. He had heard the commotion and guessed it was either Judd or Brad

Stockton, and knew that like him, the two American submariners would say nothing.

Indeed, they were trying the wet towel torture on Brad Stockton, who had passed out twice. He guessed correctly they would not want to kill him. And when, for the third time, the guard lieutenant had lifted up the cloth to check that he was still breathing, Brad had head-butted him with all of his force, slamming his forehead into the nose of the little guard chief, almost fracturing it, but not quite.

And now they were taking their revenge. Like Judd, Brad was lashed to the ceiling, taking a fearful beating. But he dealt with it in a different way from the captain. He just stayed silent and took the blows, until a smack with a rifle butt to the back of the head rendered him unconscious.

Thus far, Commander Li had only one American assistant.

2300 (Pacific Coast). Tuesday, July 11.
On board the U.S. Navy's Galaxy Air Freighter.

The 64 SEALs traveled in the rear of the gigantic aircraft as it inched its way across the Pacific. They were coming in to land now at Barbers Point, the U.S. Navy air base just along the southern coast from Pearl Harbor on the island of Oahu. The Galaxy came in from the northeast, the pilot facing toward the long rolling swells of the ocean, through which, just 23 days earlier, *Seawolf* had run with such effortless precision.

They were staying for only an hour, just to deliver an engine part and to take on sufficient fuel to last the Galaxy all the way to Diego Garcia in the Indian Ocean. The next stop at Okinawa would be even more brief.

During the outward flight to Hawaii, three more officers were introduced, both lieutenants stationed with Team Three in Coronado. Bobby Allensworth, an unarmed combat instructor, had abandoned a life of petty street crime in the South Central district of Los Angeles and joined the Marines at the age of 18. He was a black kid who never knew his father, never had a chance.

But the Marines gave him one, and he took it with both hands. Five years later he won a commission, and at the age of 29 they made him a lieutenant and gave him their blessing to join the SEALs.

Bobby was a supremely good athlete, a perfectly balanced amateur boxer with a right hook like a sledgehammer that had seen him into the finals of the Golden Gloves championships. He fought on the Marines team as a welterweight, but never considered turning pro. In his mind he was both a Marine and a Navy SEAL, and always would be. Bobby stood only five feet ten inches tall, but when he pinned on that golden Trident, he grew to be about ten feet. If he had a weakness it was a helpless sense of humor. He was always the first man to laugh, and Lt. Commander Hunter, who knew him well, said he should have been a comedian.

Bobby's cohort on the trip was another comedian, a sharp, wisecracking New Yorker from Little Italy, Lt. Paul Merloni, whose momma had never forgiven him for changing his name from Paolo.

Paul went straight from Manhattan public school to the Naval Academy, where he finished third in his class. He was a lieutenant on the guided missile cruiser *Lake Erie* when he requested an opportunity to join the SEALs. His lifelong hobby had been judo, and he had a black belt before he was 19. The SEALs liked him, and he taught Bobby Allensworth the art of unarmed combat. The two of them once cleared an entire bar in a never-to-be-forgotten brawl after a Chargers football game. They returned unharmed, except for a swelling on Bobby's knuckles sustained when he felled a 380-pound former defensive lineman with a lights-out right hook to the chin.

For this particular mission, Paul had one valuable asset—he had taught himself Cantonese while working with his judo instructors in Manhattan. He had practiced for years, and was almost fluent. Certainly he knew enough to lay up close to the prison compound when it was located and understand most, if not all, of what the guards were saying.

The third SEAL officer from Coronado was 34-year-old newly promoted Lt. Commander Olaf Davidson, who had been a team leader in Kosovo. Olaf, a huge six-foot-four-inch descendant of Norwegian fishermen in Newfoundland, had been a SEAL officer for 10 years, with no active command since the war in Yugoslavia. His specialty was boats, landing craft and the docking and operation of an SDV— swimmer delivery vehicle. Admiral Bergstrom considered him the best he had, and since it was almost certain the recon team would have to go in underwater, through the coastal shallows, wherever the jail turned out to be, the massive Olaf would hit the beach right behind Lt. Commander Rusty Bennett on the initial landing.

Two veteran petty officers were also among the final 20 SEALs who joined the flight from San Diego. One was Chief Steve Whipple from Chicago, a career naval engineer who had become a SEAL after earning a tryout as a running back with the Bears, but not making the grade. Chief Whipple, a six-foot-tall, tattooed hard man, had gone in with the SEAL team that took out Saddam's biggest oil rig in the Gulf War. He was only 21 then, and now he was 36. An instructor in jungle warfare, he had trained men for combat all over the world. Bobby Allensworth considered Steve to be the arm-wrestling champion of the inner universe.

His colleague Chief John McCarthy was another veteran, originally from Washington State. He was a quiet, shy, whip-thin mountaineering instructor who had been clambering all over the highest peaks of the Cascade Range since he was 10 years old. He was also king of the grappling irons, a czar among rope climbers, and the resident assassin among marauding SEALs. If they had to scale walls to enter the jail, Chief McCarthy would lead the way, his big SEAL fighting knife inches from his right hand at all times.

There were also three British SAS men, seconded to the SEALs for this particular mission at the express request of Colonel Mike Andrews. There was Sergeant Fred Jones from Dorset and his corporal, Syd Thomas, a 36-year-old Londoner from the East End. These two had worked deep behind enemy lines in Iraq in 1991, singlehandedly taken out two SCUD missile mobile launchers, and blown up two entire trucks full of Saddam's elite commandos on the way out. Syd currently had a half-dozen SEALs falling about laughing at stories of his antics in the desert, particularly his daredevil exploit in "cutting a goat out of some towelhead's herd, specially for our roast Sunday lunch, and Freddie went and set it on fire in the embers of the fucking blown-up truck . . . it was like eating old fireworks."

The third SAS man was one of the youngest sergeants in the regiment, Charlie Murphy, an ex-paratrooper from Northern Ireland. Charlie had been a group leader in Kosovo, operating deep in the hills, trying to drive the Serbs out. He and three troopers cleared them out of one village, destroying three jeeps, a tank and two trucks. They then stayed on and helped the wounded Kosovar civilians, holding off a determined attack by 50 more Serbs. The operation was "black," Special Forces, otherwise Charlie Murphy would have been awarded a Victoria Cross, Britain's highest battle honor. As it was, Charlie's war simply never happened.

The men in the Galaxy were not average people. And they rode together, slipping down through the cloudless sky into Hawaii with much on their minds, saying very little, each man trying to imagine what the jail would look like when it was finally located.

In the hold of the Galaxy was stowed an astounding volume of gear, big crates containing all the combat equipment they would use on this mission to split wide apart the military jail that held the *Seawolves*. There would be no Chinese prisoners taken.

Only 12 men would make the landing underwater, and each of them had packed their own custom-made, highly flexible neoprene wet suits. In fact, there were four extra suits in case of emergency. If these four men were not required, they would go in with the main team. Thus there were 16 pairs of extra-large SEAL flippers, all custom-made, all oversized for extra speed through the water, all bearing the student number awarded to each man as he passed the BUD/S course. The 16 had also packed at least two pairs of modern commercial scuba divers' masks each, their bright Day-Glo colors carefully obscured with black water-resistant tape.

None of the swimmers would wear watches because of the possibility of a glint shining off the metal through the water alerting a sentry. Instead, the SEALs would swim in holding a specially designed "attack board" in front of them. This is a small, two-handled platform that displays a compass, a depth gauge and an unobtrusive watch. Thus the swimmer can kick through the water with both hands on his attack board with the details of time, depth and direction laid out right in front of his eyes.

Because the target was as yet unknown, it was possible that the SEALs might have to go in underwater, perhaps through a harbor. This meant a heavy supply of Draegers, the special underwater breathing apparatus that leaves no telltale trail of bubbles like regular scuba equipment. The Draegers contain about 13 cubic feet of oxygen at 2,000 pounds per square inch, enough to last a SEAL for maybe four hours. The genius of the device is a recycling system for the oxygen as it is exhaled, mostly unused. This eliminates the bubbles. On land the Draeger is heavy, 35 pounds. In the water it is weightless.

The principal weapon selected for the attack was the elite German Heckler & Koch MP-5, a small, deadly accurate submachine gun, priceless at close quarters, flawless at 25 yards, the SEALs' most comforting friend. There were 60 of them crated in the hold of the Galaxy. In addition, all the SEALs would go in with their regular Sig Sauer 9mm pistol, in its strapped-down holster containing two extra 15-round magazines right above the flap.

The main assault team was scheduled to take in four machine guns, the "light" M-60 E3, which weighs more than 30 pounds with two belts of 100 linked rounds, ready to fire. But that's only 20 seconds of sustained fire for the lone SEAL machine gunners, and extra assistance would be required to carry in 12 belts per gun, providing two minutes of sustained fire in case of total emergency.

There were eight carefully knotted black nylon climbing ropes with steel grappling hooks stored in one separate crate, along with a dozen pairs of powerful night-sight binoculars. Eight light aluminum ladders, between 12 and 18 feet high, with eight extensions, had been sprayed jet black, with a matte finish, and were stored in light, strong cardboard containers with handles, easy and not too heavy for a couple of SEALs to transport through difficult terrain. A decision on ladders or grappling irons would be made by Rusty Bennett's recon team.

In special sealed cases was the SEALs' supply of high explosives, starting with six limpet mines in case they were required to take out a couple of patrol boats. The mines, complete with "back-pack" harnesses for swimming in, were packed together with their magnets and timed detonators. A couple of these little devils, strategically placed, could break the back of an aircraft carrier.

Another case contained a dozen Mk 138 satchel charges, a perfectly simple shoulder bag containing about 40 pounds of explosives, to be primed with a standard nonelectric M-7 blasting cap at the end of its fuse. Lean this innocent-looking rucksack up against the wall of a good-sized detached house, and that house will shortly be a memory.

The SEALs preferred method of blasting anything to smithereens is plastic explosive called C4. It looks like white modeling clay, and can likewise be molded into any shape. C4 works off regular M700 time fuse, the thin green plastic cord full of gunpowder that burns at around one foot per 40 seconds. You can split the end with a knife and light it with a match, but SEALs *hate* light at night and much prefer the M-60 fuse lighter, a little plastic device with a spring-loaded pin, like a shotgun. It makes only a soft thud, and right after that you start to hear the sizzle of the black powder burning along to the cap. This is an excellent time to run like hell. There was a lot of C4, and a lot of time fuse in the hold of the Galaxy.

There were also several crates of detonating cord, packed in regular 500-foot spools. "Det-cord" is known to Special Forces throughout the world. This stuff looks like regular time fuse, except it's a little thicker, a quarter-inch in diameter, and instead of burning at one foot per 40 seconds, it explodes at roughly five miles per second, because it's stuffed with some diabolically high explosive called PETN. SEALs love det-cord because they can wrap it around anything and join up different, separate lengths all to explode at the same time.

In addition to the military hardware there were cases of first aid materials, codeine, morphine, battle dressings, and bandages. There was insect repellent, water purification tablets, lactate solutions, catheter kits for IVs, and groundsheets. The SEALs have *never* left a man to die. If a colleague is badly wounded, they treat him and carry him out, no matter what. If they're trapped, they dig in and fight until there's no one left, but this, of course, normally applies to the enemy.

Other cases contained their communication equipment, which included a small, two-second "shriek" device to the satellites. There were three fairly heavy regular radios with enough range to reach the aircraft carrier, but these would almost certainly not be used because of the risk of interception. Only in the most dire emergency would the SEAL teams fire up one of these. Dire emergency to these men means the threat of certain, imminent death. There was also a case containing state-of-the art GPS systems, 20 of them, because the terrain and countryside surrounding the jail were at this stage unknown to them.

The recon team would also go in with camouflage nets to shield them while they watched, plus trenching tools to dig and bury waste and machetes to hack their way through any bad jungle they ran into. There would be the usual supply of waterproof ponchos. And, of course, two laptop computers for the SEALs who would lie in the forest recording the movements of the Chinese guards. No one is as observant as a trained Special Forces soldier.

The SEALs did not disembark in Hawaii. The refueling was completed rapidly, and the Galaxy was back in the air by midnight, growling its way west, 25,000 feet above the Pacific wilderness, through retreating time zones that would make this an endless night for the sleeping Special Forces bound for Okinawa.

When they landed it should be 9:00 A.M. on Wednesday, July 12. But of course it would not be. Instead it would be 9:00 A.M. *plus 16 hours*, which made it precisely one o'clock in the morning *the next day*, Thursday, July 13. To complicate matters even further, it was at that time midday on Wednesday in Washington. And right there, complicated matters were moving almost as fast as the time zones.

1200. Wednesday, July 12.
Office of Admiral Morgan. The White House.

"I DO NOT FUCKING UNDERSTAND IT!" raged Arnold Morgan. "WE HAVE BILLIONS OF DOLLARS' WORTH OF EQUIPMENT

FLOATING AROUND THE STRATOSPHERE, SUPPOSEDLY
ABLE TO READ THE GODDAMNED WORTHLESS FUCKING
HEADLINES IN THE *WASHINGTON POST.* AND THEY CANNOT
FIND MORE THAN ONE HUNDRED FUCKING SAILORS WAN-
DERING AROUND SOME FUCKING BEACH IN THE SOUTH
CHINA SEA . . ."

The admiral reflected mightily, pacing his office. "FUCK ME!"
he added, glaring at the portrait of General Patton on the office
wall. "YES!" he confirmed. "YOU MIGHT WELL LOOK SERIOUS,
GEORGE. BILLIONS AND BILLIONS OF GODDAMNED DOL-
LARS' WORTH OF STUFF—ADMINISTERED BY MORONS."

And he glared some more around the completely empty room.
"AND WHO IS THE CHIEF FUCKING MORON? THE LEADER OF
THE GODDAMNED PACK . . . MORON FUCKING SUPREMO!
GEORGE FUCKING MORRIS, THAT'S WHO. ADMIRAL GEORGE
R. MORRIS, C-IN-C MORON SQUADRON, FORT FUCKING
MORON, MORONLAND."

The President's National Security Adviser was beside himself
with anxiety. For three days now the American satellites had been
photographing the shores of the South China Sea in search of any
clue there might be as to the whereabouts of the crew of *Seawolf.*
The fact was, there was nothing. No sign of a major group of men
where previously there had been nothing, no sign of military activity, no sign of anything out of the ordinary. If he could have, Arnold
Morgan would have spun the Earth on its axis even faster to give
the overheads a few extra passes.

With every passing hour, his frustration mounted. He had personally sanctioned the spending of millions and millions of dollars,
sending in one of the biggest and best Special Forces team ever
assembled in peacetime. And now, he knew, they were due to land
in Okinawa and then make their way out to the *Ronald Reagan,*
presently 60 miles offshore in the company of her entire Battle
Group.

He had snatched Colonel Hart from the London embassy to take
overall command of the operation. He had spent God knew how
many thousands of dollars relocating the colonel's family back to

Washington. He had made promises to the President of the United States. And, far from having to report failure, he couldn't even find the fucking target.

"Jesus Christ!" groaned Arnold Morgan. "What the hell did I ever do to deserve all this bullshit?"

Just then the serenely beautiful Kathy O'Brien slipped into the room and inquired, "Darling. Do I detect you might be working yourself up into an absolute lather?"

"Yes," he growled. "Leave me to my misery. Can I have a cup of coffee?"

"Would you like some salad or something? You've been here since four A.M."

"You mean as well as every damn thing, I've got to pretend I'm some kind of a goddamned rabbit?"

"You can have some lovely vinegar and olive oil dressing on it. Rabbits eat it plain."

"BEEF, WOMAN!" he roared, laughing at his own ridiculous imitation of Henry VIII. "Bring me beef—rare slices cleaved by my master-at-arms, between mighty slices of rye bread, with a sizeable dollop of mayonnaise right in the middle . . . and mustard."

"You're not having beef. You eat too much of it. You can have tuna, the chicken of the sea."

"I don't want TUNA!" he yelled, still laughing. "I loathe the chicken of the sea. I want the roast beef of the land. With mayonnaise. And mustard."

"Well, you're not getting it."

The admiral stormed to the window, gazed out onto the White House lawn, and raised his arms heavenward, like Sampson. "My undying love for you, Ms. O'Brien," he said, pompously, "does not give you the right to deny me my reasonable share of the finer things in life . . ."

"The finer things in life do not include roast beef sandwiches dripping with mayonnaise and devoured about seventeen times a week."

"Fifteen," he chuckled. "Where's George, Kathy? Where is the moronic admiral who is supposed to bring me glad tidings of the battle in the South China Sea?"

"I can't say I am able to answer that," she replied, and just then the phone rang. Expertly she pirouetted around and picked up the pastel green receiver from his desk.

From the window he growled, "I speak only to the President. I'm too depressed to deal with anyone else. Anyway, I'm on my lunch break, and even that's turning into some kind of hell."

"Hello, Admiral Morgan's office . . . may I ask who's calling?

"Arnold," she said, pressing the HOLD button. "It's for you . . . you'd better take it."

"IS IT THE PRESIDENT OF THE UNITED STATES? If not, I am formally at lunch. No calls."

"No, it's not the President. It's Admiral Morris."

"WHAT!" Admiral Morgan bounded across the room like a starving panther who had sighted a roast beef sandwich.

"George . . ."

The voice on the other end was brief and clipped. "Arnold, I think we've found 'em. I got the photographs. Helicopter right outside. I'm on my way in. See you in twenty."

Arnold Morgan almost died of happiness. He lifted his right leg and flashed his shiny right shoe back and forth, pumping his right arm.

"GEORGE!" he exclaimed, chuckling. "George Morris. Doesn't seem too swift when you first meet him, mind. But he's careful, painstaking and misses nothing. The perfect detective intelligence officer. What a stroke of pure genius when I appointed him to replace me . . . pure genius."

"I thought you just said he was a moron," said Kathy, swishing across the room toward the door to order his tunafish sandwich and coffee for two.

The ensuing 20 minutes were almost more than the admiral could endure. He completely lost his appetite and, leaving even the coffee, he walked outside to the helicopter pad to wait with the security guards for the chopper from Fort Meade. And he saw it coming a long way out.

It made one small pass over the White House lawn, checked in with the control room, manned as always by Marines, and came clattering down onto the concrete square. A Marine guard moved smartly over to open the door, and Admiral George Morris disembarked clumsily, holding his briefcase and two big files, one spilling over with a Navy chart.

"Hi, George," said Arnold Morgan. "We cracked it?"

"I think so, sir. If we haven't, we've discovered something even bigger."

"There isn't anything bigger."

The two men hurried to the West Wing, where one of the agents momentarily fussed about a badge for Admiral Morris. That lasted for almost three seconds, before Arnold Morgan snapped, "I do not have time for that crap, y'hear? Get the badge and bring it to my office . . . that upsets you or your boss, run along to the Oval Office and tell the President."

And with that he hustled Admiral Morris through the door and on down the passage to his own office, never even hearing the agent mutter, "Yessir."

Inside the big carpeted headquarters of the National Security Adviser, Kathy waited with coffee. George Morris opened a file and laid a line of 8 x 10 photographs on Arnold Morgan's desk.

"Okay, sir. Let me take you through this in sequence . . . that way you'll know as much as we do. Now, take this picture shot from the overhead about three weeks ago . . . this is one of our benchmarks . . . a direct shot of a couple of islands around eighty miles west of the Pearl River Delta . . . see, we got almost nothing on it. The place is just about uninhabited save for this cluster of probably empty buildings in the north.

"Now, sir. I put a man on this. Pulled up photographs for the past five years. There's never been so much as one person in any picture we've ever had in that time. Of course I had other people studying other places along that coast . . . but this is where we got a development.

"In the past we've photographed it irregularly, but subsequent to your orders last weekend, we have intensified all our photography from the overheads, taking in this stretch of coast eighty miles east up to Houmen, and along here westerly to this island. It's called Xiachuan, and quite frankly it was right at the limit of the range you gave us . . . but we've zoomed in on it and done blowups that I'm working toward."

Arnold Morgan picked up the first two pictures and studied them, then moved on to the next.

"Now, sir. Take a look at this. See the difference? Right here . . . right here . . ."

"Where?"

"Here, sir . . . this little white spot near the buildings.

"It's too small, George. Gimme a magnifying glass, will you?"

The admiral leveled the magnifier over the spot and peered through it. "Holy shit! It's a helicopter."

"Right, sir. Now have a look at the other white mark down by the water . . ."

"Christ, George . . . it's a Navy ship."

"Right. Now take a look at the next picture . . . see, right here, the white mark's gone . . . but up here we can see it again . . . right off the coast . . . heading for Canton . . . then here, sir, we got another shot four hours later and it's back . . . see, right here."

Arnold Morgan nodded. "And what the hell, you asked, is all this military activity doing on this deserted Chinese island?"

"Right, sir. So we blew up the photographs, showing every aspect of the place. And here is the first picture. Those old buildings represent a jail . . . see . . . there's the watchtowers. And suddenly, right here, we have an outcrop of radio aerials . . . and the boat's back. Looks like it patrols for four hours and then returns. Here's a sequence of photographs taken approximately every four hours . . . and here's the blowup. We identify it as one of those Chinese fast-attack crafts . . . Huangfens . . . guess they weigh about two hundred tons . . . so far as I remember, they're fitted with Russian guns."

"George, we're getting warm . . . I feel it."

"Right, sir. But I have not finished. Now look at this . . . these are shots of the central yard in the jail. There are people, quite a lot of them, in this shot. What would you say? Maybe a dozen, wandering around . . . see this colored shot . . . they're wearing full uniform, with shouldered arms . . . dark blue . . . Navy. These guys are on duty . . . in the middle of a desert island. In company with a military helicopter, new communications, and a two-hundred-ton patrol boat. Right inside the range you and Colonel Hart gave us for the ferryboat last Sunday. Sir, we've found 'em. No doubt."

"George, if they're not guarding our prisoners, they're guarding someone else's. But the key is the set of pictures you have from last Thursday, this one here . . . no radio, no chopper, no patrol. By late Saturday, the infrared shots, right here, the stuff was all in place. That night, Saturday, the ferry leaves Canton with our guys, arrives Sunday morning . . . and your next picture sequence shows a dozen guards patrolling every time the camera clicks . . ."

"And, sir . . . in this photograph taken in the small hours of Monday morning . . . look here . . . you can see the lights in the towers are on, sweeping across this courtyard . . ."

"By God, George, you're right again. We got 'em."

Admiral Morris gathered up the photographs, left some for reference for the National Security Adviser, and made his exit, "back to the factory."

Arnold Morgan switched on his big illuminated computer screen and pulled up the chart that featured the entire area around the Pearl River Delta. He needed to think before he contacted John Bergstrom, and he needed to give himself a detailed picture of the tiny island the Navy SEALs must now assault.

He called Kathy in and asked her to bring her notebook, writing down his thoughts as he called them out.

"Okay. It's called Xiachuan Dao. It's six miles long and three at its widest point. It's set about four miles to the west of the island of Shangchuan, which is approximately twice as big. Chart reference 21.40N 112.35E. The jail is situated way up in the northeast corner of the island, which is almost on the edge, since the island is set diagonally in shallow water, northeast to southwest.

"Chart shows one big mountain in the south called Guanyin Shan, thirteen hundred feet high. There's another peak rising to sixteen hundred feet guarding the entire northern end. There's a long flat peninsula in the southwest jutting almost a mile out into the ocean.

"The western side is dominated by a long marshy mudflat, so whatever we do, we won't make any kind of a landing there. The only deep water, close in, lies between the two islands, which is how the ferry got in. And the patrol boat. There's probably twenty feet in that area, which means we probably go in from the south, and get out to the east using inflatables, four of 'em.

"Incoming from the South China Sea my chart shows a depth of forty-two feet a half-mile off the southern peninsula. Following the 112.30-degree line of longitude, I'm showing a very gentle shelf into deeper water, six miles before it gets to seventy-five feet, then another three miles to one hundred feet depth, twelve more miles to one hundred and fifty feet . . . as submarine country goes, it's approximately fucking lousy . . . sorry, Kathy, I thought you were John Bergstrom."

Kathy giggled at the steely-eyed tyrant she adored.

"To find really decent water, two-hundred-foot-plus depth, you have to be sixty miles out, which means the submarines are probably going to end up on the surface during the takeout, but by then the Chinese Navy is going to be totally involved with a nuclear catastrophe in their own dockyard. Any problems with a Chinese patrol, we sink the sonofabitch, right?"

"Right," said Kathy.

"Okay, sweetheart. Print that out for me, will you . . . then get John Bergstrom on a secure line."

He continued staring at the chart, trying to imagine the terrain the SEALs' reconnaissance party would encounter. Since the place had been uninhabited for so long, he assumed they would hit primary forest, a landscape dominated by tall, uncut trees, which creates darkness below and thus reduces undergrowth. That was good. What was also good was an ocean bottom that appeared sandy rather than rocky. If the submarine commanders wanted to take a few minor chances creeping in, in the dark, deep as possible in shallow water, they wouldn't do much worse than scrape off a few barnacles. That was also good.

The secure phone rang. Admiral Morgan picked it up and someone said, "Just a moment, Admiral Bergstrom is right here . . ."

"Arnie . . . what news?"

"We found 'em, John. Island, 21.40N 112.35E. I've made my first observations . . . Kathy's just printing 'em out . . . get 'em off the satellite in ten. George has a lot of good pix . . . you should have 'em electronically inside thirty."

"Perfect. The guys have landed. It's around oh-one hundred Thursday. They should all be on the *Reagan* by oh-four hundred. You have a time frame in mind?"

"Is the submarine ready?"

"Yessir. Right on station. Five miles off the carrier's bow, my last report. ASDV's prepared, in the shelter on deck."

"According to my charts, John, we're nine hundred and fifty miles out—which means that if we leave right away the guys will be in the area, say sixty miles south in deepish water, by Friday afternoon . . . they go in as soon as it's dark . . . and we want 'em out by oh-two hundred Sunday morning . . . Operation Nighthawk starts Sunday night. It's tight. Too tight. But it's now or never."

"You got it, sir . . . we'll talk in an hour. I got Frank Hart on the other line . . . secure from Okinawa . . .. we're all set."

Arnold Morgan smiled darkly, picked up his green telephone and hit a button connecting him to the President's secretary. "Hi, Miss Jane," he said. "Arnold Morgan here. Would you tell the President to cease whatever the hell he's doing for the next ten minutes, and report to my office with the utmost speed and stealth."

Miss Jane laughed, despite the fact that it was entirely possible no one in the entire history of the White House had ever issued such a blunt command to a sitting President of the United States.

She relayed the message verbatim to the Chief Executive, who also laughed, as much as he was capable of laughing these days, and excused himself from a meeting with Harcourt Travis and the Israeli ambassador. Then he made his way to Admiral Morgan's office with the utmost speed and stealth.

"Hey, Arnie . . . how do we look?"

"Sir, we look just about as good as it's possible to look, given our awful circumstances."

"Have we found 'em?"

"Yup, we found 'em."

"Have we got a shot at rescue?"

"It's under way, sir. Siddown. Let me fill you in."

When President Clarke returned to the Oval Office 20 minutes later, he no longer felt that the burden of the catastrophe in Canton was entirely on his shoulders. Right now he felt he was sharing it with a lot of very, very good guys, and that in the end, there was a real chance Linus would make it home. He had not felt that way before.

0330 (local). Thursday, July 13.
U.S. Navy Operational Runway. Okinawa-Jima.

The huge Sea Stallion helicopter came thundering out of the night for the third time, hovering and then touching down gently on the runway lately vacated by the Galaxy. Off to the left, standing outside in the warm air blowing southerly off the Philippine Sea, were Lt. Commander Rick Hunter, Chief Petty Officer John McCarthy, and a half-dozen other SEALs who had been supervising the loading of the gear and their 40-odd colleagues who had already made the journey out to the *Ronald Reagan*.

Colonel Hart was working high in the tower with Lt. Commander Bennett and a small staff setting up the operational headquarters on the carrier. These were excellent quarters, because Admiral Art Barry, the battle group commander, had decided the SEAL commander should work in conjunction with his own 70-strong staff in the admiral's own ample-sized ops room.

This was principally because Operation Nighthawk would be relatively short, just a few days, and it would not be worth installing a brand-new set of comms and computerized naval charts. Besides, Admiral Barry was longing to know precisely what was going on, and he very much wanted to work with the legendary Colonel Hart, around whom an unmistakable aura of mystique revolved.

Anyway, Art Barry now had the carrier under way, moving southwesterly in a long swell toward Taiwan at around 25 knots. When Rick Hunter and his men arrived they would have made by far the longest of the three helicopter journeys. But the Sea Stallion had a range of almost 600 miles and clattered along at 130 knots, eating up the now 90-mile journey from Okinawa in 45 minutes.

It touched down on the gigantic 1,090-foot-long flight deck of the carrier at 0430, and the SEALs set about unloading the last of their crates, the ones with the high explosive. There were two forklift trucks and four ordnance staff from the carrier to assist in the removal of the C4, the limpet mines, and the 40-pound satchel charges, and to ensure that they were safely stored, ready for transportation to the island of Xiachuang.

Chief John McCarthy went down in the aft lift on the port side with the forklifts in order to check and mark the explosive cases in their designated area. Several of the other SEALs, already regarded with some awe by the deck crew, stood around looking at the lines of fighter/attack aircraft, placed neatly around the perimeters of the flight deck, with the great central runway left clear for landing on at all times. The carrier's giant steam catapults can have these fighters away at 20-second intervals if necessary.

Flight crew pointed out the aerial cavalry gathered on the deck of this ferocious example of front-line United States naval muscle: the 20 F-14D Tomcats, ranged in two lines on the starboard side. Toward the stern, the SEALs could see four EA-6B Prowlers, four Hawkeyes, six Vikings, two Shadows, and six helicopters.

In two long lines to starboard was a total of 36 F/A-18 Hornets, the lightning-fast workhorse of the U.S. naval attack strike force. Out here in the black of the Pacific night, the *Ronald Reagan*, America's mighty fortress at sea, seemed to flex its rippling muscles as it pitched heavily through the rising ocean, with more than 2,000 fathoms beneath the keel. And it seemed well nigh incredible that the all-powerful U.S. military machine could not just roar in anger, right out here from this colossus of an aircraft carrier, and terrify the Chinese into returning *Seawolf* and the men who drove her.

But the subtleties of modern checks and balances of power, and the appalling ramifications of war on a global scale, sometimes render such monstrous examples of brute strength back to the age of the dinosaurs. Sometimes it works, but not always. And this was one

of the tricky ones. The SEALs' silent methods, involving high planning and low cunning, more often than not left an enemy utterly
bewildered as to the identity of the culprit.

God willing, this weekend would see them carry out their
deadly work in secrecy. And it was paradoxical that the most terrifying secret of all was already standing unrecognized, less than 100
feet away, from the on-deck SEALs. No one noticed two F/A-18
Hornets, armed, parked separately at the end of the line, both
ready to go, the second in case the first failed to start. No chances
taken.

Clipped underneath the fuselage of each Hornet was a 14-foot-
long, dark green, laser-guided armor-piercing Paveways bomb, its
warhead containing almost 1,000 pounds of compacted high explosive, sufficient to penetrate the heavy steel hull of a big nuclear
submarine.

0900 (local). Friday, July 14.
Admiral's Briefing Room. USS *Ronald Reagan*.
20.15N 116.10E. Speed 30.

THERE WERE 15 MEN IN ATTENDANCE, INCLUDING
the 12 SEALs who would make the insertion into the island
tonight, led by Lt. Commander Rusty Bennett. He sat at the main
table with the mission's forward platoon leader, Lt. Commander
Rick Hunter. In front of them sat Rusty's number two man, the
ASDV and landing boat expert Lt. Commander Olaf Davidson.
There were two lieutenants, Paul Merloni and Dan Conway; the
grappling-iron ace Chief Petty Officer John McCarthy; and the
ex–deep water fisherman Petty Officer Catfish Jones. The two
SEALs from the bayous, Rattlesnake Davies and the alligator-
killing Buster Townsend, were also there, plus four other noncom-
missioned SEALs.

Standing up behind the table was the overall mission controller,

Colonel Frank Hart, now wearing a SEAL uniform, holding a mahogany officer's baton. Behind him was a large bulletin board to which was pinned a chart of the island of Xiachuan. At the back of the room, allowed to sit in, was Rear Admiral Art Barry.

The doors were locked, and outside, two armed sentries were on duty. No one was permitted entry. And the tension inside the room was high. All of the SEALs sat silently, alone with their thoughts, not least the one they all tried to hide away: *"Tonight may be the last night of my life."*

Frank Hart was slowly pacing the width of the room in front of the chart. There was taughtness written all over his face. "Gentlemen," he said, "you all know the broad outline of tonight's mission, which you must regard as covert in the extreme. You are to land on the island, in the south, establish a rendezvous point behind the beach, and then the observation party will move northeast, a distance of six miles, probably through tall jungle, and establish two observation posts as near to the jail as possible without getting caught.

"Now I have delayed this briefing until the last moment, because it is essential that it remain fresh in your minds. For those of you who have not been told, I will now let you know formally. Inside that jail, probably undergoing the harshest form of interrogation, is the entire crew of *Seawolf*, among them the ship's executive officer, Lieutenant Commander Linus Clarke, the son of the President of the United States.

"It is unnecessary for me to explain the gravity of that situation, save to say that immediately upon your safe return to the carrier, with detailed maps, diagrams, and notes, we will be sending in one of the largest Special Forces expeditions ever assembled by the United States in peacetime to rescue the prisoners and get them out to the carrier.

"We will attack suddenly and brutally. It is entirely likely that there will be no Chinese military survivors . . . but, gentlemen, there is one thought that must never leave your minds: Discovery is unacceptable. If you should be caught, the entire mission will be over . . . because the Chinese will instantly reinforce the island with helicopters, heavy ordnance, troops and maybe even warships standing offshore . . . and they will remove the prisoners to another jail, none of whom will ever see their homeland again."

The colonel paused. Allowed his words to hit home. And he walked back across the room before continuing, "I doubt that any of you will ever undertake any mission so carefully observed from the Oval Office . . . and your watchword must be 'care'—because if you should be careless even for one split second, and you should be detected even by one guard, we will almost certainly have to abort the mission, because massive Chinese reinforcements will be there inside the hour. Should you kill the guard and get away yourselves, the result will be the same, because he'll be missed.

"I can only ask your indulgence when I say one more time . . . for Christ's sake, be careful."

He walked to the table and selected a small sheaf of papers, which he first studied and then replaced.

"In my capacity as mission controller, I will now give you our timetable. Each of you will be given a copy that you will memorize and then destroy . . . two hours from now you will embark in the helicopters and they will fly you with your gear out to the Los Angeles–class nuclear submarine USS *Greenville*, which is currently patrolling a couple of miles off our starboard beam.

"Right now, we're two hundred and ten miles south of the Chinese coast, and you will thus make the rest of the journey to Xiachuan in the submarine, running deep toward the mainland until we essentially run out of water, about thirty miles from shore. At that point, the eight underwater SEALs will board the ASDV, which you will see is in dry dock on the deck, and run in to about a half-mile from the shore when it starts to get really shallow, only about fifty feet of depth—the ASDV is thirty feet high.

"From there you will disembark and swim in. The water's warm, sandy bottom, not rough, no sharks to speak of . . . the other four will make the journey in a small Zodiac inflatable, cutting the engine and paddling in the final thousand yards. The Chinese do have a fast-attack patrol boat moored alongside on the island, but we have not observed it leaving before midnight. We'll be in by then.

"We then establish our rendezvous point dragging the boat and its cargo up the beach into the cover of the trees. Inside the boat will be two machine guns, two trenching shovels, medical supplies, the radio, GPS, ammunition, a few hand grenades and three smoke grenades, compass, laptop, binoculars, camouflage nets, and two waterproof shelters. Plus, of course, cold water and food. As you all know, it can rain like hell out here in July—it's doing it now, for Christ's sake.

"As SEALs you will all be responsible for your own weapons . . . and the observation party will leave the rendezvous point almost instantly . . . soon as you're organized."

He pointed at the chart, tracing with his baton a line from the southwestern peninsula, where they were scheduled to make their landing, to the northeast where the jail was located. "There are a couple of mountains, both of which you go around . . . but this one here, north of the jail, has slopes that look to me as if they may give some vantage points right above the jail, and that is where you want to make your OP. Don't take out the guards, because if you do, the game will be up. Try to find a nice quiet spot and mentally take the place to pieces, bring us back the information . . . and the Big Team will go in on Sunday night.

"Basically I'd like you guys in position by around twenty-three hundred on Friday night . . . and on your way out by oh two hundred on Sunday morning . . . which should give you time to assess the guards, their numbers and patrols throughout the day and night . . . you will of course leave the island quickly, the same way you entered, via the RV, swimming out to the ASDV, which you locate with the GPS and its homing beep . . . but four men will remain on the island to help the guys get in on Sunday night.

"The landing point for the main assault force will be different from the departure point right here . . . because we're going to have a lot of people leaving, and we want a beach as close as possible to the jail, which will be subdued by then.

"For the prisoner rescue, and the main force extraction, we may have some of our guys in bad shape . . . we'll have eight big inflatables working, but it will probably take two, maybe three trips out to the deeper water where our submarines will be waiting. Now I'll hand you over to your team leader, Lieutenant Commander Rusty Bennett, who will announce the detailed orders . . . Rusty?"

The iron man from the Maine coast stood up and began immediately. "If it's at all possible I want the twelve of us inside that submarine very fast. Our gear has already been transferred and the inflatable's on board. But the Chinese have their own satellites and I don't want them to get a shot of us making a transfer two hundred miles off the coast. So that means we're gonna fast-rope it, soon as the chopper gets over the deck, it's gloves on and down, then straight inside. Anyone not comfortable with that?" The SEALs stayed silent.

"Right, when we exit the submarine, into the ASDV, there will be eight of us. Lieutenant Commander Davidson will be in charge of the exit from the dry dock in company with Petty Officer Catfish, Hank, and Al. Inside the ASDV with me will be Lieutenant Merloni, Lieutenant Conway, Chief McCarthy, Rattlesnake Davies, Buster Townsend, John and Bill.

"The submarine will give us a fifty-five-minute start, while we run in at eighteen knots. Then it will surface while Lieutenant Commander Davidson, Petty Officer Jones, John and Bill very carefully lower the Zodiac into the water with all the stuff. And don't for Christ's sake let it tip over. The submarine will then disappear and you guys will run in at high speed going straight for the landing beach, located at GPS 21.36N 112.315E. You will find that the Zodiac, which is only a twenty-footer, has an especially big engine, a Johnson Two-fifty, and it will go like a bat out of hell. It also carries a lot of extra gas. We expect the seas to be calm inshore, under rainy skies, and you should knock the journey off in under the hour, even paddling in the last thousand. Don't, by the way, run over the fucking swimmers!

"I've timed it so that we should be on the beach fifteen minutes before the Zodiac. That way we gotta lot of muscle to carry the boat fast, up into the undergrowth, and establish our RV. We will then dust off our tracks on the beach, pick our spot, get the waterproof shelter up under camouflage nets, establish one of the machine guns and split up.

"The RV group commander will be Lieutenant Commander Davidson, and he will be accompanied by Catfish, Hank and Al. These four men will not leave the island when the swimmers return to the submarines. Instead they will remain on station at the RV point before moving to the assault beach where the Big Team comes in. That's located on the east side of the island, south-facing, a fraction less than a mile southwesterly from the jail, GPS 21.39N 112.38E. The small Zodiac will eventually join the four boats ferrying the guys out early Sunday morning.

"Is all that clear?"

"Sir." Everyone nodded.

"Meanwhile, the eight of us, Paul Merloni, Chief McCarthy, Rattlesnake, Buster, Dan, John and Bill, will get our wetsuits off and get into jungle gear, with camouflage. We'll travel as light as we can, but since it's always fucking raining, we'll want stuff to keep us dry, and we'll have to take a machine gun in case we get into real trouble and have to fight our way out. Likewise a radio and a few smoke grenades to help the rescue helicopters should we have to whistle 'em up. But I really hope that will not be necessary.

"Our walk into the observation area will be six miles through uninhabited primary forest. The colonel here has already supervised the loading of each man's pack, distributing the gear equally among us. We don't have to think about that. We just saddle up and leave the RV point, right? Unhappily, we do have to take a couple of shovels to get rid of any waste, *and* we will need machetes because we have to stay on bearing and we may meet impenetrable forest. We also want a coupla pairs of heavy pruning shears in case we have to cut silently. But we don't need explosives. Remember, we are a reconnaissance party and our aim is to remain totally undetected . . . now, how about questions . . . address them to Colonel Hart."

"Sir, do we know how many guards and Chinese personnel are in the jail?" asked Dan Conway.

"Not really," replied the colonel. "I was rather hoping you guys would find that out."

"Do they have any heavy guns, choppers or missile ships around?"

"The guns are, again, up to you to find. We have observed two helicopters parked right outside the jail. There is a patrol ship, a small fast-attack craft, but it's quite far from the jail. Shouldn't worry us, but the boys'll probably have to get rid of it on Sunday."

"Do we know how many of our guys are being held prisoner?"

"More than a hundred."

"How about *Seawolf*? What's happening about that?"

"I'm afraid we're going to scuttle her. Sunday night. Coupla hours before the guys go into Xiachuan."

"How, sir?"

"I'm not sure. But I know it's organized to have them think their own scientists simply screwed up the temperature of the nuclear reactor. The explosion will frighten them half to death, and that will provide a terrific diversion for us. Canton's only an hour away in a chopper. I'm hoping they won't have an American attack on their minds. They'll be too busy."

"Sir, are all the guys from *Seawolf* in there?"

"We think so. But we have no information whether they have killed anyone."

"Why do they want them, sir? They're not hostages, are they?"

"No, they're not hostages. But the Chinese have spent years trying to build a big nuclear attack submarine, stealing or buying the technology wherever they can. And now they have such a submarine captive, which they can copy—and they'll do that ten times faster if they can persuade key members of the crew to help them . . ."

"Sir, does our government have an attitude about all this?"

"Very much. But the Chinese have taken a very devious line. They're saying *Seawolf* was damaged in a minor collision with one of their destroyers. All they did was answer a call for help from its commanding officer, and now—surprise, surprise—it's developed a possible nuclear leak, and they can't release it till it's fixed, which they say won't be for another two or three weeks."

"Give 'em time to copy it, right, sir?"

"Not hardly. They'd want a lot longer than that, even if they have real help from the top technicians in the crew."

"Jesus."

"Do you think they would try to torture them? Force the information out of them?"

"Yes. Yes I do. Don't you?"

"Guess so," replied Lieutenant Merloni. "We better get 'em out. In a big hurry."

1050. Friday, July 14.
Flight Deck. USS *Ronald Reagan*.
210 miles off the Chinese Coast.

The Sea King lifted off the portside diagonal runway, its howling rotor slashing through the rain. Forty feet up, almost level with the plantation of electronic aerials at the top of the island, its nose tilted forward and it rocketed away, over the raging white wake from the bow wave, straight out toward USS *Greenville*, which could be seen on the surface two miles off the carrier's port bow.

The journey took less than a couple of minutes. They never even bothered to shut the main door before it was time to drop the two-inch-thick line out, directly down to the foredeck, right in front of the great round dry dock recently fitted to the Los Angeles–class 7,000-tonner.

All six of the SEALs wore heavy leather welder's gloves, and they lined up behind Lt. Commander Bennett as the Sea King hovered. He grabbed the rope and stepped out through the doorway, dropped like a stone for 20 feet, the line racing through his hands, then tightened his grip, applying the brakes hard, and came to a near-perfect halt two feet above the deck. By the time he touched down, Lieutenant Conway was already on the rope and on his way down, followed in quick succession by Rattlesnake, Buster, Catfish and Chief McCarthy. Three and a half minutes after the takeoff from the flight deck of the carrier, the helicopter was on its way back for the other six. That's fast-roping.

At 1104 all hatches were shut and clipped, masts were lowered, and seawater was thundering into the ballast tanks as Commander Tom Wheaton took USS *Greenville* deep and aimed her straight at the southern approach to Xiachuan Dao, seven hours away.

"Bow down ten . . . four hundred. Steer course three-zero-zero . . . flank speed."

All 12 of the SEALs were given bunks to rest on during the journey, and most of them slept. Catfish Jones and Olaf Davidson did not do so. They stayed up the whole time, poring over the map of the island, selecting the assault beach for Sunday night. They tried to watch a video, but lost interest almost immediately and returned to the charts. The two strongest men in the reconnaissance team had a lot on their minds.

At 1400 they were served an excellent lunch/dinner: thick, perfectly grilled New York sirloin steak, baked potatoes and salad. Afterward they all charged into Goliath-sized wedges of apple and blueberry pie with ice cream. It would be their last proper meal for two days.

At 1700 they changed into their wet suits, all 12 of them, including the four men who would work under the water, manhandling the ASDV out of its tunnel and then bringing in the Zodiac inflatable. They would also need wet suits in case of an accident or an attack that might put them in the water. SEALs by nature cherish the ability to go deep, where their training gives them inestimable advantage.

At 1730, Rusty Bennett and his seven colleagues, faces blackened by water-resistant oil, began to embark in the ASDV. They climbed up through the first dry hatch, which is sealed into the dry dock, and then boarded with slick expertise the 65-foot-long miniature submarine, through the hatch on its keel. The two men from *Greenville*'s crew who would drive and navigate the quiet electric boat inshore were already in position in the two bow seats.

Lt. Commander Davidson and his team waited by another exit hatch for the moment when they were informed that the USS *Greenville* could go no further, because the water was becoming too shallow.

The final four heard the call at 1752: "Captain-Sonar—I'm showing one-twenty feet on the sounder . . ."

"Captain-Navigator . . . right now we're at position 21.16N 112.315E . . . thirty miles due south of the target beach."

Commander Wheaton said quietly, "Okay, guys, this is it . . . just about as far as we can go. You wouldn't want to get back here for breakfast on Sunday morning and find us stuck in the mud, eh?"

The ship was now silent with anticipation. Anyone within range was watching the massive Olaf Davidson, who stood quietly below the hatch to the flooding compartment through which he would exit the ship. His face blackened, the veteran SEAL commander was holding his left forearm with his right hand, as if trying to take confidence from his enormous strength.

Finally he disappeared up through the hatch, followed by his three colleagues, and those working below the casing could hear the muffled bumps as they wrestled the ASDV away from the dock, out into the vastness of the South China Sea.

With Olaf's SEAL team back on board, the engines of the ASDV finally kicked into life and it moved forward, its course steady on three-six-zero, making a fast 18 knots through the warm, sandy water, 50 feet below the surface, leaving hardly any wake in the rainswept, desolate seascape.

The eight SEALs could speak to each other if they wished, but no one said anything. Their talking was done, their plans perfectly memorized. Their training had taught them that noise, any form of noise, is magnified under the water. And the silence was all-enveloping as each man dealt with the pressure in his own way.

Up front, the CO and navigator could see nothing. The entire journey was made on instruments, and it drew to its conclusion precisely where they knew it would, 120 minutes later, a little over a half-mile off the southern peninsula of Xiachuan Dao.

The CO spoke tersely. "This is about it, guys, sounder's showing we have around ten feet under the keel, but it'll shelve up quite rapidly. Time to go."

Unlike most previous SEAL delivery vehicles, which flood up completely for the swimmers to exit, this new advanced version allowed pairs of SEALs to clip on their Draeger breathing gear, and enter a small compartment that then floods. Then they just drop straight through and exit feet-first under the keel, same way they came in, leaving the rest of the submarine dry.

At this point the first pair leaves, wasting no time around the submarine, and using their precious air strictly for the swim-in. And now Lieutenant Commander Bennett dropped through the hatch, his huge flippers on, his attack board held tight in both hands. Right behind him came young Buster Townsend, on his first mission, and as he swam forward, he reached out for his leader both mentally and physically.

Buster was afraid, here in this deep water with, for all he knew, several thousand Chinese lying in wait for him on the beach. But he had been trained for this, or something very like it, for years, and he knew what to do, and he placed his right hand on the broad left shoulder of his leader, and together the two Americans kicked hard toward the prisoners of Admiral Zhang Yushu.

Rusty quickly found his course, due north as planned, and he and Buster got their kicks synchronized . . . KICK . . . one . . . two . . . three . . . four . . . KICK . . . one . . . two . . . three . . . four. Each one took them 10 feet closer, and they would need 300 kicks, one every five seconds, a 25-minute swim.

It sounds simple, but it is only simple to those who have hammered their bodies into shape on the anvil of U.S. Navy SEAL training and discipline. And now, as Rusty and Buster knifed their way through the water, they were both asking big questions of their bodies, and they were both getting all the right answers.

On a swim like this, SEALs reckon to feel tiredness late in the second mile. This short-haul run thus counted as little more than a sustained sprint, and when Rusty suddenly noticed his attack board grounding in sand, he knew it was over, and he was not surprised to see Lieutenant Dan Conway and Rattlesnake Davies pop up right behind them. Chief McCarthy and Paul Merloni came next, with Bill and John almost level.

It was nearly eight in the evening now, and the beach was in a shadowy twilight, the sun having set to the west beyond a heavily wooded headland. Rusty was glad of the last of the light, because it confirmed what they had been told: they were in a wide, gently

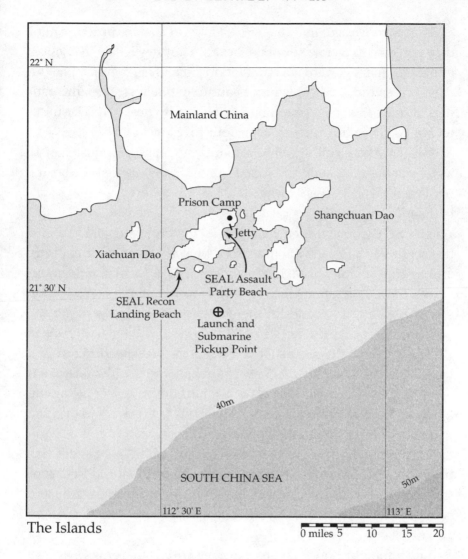

22° N

Mainland China

Prison Camp

Shangchuan Dao

Jetty

Xiachuan Dao

SEAL Assault
Party Beach

21° 30' N

SEAL Recon
Landing Beach

Launch and
Submarine
Pickup Point

40m

SOUTH CHINA SEA

50m

112° 30' E

113° E

The Islands

0 miles 5   10   15   20

curving bay, and the place was deserted, save for the jail complex six miles to the northeast.

From the land it would be impossible to spot anything on the dark water. There was no moon, and the rain clouds still hung over the entire area. Rusty sat in the shallows up to his neck in water and motioned for the others to join him. "I think we'll stay here for ten more minutes," he said. "Just until it gets really dark . . . if we make a run for it now up that wide, white beach we'd stand out like a dog's balls, if there happened to be anyone around. I'd rather play it dead safe."

Everyone agreed, and they sat silently in the warm water until they could no longer see even the beach. They never saw the Zodiac either, never even heard it as Olaf Davidson and his crew slipped the craft across the bay, with short, beautifully timed strokes, the paddles hitting the water as one, almost noiselessly, tirelessly. This quartet would have put a Harvard crew four to shame.

"Watch where you're going, you crazy fucker," said Rusty softly as the rubber boat almost bumped Buster in the back of the head.

"Jesus," said Catfish. "What the hell are you guys doing, sunbathing?"

The SEALs stifled their laughter as the crew stepped out into the shallows, and they all pulled the boat in, spinning it expertly around, the engine raised, landing it stern-first. Even in mild shore waves these boats immediately ship water over the stern if they spend even a few seconds in the shallows. The trick is to get the bow around to face the ocean.

This particular boat was moved with extreme speed, six SEALs on either side, using the specially fitted handles, positioned so that eight men could put all their strength into lifting and dragging the heavy end. They had it out of the water, up the beach and into the trees inside 90 seconds.

It was very dark the moment they left the white sand, and it was beginning to rain again. Rusty was not crazy about the first spot they chose because it afforded no cover or protection from the seaward side. In short, if anyone arrived on the beach, the SEALs could be seen.

Rusty took a short walk in company with Dan Conway, and 40 yards to the east they found an outcrop of rocks, around five feet high, running right back into the trees for 30 feet. "That's for us," said the recon team leader. "We'll get the boat in behind there, under a waterproof shelter, and we're golden . . . the watchmen can cover the beach and the landward approach with the machine gun—the guys can sleep in the boat . . . because no intruder could see anything."

For the next 30 minutes the SEALs got themselves thoroughly organized. The boat was camouflaged and covered with the waterproof shelter, which they rigged up about three feet above the hull. They took some palm branches and carefully brushed out their tracks in the sand, then used them to hide the boat even more thoroughly. They rigged up the radio in case of emergency, and fitted the ammunition belt to the machine gun.

When the exercise was complete the entire thing was virtually invisible. And when Rusty Bennett was finally satisfied with the safety of the position, he and his seven teammates prepared to leave.

They removed their wet suits and climbed into their light jungle combat gear, brown T-shirts with green and brown camouflage shirt and trousers, and long soft lace-up boots. Each man then applied light and dark green greasepaint to their faces, with the occasional splotch of brown. Rusty Bennett never wore a hat, preferring his dark green headband, which he called his "drive-on rag." When they were all fitted out they made a final weapons check: the pistol, the MP-5 automatic, the ammunition, the fighting knife. And then they shouldered up their packs, including two trench shovels, and very formally shook hands with the four men who were staying behind.

They had a radio frequency between themselves and their new base camp, but it would never be used unless something absolutely shocking happened. SEALs don't speak much. The two most lightly packed members of the team, Paul Merloni and Rattlesnake Davies, carried the big machine gun between them. Chief McCarthy and Buster had the machetes, and Rusty led the way with the compass.

It was 2104 when the red-haired lieutenant commander from Maine turned north up the peninsula, checked the bearing three-six-zero, and led his team into the sopping-wet jungle. In fact, they could have walked the first one and a half miles along the beach, but Rusty had dismissed that out of hand after studying the map. He knew it would probably have been quicker, but it also made them vulnerable to any observation from a Chinese patrol boat cruising the shoreline checking for intruders. They might even have run into a Chinese foot patrol, which would have spelled the end of the entire mission.

And so the SEALs did it the hard way, walking through the rain forest, a hundred yards inshore, out of sight, almost nonexistent. They traveled in single file except for the two men with the big machine gun, who brought up the rear. And it was very difficult terrain, heavily overgrown every yard of the way for the first half-mile. They were almost ready to start swinging the machetes, but the noise factor was uppermost in their minds, and they just kept pushing forward, stopping every 100 yards to listen. But there was always silence.

Rusty signaled a course change to zero-four-five at the head of the southeastern bay, and they moved on, keeping the ocean to the right, but remaining under the cover of the forest. It was at this point that the going became noticeably easier, with very little under-growth beneath a canopy of extremely tall trees. However, an all-encompassing darkness made it difficult not to walk into the trunks, and Rusty kept his left arm outstretched in front of him, pushing on into the great unknown. So heavy was the overhead cover that Rusty doubted it would have been much lighter at midday.

Underfoot the ground was very wet and soft. It was impossible to avoid long muddy puddles, which turned up frequently, and each man was glad of his waterproof boots. Once they almost blundered into a fast-flowing stream, but Rusty managed to call a halt just in time, which was a considerable feat since they were all confined to the merest whispers.

The water in that first stream was quite fast-flowing, and they risked a tiny flashlight to look at the map, ascertaining that the stream must have rushed down from the Guanyin Mountain, which rose to 1,300 feet somewhere up ahead to their right. This was an unnecessary obstacle and Colonel Hart had marked a route through a long flat coastal plain, bordered out to the left by wide mud flats before the sea.

Privately, Rusty might have chosen the mountain rather than a possible journey through very wet marshland. But the colonel had been insistent. If the Chinese were going to have lookout posts anywhere, they would establish them in the mountains, on the high ground to the north that dominated not only the jail, but also most of the island. If there were outposts up in those hills, it would be impossible to make a journey like this during the day. At night it would be the height of folly to risk running into one by mistake.

The colonel's legendary high intelligence often caused him to speak graphically. "Sailor," he had said to Rusty, "I'm not real happy about you and your guys getting your feet wet, but I expect you'd rather that than your ass shot off."

"I think that would be a very fair assessment, sir," the lieutenant commander had replied.

And so the flat wet plain between the mountains it was. Thus the eight SEALs were able to cover the first half of the journey without tackling any steep hills. But it was treacherous walking through deep, soft, grassy mud. At one stage as they squelched along through what seemed like an abandoned paddy field, Buster came forward and spoke in a stage whisper, "Sir, permission to draw my knife . . . this is fucking alligator country."

"Granted," hissed Rusty. "And for Christ's sake stay near to me in case I tread on one of the sonsabitches."

Everyone had to suppress his laughter at this banter. "We gotta come back this way?" asked Paul Merloni.

"Not if we can help it . . . we'll have a chance tomorrow to see if the Chinese have any guards beyond the complex. If they don't, we'll take to the hills next time."

Meanwhile they found themselves suddenly on slightly rising ground, firmer and with a definite steepness. Rusty told them softly that it was the start of the biggest mountain on the island. It was unnamed but high, and it towered over the jail, according to the pictures taken from the overheads.

The SEALs' designated route would take them right between the two ranges, north of Guanyin Shan. They now headed due east, back toward the sea, and when they reached it they angled directly north again, into the foothills, hopefully to emerge right above the complex.

And now they were into the last mile and it was almost midnight. Both Rusty and Dan Conway were using night-sight binoculars, stopping frequently, checking the terrain, watching the infrared sensors, heat-seeking, battery-operated. They never found so much as a rabbit.

At four minutes before midnight Rusty drew them to a halt, and whispered that in his view they might see the jail right over the next hill. Right now they were walking through big trees again, and they began to move extremely carefully, moving from tree trunk to tree trunk, soft ghostly figures in the Chinese night, like a scene from a children's horror story.

Rusty had the GPS system in his hand, a dim green glow illuminating the numbers. He was looking for 21.42N 112.39E. They were sufficiently far north, but the east number was flicking back and forth between 112.38 and 112.39. When that last number hardened up, Rusty reckoned they'd be in the goddamned jail, never mind outside it. They kept moving stealthily between the trees, and suddenly, dead ahead, were the lights of the prison where Captain Judd Crocker and his men were held captive.

Rusty saw the big searchlights first, the beams lancing out from the two high towers, which seemed to be otherwise in darkness. The beams were also moving slowly across the courtyard, which meant there were almost certainly two men in each tower, the light operator and an armed sentry.

"Pain in the ass," muttered Rusty, going to work instantly. "That means we gotta get up there and kill four people before we start, otherwise there's gonna be all hell breaking out, with us still outside the goddamned jail. Fuck it. We have to get rid of them."

"What now?" whispered Merloni.

"Silence, smartass . . . I'm thinking. How about over there, Dan? A little lower down the hill. See that line of bushes on the ridge with the big tree in front? We could get in there. It'd be impossible to see us from below, and we'd have a pretty damn good view of the place. I bet we could see right into the courtyard."

"We really could only be seen if someone walked up here and tripped right over us," said Lieutenant Conway, in a voice only just audible.

"Right, and we'd see him a long time before he got anywhere near . . ."

"I wonder how many Chinese there are down there?"

"Hard to say," whispered Rusty. "But if they've got one-hundred-plus prisoners, they're gonna have a guard force of thirty on duty at all times, twenty-four hours a day . . . that's one hundred and twenty people right there. Then you got all kinds of other turkeys wandering around, drivers, patrol boat crew, helicopter crews, cooks, orderlies, communications guys and Christ knows what . . . I wouldn't be surprised if there were a couple of hundred Chinese down there."

"Jesus."

"Okay, guys . . . let's just check out this hillside with the binoculars another couple of times . . . then we'll edge over to the ridge and see if we can't get ourselves organized . . . by the way, I'm as hungry as a sonofabitch."

"Don't worry about it, sir," whispered Lieutenant Merloni. "I'll just get rid of this machine gun and then I'll nip down below and order up a couple of plates of sweet and sour pork . . . you want fried rice or plain?"

The urge to laugh out loud was almost overwhelming, but no one did. They just stood against their trees shaking, with their hands over their mouths like naughty schoolboys in the presence of the headmaster.

Rattlesnake Davies made it much worse. "No need for that, sir," he whispered. "I've got the radio. I'll whistle 'em up right away . . . I expect they do takeout."

"Make mine chicken chow mein, willya . . . with extra soy . . ."

Lt. Commander Bennett knew it was all just a release for men who had been on the edge of their nerves for many hours, suppressing natural fears, wondering if they would ever get away, knowing that if they were caught unawares they would be shot dead on sight. Rusty didn't think he could give them a hard time over a few jokes about a Chinese restaurant.

"Just make sure they don't take *us* out," he said softly. "Come on . . . get low and over to that ridge . . . they just might have some asshole with a pair of binoculars like ours, and they'd pick us up very easily."

It thus took them fifteen minutes, crawling through the grass in standard SEAL operational mode. You could have stood 20 feet from them and never known they were there, until one of them killed you.

The thick bushes along the ridge were perfect for their task. They could cut small clearances and watch the jail night and day from their high position, counting the sentries, watching the guard change, timing the patrols, timing the lights, noting the time the interior jail lights went on, assessing the function of each building, establishing the building that contained the communications—the one that would go in the first SEAL assault, the one they had to obliterate, or else die when Chinese heavy-duty reinforcements came in.

To their great delight they found two low granite rock faces right in the middle of the clump. Behind these they had real cover. The jail was no more than 200 yards below them, but unless they had diabolical bad luck they would be unlucky to get caught out here. The foliage was so dense, their camouflage so professional, they would scarcely be visible even from the air. Certainly not from behind.

"Of course, we don't know whether they patrol this hill and if they do, we may have to move," offered Merloni quietly. "I know I would. If this was America and I was holding captive Mao Zedong's illegitimate grandson, I'd have guards all over this area all the time."

"So would I," agreed Rusty. "But they may not. It just might be beyond their imagination that the U.S. would launch an operation like this . . . but then, they don't *know* they have Linus Clarke in the slammer, do they?"

"And that's the key," said Dan Conway. "It's the key to why we're doing this . . . and why we have a big chance of getting away with it."

Not for the first time, Bennett believed that young Conway was going right to the top in Coronado . . . if they could just get out of here alive.

And now he issued his first formal orders. "Split into two teams. Lieutenant Conway, Bill and Buster with me. Lieutenant Merloni, Chief McCarthy, Rattlesnake, and John. The second team will now prepare a bit of food, regular cold rations for us all, then sleep until oh-four hundred. I'll take the first watch with Buster after we cut a peephole. Dan and Bill will establish the machine gun and keep watch behind our redoubt. Find the laptop, someone, and have a camera ready for first light. The sun set just before twenty hundred, and at this latitude there should be ten hours of darkness, so dawn will be around oh six hundred . . ."

Buster Townsend moved into the bushes with the pruning shears and quietly cut two gaps in the foliage.

They all used some more insect repellent, drank some water and ate some of the high-protein bars that would sustain them for the next 24 hours.

Then Rusty Bennett moved forward into the thicket, propped himself on the rocks and focused the night-sight binoculars, stop-watch in his right pocket. Buster sat behind with the laptop, ready for the commentary that Rusty would begin in around 10 minutes.

"Okay . . . there are two guards in each of the watchtowers, one of them working the light . . . the beam from each tower is activated every four minutes . . . interlocking with the others . . . it's taking forty-five seconds to traverse the yard, which allows a window of two minutes and fifteen seconds when there are no beams at all.

"There are other lights down below, midway up the tower. There are ladders leading from the roof of the long building. That's the north wall of the compound and we are observing from the west . . . range two hundred and twenty yards.

"Right now, at oh one hundred, I'm observing a patrol of four guards in the courtyard moving in twos along the inside wall of what I think is the main cell block. It takes them two minutes and nine seconds to walk from end to end, one pair heading east while the other heads west. In four crossings, the four men have stopped to talk together three times, which increased the time of the journey by three minutes.

"Dead ahead of me, to the right of the main block, there is a square single-story building with all its lights on. This building is situated immediately to the right of the main prison entrance. The door has been open since we got here and there have been people in and out, five out and three in, during the last twenty-five min-utes, but they could have been the same people. They were all in uniform. I thus conclude this is the guard room."

Rusty spoke slowly, in an impersonal but clear and steady monotone, so that his throat microphone to the tiny laptop could synthesize his voice correctly and record written words for later transmission on their portable satellite link.

"At oh one ten I observed a group of four lights moving south a half-mile east of the jail. I'm looking right across the jail toward the sea, and the jail has a marginally higher elevation than the shore-line. The four lights were on some kind of a patrol boat. I watched it head south, we must check to see if there's a jetty somewhere down there . . . action star right there."

For the next hour, Lt. Commander Bennett logged down the buildings Judd Crocker and Shawn Pearson had noted—the small building with the aerials, lit only on the first floor, the much bigger one, with seven windows lit and two dark, on the walls Rusty could see, the west and north.

He spotted two helicopters on the big round cleared area, with the fuel dump immediately to its north. His main difficulty was an inability to see what guards patrolled outside the jail. The trees below were just too close to get a view, and he could see nothing whatsoever on the west wall. The heavy jungle foliage also obscured most of the south and north walls, and the east was beyond his vision.

"I'm seeing one pair of guards walking across the entrance to the prison, always from west to east, every eleven minutes . . . therefore I'm concluding the patrol is walking right around the jail, but we'll have to go down there and get a better look a bit later. I can't tell if there are just the two or four of them. Action star right there."

The hours ticked on, and at 0355 there was the first noticeable activity. It was plainly a guard change. The first thing Rusty saw was four men emerge from the guard room in formation and march across the courtyard to the cell block. The guards Rusty had been watching for almost four hours had also formed into a square, and he observed them salute as the new men came forward. Then he saw them march off the courtyard, back into the well-lit building with the open door.

Immediately afterward the main gate to the jail was opened and four more guards emerged, obviously relieving the midnight watch. "Okay, Buster, the outside patrol is definitely four men. They changed at one minute before oh four hundred . . . the main gate opened inwards, and I thus conclude it's the only gate into the prison from the outside, otherwise they would have used a smaller one. Check in daylight. Action star, Buster."

The SEALs too changed their watch at 0400. Rusty and Buster were tired to the point of exhaustion, and they wrapped themselves in their waterproof ponchos and crashed out on the ground sheets.

Chief McCarthy and Lieutenant Merloni stepped up for duty, moving to the front of the ridge, Paul with the glasses, the chief with the computer. They took time to read the boss's notes written on the laptop screen, nearly word-perfect. And they too settled down to record every last movement of the prison that held President Clarke's son, Linus.

One hour later, at a few minutes after 0500, Paul watched the lights of the patrol boat return. There was a light southwesterly breeze off the water now, and the lieutenant had picked up the beat of engines a mile out. He also could not see where the boat docked.

At 0600 the sun rose out of the ocean directly facing Paul. At this angle it was like a red searchlight in his eyes, right above the cell block, and it was impossible to see anything for a half-hour until the sun climbed higher into the morning sky.

At 0700 Paul had a clear view of the complex, and he clarified the position of the buildings on the laptop plan. He also observed that although the outside patrol did appear to be walking around the entire jail, the main gate was constantly manned. Twice he had seen ground crew for the helicopters exit the jail, and both times the gates had been opened and shut behind them, the doors moving simultaneously. He thus concluded that there were two more guards in the courtyard at all times, on duty at the big wooden gates.

He could also now see that there were only two small windows in the main cell block, almost certainly providing only indirect light to the prisoners. From up here, staring down on a somewhat tranquil scene, it was almost impossible to imagine that the entire crew of a major American nuclear submarine was actually incarcerated in this place.

They changed watch again at 0800. Rusty came on duty, chewing another of the protein bars, while Dan Conway held the small computer. "We'll hang around up here for another hour, then we'll get in closer and get some accurate measurements. . . . We'll have one team get down near the shore, check out that patrol boat and select a landing sight for the assault force to come in on Sunday night. . . . Guess I better do that, so they got someone to blame if it goes wrong!

"You all understand the main group wants to be a lot nearer than we were when they hit the beach. There's gonna be sixty-four guys, and the quicker they deploy and get into position the better. I don't want the boats more than a half-mile away when they land— but we have to watch that fucking Chinese patrol boat, see what time it goes out and comes back all day today.

"Also, we have to select a pickup point . . . remember, these guys in the jail may be very weak . . . and there's over a hundred of them, if no one's been killed. It's a huge task to get 'em down to the shore and on board the inflatables. I know the colonel and Rick want it done as secretly as possible, but I just have a feeling we'll need to kill a goddamned lot of Chinamen to pull this one off. Anyway, we need to choose two sites, one for the assault and one for the getaway, with detailed notes . . ."

At 0830 the main gates opened again, and through them walked three uniformed Chinese servicemen. Two of them wore caps and carried documents; the third of them wore just uniform shorts and an open-necked white shirt with epaulets. He was taller than the other two, with sandy-colored hair, almost unheard of among Chinese nationals. It was easy to see that he looked different, but from where Rusty stood it was impossible to identify Linus Clarke.

Since he had cringed in terror from the towel, he had been isolated from the rest of his crewmates, and flown up to Canton each day to assist the Chinese technicians in their efforts to copy *Seawolf*. So far as Linus could see, it was that or death, and every man, he reasoned, had a right to save his own life, by whatever means.

And now he took off again on this bright Saturday morning, flying overland, back to the billion-dollar submarine he had single-handedly been responsible for losing, failing to accept the advice of either the Officer of the Deck, Lt. Andy Warren, nor indeed that of the vastly experienced Master Chief Brad Stockton. In his mind, Linus could still hear Brad's voice that night: *"You want me to let the CO know we're groping around the ass of a 6,000-ton Chinese destroyer . . . I think he should know . . . Sir, we don't know how long that towed array is.. . . that towed array is . . . that towed array . . ."*

The words echoed in his mind. They were the last words he heard before he slept, the first he heard upon waking. Sometimes he heard them in his sleep. They were words with which he must live for the rest of his life, however long that might be.

And he stared down at the hillside below, as the Helix Type-A clattered over the island, right above the "hide" that contained the Navy SEALs who were attempting to rescue him.

A half-hour later a new helicopter came in, making its approach from the northeast. Rusty watched it flying dead toward him and then at the last minute saw it swerve right over the jail and drop down over the cleared area from where the Helix had just departed. He watched four men disembark, two of them walking straight to the jail doors, which were immediately opened, the other two heading for the little house with the radio aerials. Both men carried metal toolboxes. Rusty guessed, both correctly and happily, that there was some kind of problem in the comm room.

"That little house is the biggest problem we have," he pondered. "If we are seconds late taking it out, they will have a signal away that the jail is under attack, and that will be it. We'll come under attack from the air and sea, and we may not get out alive." And he emphasized his words into the computer.

"WE MUST HIT THE COMM HOUSE BEFORE WE DO ANY-THING—THAT'S OUR NUMBER ONE TARGET. WE MUST STOP THEM TRANSMITTING A MESSAGE NO MATTER WHAT."

He checked the words out, and Lieutenant Conway, leaning on the rocks next to him, staring through the binoculars, added something else. "I'll tell you something, sir. We have two other targets just as important. Maybe three."

"We have?"

"The helicopters have radios. . . . I know they will not have any- one aboard . . . but if one of these Chinese officers is smart, and still alive when we blow the comm house, he'll rush to one of those choppers and fire up the radio. Likewise the patrol boat . . . that'll have satellite comms on board, as you know. There's bound to be someone on it, and we can't take the chance some smartass isn't going to get on the horn to the Canton base."

"You gottit, Dan," said Rusty thoughtfully. "Sometimes things that are staring you in the face need saying, to clarify a task . . . and you, baby, just said 'em. And I'm going to note them down right now."

"Remember one other thing, sir."

"What's that, kid?"

"If you hadn't pointed up the main issue, that we have to kill the comms, I'd never have either thought of it, or said it."

"That's generous of you, Dan," said Rusty, plainly admiring a young man who didn't need personal credit for things, only the sat- isfaction of getting them right.

Rusty Bennett was a keen amateur military psychologist. Not as good as Colonel Frank Hart, but he was good, and everyone knew both he and Rick Hunter were being made commanders as soon as this mission was over. If they could get it over.

At 0900 Dan Conway reported high activity in the jail. Prisoners were being marched out of the main cell block and lined up in rows of 12 in the courtyard. Other prisoners were being escorted out from the two side buildings at either end of the block. But these men were brought out individually. Rusty Bennett judged that the main block contained communal cells, and that the side buildings were places to isolate individuals, probably men under interrogation.

The SEALs were too far away for recognition of *Seawolf*'s offi- cers, but there were now no lingering doubts that this was indeed the crew of the American submarine. Almost everyone was still in uni- form, U.S. Navy trousers and shirts. But even from the hillside it was obvious that some of them had been badly treated. Three or four of the men were being supported by crewmates, among them the cap- tain, who had been brutally beaten up in the interrogation center.

Brad Stockton was still on his feet, with the assistance of Shawn Pearson and Andy Warren. Big Tony Fontana, by some miracle, had refrained from getting into more trouble and appeared uninjured.

The SEALs were not of course to know that Lt. Commander Cy Rothstein had died in the torture chamber of a brain hemorrhage, sustained when the little guard lieutenant had hit him one time too often with the butt of a rifle. After two days of sustained, unmerciful punishment, Einstein had told them nothing.

And the incident confirmed one obvious fact. The prisoners were never going to leave China to talk about their experiences. Not if Admiral Zhang had his way. Even he, the master of a massive but remote naval kingdom in the east, knew that world human rights courts these days had teeth, whoever you might be. The shocking specter of the massacre in Tiananmen Square still haunted China's rulers, 17 years later. And it would almost certainly go on doing so.

The SEALs watched from on high as a new figure emerged: Commander Li strode out in his high boots from the little house with the aerials. The gates were already opened, and he marched forward, plainly to address the prisoners. Rusty and his men could not hear what he said, but it sounded angry. A few minutes later Li turned on his heel and exited the jail.

"You want me to shoot the little prick right now, sir?" asked Lieutenant Merloni.

"Perfect idea, Paul," replied Rusty. "Which do you prefer, sudden death from a Chinese fighter plane, or court-martial when we get home? If we get home."

"I'll take the court-martial, sir. But not by much."

And now they could all see the guards moving forward. There were 30 of them now, and they were separating some men from the lines and marching them forward toward the other big house inside the jail walls, right opposite the guard room. That was the one building they really could not see from the hillside, but Rusty hoped to get a closer look sometime in the afternoon or early evening.

By 1015, Rusty judged it time to move. "We have seen no sign they are patrolling anywhere beyond the immediate outside wall of the jail," he said. "No guard has made one move into the forest . . . which is good, because we have a lot of work to do. . . . Dan and my team will make our way back into the trees and then head on down to the beach, check out the details of the patrol boat and its jetty. Then we'll stay within a half-mile of the jail and look for a landing site for the main group.

"I can't see what the undergrowth is like, but we may have to clear some kind of a path for the guys to come through . . . remember, it will be pitch dark when they get here, and we want to get a landmark clearly positioned, and on the computer with full GPS numbers.

"You'll see from this diagram I've made right here . . . Colonel Hart has given us his suggestion for a spot . . . really, we just gotta check out that it's safe, and if not, locate another one . . . just so you guys know where we're working.

"Tonight we'll go and have a look at the water, right after dark. We don't want to guide the inflatables onto a pile of rocks. Meanwhile, Paul, I want you take Chief McCarthy and try to get some accurate measurements of the jail size, and distances between points. Try to get an accurate fix on the height of the walls, the gate and the towers. And try to find out how they lock the fucking door, since we need to blow the sonofabitch off its hinges tomorrow . . . I still think we'll go with det-cord. . . .

"Rattlesnake and John, stay up here and keep watching . . . recording all movements down below. I noticed through the glasses the Chinese have obviously been trying to clear some areas of vegetation, but they haven't done much of a job . . . and luckily there's a lot of very good cover, very close to the jail wall in several spots. Mark them on the laptop. So Dan and the chief should be able to get in close . . . but not too close, for Christ's sake. We'll meet back here and compare notes at, say, fifteen hundred."

"Okay, sir, we'll get moving now."

The SEALs split up, six of them heading back up the hill into the trees, making a circular route to their allotted operational areas. All the routine tasks with which they were charged were

achieved in silence and stealth. The area for the assault chosen by
Colonel Hart was perfect. Rusty and Buster planted a rock in front
of the trees where the big team would enter the forest. Behind
there, in deep shadow, they cut a clearing for the boys to gather
tomorrow night and sort out their positions.

Two hundred yards away Bill lay on the bank of a stream that
flowed past the jail to the north and watched for interruptions. If
anyone approached either him or the beach, he would duck back
into the trees and make contact with Dan Conway, who would race
to alert Rusty and Buster to keep the noise level way down.

But not one of the Chinese guards ventured anywhere beyond
the jail compound, except to patrol the outside wall. It was, as Lt.
Commander Bennett had said earlier, beyond their imagination
that the Americans would actually attack their own jail, on their
own remote island, right offshore, surrounded by thousands of
miles of the South China Sea, plus half of the Chinese Navy, just a
few miles from the city of Canton.

By the time they regrouped in the hide they had a ton of information. The patrol boat had gone out shortly after 1000 and stayed
out until 1400. There was a long stone jetty where it moored alongside, 600 yards precisely from the assault point. They'd send a couple of SEALs over the side of the incoming Zodiacs and have them
stick a couple of limpet mines on the hull, timed to detonate precisely when the choppers went up and the comms room did an imitation of Hiroshima.

By then, thought Rusty, *we'll hopefully be up and in the compound, and the outside patrol should be dead.* The rest, he
decided, might be a bit more problematical. And he did not like
Chief McCarthy's report on the watchtower situation. Not one bit.

John McCarthy was a very experienced mountaineer and he
could throw a long grappling iron like Peyton Manning going for
the end zone. But he was plainly worried about this attack.

"The walls are fifteen feet high, made mostly of smooth concrete, but with a flat wooden frame right to the top, like beams in
an old house. I can hit the top beam with a grappling iron and
climb up the knotted rope inside one minute. But we do not have

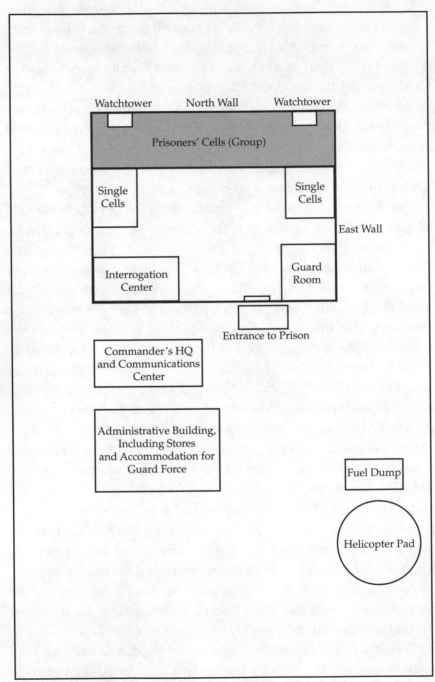

The Prison on Xiachuan Dao

long. I think we'll have to take out the outside guards first, which is not good. I would have preferred to have four climbers on top of the wall, unseen, and then climb the ladder to the tower top.

"Quite frankly, I cannot imagine our four men all getting to the top without being seen by the tower watchmen. Then we'd have to shoot them, and that would make noise, ten minutes before we want anyone to know we're there. In my view, we desperately need those ten minutes, and the only way I can see to nail the tower guards in silence is if it rains. And I'm recommending we wait until it does."

Rusty did not like it, but he understood. "The noise?" he asked, knowing the answer.

"Yessir. When we had that very hard rain shower around thirteen hundred today, I was lying in the undergrowth right below the northwest tower. I was about thirty feet away, across the path watching the guards. As soon as it rained, they both pulled on a kind of plastic cape, hooded. The rain was blowing right in, and it must have affected their hearing.

"Sir, if we attack in heavy rain, I believe we could all get up there and take the guards out, then we could operate the lights for a few minutes, just enough time for the guys to swarm up the walls, take out the four duty foot guards from the top, while another couple of our guys eliminate the guard room. At that moment we blow all forms of Chinese communication.

"But if we are caught on the way up the watchtowers we've had it, we'll have to open fire . . . and there's comms in the watchtower, I could see the electrics. As soon as we pull a trigger, all hell will break out, and they'll have time to regroup, get going with a couple of machine guns and mow our guys down on top of the wall. Plus they'll have that few minutes to alert Canton they're being attacked . . . then it's over. We'll never get out."

Lt. Commander Bennett was thoughtful. "I guess this entire operation depends on taking those watchtowers quietly."

"Correct. And we can't use grapplers to get up the last bit, we'd probably hit one of the guards in the back of the head."

"Do you have a recommendation, Chief?"

"Yessir. I think we should get four guys up there early. And I think we should use ladders. They're quieter, and faster. The wall's a consistent fifteen feet high, so we want four fifteen-footers, nothing bigger so it doesn't jut above the parapet. There's a four-foot strip right along the rear of the cell block flat roof. It's in perpetual pitch dark, literally under the towers. The guards can't see anything there. The boys can pull the ladders to the roof and then make a synchronized attack, straight up the sides of the towers, exactly where no one would dream of looking."

"Aluminum ladders rattle a bit," said Rusty, somewhat wryly.

"Not if they're ultralight and bound in thick black cloth. Those guards aren't sharp. They're just up there, bored to death, trying to stay dry. Wouldn't be surprised if one of 'em was asleep while the other guy worked the light. If we can wait for rain, sir, I have a high level of confidence in this. We'll make it."

"I'm not sure we have much choice . . . and I agree with what you say. We have to take the watchtowers, and we have to take 'em quietly."

"The thing is, sir, if we can get those towers without anyone knowing, the guys can take out the patrol in the courtyard and then hit the guard room. The moment that explosion is heard, we slam the boat, the choppers and the comm room. With any luck, they may *never* get a signal away."

"Now that would be fantastic, because it would give us another hour to evacuate the place in peace."

"Not sure I'd go that far," said the chief. "This thing's likely to resemble a major war, at least for fifteen minutes."

"Right. And now we have just two priorities left—the big building opposite the choppers . . . we don't know much about that, and we have to find out whether the patrol boat goes out in the evening . . . we know it goes in the early hours . . . meanwhile we have to keep watching that big building, and we should get down there when it's dark. Luckily it is the farthest point from the main Chinese patrol."

And so, as darkness fell over the prison, the SEALs once more moved into the trees and made a circuitous route to both the complex and the jetty. It was raining again, which made their tasks less hazardous but no pleasure. Rusty, Rattlesnake and Buster found a position at the back of the building and quickly worked out that it was a dormitory for the guards. Rusty did not much like the idea of killing men sleeping in their beds, but if he left them they'd rush out and start killing Americans. As usual, on SEAL missions, there was no alternative to the harshest possible course of action. Anything less, you're likely to end up dead yourself.

They had a while to ponder the situation, keeping the stopwatch on the guards, checking the watch change at 2000. Outside the dormitory there was just one guard, and he was relieved every two hours, the door being mostly open with men obviously sitting around on their off-duty evenings.

And then, at exactly nine minutes after nine, one of those million-to-one chances actually happened. The single guard suddenly began to walk right toward the precise piece of ground where the three SEALs were lurking. They all saw him coming. The distance was only 40 yards, and in the light from the building, they saw that his rifle was slung over his shoulder, and his right hand was unzipping his fly. The guy was just coming over for a pee in the undergrowth.

The SEALs froze and the guard kept walking, straight at Rusty, who flattened himself into the ground facedown. The other two were four feet on either side of him, and there was no escape. They could not run, they could not slink back into the woods because they would be seen, and they certainly could not shoot him. The noise would cause an uproar. Even stunning him or throttling him was no good because he would be missed.

"Holy shit!" whispered Rusty. "He's gonna walk right over us." And he was perfectly correct. The guard, ready now to take aim into the bushes, actually stood on Rusty's right leg. He probably thought it was a body, but Rusty did not move. The guard turned, startled, as if to call out, but he never made it. Rattlesnake was on him, cleaving a four-inch slit right across his throat, severing his windpipe, his jugular and his vocal cords with one devastating movement. The guard was dying before he hit the ground, but the one thing he could not do was call out. And now the SEALs had a major problem.

Lt. Commander Bennett instantly took over. "Quick, one of you on each arm and drag him back into the woods. And for Christ's sake don't get covered in blood . . . steady, guys . . . keep going . . . get him well clear . . ."

Forty yards later they stopped. "Hold it," said Rusty. "Look, the biggest danger right now is that trail of blood . . . we have to get rid of it. Buster, get back up the hill and come back with a machete, pruning shears and the two trenching shovels, and one of those rubberized ground sheets."

"Aye, sir."

It took him nine minutes and he slipped back through the trees so silently that no one picked him up until he was back, standing next to Rattlesnake. "Jesus, Buster. Where the hell did you come from?"

"Just practicing."

"Okay, guys . . . we can't clean this scrubland like a carpet, so we'll obscure the blood instead. Cut some of that palm tree stuff with the shears and we'll put it all over the grassy area where it happened. Right here it's not so bad, just earth. They won't know what's happened to him and I doubt they'll search before the morning. Meanwhile we'll drag him down toward the beach and bury him deep. When we get there we'll get his boots off and his cap and rifle and place it somewhere where it'll be found . . . with a bit of luck they'll just think he went for a swim and drowned, or deserted."

What had seemed like a quiet night had turned into a very dangerous situation, and they were all tired when they finished digging the grave and then walked the six miles back to the original rendezvous point. But it was midnight now and the eight SEALs had to go. They handed over the computer with its notes and diagrams to Lt. Commander Davidson, and told the holding team that with any luck they'd be back around 2300 at the assault beach as planned.

Commander Davidson and his men had had a dull watch, never seeing anyone, but they did spot the patrol boat about a mile offshore around 2100. According to the combined data on the satellite and their laptop, it was due to go out again at 0100 until 0500. This was a good moment to set up the satellite dish and send the report back to Colonel Hart.

Olaf and Catfish walked down to the water with Rusty and his men as soon as they had changed into their wetsuits. They carried big palm fronds to cover up the footprints in the sand, and they shook hands on the dark soundless beach. It was still raining slightly as they moved into the water, carrying the attack boards, breathing through the Draegers, and there was still no sound as they glided into deeper water heading out to the ASDV that awaited them, issuing its friendly little sonar bleep every 30 seconds.

0939 (local). Sunday, July 15.
Office of Southern Fleet Commander. Zhanjiang.

Admiral Zhang was thoughtful. He and Admiral Zu were looking at the daily report from Commander Li. It was mostly routine, mentioning any critical information they had been able to glean from the prisoners, and data on the general running of a temporary military facility. Costs, requirements, arrivals, and departures.

However, at the bottom of the report, which came in on the fax at 0900, there was a final paragraph which ought not, really, to have exercised anyone unduly. It stated, "One of the Navy guards at the dormitory has gone missing. He did not report for duty at 0200, and his bed had not been slept in. At first light we conducted a thorough search, and unhappily discovered his boots, socks, trousers, cap and rifle on the beach. However, there was no sign of him, and we have therefore concluded he went for a swim, late at night because of the heat, and either drowned, or deserted. We have alerted police at Shangchuan Dao to watch for a body along the western shore of the island, since that is where the tide would undoubtedly carry him."

Admiral Zu had read the entire report carefully, especially making notes regarding costs and requirements. Only as an afterthought did he remark, "They lost a guard last night. Apparently drowned or deserted. Found his clothes on the beach."

Admiral Zhang held out his hand. "May I see?"

"Of course, last paragraph."

"Hmmm. That's rather worrying. Because the man could have been an American agent, working against us. Somehow getting information on the prisoners back to the CIA."

"Ah, Yushu . . . you are seeing too many Americans."

"Am I?"

"Well, a few days ago you did decide to rebuild an entire jail at Chongqing, just in case the U.S. elected to storm the island of Xiachuan and release their men."

"Yes, I did," said the C-in-C. "And I have proceeded on that basis. The Americans will stop at nothing . . . we both know that, to our cost."

"I realize that, Yushu. But I have tried to reason it all out on the basis of military probability. Ask yourself, how many people do you think it would take to overpower our forces? And how on earth would they get here? And how would they ever know the crew of *Seawolf* was even on the island in the first place?

"And you could add, and how would they get everyone away? They'd need a major warship, and the water is too shallow, and anyway we'd know it was trying to come inshore hours and hours before it got here. In my opinion you are staring at a military impossibility. And Yushu, as always, you are staring very hard."

"It's my job to stare very hard, Jicai. That's my mission on behalf of the Chinese people. And this drowned naval guard, I don't much like it . . . allow me to look at that last paragraph once more, please . . ."

Zu Jicai handed over the fax once more, and again the C-in-C read it through, pacing the floor, a deep frown on his wide, stern face.

"First of all, I would like you to get a full report on the drowned man; his home, his family, his background, his length of service . . . just to see if there is one tiny shred of evidence that he could have had contact with Americans."

"Very well. I think most of the guards are attached to the Southern Fleet, which means his complete record will be here at Zhan-jiang. If that is so, we will have it in fifteen minutes."

Admiral Zu summoned an assistant, gave him the fax and instructed, "Call Xiachuan and get the name of the man mentioned in the last paragraph, then pull up his record."

The two admirals sipped some more tea and waited. Twelve minutes later the missing guard's record came in. Admiral Zu scanned it, mentioning information as he read. "Well, he's twenty-eight, married, with a young son. They live in Guangzhou . . . next of kin listed as his wife . . . parents live in your hometown of Xiamen. He was born and brought up there . . . served at sea in destroyers . . . so far as I can see, never been out of Chinese waters."

"How about his wife?"

"Same. Come from Xiamen. Not much education. Moved to Guangzhou when he received his last posting. No applications filed for any future career changes . . . he wouldn't be a classic CIA spy candidate," he added, an edge of wryness in his voice.

Admiral Zhang smiled for the first time. "No. I agree there. However, something is worrying me. That report lists his clothes on the beach in some detail, right down to his socks. But it makes no mention of his military jacket or uniform shirt . . . "

"So?"

"Who goes for a swim in their shirt and jacket, having taken off their boots, socks, trousers and cap?"

"Well, he may not have been wearing his jacket."

"True. And if that's the case, it will be in his room."

"And if it's not, what might you then assume?"

"Nothing, really. Except that he could have been shot or stabbed, covered in blood, and the murderer dumped some of his clothes on the beach and then got rid of the body and the incriminating evidence of the bloodstained clothes."

"Sir, not even Lee Chang," Admiral Zu said, referring to the famous Chinese film detective, "was as imaginative as you."

Admiral Zhang laughed. "I am only half playing the devil's advocate," he said. "But I really do wonder why a man goes for a late-night swim wearing his uniform jacket."

"Perhaps he wished to commit suicide, Yushu. And kept it on to help weigh him down."

"If he had wished to end his life, surely he would have tried to swim with all of his clothes on. Why take off his boots and trousers?"

"Well, yes. I suppose so. But these are all just assumptions."

"I understand that, Jicai. But let's get a call in to Commander Li . . . and have the man's room searched . . . see if his jacket's in there and maybe his shirt, too. Perhaps he just took those things off and walked out into the hot night down to the beach."

"Certainly, I will do it, sir. But I still cannot believe he was a CIA agent, nor that there is a homicidal maniac lurking in the jungle of Xiachuan Dao, killing armed, trained Chinese soldiers."

"Unless the Americans have already landed, Jicai."

"Landed!"

"Well, stranger things have happened. And of course I know there is little chance of these things being true. But they could be, and we must run our checks on that basis. Not on what is likely to happen. But what *could* happen."

A further 15 minutes went by before Lee returned with a fax that read, "Room search completed. No uniform jacket. No uniform shirt."

"Then he died with his shirt and jacket on," said Admiral Zhang. "Either in the water, or at the hands of a murderer. Perhaps from a foreign power?"

"Of course, he could have been murdered by one of his colleagues, sir."

"Yes. He could."

"And so, what would you like me to do about it now?"

"My friend Jicai, nothing more. However, this disappearing guard is on my mind, and it is likely to stay there. I am thus making all haste to have the American prisoners removed from this vulnerable island."

"You mean you really did activate the renovation of the jail in Chongqing?"

"I did. Six days ago."

"And the jail is ready to receive prisoners?"

"Tuesday. But I have decided to move them at first light on Monday morning, that's tomorrow. They will travel by road and it will take two days to get there, up through the mountains. And then my worries are over. Because they will be in a place where no one will ever find them. Not in a hundred years."

TWO DAYS BEFORE THE SEAL RECONNAISSANCE
team took off for Xiachuan Dao, the first half of Admiral Morgan's two-pronged attack on the Chinese Navy had moved into
operational mode.

It was Wednesday, July 12, 12 noon, the precise moment the
SEALs began to arrive on the flight deck of the *Ronald Reagan*.
But this was 8,000 miles away, in a time zone 13 hours earlier, in
the sunlit Southern California city of San Diego. John Bergstrom
was going to the zoo.

Deep in the sprawling cultural center of Balboa Park, less than
three miles from his Coronado base, the King SEAL had already
paid his respects before the great Veterans War Memorial. And
now he strolled along Zoo Drive, heading essentially for the monkey house, directly opposite the bears.

He wore white shorts, a dark blue tennis shirt, no socks and
expensive-looking boat shoes. In his right hand he carried a plastic
shopping bag in which there was a brand-new cassette player, still
in its original heavy white cardboard packaging. A deeply tanned

man with smooth, just graying hair, Admiral Bergstrom was an imposing figure, lean and confident, the kind of man accustomed to being obeyed.

Sitting on a bench outside the monkey house, surrounded by tourists, was not a natural setting for him. But that was his position right now, in the great scheme of the upcoming attack on the Chinese Navy. And he sat impassively, awaiting the arrival of Richard White, a 43-year-old investment executive at the Bank of California in Hong Kong. Richard White, like the admiral, was not quite what he seemed after 20 years of covert operations for the CIA in the Far East. Not even the board of the California Bank knew anything of Mr. White's activities.

When he arrived, the admiral knew, there would be a third party, Mr. Honghai Shan of the China International Travel Service. He and Richard White were traveling back to Hong Kong together, but it would be the Kowloon native who would carry the cassette player through the notoriously difficult Chinese customs at Hong Kong International Airport.

The rendezvous would take place on the bench, beneath the swaying excitement of the zoo's Skyfari, the aerial tramway that trundled through the treetops above the lions every 20 minutes. Here Richard White would accept the package and introduce Admiral Bergstrom to the brave American agent whose work for the official "external arm" of the Chinese tourist industry made him immune from the Hong Kong customs.

Honghai Shan's parents, both schoolteachers, had been murdered by Madame Mao's Red Guards in the Cultural Revolution, and he had worked as a CIA liaison man since he was a boy. Three years from now, he and his wife would retire to a hillside house in La Jolla, courtesy of a grateful intelligence agency.

They arrived separately, the American first, sitting on the bench immediately and starting to read the *Wall Street Journal.* He said softly, from behind the newspaper, "Hi, Admiral. Rick White. Shan'll be here momentarily."

John Bergstrom made no indication of recognition. But three minutes later, a perfectly dressed Chinese businessman, wearing a light cream suit in the 90-degree heat, walked slowly forward and joined them sitting on the far end of the bench, studying his zoo guidebook, presumably searching for pandas.

Still behind the wide pages of the newspaper Rick White spoke again, almost in a whisper. "Admiral, this is Honghai Shan, a deeply trusted man. We are traveling back to Hong Kong together. I will take the package all the way, but when we disembark the aircraft, Shan will go alone, carrying it with him. He will drop it off to me at my office."

High above them, the Skyfari moved slowly by; the CIA agent, photographing the three men on the bench, blended in perfectly with the crowds watching the other lions.

Admiral Bergstrom said nothing. He just stood and walked away, leaving the plastic shopping bag behind. Then Richard White too stood up and left, carrying the bag. He walked slowly back through the zoo entrance, back toward the Veterans Memorial, but before he reached the huge edifice, he slipped into a black sedan that sped him across the city to Lindbergh Field, home of San Diego's International Airport.

Honghai Shan used a different car, a dark green limousine that took him away from the city straight up the freeway, north to Los Angeles International Airport. The next time the two men saw each other, they were in adjoining seats on the United Airlines flight to Hong Kong. The cassette player was on the floor, right next to Rick White's left leg.

The flight took off at 10:00 on this Wednesday evening, but because of the 10-hour time difference, they would actually arrive in China at midnight Friday. The journey itself was 16 hours, like flying from New York to Paris and back, and the two American intelligence agents spoke quietly about life in Hong Kong, about the old days of British rule, and about the continuing buildup of the Chinese military.

They were old friends and had faced danger before, but to each of them there was something lethal about the package they must get into Hong Kong at all costs. Shan was not worried. As the senior Chinese overseas tourist executive he was responsible for bringing millions and millions of American dollars into the People's Republic every year. He was a privileged traveler, with many friends in the highest reaches of the Communist Party. Most of the customs officers knew precisely who he was, and it was literally years since anyone had asked him even to open a bag, much less search it.

The chances of someone asking him to open the plastic bag were remote. Requesting him to break open the packaging to the cassette player, and then ordering it to be dismantled, were odds too great to calculate.

And so it proved. Honghai Shan walked straight through customs at Hong Kong International, receiving a nod and a bow of greeting from the officer in charge. Rick White's suitcase was routinely opened but not searched. And both men were home by 8:00 A.M.

At 9:30, Shan left his office on the 10th floor of Swire House along Chater Road, and walked briskly through the Central District to the offices of the California Bank. There he met Richard White in the lobby, and handed over the package they had transported halfway across the world.

The two men smiled and shook hands, and the American hurried back to his office on the sixteenth floor, where he instructed his secretary Suzie Renrui, a Chinese-speaking divorcée from San Francisco, to render him unavailable to anyone.

He locked the door and unpacked the cassette player. Then he took a small screwdriver and began to undo the slim holding bolts that locked the outer casing together. Inside there were no electronic working parts, just two sealed black plastic bags, ingeniously fitted into place, one of them containing a heavy six-inch-long box, about four inches wide and an inch deep. The other felt as if it held a five-inch-square box plus a round camera lens of some kind, plus wiring, plus screws or bolts that rattled against each other.

Rick White did not know what was in the bags, and he never would. Meanwhile he took from a shopping bag a fine-looking melon, which he had cut in half and then spent a half hour hollowing out before he came to work. He had dried it carefully, and now he placed the two plastic bags carefully inside. When he put the upper half of the melon on top of the lower half, it fitted perfectly and the contents were completely hidden.

He had another look inside the hollow cassette and found what he needed, a small length of inch-wide plastic adhesive tape, black and yellow in color. He spread it out, ripped the protective covering off the sticky part and wound it carefully around the circumference of the melon, binding the two halves together. The words around the melon now read SOUTH CHINA FRUIT.

He repacked the parts of the cassette player into its original box, and with the melon in a separate plastic bag, he slipped out of the office, told Suzie he would be gone for less than 30 minutes, and headed for the elevators. On the way, he dumped the box down the incinerator.

Once outside he moved fast, walking quickly between the skyscrapers, and then heading into more intimate streets, toward the market stalls down between the teeming shoppers in Li Yuen and Wing Sing streets. It took him 10 minutes to find the stall he wanted, Jian Shuai Fruit and Vegetables, which comprised three long barrows, containing every possible kind of produce. At one end was a pile of melons, several of them bound with the black and yellow plastic tape of the South China Fruit Corporation.

Mr. Jian himself came toward him. "Good morning, Mr. White. Hold open bag, please," he said, picking up two of the melons and placing them carefully inside. Even Rick hardly noticed him remove the other one and deposit it back next to the till, so swiftly did the fruit seller operate. Then he came forward with a handful of yen. "Your change, Mr. White, thank you . . . thank you very much . . . next, please . . . you like some snow peas, madame? . . . ah . . . good choice."

Rick White vanished into the crowd, heading back through the streets into the skyscrapers. Back on the sixteenth floor he made Suzie a gift of the two new melons and settled down to work, his task on behalf of his government now complete.

Back in the narrow throughway off Li Yuen Street, Jian Shuai temporarily handed over the fruit-selling operation to his wife and daughters. Then he packed a box full of mixed produce, cherries, snow peas, peppers, rice, lichees, spinach, broccoli and one melon.

Still wearing his white apron, he stopped a passing taxi at the end of the street and had the driver take him down to Aberdeen Harbor, a couple of miles away on the southwestern coast.

The sheer impossibility of finding anyone here in the crowded madness of this waterborne community, where 80,000 people make their homes on floating sampans, did not daunt Shuai. And he hurried through the insane commerce of the place, past the floating restaurants, looking out at the gentle chaos of the East Lamma Channel, dodging trucks and delivery boys, searching for the big fruit and vegetable junk owned by his friends Quinlei Zhao and Kexiong Gao.

These two were familiar traders on these waters, buying fruit from all of the remote farmers on the fertile islands in the area. Their boat was a big heavy-sailed 40-footer, and with a decent quartering wind they could slice along at 10 knots. They were expert seamen, and careful buyers of the best produce. They had also worked for the CIA for years, yet still moved busily through the trading channels, no suspicion of any kind attached to either one of them. Zhao and Gao, both fortyish, were the consummate field operators in an area swarming with Chinese spies.

And now they waited, scanning the dockside for the sight of Shuai, carrying his box along the waterfront, watching for the familiar figure of the CIA's most successful messenger. Gao saw him first, and stood up, yelling, "Over here, you idiot . . . you're late and we're in a hurry . . . SHUAI! OVER HERE!"

In the frantic race for sales that kept Aberdeen Harbor in a day-long turmoil, this was normal banter between traders. Perfectly normal. Just the way Zhao and Gao liked it.

Shuai came on over, carrying his box, and handed it over, shouting, "All right! All right! Who you think you're yelling at, hah! You don't order till yesterday—you think you own my company? Here, take it . . . and mind you pay on time, for a change."

And with that he disappeared back into the throng, Gao yelling behind him, "You don't get a move on, we don't order no more . . . you hear me?"

He took the box of produce and placed it in the middle of

another pile. Then he began to cast the lines and pull up the big gaff-rigged sail. Within moments they had caught the nice south-west monsoon breeze, which drove them out into the Pearl River Delta, where they headed the junk northwest, up around Lan Tau Island, and then on upstream toward Canton.

These were treacherous waters for all but Chinese nationals. Heavily patrolled by the coast guard, the seaways through the Delta are not open to foreign shipping. The Chinese authorities have ruled that the Lema Channel, which is, effectively, the southern approach to the Pearl River, is closed to all non-Chinese vessels. This wide-spread paranoia by successive governments reached back to the Opium Wars with Great Britain 150 years previously.

If you want to sail upriver to Canton you have to be Chinese, in a Chinese boat, with a special permit to navigate the waters. And even then you may well be stopped and questioned. Only the trading regulars, local men, well known to patrolling customs and river police, were never harassed. Which was why Zhao and Gao rode the southwesterly without a care in the world, for hour after hour, selecting a course up the center, staying clear of the shoals along the left bank where two major rivers split into a thousand tributaries and then meander across green wetlands, only about a foot above sea level for almost 50 miles.

As the sun set, the breeze dropped slightly. The vegetable junk had been running since midday, averaging nine knots, which now put them in the vicinity of the city. When the river split 12 miles downstream from the center, Gao steered for the north fork, keeping to the right in a line of other small boats heading into the wharves of Canton.

And for the next mile they were just another trading junk, bringing the freshest produce from the lower Delta up to the hotel and wholesale agents who awaited them each evening. But now Zhao for the first time switched off his navigation lights and left the convoy, sliding into the shadows, not yet lit by the rising moon. The little sonar sounder soon showed them in less than five feet of water, and Zhao brought the junk about, heading back along the shore, below the industrial suburb of Huangpu.

It was lonely along here, out of the main north fork throughway, but it required a lifetime of knowledge to avoid running aground, even in a skiff that drew no more than two feet fully loaded. The warm, light breeze hissed through the miles of bullrushes off their port beam, and Gao watched the sounder, edging along through the dark shallow water. Every time it showed only four feet below the keel, he told Zhao to "pull," nosing the boat to starboard into a fractionally deeper channel.

And now they could see a familiar clump of willow trees hanging almost above them, and Zhao pulled in the sail, cutting the speed to only two knots, and they drifted quietly in toward the land. Up ahead was another boat, and Gao picked up three quick flashes of light. "That's him," he hissed. "We're right on target."

And now they could hear the splash of oars as the little rowboat made its way towards them. "Dong! You there?"

"Okay, Zhao . . . I'm coming alongside."

The two boats bumped together. They shook hands, and the box of fruit with the single melon was handed over. "Hurry now, Zhao . . . you go quick . . . go now . . . there's patrols everywhere."

"Good-bye, little brother . . . take care now."

Zhao laid the big junk onto a southwest course, and the light breeze gusted now over his port bow. The sail was already tight and he kept it there, heading the boat up, steering out into the channel, switching the navigation lights on again.

And far away, in distant San Diego, three separate checks, each one for $10,000, were being deposited in three separate bank accounts, owned by Zhao, Gao, and young Dong, three Chinese nationals preparing for a new life in the USA, a country none of them had ever even visited.

Quinlei Dong rowed to the shore, leaving the old boat surrounded by reeds, moored to an iron bar he had hammered into the muddy shallows long ago. From here to the road was almost a mile, but the grasses were tall and Dong wore high gumboots as he squelched his way forward, carrying the box, splashing his way back to his car.

It took him 25 minutes in the pitch dark, and then he stood in a clear stream that ran under the road, cleaning off his boots. He put them in the trunk with the box of fruit, reversed the car out of the woods and hit the main road into Canton. It was almost 10:00 P.M. and he looked forward to a late dinner at his small home in the market area, right off the Liuersan Road, by the Shamian Island bridge.

He and his wife, Lin, had lived there for 15 years, since they left college in Beijing. Both of them had been in Tiananmen Square in 1989, and they had seen several friends and one cousin shot down and killed by the military. As such they had elected to get out of the capital and move to the quieter, warmer city of Canton. And there they had nursed their grievances against the ruling Communist party, vowing one day to leave China for the United States, as so many of their friends had done over the years.

Young Quinlei had been recruited by the CIA before he left the university, during the six months following the massacre in the square. And in the ensuing 17 years he had built up a nest egg of almost $450,000 in his bank in San Diego, keeping Langley informed of the arrivals and departures of ships, personnel, and a myriad of other naval detail.

Dong's degree in electronics saw him rise rapidly in the Navy dockyard, not working on the ships, but in the many operations rooms on the shore. He had made himself a computer systems expert, and had personally installed many of the major lighting grids throughout the yard. At 37, he was the deputy chief electrical engineer, a civilian position, but always working closely with the Navy executive.

Each day he reported for work at 8:00 A.M. finishing at 5:00 P.M. He was subject to random searches by the guards on the way out, but not on the way in. And now he was preparing for his biggest task yet on behalf of his American masters. By Monday morning he and Lin would be on their way. They had just two more nights left in the little house near the Shamian Island bridge.

Many of their possessions were already packed. Their nine-year-old son Li was asleep, and Lin had gone to much trouble preparing what might be their last meal together in China—a superb Shao Xing chicken, cooked whole in Hua Diao wine, accompanied by flat rice noodles.

They dined together at the end of the small kitchen, drinking only water and saying little, as if afraid even the walls might have ears for their conversation. For tomorrow morning Dong would begin arguably the most dangerous mission ever attempted by a local CIA field operative in this part of the world.

They cleaned up after dinner together, and were in bed before midnight. Neither of them slept much, and by the time dawn broke over the city, Dong was already up, unzipping the melon and removing the electronic parts it hid so efficiently. He ripped open the black plastic bags and studied the small black box, the power pack that would last for around six hours. He checked the terminals, checked the wiring, checked the length of wire he had been given. Then he checked the main fitting, walking to the window, staring through the lens, focusing the cross-hairs, fitting the lens to the square box, then checking the connection between the power pack and the square box, nodding with satisfaction when he flicked the switch and watched the green light flicker, then glow firmly in the morning light. He was getting a half-million dollars for this. There had to be, he knew, no mistakes.

He carefully placed the black electronic parts in the lower section of his toolbox, hiding them among rolls of wiring and tape, keeping them separate, to look like random pieces of an electrician's box of tricks. At 7:30 on this Saturday morning, his telephone rang and when he answered, a voice said simply, "Yes." He knew who it was, the same man he had worked with for many years, an American broadcast executive downriver in Hong Kong.

Rarely has the word "yes" signaled so much. It meant that the American satellite operators in Fort Meade, Maryland, had picked up the red infrared "paint" on the pictures from space, showing that *Seawolf*'s nuclear reactor was running again as she lay alongside in the Canton base.

It meant that the electronic laser beam that would illuminate the precise area of the deck above the reactor should now be fixed in place.

It meant that Arnold Morgan was about to do what he had said he would do. He was going to hit *Seawolf*, and put Canton's naval dockyard out of action with it.

Quinlei Dong said good-bye to Lin, who was trembling with fear but refusing to cry.

"Please, please be careful," was all she could manage.

He placed his toolbox in the trunk and started his little car. He drove briskly east, along the Liuersan Road, and crossed the People's Bridge. From here it was a straight 15-minute run down to the dockyard, and when he arrived the routine was simple.

"Hello, Mr. Quinlei," said the guard at the gate. "You work too hard—it's Saturday . . . should be home with the family."

"No, Sun . . . not too hard . . . too slow . . . should have been finished last night!"

The guard laughed and waved him through, shouting, "You hurry up, now . . . nice day to take out the family."

Dong drove slowly through the grim dockyard buildings, noticing as he had done constantly these past few days that the place was literally crawling with guards, all along the jetties, and then in a mighty regimented group near the American submarine. Quinlei the electrician, his privileged status displayed in a red and white sticker on his windshield, stayed away from the main dockside areas, driving along the quiet streets between the buildings a block from the water, a block from the submarine.

He had deliberately left incomplete a rewiring job he had been working on all week, up in the ceiling above an ops room. And now he made his way up the stairs once more, nodding to the guards at the doorway, and mentioning that he was going up to finish the new terminal for the main computer. The guards had seen him coming and going for two weeks and scarcely responded, just smiling and saying, "Okay, Mr. Sparks."

At midday, he walked downstairs again, carrying his toolbox and his small lunch bag. He turned to the senior guard and said, "I'm going to have lunch down by the water, but I'll be back. I've run into a problem, so don't lock up . . . this thing has to be running for Monday morning. Right now I'll be lucky to have it running by New Year!"

"What was it, sir . . . that main cable they dug up last month?"

"I thought it must be . . . but I'm not so sure now. I think there's a fault inside the building. I might ask one of you to give me a hand for ten minutes this afternoon."

"No trouble, sir . . . glad to help."

Quinlei Dong strolled quietly back toward his car and moved around to the far side, out of the view of the guards. Then he rounded the corner of the building, checked to see that no one was watching, and sprinted across the street to another tall brick building in which there was a small, gray steel back door. This was the old dockyard stores, derelict now, unused for the past five years, and because of budget restrictions likely to stay that way for the next five. The modern Chinese Navy spent money on new ships, not old buildings.

Dong knew it was open. He had deliberately wrecked the locking mechanism five days earlier. And now he grabbed the handle and twisted, pulling the door outward and slipping inside, closing it behind him softly.

He crossed the dark, deserted floor, making for the iron stairway, which led right up to the roof seven floors above. He walked slowly, not knowing quite how he would deal with the locked door at the top. When he got there, the problem solved itself. The door was jammed shut with two big bolts, top and bottom. All he had to do was open them, and he was on the roof.

He stepped out carefully, crouching low, moving slowly inside the parapet. At the southern edge, overlooking the main submarine jetty, there was a chimney block, and he pressed back against it, staring down at the guard patrols in front of USS *Seawolf*. If one of them took a real hard look at the roof, they would see him. That was his main assessment.

But now he opened the toolbox and took out the round viewing lens. He took his measurement, knowing that the spot on the deck he sought was exactly half the distance back from the rear of the sail, as the total height of the fin: i.e., if the sail was 40 feet high, he was looking for a geometric spot 20 feet back. The actual numbers were irrelevant. It was that half-distance stat that counted. Dong could not measure feet and inches, but he could measure halves and doubles with his eye and his steel ruler.

He put his thumb on the ruler at the halfway mark. Then he took it horizontal instead of vertical, and there in front of him was the precise spot he sought. He held the ruler steady with one hand and lifted the lens to his eye, with the other focusing the crosshairs precisely at the end of his own thumb. Directly below that, he knew, was *Seawolf*'s nuclear reactor. Now he had only to fix the device to the chimney block, which was the difficult part.

A small bracket would need to be drilled and screwed into the brickwork at a spot just above his head. If he stood on the toolbox he could manage that. It was the noise that worried him, but it would not take long, just two holes, about an inch and a half deep. He could do that.

Dong removed the black parts from the box, and took out a screwdriver and a portable drill. Then he took off his jacket and wrapped it tightly around the drill to suppress the high-pitched whine of the electric tool. Then he stood up on the toolbox, held the bracket in place and hit the button on the drill, which bit into the brickwork. The jacket kept the noise to a minimum, and the gusting southwest wind scattered what sound there was high and away. Twice he went into the wall, and then he stopped and ducked right down, and stayed there for 10 minutes.

Finally he stepped back onto the toolbox, and, using a hammer and a thin Phillips screwdriver, rammed the plastic plugs into the drill holes. Then he lifted up the bracket and screwed the first bolt into the first plug. Then he did the second, fixing the bracket firmly to the chimney.

Five minutes later he slid the main fitting onto the bracket. Then he climbed up the sloping part of the roof, keeping one foot on the toolbox, and stared down at USS *Seawolf*, placing the crosshairs exactly at the end of his thumb, aiming directly at the spot above the reactor.

Dong connected the wires between the main box and the power pack, tightening the terminals with small electrician's pliers. Then he slid the power pack into the bracket where it fitted perfectly. He turned on the switch and watched the green light flicker and harden up. Then he climbed up the roof again and checked his bearing, checking again the accuracy of his measurement.

It had been a fairly simple job, but for something this important, nothing was simple. He took a section of gray plastic out of the box and wrapped it carefully around the device, securing it below with a trash-bag tie. Now all he needed to do was escape.

Back down the iron stairway he went, opening the door slowly, and ensuring that the coast was clear. Not a soul was in the back street behind the building, and he closed the door carefully, walking back to the building in which he was officially working.

The guards were still there, and he went inside again, and climbed the stairs. In fact, he needed only to clean up, but he needed an excuse to return again tomorrow, and he parted several wires, leaving them exposed on the carpet.

Fifteen minutes later, he went back downstairs and said good-bye to the guards, telling them he'd come back to finish tomorrow afternoon, because he had to replace a faulty switch that was the cause of the problem. He'd need less than an hour.

No one bothered to search him on the way out, and the same guard who had advised him about the quality of life on the way in now did the same on the way out. "Good day for family, hah? You go have a nice time, Mr. Quinlei . . . I'll hold the fort here . . . ha-ha-ha."

2200 (local). Saturday, July 15.
Office of Admiral Morgan. The White House.

The President's National Security Adviser right now answered to no one. He had been given firm orders by the Chief Executive to get Linus back no matter what. The President understood that this meant *Seawolf* had to be, essentially, scuttled. And that the Navy SEALs team would have to go in guns blazing to break open the jail and subdue whatever opposition there was.

The military details did not need to be relayed to this particular President in this particular incident. He wanted his only son back, and that was the end of it. Admiral Morgan had been tasked to mastermind the rescue, and that he had most certainly done. So far.

And now he was in conference with his most trusted operators: Admiral George Morris, Director of the National Security Agency at Fort Meade, and Jake Raeburn, head of the CIA's Far Eastern desk. It was midnight in Washington, one o'clock the following afternoon in the South China Sea.

Admiral Morris had reasonable news. *Seawolf*'s reactor had been running steadily now for three days, and was still doing so. The satellites showed no visible sign of increased activity inside the jail on Xiachuan Dao, nor was there any sign of a transfer of prisoners, although it did seem that certain members of the American crew were being relayed back and forth to the Canton dockyard. The Chinese naval hardware had not increased, but still consisted of one fast attack patrol boat and two helicopters, occasionally only one.

Admiral Morgan himself had a signal from John Bergstrom in Coronado. And that was excellent news. Nothing elaborate, no details, just a coded *Nighthawks roosting*. Which meant that the SEAL reconnaissance team had been into Xiachuan Dao, done their business and were safely back in the *Ronald Reagan*. Arnold Morgan was hugely relieved.

Jake Raeburn also had good news. His man in Canton had collected the laser marker and established it high on a building overlooking the submarine. If there were no hitches, he would switch it on at 1900 local time the next day, and the bomb would hit two hours later.

This meant Nighthawk was GO. Lt. Commander Rick Hunter's big SEAL team would hit the beach at Xiachuan Dao sometime before 2300. After that it was in the lap of the gods. But the SEALs had done it before, and the admiral believed they could do it again. Admiral Bergstrom was confident. In Colonel Frank Hart they had the best possible overall commander. The only question was how close inshore the submarine commanding officers could go before they had to surface.

Arnold Morgan was counting on the fact that the massive diversion in Canton Harbor would cause such a commotion that there would not be a warship anywhere around the prison island with the slightest inclination to be looking for American submarines. The crisis up the Pearl River would be all-consuming, and a whole lot worse than Three Mile Island.

The three men continued to speculate in hushed tones as to the possible outcome of the mission. But shortly before 0100 the telephone rang, and this time the news was somewhere between suspect and bad.

The call was for Admiral Morris. One of his operators studying satellite pictures had made a shrewd observation, that a fleet of Chinese Navy trucks had suddenly appeared out of nowhere in the town of Yangjiang on the mainland, some 45 miles northwest of the jail. The operator counted a total of 12 trucks, painted in dark blue naval livery. In addition, a large Russian-built troop transporter helicopter had just landed at Xiachuan.

"I just wondered, sir, whether this might add up to a movement of the prisoners—you know, perhaps leaving the island and heading off to some inland jail. Neither the trucks nor the chopper was anywhere in sight four hours ago, and there's a fairly good road between Yangjiang and Southern Fleet Headquarters at Zhanjiang."

"Thank you, Lieutenant . . . very well observed. I'm grateful. Let me know if anything else catches your eye, will you?"

"Who's seen what, George? Lay it right on me," rasped Admiral Morgan.

"My guys think they might be getting ready to move the prisoners."

"WHAT? NOW?" thundered Arnold Morgan. "JESUS CHRIST! NOT NOW!"

"Well, it's two in the afternoon over there. I suppose it's possible. But it is Sunday. I shouldn't think they'd do much until Monday morning. And if they did, there wouldn't be a damn thing we could do about it, except watch."

"But what have your guys seen?"

"A convoy of twelve Navy trucks arrived in Yangjiang, which is just about the nearest major town to the island, about forty-five miles away to the northwest. And a big troop transporter helicopter just landed at Xiachuan . . ."

"That's not bad. That's fucking terrible," snapped the admiral.

"Well, not if they don't plan to hit the road until Monday morning. If that's the case, we don't care one way or the other."

"No, I suppose not. And anyway, there's not much we can do about it—just zap the submarine and the dockyard, and let the prisoners go. Which will not please the Chief."

"No, I suppose not, Arnie. But even Linus Clarke cannot be worth a war with China, a war in which they might feel compelled to slam a West Coast city in retaliation."

1000 (local). Sunday, July 16.
Admiral's Briefing Room. USS *Ronald Reagan.*

With four hours to go before departure back to the island, Lt. Commander Rusty Bennett was operating on pure adrenaline. Like his seven colleagues, he had slept most of the way from Xiachuan to the carrier, and he would try to sleep going back in this afternoon.

However, right now he was in a maelstrom of activity. The weather forecast was perfect, more heavy rain before midnight, sweeping up from the southwest the way it had been for over three weeks. The senior SEAL officers were poring over the maps they had drawn of the jail, studying the precise distances from the new assault point on the beach, a half-mile from the watchtowers. Rusty and Colonel Hart were noting the heights and times on distance and assessing the Chinese guard strength. Rusty could tell that the colonel was on the edge of his nerves as he paced the room, anxiety written all over his face.

Lt. Commander Rick Hunter sat silently with blowups of the maps, measuring distances with a steel ruler, hitting the STOP-START buttons of his stopwatch, counting out the seconds, trying to imagine in his mind the time it would take his men to cross the outer track and scale the wall, dragging the black padded ladders behind them.

Over and over he checked the patrol times, writing in his notebook the precise whereabouts of the guards when his boys would bolt across the rough ground to the wall. He counted out the seconds it would take for the guys to take out the four tower guards and then get the ladders back to the ground, ready for the second assault wave on the jail wall. This would be made by the men who must remove the patrolling guard inside the wall without being heard by the patrol outside the wall. He and Frank Hart had long decided that the three silent killers required for this move would be the SAS men from Bradbury Lines in England, Sergeant Fred Jones and his corporal, Syd Thomas, plus the ex-paratrooper Charlie Murphy.

At this point, all three commanders knew they must be prepared to "go noisy." But Rick Hunter and Frank Hart were desperately trying to buy a few more minutes to blow up the guard room, before the patrol boat, choppers and comm room were taken out simultaneously.

"I don't think we can expect them to wipe out the guard patrol and then get across the yard without being spotted by anyone, and then hit the guard room." That was the colonel's assessment. Rick thought it might be possible, but agreed it was unlikely. "Better to get three more guys up and over while we hold the watchtowers and slam the guard house right on time . . . exactly when the others explode."

Both men knew the problem. There just might be a telephone or even a radio in the guard house. If the three SAS men were seen by anyone, the alarm would be raised and the Chinese just might get a signal away before the rest of the communications went out. Three extra men inside the jail could dictate the life span of any guard house communications. "And that way," said Rick, "the SAS guys can concentrate on opening the main gate, either with explosive or peacefully, depending on the opposition."

"Okay," said Rusty. "That means we leave the ladders in place after the guys clear the wall. How many seconds do we have before the patrol rounds the corner and sees them?"

Rick studied his notebook. "Thirty . . . max. Look, the guard is right here when the SAS guys go in. It takes 'em forty-seven seconds to walk down this side before they get to the corner. I've got seventeen seconds from the bottom of the wall . . . they're taking grapplers, right? For the fifteen-foot drop over the other side. . . . Okay, make sure the next three guys with the satchel bombs know exactly where the grapplers will be. If they're quick, they can kick the ladders over flat when they reach the top of the wall. They have about thirteen seconds before the outside guards have any view at all . . ."

And so it went on, into the third and fourth hours, the detailed notes, the fractional times, the assessments, the risk element, the need for sudden noisy brutality, the contingency plans: "What if these guys are spotted . . . what's our number one priority if someone blows the whistle before we're quite ready . . . THE COMMS, always the comms. Hit that and they cannot get reinforcements. Fail to hit that, and we're all dead."

On an intellectual level, the colonel had a serious problem with the limpet mines on the patrol ship, which would need to be fixed with a timed detonation of, perhaps, 60 minutes while the SEALs put everything else in place. Which made that timing device in the water under the ship extremely important.

"Too important," said the colonel. "The timing of the entire mission is dependent on a limpet mine. Because when that blows, *we have to go noisy*. And that means everything else we do is absolutely dictated by the moment the limpets will blow. I'm unhappy with that. But I'm even more unhappy with the sequence if something goes wrong."

"How do you mean, sir?"

"Okay . . . we all realize there may be a point when some Chinese guard blows the whistle, perhaps twelve minutes before we're quite ready. Let's say he yells, at which point we go automatically . . . the guys with the bombs outside the comms room hurl 'em in, someone blows the choppers, we hand-grenade the towers, blow the gates and fight our way in, firing at will, making the absolute maximum of our surprise element.

"BUT, down on the jetty there's a patrol boat with a fully active radio system. Inside the boat there may be a trained operator, plus a couple of guards. They hit the military airwaves and announce that the jail is under severe attack. Because right now it's going to sound like World War Three . . . the boat has of course only ten minutes to live, but that ten minutes could be enough, and I don't like it. Because if they get a signal away, you guys are dead."

"Hmmmmm," said Rick Hunter. "I don't like it either."

"Well, it's easily solved."

"It is?"

"Sure. Let's not use limpet mines at all. We'll put two guys behind the jetty with antitank weapons, those very light, hand-held launchers . . . either when they hear the first bang or on your radio command, they slam a couple of those babies straight into the ship fore and aft, and no one's making any phone calls."

"Beautiful. That's a great call, sir. Same with the choppers?"

"Definitely. We don't want any fixed time detonations. Because in the end they could turn out to be a real PITA."

"A what?"

"PITA. Pain in the Ass."

Lt. Commander Hunter shook his head. There really was something about Frank Hart, super brain, always on top of the situation, always with time enough for the wry quip. Bergstrom said his appointment had come direct from the White House.

He was honest, too. "Rick," said the colonel, "I like the euphemism PITA so much, I would like to claim it as an original, complete with copyright and exclusive usage clause. But I cannot do so."

"Why not?"

"Admiral Morgan invented it, and he likes it more than I do. But I'm still using it."

Down below, the SEALs were preparing to go, checking their weapons, cleaning and lightly oiling their guns, adjusting their camouflage. Some were already blacking their faces and hands, tightening their belts, standing alone, practicing their readiness to attack. You could have cut the tension in those rooms with a kaybar fighting knife. Petty officers walked among them, encouraging, warning, urging them to be alert at all times, remembering always the creed of caution, of silence, forbidding the wearing of any jewelry, checking pockets for loose change that might rattle and cost someone his life.

Almost no one spoke now, as the final minutes ticked by, save for a master chief who was murmuring quietly, "You have been trained for many years to undertake such a mission. No one in the history of military conflict has ever been better trained . . . if you stay sharp, you guys are invincible . . . just remember everything you have been taught about care and attention to detail . . . take no chances unless you have to . . . and if you have to kill, do it hard, quick and silent, because if you don't kill him, he'll sure as hell kill you. I have complete faith in every one of you . . . and I want you back, every one of you. Don't let me down, guys. Now go get 'em."

The master chief slapped a few of them on the upper arm as he walked out, and a buzzer went off three times. Slowly the SEALs followed him out to the companionway leading to the flight deck, where the big choppers would roar them out over the water to the waiting submarines.

Colonel Hart and Lieutenant Commander Hunter remained in conference until the last minute. Through the high windows they could see two nuclear attack submarines, USS *Greenville* and USS *Cheyenne*, waiting a mile off the carrier's port beam, with the helicopters hovering intermittently above them, the SEALs hot-roping down onto the deck. He could not see the third submarine, USS *Hartford*, another 7,000-ton Los Angeles–class nuclear boat, which was cruising with a minimum crew at periscope depth a half-mile further to the west, and would be utilized almost entirely as a rescue and hospital ship for the crew of *Seawolf*.

Finally it was time for Lieutenant Commanders Hunter and Bennett to leave, and they shook hands with Colonel Hart before striding out to the elevators, down to the flight deck and on out to the submarines for the next leg of the journey to the prison on Xiachuan.

1400. Sunday, July 16.
South China Sea. 190 miles offshore.

Both submarine commanding officers planned to dive and join *Hartford* below the surface as soon as the SEALs were safe aboard for the six-hour journey inshore. *Greenville* went first, diving down to 400 feet and then making flank speed on bearing three-six-zero, heading due north to the island in 200 fathoms of water. *Cheyenne* followed, at the same course and same speed, about 1,000 yards astern, using a low-power active sonar pulse to keep station. If necessary they could communicate on the underwater telephone, but only in a case of extreme emergency.

The SEALs who had seen the jail were divided into two groups of four, Rusty Bennett, Dan Conway, Buster Townsend and John in *Greenville*, Paul Merloni, Rattlesnake Davies, Chief McCarthy and Bill in *Cheyenne*. Hopes of sleep declined rapidly. In each ship there were 28 other SEALs whose curiosity was getting the better of them with every passing mile.

The maps and charts were excellent to study, but the opportunity to speak to colleagues who had actually been in the place was overwhelming. And the issues they all wanted to discuss were (a) the number of guards, (b) was the jail nearly impregnable, short of blowing it up? and (c) did they have a real chance of success?

The veterans were accurately optimistic. So far as anyone could tell, the Chinese had no idea there was any danger. The guard was moderate but not scarily large, and all of the men who had been in there thought success was nearly certain, as long as they could smash up the communications system thoroughly.

And all the way in, both Lieutenant Commander Bennett and the vastly experienced Chief McCarthy went over and over the lesson: If we hit the comms hard and fast, we're golden. If we fail to do so, we have a very good chance of dying. None of the SEALs liked the latter option at all.

1800. Sunday, July 16.
Liuersan Street. Canton.

Quinlei Dong carried his toolbox out to the car and stowed it in the trunk. In his hand he carried a square white box that contained a brand-new electrical switch. He started the engine and turned along the old familiar way to the People's Bridge, and then took the road to the dockyard. It was a bright warm evening, the sun still high, as the master electrician pulled up to the gate.

The guard walked up to him, a different man from yesterday. "Hello, sir. Where are you headed?"

"Same place as yesterday and all last week, the ops room in B Block, where the electrics are still in chaos."

"Why are you here on a Sunday?"

"Mainly because, on pain of death, I have to have the system up and running by tomorrow morning at 9:00 A.M. sharp . . . orders of the commandant . . . you think I like being here?"

The guard smiled. "Do the guards at Block B know you're coming?"

"They do. I told them all yesterday. Here, you see this switch . . . this is the new part. I was just about ready to have the whole yard dug up to find the fault when I noticed the old switch had burned right at the back. Now I have to put this little devil in place. Thirty minutes and I'm out of here. Come and help me if you like—I need an assistant."

The guard laughed, checked the windshield sticker and said, "Okay, Mr. Quinlei . . . see you a bit later."

Dong drove on slowly through the empty yard, empty, that is, except for the waterfront, where there was the usual army of personnel surrounding the American submarine. He parked his car in his usual spot, way along the back street, much nearer the derelict stores building than the ops room where he was working.

He walked back briskly to where there was one single guard at the bottom of the B Block stairs. The two men greeted each other cordially, recognizing each other from the previous day's meeting.

"Got the new switch, heh?"

"Right here. I'll be about a half-hour."

"Okay."

Dong climbed the stairs and began to clear up his mess. The new switch was unnecessary but he fitted it anyway and then made his wire joins, cleaning up the clutter and replacing the ceiling panels. He checked the electrics all through the room, dumped the trash in a bin and strolled downstairs. It was exactly fifteen minutes before seven.

"That it?" said the guard.

"That's it for me. You can lock up now. I won't be back. Lights all working, computers all working. See you tomorrow."

"'Bye, Mr. Quinlei."

Dong walked back along the street to his car, went to the driver's side and stared back the way he had come. The guard must have gone into the building, because he was no longer outside. So far as he could see, the street was completely deserted. And he dashed for the big building, pulling open the door and ducking inside, his heart pounding.

And now he had to hurry, because the guard could return at any moment and he would wonder why the car was still there, maybe even walk along to find out.

Dong hit the iron stairs running, taking them two at a time, charging upward to the seventh floor. When he arrived he shot back the two bolts and stepped carefully out onto the roof. He ducked down and edged along to the chimney block, then reached up and undid the trash tie, removing the gray plastic cover in one movement. Then he edged up onto the sloping part of the roof and stared through the lens at the crosshairs. The submarine had not moved, nor had the viewfinder, and he was looking at the precise spot on the deck of USS *Seawolf* he had fixed on yesterday.

Then Quinlei Dong, husband of Lin, father of nine-year-old Li, switched on the laser machine that would guide an American bomb toward the first major nuclear catastrophe in the entire history of Canton. He watched the little green light flicker, then harden up, and he knew the invisible laser beam was lancing across the jetty, over the heads of the massed ranks of China's naval guards, pinpointing a spot on the ship's casing, illuminating it for the incoming bomb, which, right now and for the next six hours, could not miss.

He waited for a few seconds, looking out over the parapet at the American submarine. Even at this hour, early on Sunday evening, there was unusual activity around the great underwater ship. He could see a group of four men in white laboratory coats talking to uniformed officers on the casing; three other men were walking back across the gangway. He could see, on top of the sail, at least four uniformed figures on the bridge. Guards were everywhere.

Dong ducked down before they saw him and moved quickly back to the door, quietly bolting it behind him. He flew down the stairs to the first floor and reached the steel door to the outside. He pushed it open a crack, and to his horror heard voices and footsteps. For one appalling moment he thought he had been seen, and that a patrol was on its way in to search for him.

He eased the door shut and waited. Then he opened it again and there was silence. Up ahead he could see two guards disappearing around a corner. He checked again that the street was clear; then he slipped outside, and walked resolutely the 50 yards to his car. He started it quickly and drove around the back of C Block, avoiding the guard to whom he had spoken earlier.

At the main gate, he was stopped and asked if he had finished his work. Dong replied that he had, and that he had advised the other guard that he could lock the building up.

"Okay, sir . . . see you tomorrow?"

"'Specially if the lights don't work in B Block!"

The duty guard laughed and waved him through the gates for the last time. Thirty minutes from now, he and Lin and their little boy would be on the road south toward Kowloon, where the American agent had new identities for them all. Dong and his little family would be on the evening flight to Hawaii, and then Los Angeles.

2015. Sunday evening.

Lt. Commander Olaf Davidson and his team had deflated their Zodiac, buried it with most of their equipment, and left the original rendezvous point on the distant southern peninsula of the island. And now Catfish Jones and Al, fully armed, faces blackened, carrying the big machine gun, were moving into a spot right above the new landing beach a half-mile from the jail, still in sight of the patrol boat, which had just left the jetty.

Olaf himself was up in the SEALs' hide with Hank, overlooking the jail, checking off Rusty Bennett's list of guard times, numbers and patrols both inside and outside the wall. The slightest change in the pattern would be noted and assessed. But so far the SEAL commander had recorded every movement precisely as it had been for the previous two days and nights. The only minor variation was the seven-minute lateness of the patrol boat's departure and the arrival earlier in the afternoon of a big Russian-built helicopter. There were, however, still only two on the landing pad, as there usually were, according to Rusty's report.

Down at the beach, in the gathering darkness, Catfish had the night-sight binoculars trained on the jetty, where two seamen had cast off the patrol boat's lines and now stood talking. Rusty's notes said they always left the area as soon as the boat departed and returned to the dormitory. Catfish hoped they would do the same in the next half-hour, otherwise he and Al would have to kill them.

Meanwhile Al made ready the signaling lights and established the machine gun in a position covering the approach to the jetty. If the big SEALs landing party was sighted and the Chinese swarmed down to the beach to repel them, the first 50 of them would never get past the wall of .50-caliber bullets that would spit death at them, straight out of the jungle.

Up in the hide, Olaf Davidson checked his watch. It was 2103. The guard change outside the jail had taken place right on time, and he could see the four men walking in pairs slowly around the jail. If things went according to plan, this was their last patrol. The boys would be in less than two hours from now.

2109. Sunday evening. South China Sea.
The Flight Deck. USS *Ronald Reagan*.
18.25N 112.35E. Speed 25. Course 225.

Lt. Commander Joe Farrell glanced up at the island. The red light signaled four minutes to launch. Ahead of him, through the cockpit window, he could see the brightly lit runway stretched out in front. All around him the launch men were moving into position. Even stationary, the big engines screamed at the slightest touch on the throttle of the supersonic F/A-18 McDonnell Douglas Hornet.

The aircraft would effortlessly carry 7.7 tons of bombs if necessary, but tonight she carried just one, the 14-foot-long Paveway with its laser-guidance system and 1,000-pound high-explosive warhead.

Two minutes went by, and now the light blinked to amber. The crewman crouching right below Joe, next to the aircraft's nose, signaled him forward and moved underneath the fuselage, locking on the thick catapult bridle.

High above him the light turned green. The "shooter," Lieutenant Dale, pointed his right hand at the pilot and raised his left, extending two fingers: *Go to full power right now.*

Joe Farrell opened the throttle, releasing the howling, murderous energy of the engines. Lieutenant Dale flattened out the palm of his hand, staring hard at the pilot: *Hit the afterburners.*

Lieutenant Commander Farrell saluted formally and leaned forward, tensing for the impact of the catapult. The shooter, his eyes locked into Joe's, saluted back. Then he bent his knees and touched two fingers of his left hand onto the deck.

He gestured *Forward!* and the crewman on the catwalk just to the left of the aircraft hit the button on catapult one, and ducked low as the massive force of the wire flung the big fighter jet off the blocks.

Joe Farrell, throttles open wide, gripped the stick, his knuckles ivory as the Hornet screamed flat-out down the catapult, leaving a hot blast in its wake. Every veteran pilot and air crewman watching the takeoff held his breath. Up in the island, Colonel Frank Hart, standing with the admiral, found his hands shaking at the sheer formal drama of the moment as Joe Farrell set off to destroy USS *Seawolf*.

The nose of the Hornet rose as she thundered forward, and a collective sigh of relief broke out as the spectacular U.S. Navy fighter attack aircraft rocketed off the deck and then lumbered into the night sky, carrying her deadly steel burden below, making almost 200 knots, climbing out to port. "Tower to Hornet one-zero-zero . . . good job there . . . you're cleared out."

"Hornet one-zero-zero, roger that."

**1919. Sunday evening.
Cockpit of the Hornet.**

L IEUTENANT COMMANDER FARRELL HAD HIS EYES down on the instrument panel as the fighter attack aircraft screamed across the South China Sea, 250 feet above the waves, covering six and a half miles every minute. This was the most demanding part of the combat flyer's art, staying low, below all military radar, knowing that one too-firm touch on the stick will send you hurtling upward onto the screens of the enemy, or alternatively straight into the sea and instant death in a pirouetting fireball.

U.S. Navy pilots practice low-level flying constantly, but the dangers remain, and the concentration required to stay precisely 250 feet above the water at high speed is nothing short of awesome, especially at night.

Farrell's Hornet was cruising at only 400 knots, but any time he saw a light on the ocean up ahead, say 1.5 miles ahead, he was past it in 13 seconds. And he held the stick hard, his gaze switching from course to height, from windshield to trim, murmuring occasionally into his microphone, back to the carrier, which was now 120 miles astern, 15 minutes into his journey.

And now he made a course change, just as he howled across the unseen line of longitude at 113.30 degrees, due south of the port of Macao. He turned the aircraft north for the 30-mile run up to the mouth of the estuary to the Pearl River, straight over the Wanshan Dao, less than five minutes flying time.

He saw the island lights right below, and over to the left was the brightness of Macao. He swung nine degrees west of due north, settling momentarily on course three-five-one, hugging the shore in the shadow of the 1,500-foot mountains west of the city of Sanxiang.

One touch on the stick and he was out over the central channel of the river, east of Kowloon, passing the island of Qiao, and then he turned back with split-second timing onto course three-five-zero, right over the vast wetlands. He rammed open the throttle and felt the surge in power as the Hornet accelerated to a speed just below 600 knots, just short of the speed where she might make a giveaway sonic boom. He had her on a beeline for the Canton dockyards right now . . . and he was ten miles southeast . . . nine . . . eight . . . seven . . . the miles scorched by under his wings . . . and now it was six. His automatic preset bomb sight, counting down the seconds, told him to pitch up.

Lieutenant Commander Farrell reached out with his gloved right hand and made the PERMISSIVE button. He pulled back on the stick and the Hornet, for the first time, gained height, coming up on a precise 45-degree climb angle. Right below the fuselage, the bomb automatically released, and the big Paveway 3 was flung upward by the sheer force and momentum of the aircraft 3,000 feet farther into the sky, whistling through the darkness at a decreasing velocity, the first mile in four and a half seconds, the second, third and fourth in less than 30.

And now, as it reached the top of its trajectory, it began to head down into its long flight to the ground, its laser guidance system scanning the terrain below, searching for the tiny illumination so meticulously aimed by Quinlei Dong.

Lieutenant Commander Farrell made an Immelmann turn, racing higher in the sharpest loop he could, upside-down and then rolling out, carefully easing back down to 250 feet above the wetlands. Then he gunned the aircraft back over the central channel, turning south toward the open ocean. Still making almost 600 knots, he was past Kowloon just a few moments before Quinlei Dong parked his car at Hong Kong International Airport.

And like Dong, he would keep going until he touched down on American soil, or at least American steel.

Meanwhile the bomb hurtled downward through the darkness, silently locking onto Dong's laser illumination, its fins making the course adjustments as it fell, steering the dark green killer immaculately toward its target. No one could see it. No one could hear it. No one could possibly know it was coming.

There were six guards on the foredeck, six Chinese technicians in the sonar room, and twenty other submarine experts in various parts of the ship, several of them Russian. No one knew a thing about it when the Paveway 3 smashed into the casing at 2140 precisely. It came in making a strange, soft, eerie whistle. Inside one millisecond its armor-piercing head had smashed straight through the pressure hull and into the massively protected reactor compartment, exploding with a dull, shuddering K-E-R-R-B-A-A-M six feet from the seething mass of the reactor core.

The actual explosion of the Paveway was brilliantly contained by the iron grip of the American-built compartment, but the bomb wreaked fearsome damage internally, catastrophically rupturing the steel pipes of the primary coolant circuit in four places. The water system driving through the reactor under pressure of 2,300 pounds per square inch blew open, flashing off to steam instantly, blasting into the compartment.

The pumps stopped as the control rods automatically dropped into the core to scram the reactor. Both of the big isolation valves, failing safe even after the explosion of the bomb, slammed shut, automatically sensing the cataclysmic drop in pressure in the circuit outside the steel reactor vessel. And now the reactor was being starved of the purified, pressurized water that takes away the heat caused by the fission of the enriched uranium-235 in the core. Control of the lethal fast neutrons was quickly slipping away as the core grew hotter and hotter and hotter.

There was only one chance to save the reactor, and that was the automatic emergency cooler system built to cope with occasions such as this—catastrophic failure of the primary coolant circuit. This, too, has two big valves and is designed to suck in seawater—any water, for God's sake—and drive it through the core, for its hydrogen content to fight the diabolical energy of the neutrons, the basic energy of an atomic bomb. And the water was life-giving in more senses than one: its sheer cooling effect is designed to prevent the meltdown of the whole core.

The incoming water is known as the "cold leg." By the time it powers away from the mass of seething silver-colored uranium-235, it is outrageously hot, and will be driven out through the pipes of the second part of the system, the "hot leg." But, thanks to the thoughtful activities of Judd Crocker and Mike Schulz while *Seawolf* was being towed into Canton, the isolation valve had been sabotaged to drift open, and now the ship had two hot legs, which represented a total disaster.

The emergency cooler circuit was dead. And the Chinese in the machinery control room, already terrified by the tremor of the bomb's blast, now saw to their horror how dead it was. They could see the core temperature rising spectacularly, racing upward toward inevitable meltdown. This was a Chinese Chernobyl.

They struggled against it, praying to whatever god might be available on this Sunday night that the emergency system would suddenly kick in. But Mike Schultz had made no mistake. Nothing was kicking anything, except for the bomb, in the context of Chinese ass.

Four minutes later, all indications of any possible salvation were lost, and the core temperature was now well above the danger level. Deep in the reactor room the residual radiation and heat were beginning to melt away the casing, and at 2148 the white-hot mass of uranium and stainless steel burned clean through the 15-foot-wide fortified bottom of the reactor vessel and dropped down onto the hull of the submarine.

In a few seconds, it reduced that colossally strong five-inch-thick steel casing to melted butter and dropped into the waters of Canton Harbor. On its way it turned *Seawolf* into a death trap, the radioactive fallout filling the reactor compartment and beyond. The waters of the harbor would be lethally unsafe for a minimum of 40 years.

Up in the control room, the scientists were fully aware of the scale of the disaster. There were radiation alarms sounding everywhere, and there was a weird glow in the water. The warning, "CORE MELTDOWN . . . CORE MELTDOWN," had already echoed through the ship, where mass panic now ensued.

The acting CO ordered "ABANDON SHIP! . . . WE HAVE CORE MELTDOWN!"

There was a stampede to disembark as technicians, scientists, and seamen alike raced for the hatches and the gangways. *Seawolf* still floated, even with her reactor compartment flooded with seawater, but anyone who spent more than 10 minutes on the ship right now was a dead man, probably with a maximum of three weeks to live.

Admiral Zhang's dream of copying the great American emperor of the deep was over, and suddenly, in the space of just 15 minutes, they were in a desperate damage-control situation. The officer in command literally ran for his life, followed by the scientists, and he roared at them to keep running to the most distant of naval offices right out by the gate.

When he arrived the office door was locked, and he blew the lock off with his service revolver. They all headed for desks and telephones and opened up a conference line to Fleet Headquarters at Zhanjiang, direct to Admiral Zhang Yushu.

The C-in-C was stunned, and he found himself in an argument with the on-the-spot nuclear physicists, who felt that the only way to cope with the catastrophe was to sink *Seawolf* right here, letting her subside and settle on top of the reactor core. Then somehow, they could isolate the area for possibly 500 yards and perhaps contain the water around the submarine, possibly with a dam, anything to stop the contamination from spreading into the city.

However, there were technicians who very much wanted a second shot at the American boat, and they wanted to tow the submarine out into the open ocean and try to remove the key systems from it.

For Zhang this was a ray of hope in the darkness and now, yelling on the increasingly hysterical conference line, he demanded they do as he ordered, tow the submarine out and then board it and have one more try at removing the critical parts.

Dr. Luofu Pang, the senior physicist and one of China's most respected scientists, finally agreed, or at least he seemed to agree. "Admiral," he said, "if that is what you order, then I am not in a position to tell the Navy what to do. And so be it."

But he added, "I will, however, issue to you my final thought: any man who boards that submarine for just ten minutes will die. If you send in many of our expert technicians, we will lose them all. I deeply regret to inform you, sir, that this is not a practical proposition. And if you do issue an order that knowingly sends our best men to their immediate death, after an accident in which I have been personally involved, my advice must be properly recorded, and I shall take immediate steps to ensure it is."

And then his voice hardened. "Admiral," he said. "Forget it."

Zhang knew bald-faced reason when he heard it. And he just said quietly, "Very well, Dr. Luofu. I am disappointed, as a military man. But I bow to the great scientist. Please do everything you can to ensure the safety of everyone in the area. And sink the submarine as you see fit."

They were big words from, essentially, a big man. Admiral Zhang had not become the youngest-ever Commander-in-Chief of the People's Liberation Army/Navy by some kind of fluke.

At this time, in the minutes before 10:00 on this Sunday evening, July 16, 2006, the big Navy yard began to react, its nuclear accident organization activating the predetermined plan to deal with such disasters—radiation monitoring and decontamination teams, fire and medical squads, wind and weather checks.

Back in the central area of the city they slowly learned there had been an accident on the base. The police moved quickly to evacuate and cordon off the immediate areas around the submarine, particularly downwind and into the city. Their principal concern was to avoid mass panic.

The police chief called his Beijing headquarters to inform them of the disaster, and already the media were trying to make contact with the Navy itself. It took only another few minutes before Admiral Zhang Yushu was on the line to Beijing, informing his government that somehow or another, the big American nuclear submarine in the Canton dockyard had suffered a serious nuclear accident while engineers were working on the reactor.

They already knew that the dockyard was heavily contaminated, but so far there was no evidence of radiation spreading to the city itself. The police felt it would be unwise to allow any flights into Canton airport until a proper assessment had been made over the next two days.

Back in Zhanjiang, Zhang had his own private worries. His first instinct was that his own scientists had somehow screwed the entire thing up. There must have been American reactor protection systems capable of dealing with this sort of problem. So the scientists had "done a Chernobyl"—deactivating safety systems in order to carry out some crass experiment of their own. Zhang shuddered. Surely not.

Maybe the Americans had an automatic booby-trap device fitted into the submarine, and they had known all along that it would ultimately self-destruct. Hence the polite, devious messages through the diplomatic channels. Being made to look a complete fool was a condition to which Zhang was not accustomed. Nor was he appreciative.

He summoned Admiral Zu Jicai and briefed him on the disaster in Canton. Jicai was thunderstruck, his natural calm evaporating in emotional turmoil. To Zhang's repeated question—was *Seawolf* booby-trapped?—his answer was a qualified no. Both men knew they had the cooperation of one of the senior Americans, the executive officer, no less, Lt. Commander Bruce Lucas.

On one evening he had quite agreeably spent the night on board the submarine and had shown no sign of nerves that the ship might self-destruct. He had even been questioned about such a possibility. Both Zhang and Zu had read the report, and the American had assured them he had never even heard of any American warship being so protected.

Nonetheless, both Chinese admirals felt a certain contempt for the American officer who had given in to their demands for information about the inner workings of the great underwater ship. It was connected to the innate Chinese phobia about loss of face, pride in your standing and position. Like all Chinese military men, they had a grudging respect for men like Judd Crocker, Brad Stockton and the unfortunately deceased Cy Rothstein, men who were unshakeable, to the death if necessary, in their loyalty and patriotism.

For Bruce Lucas they had little time, and it was with a certain sadistic pleasure that Admiral Zhang picked up the telephone and opened up the line to Commander Li, who was just dining in his private rooms, above the comm center, outside the jail in Xiachuan.

"Good evening, Li," he said. "I am sorry to call you so late, but you may not have been notified that there has been a major disaster at the Canton base."

"No, sir. I have not been informed."

"The American submarine has had a serious nuclear accident and contaminated most of the dockyard. It was apparently a reactor meltdown. Privately, I think our scientists may not have been quite competent to work on it without willing American assistance, and that they ran it too hot or something. However, we must be aware that the ship may have been booby-trapped to blow itself to pieces if it ever fell into foreign hands."

"We did question Lieutenant Commander Lucas about this, and he professed to know nothing of such a scheme," replied Li.

"However," said Zhang, "he is clearly a cowardly man who may be dishonest, and I think you should have him removed to the interrogation room again as soon as possible, tonight. Keep him awake. Try the wet towel again, hah? That way we may get a serious answer. . . . Thank you, Li. Let's speak tomorrow early before the prisoners are moved."

2215. Sunday evening.
South China Sea. 21.12N 112.35E.

All three American submarines were now at periscope depth, making 8 knots through 150 feet of water, some 30 miles south of the
assault beach. The depths on the fathometers steadily lessened. In
all three boats, the attention of the commanding officers was fixed
on the voices calling out the depth below the keel—the ever-
increasing proximity of the soft sandy ocean floor as it sloped up
to the mainland.

Minutes passed, and then . . . "Fifty-feet on the sounder."

At 2250, *Cheyenne* was calling less than 20 feet under the keel;
one more mile and they would surface, running in toward the landing beach. *Cheyenne*'s satellite comms had already established
that the Xiachuan patrol boat was back on the jetty, and there was
no sign of a further Chinese warship.

And so, in heavy rain and a light wind, the three Los Angeles–class
boats came sliding out of the dark ocean into the hot, wet night air of
the south China tropics. They pushed forward on the surface for
another four miles, watching the ESM, checking that there was no
shore-based radar along the desolate coastline, which there was not.
And then they came almost to a halt, riding on an easy swell in 50 feet
of water, four miles off the southern beaches of the island.

The SEALs were ready and began to climb out onto the deck,
each one wearing heavy black camouflage cream on his face.
Already on deck, members of the submarine crews were inflating
the much bigger Zodiacs, priming the engines, checking the gas.
Then, from the decks of *Cheyenne* and *Greenville*, 32 SEALs each
expertly manhandled them into the water and climbed aboard for
the three-mile power-assisted run into Xiachuan. The last mile they
would paddle, just as Olaf Davidson's recon team had done two
nights previously.

Each of the big rubber boats was now commanded by one of
the SEALs who had reconnoitered the island. Lieutenant Commander Bennett was in the lead, followed by Lt. Dan Conway's boat,
then Buster Townsend, then John. Chief McCarthy would lead the

four from *Cheyenne*, followed by Paul Merloni, Rattlesnake Davies and Bill.

Eight SEALs traveled in each boat, which was a tight squeeze because they all had to bring equipment: machine guns, ladders, satchel bombs, det-cord, antitank launchers, grappling hooks, grenades, and a box of flares to light the place up once they'd gone noisy. In addition, there were small hand-held radios, already primed to connect with the bigger one that would be carried by Lt. Commander Rick Hunter's personal bodyguard and would act as the command post for each of the marauding SEAL teams. In addition, there was the navigation kit, compasses, GPS systems, medical supplies, and light aluminum stretchers.

The engines kicked into life, the noise surprisingly quiet for such powerful engines. But the word from the sonar and radar rooms was excellent. There were no Chinese ships within 25 miles, save for the parked patrol boat on the jetty at Xiachuan.

And so they set off at a low growl, running fast at 20 knots, heading due north for the beach where Olaf and Catfish would signal them in. Rusty knew the light on the southern headland of Shangchuan Dao would be their guide, and he spotted it after eight minutes, a fast bright flash to starboard every five seconds. He checked his watch, and kept going, the other seven boats line astern. Six more minutes and he would signal to cut the speed, and he thanked God for the rain, which tended to deaden sound on the water.

At 23:45, they drifted silently to a halt and the SEALs took up the paddles, perching on the broad rubberized gunwhales of the Zodiacs and pulling long, quiet strokes through the water. No lights, no sound, guided only by the compass and the soft green glow of the numbers on Rusty Bennett's GPS system.

At 23:55 Lieutenant Commander Bennett spotted his second bright light of the journey, right off their port bow, three quick flashes every 20 seconds, the agreed-upon signal . . . *"There he is, it's Olaf and Catfish right in there . . ."*

He muttered in the dark, "Starboard four, two strokes," and he felt the boat swing to port. "All pull now . . . six strokes and wait . . .

starboard side, two . . . portside, one . . . all pull again ten strokes and easy . . ."

And then he felt the boat moving on its own as Olaf and Catfish grabbed the bow handles expertly and hauled the Zodiac inshore, through the shallows and onto the beach. The SEALs jumped out and grabbed the handles, two men peeling off from each boat to assist the next one in.

Rusty, now assuming command on the landing beach, ordered two crewmen to remain with each boat, a total of 16 valuable SEALs. But the getaway beach was a mile to the north, up beyond the jetty, the closest possible water to the jail. And the moment the patrol boat blew, the eight Zodiacs had to be floated out and driven with all speed right past the wreck to the point where *Seawolf*'s stricken crew would begin to arrive. And theirs had to be the shortest possible journey because of the wounded.

Meanwhile Hank and Al came ghosting out of the jungle, shook hands quickly with Lieutenant Commander Hunter, and led the way back to the point in the trees where they had cut sufficient undergrowth to form a muster point. Rusty Bennett supervised the unloading of the gear, and Lieutenant Conway was in charge of moving it up the beach into the cleared area.

Conditions may have seemed awful, pitch dark and driving tropical rain, but for this operation, conditions were perfect. The only lights anyone could see were on the distant patrol boat, moored at the jetty. And now Lieutenant Commander Hunter began to assemble his teams, three of them, 16 men in each.

Team A would be led by Rusty Bennett. Under his command would be Chief John McCarthy, the three British SAS men, Buster Townsend, two expert climbers, John and Bill, plus eight regular seamen. Their task was the initial assault, taking the watchtowers, scaling the walls, taking out the guard patrol inside the jail, blowing up the guard house and the main gates, and then moving in to assist in prisoner release. At this point Chief McCarthy would take over command while Rusty peeled off to command the exit beach.

Team B would be led by Lt. Dan Conway. His second-in-command was Lt. Paul Merloni, and the team included Rattlesnake Davies,

Petty Officers Catfish Jones, Steve Whipple, and Rocky Lamb, plus Hank, Al, and eight other SEALs on their first mission. Their critical task was to attack the camp headquarters, and destroy all communications equipment; attack the combined administration and dormitory block, preventing any of its inhabitants from influencing events; and kill any guards patrolling outside the walls of the jail.

Team C would be commanded by Lt. Commander Olaf Davidson. His second-in-command would be Lt. Ray Schaeffer. They would be assisted by Lt. Junior Grade Garrett Atkins and a team of SEAL veterans because this group was the uncommitted reserve, and they had to be ready for anything, particularly in the event of a crisis. Their principal tasks were to destroy the patrol craft and the two helicopters, and thereafter to move right in close and provide backup to both Team A and Team B in the release of the prisoners. They were also in command of the medical supplies, plus the lightweight stretchers

Lieutenant Commander Hunter would man the command post, which would be situated on a section of steep, wooded ground 40 yards southwest of the helicopter pad, just left of the track down which the prisoners had first marched. The recon team had spotted this ideal place because of its clear view of the main gates. Rick would be assisted by Lt. Bobby Allensworth, who would also act as his personal bodyguard, plus two other SEALs during the initial phases of the attack. They would provide the radio contact for all three teams. If there were any problems, Rick Hunter would decide on the length of delay.

Only when the outer buildings were destroyed, the inner guards subdued, and the gates blasted open would Rick Hunter and his team move into the main courtyard of the jail and organize the exit of the prisoners down to Rusty Bennett's beach.

Right now, it was still pitch dark and raining like hell, and the equipment was arriving agonizingly slowly in the jungle clearing. But SEALs hate mistakes, hate leaving anything behind, hate unchecked lists, hate forgetting anything, hate surprises. Lieutenant Conway was working with a small waterproof laptop, checking *everything* under its subdued light, and Olaf Davidson was moving each piece of equipment to the appropriate team, each of which was now occupying a separate section of the clearing.

Rick Hunter walked among them, whispering instructions to each leader, particularly in terms of the radio signals. The lieutenant commander wanted no words unless, as he put it, "the fucking roof's falling in." His preferred method of communication was quick bleeps from the hand-held sets, one for *nearly ready*, two for *ready*, three for *minor problem*, one long beep for *crisis*.

It was almost 0030 before they were ready to move, which meant they were around an hour behind schedule, but that was built in to the mission. Colonel Hart knew they would be an hour behind, but he thought they would catch up once they were under way. And now Rick Hunter ordered everyone forward into the soaking-wet darkness, and they moved silently in different directions, each leader carrying his map of the jail, his map of the island, and his timing notes made so carefully by Rusty and the recons.

The watchword was H-hour—"H" for HIT. They were expected to be in position one hour from now, and that would be H minus 15, or 15 minutes from the opening attack. Thus, right now they were looking at H minus 75, SEAL time.

Down along the shore, Ray Schaeffer and Garrett Atkins led two other SEALs through the trees at the top end of the beach, and they walked with stealthy steps, a special SEAL walk, light, moving weight forward at the last moment, avoiding the breaking of small twigs. In full daylight they would have looked a bit like extras from the *Pink Panther* movies, but they traveled deceptively fast and made no sound. In addition to their personal weaponry, each of the four men carried two light plastic disposable antiarmor rocket launchers, the M136-Bofors.

Their program was vital and simple. On the command, precisely at H-hour, Ray and Garrett would fire one shell each at the patrol boat. Each one would hit the port side, one below the waterline, one above. Depending on the damage, they would then fire two more. Of course, if the first two reduced the ship to matchwood, no further action would be necessary, although Ray would put two SEALs with their light machine guns within 40 feet of the end of the gangway, specifically to cut down any Chinese crew who were able to make a run for it. The objective was plain: to ensure that no one could possibly get a radio message off that ship. Being SEALs, that meant the total destruction of all radio equipment plus anyone who might be able to work it.

And still they slipped through the edge of the jungle, watching the lights from the ship draw nearer. With 200 yards still to walk they swung deeper into the trees, following the route Rusty Bennett had suggested. Then they turned in, back toward the ship, coming at it softly, step by step, finding their position, looking straight at it from the cover of the foliage. Time was running out for the Chinese ocean patrol.

The walk had taken them 40 minutes. It was H minus 35, and out on the edge of the jail's precincts, the other members of their team, Lt. Commander Olaf Davidson and his veterans, were staring down at the two helicopters from a hillside southeast of the prison. Olaf knew that Colonel Hart was not in favor of timed detonations because once they were fixed they had to stay fixed. He instinctively agreed with that, realizing that if there was a hitch and they had to delay the start, they would have to deactivate the charge, which aside from being a PITA was also bloody dangerous, and they might get caught under the choppers.

Thus he placed two men with the light portable antitank launchers in prime position, less than 50 yards from the choppers. The first moment the operation went noisy, they would rip a high-explosive shell straight through the cockpit of each aircraft, both of which were full of fuel and would unquestionably explode in a massive fireball. The guys would want to stand well back from that one, especially as the blast might send up the fuel dump as well.

Olaf watched his men move into place. Then he moved on through the rain and set the rest of the team up in two strategic locations. Group one would conceal themselves in a position opposite the southeast corner of the wall, ready to follow the first assault force through the main gate. Group two would provide covering fire and backup to the force that would attack the dormitory, where there could be resistance. Olaf ordered his men right around to the western hill, from where they could if necessary destroy the entire building. By the time they were settled, it was H minus 25.

Dan Conway's Team B had to move a lot of high explosive, and they were slower through the jungle than Olaf and Ray Schaeffer. There was a pile of satchel bombs, four of them containing special compressed gas with which to blast open the administration block. The regular high explosive was for the commandant's quarters, which also held the communication center. The satchels weighed 40 pounds each, and they were life or death to this mission. There was a contingency plan for each one of them—*What if two SEALs were gunned down on the way in? That would require two more, maybe four.*

There were four buildings to be hit, and whereas 8 bombs would do the job just fine, they had to bring 16, just in case. That was a 320-pound insurance policy against the lives of 170-odd Americans that Dan and his team carried. Fit as mountain lions, they hauled their burdens through the wet, clinging jungle. SEALs walked out in front with machetes, cleaving some kind of a path for Rocky Lamb, Rattlesnake Davies, and the gigantically strong Catfish Jones, who carried two satchels on his own, as did Steve Whipple. And the rain beat down, and the SEALs slipped and cursed softly, and they prayed that it would not stop pouring on this night of the Nighthawks.

By the time Dan had deployed his team it was H minus 20, and they were almost ready. Lt. Paul Merloni, in company with three other SEALs, was the last man in place, completely concealed in a hollow opposite the north wall, right in the area where he would attempt to kill all four Chinese guards, or six if necessary. Olaf's note had reported two extra guards on duty in the afternoon, but of course he had no way of knowing whether the same would apply after midnight. Nonetheless, the warning was there.

Rick Hunter himself, traveling lightly, was established in position first, the big radio placed next to him by Lt. Bobby Allensworth. That radio was the link between Rick and all of the SEALs; through its VHF transmissions would flow all commands and minor plan changes. In a crisis the radio was the SEALs' only lifeline, the only way they could access the carrier and send for help if the Chinese managed to bring in reinforcements. But the odds against that happening were heavy.

Team A also had a long walk to the north wall of the jail. They were there a few moments before Paul Merloni was almost shot dead by Buster Townsend, when the Italian New Yorker hissed, "Velly good work, Mr. Buster . . . velly fine job . . . you like my sister? She velly clean . . ."

Chief McCarthy almost exploded trying to stop laughing, not so much at Paul's sophomoric humor, but at Buster's instant assessment that this might be a real live Chinese person. They all needed a laughter break, even Rusty Bennett, and they chuckled silently together, standing under the trees, 100 yards from the north wall, still holding the seven heavily padded, black-covered ladders. Paul Merloni and two other SEALs had to leave immediately, since they were delivering satchel bombs to the members of Team A on the east side.

It was H minus 16 when Rusty ordered them to close into the wall, as soon as the two-man patrol vanished around the northwestern corner. And both he and Chief McCarthy, with John and Bill, eased forward, crawling on their stomachs, while two other SEALs established a big machine gun aimed straight at the northwestern watchtower. The other machine gun was already in position, aimed at the northeastern watchtower, and also in position to open fire anywhere along the eastern wall. The three British SAS men were hiding 40 yards from that wall, faces blackened, gloved and armed, ready to go over the top. Three other young SEALs, each of them holding one of the 40-pound satchels, were hidden five yards to the left of the SAS men, ready to follow them over the wall 13 seconds later. Right now it was H minus 15.

1300 (local). Sunday afternoon.
Office of Admiral Morgan. The White House.

The admiral was on his way back from the Pentagon, and inside his office there were only two people, Kathy O'Brien and the President of the United States, who was, by any standards, totally distraught.

In the mind of the most powerful leader in the West, there was but one image, that of his only son Linus in a Chinese torture chamber, possibly having his fingernails ripped out or electrodes attached to him, all the grisly ideas used in both factual and fictional accounts of interrogation in Far Eastern countries.

And all he could think of was the terrified face of his little boy, and he couldn't fight his own fears any longer, and his great shoulders heaved as he wept uncontrollably at the desk of his National Security Adviser.

Kathy had her arms around him, and she was desperate to stop the complete disintegration of the Chief Executive, desperate that no one should come in and see him like this. She had locked the door, and she was saying over and over, using his Christian name for the only time in her life, "No, John, please don't. You mustn't be this upset. Arnold says we have the matter in hand . . . he's certain the SEALs will free him tonight. . . . Arnold will be back in a few minutes . . . he's already left the Pentagon. . . . Just please don't give in, sir . . . we have to have faith . . . I don't know where I'd be without mine."

The President made a huge effort, and he took from his pocket a large white handkerchief and wiped his tear-stained face dry, trying to regain his composure, trying to fight from his subconscious the reflection of Linus as a little boy. "Are you a Catholic?" he asked Kathy.

"Yessir. I am. My Irish family has been for centuries. How about you, sir?"

"I wish I was," he replied. "They seem to gain a greater strength from their religion in times of trouble."

"Oh, I think that's to do with faith, sir. The stronger your faith, the easier it is."

"But I was brought up to have faith. I just somehow wish it was the Catholic faith. . . . Kathy, what would your priest tell me to do right at this moment?"

"I cannot be sure, sir. But he would certainly mention that you must trust in the Lord, and that the Lord loves Linus as well as you, and that in the end he will keep him safe."

"But he does not keep everyone safe, does he?"

"In his own way, he does. But that's part of faith. You have to have it. That's what trusting in the Lord is. And you must pray for him . . . my priest would tell you that . . . just one still, small voice . . . but it will be heard . . . I know that's true, sir . . . you must pray . . . I am sure of that . . . why don't we just pray now for the safe deliverance home of Linus . . . here, now, together. Two voices might be better than one . . ."

"Two still, small voices?" he smiled.

"Yessir. Here and now . . . and I think we should kneel."

And so they did, and Kathy O'Brien said the words of a prayer she had been taught . . . and she recited them quietly. And then they prayed silently, until Kathy said, "Please, God, bring him home safely . . . with all of the others . . . in the name of our Lord Jesus Christ. Amen."

As if on cue, the Archangel Gabriel from the Pentagon arrived outside the door and thundered on it with his right fist. Kathy stood up and opened it, and Admiral Morgan charged in, his left fist raised.

He glanced down at the President, but seemed not to notice that the great man was on his knees, and snapped, "This is it, sir. We got the bastards on the run now. You want the good news or the even better news?"

"I'll take the good, then the even better."

"Right. Now, the Russian news agency is reporting a major nuclear accident in the navy yards at Canton. That's the end of *Seawolf*, and it has plainly caused the most gigantic diversion in the South China Sea. Our pilot is safely back in the carrier.

"Next, the Special Forces are in, right now surrounding the jail, everything is in our favor, and everything is in place. This is a classic SEAL operation. They attack in ten minutes, and I shall personally be astounded if the submarine crew is not free and on its way home in the next two hours. How's that?"

"I'd say pretty darned good. But tell me, why the overwhelming optimism?"

"Well, sir. Hitting the submarine was very difficult, but now we know the Chinese have something to be massively concerned about. I suspect all of their energies are being diverted to the disaster in

Canton. In addition, the recon and then the insertion of the big Special Force were always the most dangerous. It's getting in and remaining unseen that's so critical. Once the guys are in, safe, and armed to the teeth with all the explosive they need, it's dollars to doughnuts they'll succeed against an unalerted enemy. And that's the way I like it."

"As a matter of fact, that's the way I like it, too," added the President as he prepared to return to the Oval Office. "By the way, Kathy, you don't have a direct line up there, do you? Because it sure seems like you do."

"No, sir. Not direct. But he does hear us."

"Yes, Kathy. I guess he really does."

H minus 13.
Outside the Jail on Xiachuan Dao.

Tonight there were two Chinese guard patrols outside the jail. One consisted of four men who walked "two walls" in front of the two-man patrol; thus one patrol never saw the other, since they each arrived at diametrically opposite corners at the same time. In fact, Rusty had noted that after about one hour, the four-man group did tend to catch the other up, and then would quite deliberately wait until the gap between them was again correct.

Tonight, in the heavy rain, it was taking each group 53 seconds to walk along the 50-yard-long north wall. The shorter east and west walls then took only 43 seconds, which meant that tonight there was a window of only 43 seconds for the four SEALs to cross the track completely out of sight of the guards, scale the wall and drag the padded ladders up behind them.

It was plenty of time, but Lieutenant Commander Bennett knew the closer to the wall the four climbers hid, the more time they would have. And now he urged his three colleagues forward again, into the long grass, only 60 feet from the base of the prison wall.

And as he did so, he hit the radio buttons to Lieutenant Commander Hunter, one short sharp bleep, *almost ready*. It was H minus 12, and the rain kept pouring down. Up in the watchtower he could see the four men in the reflected glow of the big searchlights that swept the prison yard. It looked even wetter up there. Just moving around the corner from the east was the four-man patrol, and the SEALs held their collective breath, flat in the grass. The Chinese passed, walking firmly, rifles over their shoulders, looking ahead, and using, Rusty noted for the first time, a flashlight to illuminate the wet ground, with its now deep puddles. He also noted that they were not using the beam to sweep across the rough low jungle on the righthand side. Which was excellent news. The north side of the jail was the darkest by a long way, out of range of any light.

Rusty watched the guard walk on toward the end of the wall. Then he hit the radio button twice . . . *ready.* Instantly the single bleep from Rick Hunter came back . . . *GO.*

"This is it, guys . . . we're outta here." Rusty's words were typically SEAL, militarily unorthodox, sharp, to the point, with overtones of buddies, not officer to men. And with that they picked up their ladders, and raced silently across the rough ground, Rusty and John running diagonally west, Chief McCarthy and Bill to the other end of the north wall. They reached it in four seconds.

All four 15-foot ladders were placed against the wall within .0001 of a second of each other, and the SEALs climbed them in the dark at the pace they had been taught, fast but not too fast, no mistakes. They reached the top of the wall in 12 more seconds, rolling flat over the narrow parapet onto the jail's long flat roof, into the pitch dark beneath the watchtowers. Each SEAL lay stone silent below the tower guards for 10 seconds, and then they reached back over the outside wall and pulled up their padded ladders.

Less than half a minute had elapsed since Rick Hunter's beep, but now they had to wait until the two-man patrol passed by. It would be in just a few seconds, but they did not want to be working right above the heads of an armed foot patrol. The plan was to let the guards get back around to the west wall before they scaled the second half of the climb to the towers.

Timing was critical. Rusty Bennett peered over the wall, watching the guards walking by. In his hand he held his little radio, tuned to the frequency of Chief McCarthy.

The final guard turned the corner, and Rusty hit the button. John McCarthy's radio light blinked. They each counted to five and placed the four ladders softly against the upper wall surrounding the guards at the top of the tower. And then they set off, climbing more slowly, more carefully through the rain, one man on each side of the crow's nest where the Chinese worked the lights.

At the top, there was no more hesitation. Rusty Bennett could see the nearside guard with his back to him, and he pushed off the top rung, his fighting knife ready, jumped over the waist-high wall, rammed his arm around the man's head and sliced his throat almost in half. Three feet away Bill did exactly the same to the second man. There was no sound, but the mess was awful as two Chinese jugulars pumped out blood onto the floor.

Bill was in charge of what Rusty called "blood control," somehow dragging the two bodies into a corner while Rusty himself manned the light, keeping its pattern passing regularly across the courtyard.

Over in the other tower, Chief McCarthy and John were in exactly the same position, trying to stay away from the blood, the chief trying to synchronize his searchlight with that of Rusty in the other tower.

Back in the command post, Lieutenant Commander Hunter, watching through his night-sight glasses, knew the watchtowers were in American hands, which gave the all-clear for the guys to storm the wall. It was H minus 2.

And it was still quiet.

The two-man Chinese patrol was just passing the main gates, 15 seconds from the corner that turned onto the eastern wall, the wall the British SAS men were shortly to scale. Rick Hunter could see the patrol, but Buster and the men from Bradbury Lines could not. They had already signaled *"Ready."* But they could not move forward with their grapplers and ladders until the bleeper bleeped on Buster's radio. And right now there was silence.

The SAS troops waited in the grass. There was more light out here, and they saw the patrol as soon as it rounded the corner, flattened themselves into the ground, and gripped their MP-5 light machine guns. They were so close they could hear the guards' boots on the gravelly area below the wall, and watch them walk past. There was no danger to life, because if the guards had made one move of recognition the SEALs would have shot them both dead, but then they would have been in a very different kind of mission, a standup firefight they would probably have won, but at what cost?

Syd, Fred, Charlie and Buster stayed very quiet indeed, holding their breaths while the rain beat down on their backs. They watched the guards walk on to the far corner, and as they rounded it, Buster's "go-light" flickered on his radio. This signified two aspects of the attack: one, Rusty and the guys had taken the watchtowers, and the searchlights, which they now watched slowly sweeping the jail, were in American hands; two, this was it.

"Move it, y'all," snapped Buster in his deep Louisiana drawl.

"Right-ho, y'all," hissed Syd in his cockney dialect. "I'm just getting the old arse into gear . . ."

And with that the three SAS men flew out of the grass, and charged for the wall, leaving Buster half-laughing, half-petrified. The fate of the entire mission hung in the balance for the next 10 minutes. H-hour was right now.

It took Fred and his men 4 seconds to reach the wall, 3 more to put the ladders in place, and 10 more to climb to the top of the wall with the grapplers. The four-man Chinese patrol was still 28 seconds from the corner, and before they reached it, three more SEALs had raced out from the undergrowth and retrieved the ladders, because they could not have been left there, either knocked over on the ground or left against the wall.

Up on the parapet, Fred, Syd and Charlie lay flat in a long line, no one moving. In the watchtowers, Rusty and Chief McCarthy made minor adjustments to the range of the lights, stopping them short of the east wall where the SAS men were flattened into the shadows.

The trouble now was finding the patrol inside the jail, and right now no one could see anything. There was no reason to go over until they could at least see their target. Rusty and John McCarthy knew the problem: They couldn't spot the Chinese guards at this moment, either. And they probed the inner shadows with their searchlights.

After two minutes they spotted two of them emerging from the building opposite the guardroom, the mystery building they had never been certain of. They were regular uniformed Navy personnel and they took up positions on either side of the main gate, lit up by the lights from the open door of the guardroom.

The SEALs knew there was a regular patrol crossing the long front of the main cell block, but it was taking its time arriving, and on top of the wall, Charlie had already muttered, "Bastards are on their tea break."

He may have been correct, and it was 90 seconds later when the guards emerged from the shadows. Two of them quick-marched from west to east, then swung right up the short block at the end. The other two waited until they were ready to march back, much more slowly, and then they also set off. The two patrols would pass each other exactly in the center of the main block. Sergeant Fred Jones elected to take them out in pairs.

He hoped Rusty and Chief McCarthy were watching, and he signaled with his right arm to keep the lights away from the eastern side of the jail. Then he ordered the grappling irons in place, and he and his men climbed softly down into the jail yard, right between the single-cell block and the guardhouse, which had no windows on this side.

The wait was 24 seconds, but it seemed like four hours. Finally the two Chinese guards began to walk up the front of the single-cell block and as they reached the end, big Fred Jones and Syd Thomas suddenly appeared, bang in front of them. Each SAS man clamped his hand over the guard's mouth and dragged him into the dark space between buildings, permanently dark now, because the lights were not sweeping that far.

The killing was classic SAS, a deep thrust with a big fighting knife straight into the heart, cleaving it in half. Fred and Syd kept their hands rammed tight over the guards' mouths until the men died, a matter of a few seconds. Charlie Murphy slipped silently out of the shadows and helped drag the men to the deep darkness beneath the main wall.

By now, the other two were on their way along the main cell block, and Fred Jones knew they would realize something was amiss when they did not pass their colleagues at the halfway point. This was a critical point in the mission. And Fred could not afford a mistake. If the guards turned and ran from the courtyard back to the guard room, the three SAS men might find themselves surrounded and outnumbered. By now he knew there were three more SEALs on top of the eastern wall, and that they would probably survive a firefight.

But he did not want a firefight. And suddenly he knew they would have to go after the two guards right now. And he ordered Charlie Murphy to draw his light machine gun and cover them while he and Syd raced silently along the wall and took them out. He heard three more SEALs clear the wall with the satchel bombs for the guard-house, and then they set off.

They made the end of the single cells and swung left along the dark front of the main cell block. Up ahead the two guards were coming right at them, but they were talking and looking at each other. That little conversation bought the SAS men three more seconds. And they would not need much more.

"GO, SYD, GO!" hissed Fred, and now they ran flat-out, straight at the two guards, whose weapons were still shouldered. There was a 15-foot gap between them, and one suddenly saw two fearsome, blacked-up monsters right in front. He had time to say, not shout, in Chinese, "What the . . . ?" But it was not loud enough, there was no one near, and Syd Thomas was on him, a full frontal assault. He slammed the butt of his fist hard into the man's nose, grabbed his hair, jerked back his head and sliced his throat wide open.

The other guard turned to look, in total amazement, and he never really saw Fred Jones clearly as the Dorset sergeant crashed into him, driving his knife right between his ribs, killing him instantly. The guard was dead before he hit the floor with Fred's right hand rammed across his mouth.

"Leave 'em, and get back between the buildings," he snapped. And both men ran back along the shadows, to regroup with Charlie and the three newly arrived SEALs.

Fred Jones now decided it looked a bit different from down here, and that it was impossible to take out the main gate guards quietly with knives. The whole area along the front of the prison was bright, light flooding out from the guardroom and from the building on the right. They'd never get across there without being seen.

"That means we bomb the guardroom and shoot the sentries at the same time?"

"Better yet," said Syd, "let's just shoot the sentries and send in Charlie here with the det-cord to blow the gates. As soon as he gets to the gates, we blow the guardroom."

"Don't be a prick, Syd, we'd also blow Charlie. Sorry, lads, it's guardroom, sentries, gates in that order. Right now. I've got H plus seven."

Two SEALs prepared the blasting caps on the Mk 138 satchel bombs. Then they slipped around the corner, pulled the pins and hurled one through the lower window and one through the upper, diving back with the others flat on the ground, in the shadow of the single-cell block wall.

The detonation was savage. It blew the building to bits with deafening impact. The entire front wall caved in, and so did the roof. All that was left was a pile of smoking rubble. From the guards inside there was not a sound, since there were no survivors. As the dust and smoke cleared, the two gate guards could be seen running toward the obliterated building, but not for long. Fred Jones shot them both in their tracks. Another SEAL ran in behind Charlie Murphy and hurled a hand grenade into the lighted window in the mystery building to the right of the gates. Both SEALs flattened themselves to the ground as it exploded, killing all six of the Chinese interrogators, who were sitting drinking tea in the room to the left of the front door.

Instantly, Charlie Murphy reached the gates and wrapped three lengths of det-cord around the big jutting hinges and the central locking system. Then he retreated fast, playing out the det-cord behind him. He lit it at a range of 40 yards and blew the huge gates 10 feet into the air. At this point the SEALs had control of the interior of the prison. It was outside where the action now was.

As soon as the guardhouse was blown, Rick Hunter hit the GO button on Dan Conway's wavelength. The young lieutenant from Connecticut snapped, "GO!" and Petty Officers Catfish Jones and Steve Whipple charged around the corner and hurled two 40-pound satchel bombs straight into the upper and lower windows of the commandant's HQ and the main communications room above it. As with the guardroom, the impact was staggering; all four walls of the building were blown out and the roof just collapsed. Debris was flung everywhere, and it rained in through the trees, some of it close to where the SEALs were standing.

Rick Hunter put his head up into the dust cloud and tried to see something, but the dust was choking and the smoke made vision impossible. However, Rocky Lamb, Hank and Al were racing through it, Rocky's gun firing round after round through the doorway of the accommodation block, driving back the guards who were fighting to get out, pulling on coats, grabbing their rifles.

Lieutenant Conway came in right behind them, and he hurled three hand grenades one after another into the hallway. The one thing the ex-catcher could do was throw, real hard and dead straight. And the entrance hall was now a mass of fire, dust and bodies. Around the back of the building Hank and Al were priming their smoke bombs, which contained poisonous but not lethal gas that would knock out anyone for 24 hours and leave him very sick, with a shocking headache, but not dead.

They flung in two each, on both levels. The idea not to kill civilians had been Frank Hart's. But no matter what, no one was walking out of the dormitory right now, and those guards who had tried were no longer alive.

Simultaneously, the lights were flickering on the radios of Ray Schaeffer and Olaf Davidson. And it was Ray who moved first. In the last half-minute he had heard the succession of explosions, and now he whispered to Garrett Atkins, "Okay, buddy. Right now . . ."

And both men squeezed the triggers of their antitank launchers, and the two armor-piercing canisters came rocketing down the tubes, past their ears, and straight out into the night, straight at the Chinese patrol boat.

Garrett's slammed in and exploded bang in the middle of the super-structure, blasting the radio room to pieces. Ray's shell hit the guided missile launchers at the stern, which blew the ship apart with a thunderous explosion. Down by the gangway, the armed SEALs waited for any Chinese crew to show themselves. But there was nothing. Rusty Bennett had estimated there would only be three men, four at the most, and they probably had not survived. If one of them had, he would not be making radio contact with anyone.

Up on the hill overlooking the helicopters, Olaf ordered his men to fire. And they too unleashed the antitank weapons, demolishing both aircraft in massive fireballs that caused the nearby SEALs to move back, away from the heat. A half-minute later the fuel dump went up, sending a rolling ball of flame 100 feet into the air.

Rick Hunter looked up at the massive cloud of black smoke and muttered, "Jesus Christ! We might have overcooked this . . . you could see this fire in Shanghai."

So far, no prisoners had been either located or released. But the SEALs had done that which they were best at: brutal demolition of any installation they wanted removed, and any guards who might get in the way. The jail on Xiachuan was well and truly in American hands. At least, for the moment it was. The navy guards in the cell blocks were unlikely to be a match for the SEALs and their SAS colleagues.

0214. Monday morning, July 17.
Office of the Southern Fleet Commander. Zhanjiang.

Unsurprisingly, Admiral Zhang and Admiral Zu had not gone to bed, as the crisis in Canton continued to unfold. Already there were reports of badly burned men, of colossal levels of radioactivity. And now there was a further problem.

A young lieutenant was standing in the room informing the C-in-C that they were having trouble making phone contact with Xiachuan.

"How long have you been trying?" he asked.

"About ten minutes, sir. Since you asked us to inform Commander Li you wanted to see him in the morning."

"What kind of response?"

"That's the trouble, sir. No response. We can't even get the phone to ring."

"You mean the usual one in the main comms room?"

"Well, that one, and the private line to Commander Li, sir. It's not that they won't answer. It just won't ring out."

"Try the patrol boat. We've done that before."

"We've tried it, sir. Same result."

"How about the radio?"

"Nothing, sir. We have three technicians on it now, but they're not having any luck."

"So the problem is not just electronic, the phone wires. It's also affecting the airwaves."

"Yessir."

"Have you left satellite comms in place?"

"Yessir. And the replies usually come back very quickly from Xiachuan. But we're getting nothing."

"No phones. No radio response. Nothing on the satellite," the C-in-C murmured, a chill feeling of sheer dread pervading his entire body and mind. "And the American submarine blows up a few hours before."

He stood up, and said, "Thank you, Lieutenant." To his friend Zu Jicai, he said, "Jicai, we are under attack. The coincidences are too great."

Admiral Zu looked slightly helpless. He stood up and said, "You mean the Americans?"

"Who do you think I mean," he snapped, "the Tibetans?" All semblance of self-control was receding with the onset of the admiral's mounting anger.

"You mean they are on the island?"

"I don't know. But I think it's possible."

"Well, how did they get there? Is this an invasion?"

"I underestimated them," he muttered. "Jicai, I underestimated them. And I have done it before. No one knows how ruthless the Americans are when they have their backs to the wall. I just wonder, is there anything left for me . . . what can I do . . . how can I save face?"

0217. H plus 15. Monday, July 17.
Xiachuan Island.

Lt. Commander Rick Hunter could now hear only sporadic fire as Lieutenant Merloni and his men tried to wipe out the six guards on the outer rim. The first four had been simple, gunned down as they raced back clockwise from the north wall at the first sound of the guardroom blowing up.

The last two had come around the other way, very quickly, seen the direction of the SEAL machine gunfire, and opened up in the correct direction. They had not hit anyone, and one of them had gone down. But he regained his feet and ran back around the wall with his colleague, and they had escaped in the confusion.

Rick Hunter and his men had loosed off ultrabright flares to illuminate the area, and Lieutenant Merloni had pursued. But it was not successful, and they all believed both the Chinese to be still alive in the woods, which was bad news, but unavoidable. And it was both pointless and dangerous to continue pursuit in the darkness of the jungle, where anyone could be hit and killed.

Rick Hunter decided that now was the time and, signaling for Bobby Allensworth to bring the big machine gun, he and two other SEALs began to work their way down the hill and across the still dust-blown area in front of the buildings. For the first time, he noticed the rain had stopped.

And now the massive SEAL commander walked down by the light of the burning fuel dump. All around him were the men who had caused such havoc in the Chinese jail, falling in with him, walking tall, their submachine guns held out in front of them, many of them with their bandanas scorched black from the smoke, especially those who had been close to the burning fuel and the explosions inside the jail.

Rusty Bennett appeared from nowhere, covered in blood, and announced that he was on his way to the pickup point of the beach.

"You hurt, Rusty?" asked Rick, somewhat alarmed at the sight of his 2 I/C, who looked as if he had just gone three rounds with Mike Tyson.

"No, not me. I'm fine."

"Guess someone must have got hurt right next to you, huh?"

"Guess so. See you later, Chief."

The searchlights were still on, but Chief McCarthy and his men were coming out of the main gates now, and all three of them were variously splattered with blood.

Rick just shook his head at the unending courage of the men he fought with. "Great job, guys," he said. "Just a great job."

Olaf, Catfish, Buster, Rattlesnake, Syd, Fred and Charlie arrived outside the gates next, all of them covered in either mud, dust, blood, or smoke burns. As soldiers go, they looked ghastly with their black faces, grim expressions and long strides forward.

"Terrific job, guys," said Rick again. To the three bloodstained SAS men, he just said, "A special thank you, gentlemen. We're all grateful for the real rough end of the mission you carried out."

"Don't mention it, Ricky my old son," said Syd jauntily. "All in the line of duty."

"A bit beyond that," said the SEAL commander. "Now, gentlemen, let's go and get the guys free . . . and for Christ's sake be careful inside the cell blocks. There's armed Chinese guards in there, as we know, so don't fire randomly or we might hit the prisoners.

"Let's go . . . nice and careful . . . fire to kill, but selectively."

0218. Monday, July 17.
The Jail on Xiachuan Dao.

L T. COMMANDER RICK HUNTER ISSUED HIS LAST
orders before entering the wide gap where the main jail gates
had been a few minutes earlier. "Okay, guys . . . we know there are
still Chinese guards in here, in the cell blocks, and possibly in the
building on the left as we enter. Therefore we go in as if we're attacking a fortified area . . . strong frontal attack, heavy covering fire
against the cell block, but don't, for Christ's sake, hit anyone inside."

"Sir, what's the door to the main cell block made of, and is it
likely to be locked? Don't wanna get caught outside against the
wall with our shorts down, right?"

"I'm assuming it's steel, Paul . . . anyone know better?"

"The door on the individual cell block on the right is steel," said
Syd Thomas. "And it was locked. I gave it a shove, turned the
'andle and it never budged."

"Okay, let's blow it right now. Det-cord, someone . . ."

"Right here, Rick." Dan Conway had a big reel he'd been carrying around for five minutes in anticipation of this.

"Who's going?"

"I'll do it," said Buster. "I got fucking speed to burn."

They all laughed as the SEAL from the bayous grabbed the loose end and told Dan to hang on to the reel and play it out. "Right now I'm gone . . ."

Buster flew through the lefthand side of the gateway and made for the small cell block on the left, racing into the shadows. He paused for a moment and then ran along the edge of the wall, just as a machine gun opened up from the main cell block window. They all saw Buster go down, and Rick ordered instant gunfire at the window from which the fire had come.

Steve Whipple delivered it from the big machine gun he had positioned just inside the gate behind the rubble of the guard room. The clatter of the gun silenced the Chinese resistance for the moment, and as it did so, Buster sprang to his feet and charged on to the door, still holding the end of the det-cord.

They all saw him reach the door and start winding the stuff around the handle and the gap around the lock. He reached for his knife, wound another length in around the hinges and then spliced the ends together.

Then he turned and raced back the way he had come, just as Steve pounded another 25 rounds through the silent window.

"Fuck me," said Rick. "I thought they got you."

"What? Those assholes? I've fought fucking alligators a lot more scary than them. Blow it out, Dan."

Lieutenant Conway cut the length of cord and hit the fuse, instantly blasting the steel door off its hinges and leaving it leaning halfway into the cells.

Rick Hunter signaled his 20 troops in, and they set off at a jog for the main cell block, with Steve Whipple still firing short, steady bursts at the window where once there had been machine gunfire.

Twenty yards from the block, the giant SEAL leader increased his pace and made for the door. He slammed his boot into it, kicking it in, and swung right, firing from the hip straight down the outer corridor, at the same time yelling, "All right, guys. This is a force of the United States Navy here to liberate our prisoners. Any Chinese guards, come out with your hands high."

Dan Conway stood at Rick's shoulder just as the two duty guards burst from cover at the end of the corridor and opened fire. At least, they tried to open fire, but Rick Hunter and Dan Conway cut them down in their tracks with their trusty MP-5s. Each of the Chinese guards took 10 rounds before they hit the floor.

"That's pretty good shooting, pal," said a deep American voice from inside the first barred cell on the left. "I'll say one thing, you guys sure know how to make a fucking noise."

Rick Hunter could have died with relief. This was the first real hard evidence he and his team had that the American crew were here at all.

"Cover that end of the corridor, Dan, Bobby," he said. "Anything moves, blow its head off."

Then he turned toward the cell, and saw a brawny arm sticking through the bars.

It was dark inside, and the face was hard to see, but the voice was firm and the grip strong.

"Am I glad to see you. I'm Captain Judd Crocker, USS *Seawolf.*"

"Hello, sir. Lieutenant Commander Hunter. SEALs."

Judd looked at his blackened face, battle dress, bandana, hot machine gun. "I didn't think you were from public relations," he said, chuckling.

All the SEALs within earshot laughed at the still-droll submarine commander. "I suppose we haven't got any keys, have we?" said Rick.

"If we had, we probably wouldn't be here . . . and I don't think the guards carry any. When they open the cell doors, which ain't that often, a special little lieutenant comes in and does it himself."

"Okay, sir . . . I thought we might have that problem. We've got plenty of small charges, and the little lieutenant is probably dead somewhere. Rattlesnake!"

The other SEAL from the bayous came forward and stuck a handful of white plastic C4 on the lock. "Stand back, sir . . . geddown over there against the wall. . . rest of you get back while I fire this . . ."

He fixed the firing cap and the C4 blew the lock clean off the door. *Seawolf*'s CO was free.

Judd came out and shook hands with his rescuer, telling him, "There's just two single cells here, the rest are communal, I think eight of my guys in each one—some of 'em not in great shape, but I think we're mostly alive."

Rattlesnake blew the next door lock, and then shouted back, "Hey, sir . . . there's no one in here."

"DAMN!" snapped the captain. "That's Linus. I thought I heard them move him about an hour ago. You guys didn't destroy the big building to the right of the gates going out, did you?"

"No, sir. We hit one room only, left of the front door."

"Good. That's where the interrogators sit. I think we might find a couple of our guys in that building, down at the other end—my XO and the combat systems officer, Cy Rothstein."

"Okay, sir . . . lemme just hand this locksmith crap over to Lieutenant Conway, then we'll put Lieutenant Commander Davidson to work on the other two smaller cell blocks . . . meanwhile, let's just sweep this place for guards, then we'll go and find the two officers in the interrogation block. . . . Quick, Buster, Paul, Bobby, come with me . . . Rattlesnake, try not to blow us up as we come by."

The four SEALs moved to the end of the corridor. From inside the end cell, a voice said quietly, "Careful, sir . . . there's one of them still around that corner . . . the lieutenant . . . little bastard."

"Any of our guys in that area around the back?"

"Nossir. We're all in the area along this corridor. Ten big cells, eight of us in each. I'm Lieutenant Warren, sir. Officer of the Deck."

"Okay, old buddy. We'll have you all out of here in a minute."

"Are you guys SEALs?"

"'Fraid so."

Rick Hunter turned to Lieutenant Merloni and said, "No reason to take chances . . . gimme one of those hand grenades, willya?"

He gripped it in his hand, which was like putting a marble in the joint of a leg of lamb. Then he pulled the pin and hurled it around the corner. The impact inside the building was an ear-shuddering thud, and the guard lieutenant died with his boots on.

"That's all of 'em, sir," yelled Andy Warren. "I count the little pricks in every night, and I count the little pricks out again in the morning." Arnold Morgan would have been proud of his phraseology.

By now Rattlesnake Davies had found a rhythm, and he was blowing locks at a fast rate. Lieutenant Conway was going inside each cell, occasionally calling for Olaf's team to bring in a stretcher. The men from the first cells, nearest the obliterated door, were beginning to file out into the yard, and Chief McCarthy was suggesting they line up in some sort of order in case there were people missing.

"Right here we got a crew list," he said. "I've given one to the captain, but we really don't want to leave anyone behind, so can I ask you to get into lines . . . anyone want a crew list, I have 'em right here . . . anyone knows of a missing person, lemme know, okay?"

"They shot Skip Laxton dead on the first day," someone called.

"And we haven't seen Brad Stockton or Cy Rothstein for a coupla days."

Chief McCarthy noticed that the men looked terrible, hollow-cheeked, haggard, many with bruises on their faces, some with blood. The second stretcher was coming out with a crewman strapped in, his leg fractured by a rifle butt. The first one had contained another crewman who kept drifting in and out of consciousness after a very bad beating. He had worked for Lieutenant Commander Rothstein.

Captain Crocker himself looked pretty battered. Both his eyes were blackened, and his right cheek was swollen. There was blood caked around the corners of his mouth. But he seemed to be able to move around without pain, and now he emerged from the cell block with Rick Hunter.

Before him was a scene of chaos. A thick pall of smoke hung over the jail, and there was still fire, which could be seen above the walls, from the exploded helicopters and fuel dump. There were scattered bodies all over the place, none of them SEALs.

Judd and Rick walked past the men, heading for the interrogation block in company with SEALs Buster Townsend, Paul Merloni and Bobby Allensworth.

At the door, Lieutenant Commander Hunter said, "Sir, you'd better not come in here . . . we might get resistance."

"If I don't come in, you might get killed. I'm an expert on the layout of this place and I'm the only one you've got."

"Okay, sir," said Rick, drawing his service revolver. "You know how to use this thing."

"Expert," he said. "I'm the fucking Wyatt Earp of the deep. Okay, follow me into the hallway, which you seem to have already demolished. Then I'll follow you guys down the passage."

Judd Crocker stepped over the rubble, followed by Rick and Bobby. But before they reached the end, Lieutenant Allensworth put his hand on the captain's shoulder and said, "Wait, sir. Let me just stick a gun barrel in that doorway, see if anyone's left alive. It's better I shoot him than he shoots you."

"No argument from me," said Judd.

Bobby shoved his MP-5 around the corner and opened fire immediately. But there was no need. Whoever had been in there was no more, buried beneath the rubble.

Judd led the way down the corridor to the three rooms. Two were open, with lights on, the doors just ajar. The third room was closed. Buster came forward and booted wide the door of the first room. He entered and hammered four rounds into the panel of the door just in case someone was hiding behind it. Then he did the same to the second room, and there was no one there either. Which left the room where the door was shut.

"LIEUTENANT COMMANDER LUCAS!" yelled Judd.

"In here, sir," came a muffled reply.

"Steady, sir. Don't touch the door . . . leave it to us . . . Paul . . ."

Lieutenant Merloni, unrecognizable in the dust and smoke, stepped up beside the mission leader.

"Ready?"

"Sir."

Rick Hunter, with an outrageous display of strength, booted the door off its hinges with two massive kicks, one high, one low. And as he did so he jutted his machine gun, but not his body, around the corner, and they all heard the Chinese guard open fire, straight at the barrel of Rick's MP-5.

Unhappily for his family, the guard did not see Paul Merloni slide around the doorway on the floor and open up, shooting from low down at point-blank range with a wall of fire that killed the guard instantly. And now they could see Linus Clarke tied to a chair, a soaking-wet bath towel on his lap.

The second guard, Commander Li himself, dropped his rifle and put his hands in the air, just too late. Judd Crocker came through that doorway like a charging bull, fueled by the frustrated fury of almost two weeks of captivity. He rammed his left hand hard up under Li's throat and carried him back ten feet from the wall, holding him suspended three inches above ground level, his feet kicking wildly.

Then the CO drew back his right fist and smashed it into the Chinese commander's face, letting him drop to the floor.

"STAND BACK, SIR! RIGHT NOW. HE'S STILL ARMED . . . WATCH THAT PISTOL . . . SIR . . . SIR . . . STEP ASIDE!" Paul Merloni was not joking.

But Judd Crocker was not stepping aside for anyone. He drew Rick Hunter's service revolver and shot Commander Li clean through the forehead, twice.

"That's for a young friend of mine named Skip Laxton," he said. "You murderous little bastard. Call it frontier justice."

As he stepped away, Rick Hunter could see tears rolling down the CO's bruised and battered face.

By now, Buster had cut the XO free and Linus Clarke finally stood up, throwing the towel to the ground. He did not look anywhere as beaten up as the rest of the crew, but it was clear that he had been through some kind of trauma. He was shaking, but he was clean and looked better fed than the others. Also, he was wearing a Chinese uniform shirt and shorts.

However, there was no one else left alive in the building, and Rick Hunter ordered everyone out, back into the courtyard to assess the damage done to Judd Crocker's crew.

By the time they retraced their steps along the corridor, the lights were beginning to fail, and they kept fading, then surging back on again. This was scarcely surprising, given the general pounding the place had taken. Both searchlights had now gone out, and the lines of men now stood in almost complete darkness.

Judd Crocker shouted to ask if anyone had seen Lt. Commander Cy Rothstein, but no one had. He turned to Rick Hunter and said, "That's the combat systems officer, cleverest man on the ship. He was under heavy interrogation . . . I'm extremely concerned about him."

The SEAL leader asked if everyone was out of all three cell blocks. "Affirmative, sir," replied Chief McCarthy.

"Make one more search, Chief . . . take flashlights . . . we gotta very important guy missing . . . Lt. Commander Cy Rothstein . . . start calling out his name."

"Aye, sir."

"Anyone else, Chief?"

"No, sir. All present and correct, sir. Except of course for Skip Laxton."

"Anyone know if he could have been taken off by air?"

"Nossir," said Lt. Shawn Pearson. "He and I were communicating through the wall until about three days ago. He's been in the interrogation block, and I saw the same guard take him back there . . . it's just that I haven't heard from him since . . ."

"Jesus Christ," said the CO. "The little bastards have killed him."

A few more minutes passed, and then the searching parties began to arrive back. "There's no one left in the cell blocks, sir. No one alive."

"Well, there's no one in the interrogation rooms, either," said Rick. "We've checked them. The guardroom's rubble. The comm room's rubble, the dormitory badly damaged, but most of the personnel have been gassed, and anyway he couldn't be in there. I must therefore conclude that Lieutenant Commander Rothstein has been killed. And in any event, I'm afraid we cannot remain a moment longer or else we'll all end up dead. We have to get off this island."

"Right, Lieutenant Commander. I understand that. Judging by

their methods of interrogation, I hold out absolutely no hope what-soever for his rescue."

Just then a sporadic burst of gunfire burst from the hill over-looking the southern wall of the jail. The bullets flew into the big crowd in the jail yard and two seamen went down out on the left.

"IT'S THOSE TWO LITTLE BASTARDS WHO GOT AWAY FROM THE OUTSIDE PATROL!" yelled Bobby Allensworth.

"GET IN UNDER THE WALL, EVERYONE . . . TAKE COVER RIGHT NOW . . . BOBBY . . . GIMME ONE OF THOSE FLARES . . ." Rick Hunter was moving fast. He lit the flare and held it in his gloved hand, letting go at the last minute when it sparked and made liftoff. They all watched it head into the night sky, burst and illuminate the entire hillside.

Buster yelled first. "THERE THEY ARE, SIR, RIGHT UP THERE . . . LEFT OF THE TREES . . ."

"Paul, Rattlesnake, Buster, Steve . . . follow me. We have to get rid of them. Bring the big machine gun . . . otherwise they'll try to pick us off all the way to the beach . . . take care of those two wounded men, Olaf . . . THE REST OF YOU STAY AGAINST THE WALL TILL WE GET BACK . . ."

Rick Hunter headed left, up the hill, in the cover of the trees, running softly through the dark, followed by four of his most trusted men. "Keep right on this treeline till we get above them . . . cut 'em off from cover . . . keep 'em pinned down on the hill . . . so their only way out is toward the beach . . ."

Rick issued his orders as he ran, and when he was high enough above the last known position of the two remaining Chinese guards, he told Paul to loose off another flare, this time through a proper launcher, rather than hand-held.

It arched like a big rocket high up over the hill, and burst in a dazzle of light. "There they are, sir . . . right down there . . . nearer the jail than when we last saw them . . ."

"TAKE 'EM OUT, STEVE . . . MACHINE GUN . . ."

The big petty officer opened fire immediately. Paul sent up another flare and they all saw the last of the patrol guards get up and run for higher ground. But they never made it, and the five SEALs packed up their flares and ammunition belts and headed back down to the jail.

0300. Monday, July 17.
Office of the
Southern Fleet Commander. Zhanjiang.

In the mind of Admiral Zhang Yushu, all was lost in this ill-fated adventure. The American submarine was gone, indeed the entire Canton dockyard was almost gone.

And now it was obvious to him that the forces of the United States had landed on Xiachuan and taken the jail. There would be, he knew, many, many casualties, and much worse, no prisoners.

So far as he knew, only two of the Americans had actually died. And they were the only two Americans who were safe, so far as he could tell. The rest of them, if they escaped, which they now seemed certain to do, would sing out to the whole world what had befallen them after their ship had been essentially hijacked in international waters.

It was not, and had never been, the policy of the regime of Communist China to give a damn what the rest of the world thought. But increasingly, in the interest of international trade, they had tried to be at least agreeable to world opinion.

This looked to Zhang like trouble on a grand scale. In fact, this could turn out to be Tiananmen Square in the jungle. For the first time in his entire life, Zhang Yushu thought his career might be on the line here.

He was simply uncertain whether any C-in-C in any part of the People's Liberation Army/Navy could afford to be the only person responsible for a disaster of this magnitude: nuclear catastrophe, many Chinese deaths; failure to incarcerate prisoners, many more Chinese deaths; loss of two massively expensive helicopters to foreign enemy on Chinese soil; loss of a highly expensive guided missile patrol boat in Chinese waters, on a Chinese jetty, to the same foreign enemy; and worldwide public condemnation of Chinese methods of interrogation of a most important friendly trading partner.

And only one solitary person to blame: Admiral Zhang Yushu himself, architect of the entire, hideous comedy of errors.

Admiral Zu stood up and walked across the room, wearing a deep frown.

"Is there any point speculating that the Americans may not actually have attacked our island, and that we are just experiencing some kind of major power cut?"

"None. No power cut would affect the radio or the satellites. The reason we are unable to contact Xiachuan is because the Americans have attacked it. There is no other explanation. And I know them so well."

"But how?"

"We've seen no large helicopter platform within two hundred miles of the coast. Therefore, they can't be using helicopters. So they must be using ships. And only submarines could get close enough without our seeing them. And then small landing boats to bring them to shore."

"But they cannot overpower our forces. We have more than one hundred fully armed guards and many other personnel."

"Well, we may have beaten them, driven them off. But somehow there's been a battle. That's why we cannot make contact with the island. What worries me is the coincidence with the submarine's demise. Just a few hours ago, we lose the ship, and now the island is completely inaccessible."

"Well, what do we do? Send in reinforcements? Helicopters? Troops? Artillery?"

"No, Jicai. It's much too late for that. It would take us two hours to prepare at this time of night, and another hour to get there. No, our only chance is by sea, because if the Americans are there, they came in submarines. And if they came to rescue the prisoners, they will have to leave in submarines. They could not have used surface ships or we would have seen them long ago.

"Jicai, this is a Navy problem. If we want to catch and punish the Americans, it will be on the sea. If we can catch them in Chinese waters, we are at liberty to attack in self-defense. We may even have the chance to put a couple of American nuclear boats on the bottom of the ocean."

Admiral Zu looked across the room at the now-distraught Commander-in-Chief as he strode back and forth, reflecting on this local but Homeric struggle between two of the world's great powers.

"But how, with what?"

"Jicai, if they are about to evacuate Xiachuan, they are almost certainly on the surface or in shallow water. Our destroyer, when it gets there, could attack very effectively."

"Well, sir, let's look at the charts. Right here is Xiachuan. If the Americans came in underwater, they would be around here, where it's forty meters deep. Plainly we cannot get ships out of Canton at the moment, since the entire waterfront is radioactive . . . so whatever ships we send to intercept will have to come from here . . . four hours away."

"What ships do we have available, Jicai? The big new destroyer for a start, eh? *Xiangtan*. It carries guns, torpedoes, surface-to-surface missiles and two ASW helicopters. Also, she makes over thirty knots through the water, and she has reasonable sonar."

Yessir. And the light Jianghu-class frigate *Shantou* is ready to sail immediately."

"She carries A/S mortars and depth charges, correct?"

"Absolutely, sir."

"Then I think we must proceed, Jicai. Send for both commanding officers. I think we should explain to them personally precisely what we expect of them. We could, with good reason, hit an American submarine."

"Good reason?"

"Certainly, a big American nuclear boat in Chinese territorial waters, an island that had been attacked by an obviously American force from the submarine . . . oh yes, Jicai . . . we could make that sound very plausible. We could even claim hot pursuit, continuing to chase them in international waters and demanding their legal arrest."

"I am just not sure where any of this is taking us, Yushu. Let's face it, if the Americans have their prisoners back, why not just let them go? They're going anyway, and *Seawolf* is lost."

"That has to do with loss of face, Jicai. I agree that the prisoners are probably going home. Mostly. And I understand that they will talk about us and our methods of interrogation. But I would prefer that not all of them went home. I would just feel better if we were able to sink an American submarine, which would take a few dozen of the prisoners down with her . . . that would be more satisfactory to me. I would feel that I had not been completely humiliated. And in the halls of power in Beijing, that might look much better for me. I might even retain my job."

"Yushu, in all the years I have known you, I have never heard you speak like that before, considering yourself above the principal military picture."

"Jicai, I have never had to. Now it's different."

"And what of the warships now on their way? What will I order them to carry out . . ."

"Jicai, you will tell them to sink any American submarine, no matter what the risk, no matter how difficult. As many as they find."

Just then, Admiral Zu's young lieutenant assistant came in, carrying a single sheet of paper. "Just in from Canton city, sir . . . a very short signal. Telephone communication from a village elder on the island of Shangchuan, just across the bay from the jail. He says his sons sighted a very bright glow in the sky about an hour ago, says it looked like a very large fire . . . he telephoned the police in Macao, and they networked it through their headquarters in Canton."

"Thank you, Lieutenant. That will come as no surprise to our learned Commander-in-Chief."

Admiral Zhang continued to pace the room. "We must get one of them, Jicai. We must hit one, and put a lot of Americans on the bottom of the ocean. It is essential that we do that."

"Just for loss of face and your career, Yushu? Do you not think there may have been enough bloodshed already?"

Admiral Zhang hesitated. And then he unloaded on his oldest

friend, control slipping away as he spoke. "SILENCE!" he roared. "SILENCE, Jicai. I must have revenge, do you understand me? REVENGE! For God's sake, am I not entitled to that, after all I have done for this country? I understand I may be relieved of command, but don't deny me my pride. If I go, I must go as a warrior, as a commander who fought the enemy to his last breath. Not as a poor, pathetic creature, beaten and humbled by the American imperialists, pounded into defeat and then sent away to rot in obscurity.

"Don't begrudge me my pride, Jicai. I must save face. And the only way to do that is to make sure we hit the Americans. If I could, I'd do it myself. Nothing would make me happier than to smash a Chinese torpedo right into the heart of an American ship—I hate them, Jicai. My God, I hate them."

For the first time, Admiral Zu was actually quite concerned about the state of mind of the Commander-in-Chief of the People's Liberation Navy. His own instinct was to let the damned American prisoners go, clear up the mess, apologize to Washington for the destruction of *Seawolf* in the accident in Canton, blame the damage on the collision with the destroyer, and get on with life, trade and prosperity.

Yushu's pride, he thought, might prove expensive.

1415 (local). Sunday, July 16.
Office of Admiral Morgan. The White House.

The hotline from the Oval Office rang yet again.

"Hello, sir," said Arnold Morgan. "Sorry, no word yet. But no news is good news . . . there was never going to be communication until the prisoners reached the first submarine, unless there was a crisis. So far there has been no communication, and they have been on the island for two and a half hours. That means the jail is in American hands, sir. Trust me. Otherwise we'd have heard."

"But are the prisoners alive? That's all I want to know . . ."

"If they'd found anything untoward, they'd have let us know by now. Sir, we have to continue to think the operation has been successfully carried out, and I'm not moving from this chair until we hear. I'll call you the first second I get any news whatsoever."

"Okay, Arnie. I know I'm being neurotic. But I don't know what I'd do if I lost him . . ."

The admiral put the phone down and picked up his direct line to Admiral Mulligan's office in the Pentagon. "Hi, Joe, anything yet?"

"Uh-uh. Just heard from George Morris, though. We got a picture from the overheads showing a large fire on the island of Xiachuan. Lotta black smoke, looks like fuel."

"The fire's probably a good sign. It should mean they're in and attacking. Let's face it, Joe, no one can deal with the SEALs when they're in full cry."

"That's where my money is . . . I'll call you back as soon as I get anything."

0312.
The Jail. Xiachuan Dao.

Captain Crocker went over the crew list one final time. Only Cy Rothstein and Skip Laxton were still missing. Rick Hunter said, "I gotta brief your guys."

"I got eight fast inflatables on the beach," rapped the SEAL leader. "Each boat takes eight with one on a stretcher, nine without. I'm takin' three boats with nine guys, that's twenty-seven. With five stretcher cases, we got forty more places in the first wave . . . that's a total of sixty-seven I want ready to leave right away. Do *eggzackly* what my guys say. They say *DROP,* you drop. They say *JUMP,* don't stop to ask how high. You jump.

"They'll carry the stretchers, guide you down to the beach. There's a team there to get y'all aboard. Then you got a thirty-minute ride to a submarine. GO, TEAM."

Judd Crocker added, "Shawn, do the head count. Andy, take care of Brad. He's on a stretcher for the ride."

Rick checked the courtyard for American guns or equipment that might have been dropped in the general melee. Dan Conway and Buster Townsend led the orderly stampede down the half-mile to the beach where Lieutenant Commander Bennett awaited them, still covered in mud, blood and gunpowder. With his face blackened and his "drive-on rag" spattered red, he looked like Crazy Horse's half-brother after Little Bighorn.

The night was still hot, but, as if on cue, it began to rain again, and it was slanting, tropical monsoon rain that lashed down on them, refilling the long puddles in the courtyard and soaking the winding column of men that had formed behind the lead SEALs.

Dan and Buster led them to the north for a very slow 400 yards along a rough path hacked out of the undergrowth by Olaf's men an hour earlier, as soon as the jail had fallen into American hands. But the jungle was lower here as the land fell away toward the sea, and there was a lot of overhang, wet branches and undergrowth. The rain was belting down so hard it was forming small lakes instantly along the little track, and the SEALs up front, carrying the five stretchers right behind Buster, were slipping and sliding and cursing in the pitch dark.

Progress was painfully slow. It took 10 minutes to cover that first quarter-mile, and nothing much improved when Dan changed course, now heading northeast. The terrain was, if anything, worse as the jungle thinned out above this particular stretch of beach. There were deep puddles and areas that were almost a quagmire, and they were unavoidable because nobody could see them until they were in them, up to their ankles in mud. It was very tough for the stretcher-bearers to keep their balance, and sometimes they didn't. But no one capsized and 17 minutes after they had left the jail, the long column of Americans reached the beach.

"Christ, we thought you'd never get here," said Lieutenant Commander Bennett, walking up to meet them. "Better hurry before the boats fill up with rainwater and sink."

Dan Conway chuckled and followed the SEAL beach boss down to the water where the Zodiacs were moored on the sand, with their bows facing the short surf rolling in from the east. The little waves caused each boat to rise very slightly with the tide, but only the first three feet of the Zodiacs was in the water.

"Okay, guys," called Rusty. "Let's get one stretcher in each of the first five boats, and while we're doing that, Buster, count out the next twenty-seven men and have them report to the last three inflatables in the line. I got two guys on each boat, the driver and one other to help with the launch . . . only the drivers go."

Since everyone on the beach was in the Navy, it was a well-disciplined operation. Only the stretchers were difficult, but the SEALs had done it before, and they laid each one flat on the temporary decking they had fitted to the frame before last night's launch. They centered the stretchers forward, which would allow other passengers to sit or kneel in a line facing aft, holding onto the handles if the sea got up.

It was complicated, but by the time Rusty had the operation halfway complete, the three boats at the far end were loaded and ready. Lt. Commander Linus Clarke was in one of them.

Rusty sent them ahead. This was no time to hang around. It was already 0335 and it would be light in less than three hours, and that was really bad news, because if the Chinese wanted to wipe them out, they could bomb and strafe this beach with absolute impunity as soon as their helicopter pilots could see the evacuation taking place.

He walked down to the end Zodiac, which was now floating 30 feet out from the beach, its painter held by a SEAL standing up to his chest in the water. And he called out through the rain, "Okay, guys, start the engines and head on out . . . southeast for three miles, then sou'sou'west, course two-zero-two for six . . . you gottit all on the GPS tracks . . . just remember what I told you . . . when you've been running at twenty knots for nine miles—nearly half an hour—*Hartford* lies right at that point . . . you'll pick up her beacon . . . that's all . . . GO NOW . . . and don't fuck it up."

All the SEALs loved the last phrase. It was a Rusty Bennett trademark, and since they all hero-worshiped the iron-souled lieutenant commander from the coast of Maine, each driver felt that it was a personal goodwill message to him alone. Which is, in a sense, what real leadership is all about.

Back on the beach, the remaining personnel heard the big powerful engines on the Zodiacs growl into life. And they heard the long straining beat of the motors as they fought to lift their heavy loads up onto the "stump" of the wash. Then they heard the acceleration as the inflatables found their high-speed trim and literally flew over the calm water, all three together, racing beam on beam, bearing the President's son and 26 other crewmen to safety.

When the next two boats, carrying stretchers, were ready in the water, held by SEALs, Rusty ordered them to leave. That way he had three out in front, two a couple of miles back on the same course, and there would be a group of three Zodiacs bringing up the rear. No one would be far from help if anything went wrong mechanically. Which it had better not, otherwise the engineers, who had meticulously prepared the Zodiac outboards, would probably end up on the wrong end of the modern-day equivalent of a thousand lashes. At least that's what Lieutenant Commander Bennett told them would happen.

And now, as the last of the engines died away in the rainswept distance of the South China Sea, there was little more they could do but wait for an hour for the boats to return. The next time, the eight boats would take 72 more off, but by then it would be 0445. And there would still be 30 men on the beach, with no hope of escape before 0555, a few minutes before dawn. And then they would be running south for almost a half-hour in gathering daylight.

"This," muttered Rusty Bennett, "is going to be tight. Fucking tight. 'Specially as me, Rick and Ray Schaeffer will be in the last boat to leave."

But the new column was arriving now, more than 100 men walking slowly toward the beach in the dark and rain, the SEALs, weapons at the ready, marching to the side, watching the jungle edges, even though they knew there could not be any more Chinese guards on the loose. Not unless there was a parachute drop they didn't know about. Nonetheless, a stranger would have thought the crew of the late USS *Seawolf* was under close arrest, rather than U.S. Navy protection.

By the time everyone was on the beach, almost 20 minutes had passed since the last Zodiac had left. The jail was now deserted, and would remain so until the gassed personnel in the dormitory began to recover in the small hours of tomorrow morning.

Judd Crocker was still on the island, and would leave in the last boat carrying his crew members, sometime in the next 45 minutes. Like the final dozen men in the first eight-boat flotilla, Judd would be transferred to the USS *Cheyenne*, which now waited on the surface only six miles off the southern beaches of Xiachuan, in less than 100 feet of water.

He was talking to Rick Hunter right now, expressing his concern over the condition of Brad Stockton, who had been savagely interrogated, mainly because the Chinese thought he was the most senior man in the crew, aside from the CO.

"I wouldn't worry too much, sir," said the SEAL leader. "We have a Navy doctor who specializes in torture-type damage in each of the submarines. They'll get him fixed up. Anyway, we're making the transfer to the carrier within a very few hours, and there's a full-blown hospital in there."

Judd Crocker nodded, and Rick Hunter asked suddenly, "Was it bad, sir?"

"Well, it wasn't great."

"What did they want from the crew members?"

"They really wanted information. But they wanted it in a very specialized form . . . you know, they wanted a guided tour of the combat systems by Lieutenant Commander Rothstein. I expect you know this, but these are among the most complicated systems on the ship . . . and while they would certainly be able to copy them, make plans, and for all I know, remove certain parts, there's nothing like having the man who works them in your corner."

"No, I guess not . . . so those little bastards really wanted to get ahold of all of our specialists on the ship, and get them to spill the beans on all the subtleties of the electronics—so they could make a submarine of the same standard as *Seawolf* . . . ?"

"Lieutenant Commander, you have it right there."

"Jesus Christ, cunning little bastards . . . but what I don't know is how they managed to capture the submarine in the first place, sir . . . what happened?"

"Well, it might be classified, but since ten thousand Chinamen and more than one hundred crew and half of SUBPAC know, I guess there's no harm in my enlightening the officer who rescued us . . ."

Rick Hunter chuckled in his deep, quiet Kentucky manner. "In any event, sir, you may count on my discretion . . . we'll say it was passed on under the 'need to know' syndrome, since we're not out of this fucking hellhole quite yet."

Judd Crocker laughed. "May I call you Rick?"

"Of course."

"Well, Rick, I am about to impart to you a brief shining example of a monumental snafu. On a dark night, way out there in the South China Sea, we managed to wrap our propeller hard around the long towed array of a six-thousand-ton Chinese destroyer."

"Holy shit!"

"To the best of my recall, those may have been my own precise words when I realized what had happened."

"Did you have the conn, sir?"

"Hell, no, I was asleep. I'd just come off watch."

"How'd you find out?"

"Are you kidding? When something like that happens in a big nuclear boat, everything suddenly changes. You lose propulsion and it goes kinda quiet, the trim changes, and machinery sounds that you all live with all the time are suddenly different, even the angle of the boat is different . . ."

"Who had the conn, sir?"

"That, I am afraid, is classified. But the truth will in the end come out, I'm sure of that."

"Do you think there will be a Navy inquiry?"

"Christ, yes. A full one first, listening to the evidence of everyone, plus his wife and his dog. That'll take God knows how long. And there'll be a recommendation, if they think someone failed in his duty: possibly that certain officers of *Seawolf* were guilty of gross negligence, perhaps even leaving their place of duty in the face of the enemy . . ."

"You mean they may court-martial you, sir?"

"They just might. Unlikely, but possible. Any commanding officer who manages to lose his ship faces deep trouble. But in the light of the evidence, I hope they will find me not guilty . . ."

"I would, sir."

"Thank you, Lieutenant Commander. I hope they'll be as under-standing."

"Well, if they're not, I'll come forward and tell 'em you took out the armed camp commandant singlehanded right there in the death cells."

"Don't do that, for Christ's sake. Some left-wing politician would probably want me charged with murder under the new Act to Prevent Unreasonable Cruelty to Far Eastern Dwarves."

Both officers laughed, although somewhat grimly.

0430.
On board the destroyer *Xiangtan*. 111.29E 21.13N.
Course zero-six-zero. Speed 30.

Colonel Lee Peng was mainly concerned about his orders. Person-ally issued by the Commander-in-Chief, they were coldly specific: "Seek and pursue any suspicious vessel in the area six miles due south of Xiachuan Dao. You have authority to open fire on, and sink, any United States naval vessel in national waters, or, in hot pursuit, in international waters."

And now he stood on the bridge, continuing a short conference with his executive officer, Lt. Commander Shoudong Guan, and his combat systems chief, Lt. Commander Anwei Bao. And the discus-sion bore a somewhat fatalistic edge.

All three of the senior officers on board knew that the main trouble with the American Navy is that it is likely to hit back, very fast and very hard. They also knew that even if they man-aged to get helicopters up and were able to blitz the Americans with depth charges, depth bombs and maybe even torpedoes, an American SSN could still fire three or maybe even four torpedoes right back, hard and accurate. They'd keep well clear. And pri-vately, all three of the Chinese officers thought that to open fire on a big, fast American warship of any kind was something very near to suicide.

Colonel Lee, however, was adamant. "The C-in-C left no room for manuever," he said. "He told me to open fire and sink it."

"Did he have a view about losing the best surface ship in our Navy?"

"No, Guan. He did not. He seemed not to listen, or at least not to hear. Then he told me the honor of my country was at stake. The only thing that mattered, both to him and to his masters in Beijing, was that we hit and sink a major American submarine. And he was certain there was at least one out there, possibly two . . ."

"Well, he may not know it, but I do," replied Lieutenant Commander Anwei. "The Americans, if we find them, will hit back. Like mad dogs, probably. I think a lot of people may die out there this morning."

"Have you considered the possibility of just ignoring everything and denying we ever saw anything?"

Colonel Lee smiled. But he said, "My old friend Guan, I must be honest. Yes, I have. But consider those consequences. It would be known that we saw something, possibly overhead, certainly among this very large crew. If we were to turn a blind eye in the face of the enemy, the entire senior command of this ship would be 'disappeared,' possibly jailed for life in national disgrace . . . I think we would all prefer to take our chances with American retribution, and return as heroes."

"Hopefully not in a coffin," replied Guan. "Anyway, we may not see anything."

"Indeed."

"Anyway, how do we look now, navigator . . . ?"

"We're fine, sir. Making very good time, just approaching longitude 111.30, just a little less than two hours to go, sir. This is a very fast ship. We'll be in the area at a little before oh-six-thirty at this speed."

1530 (local). Sunday, July 16.
The Oval Office.

It was the first time in living memory that anyone had marched along the corridor and just barged straight into the President's private office without even knocking, regardless of who might be in there. Even President Clarke's secretary was slightly taken aback as Arnold Morgan made his entry.

The Chief Executive, unused to being interrupted this brutally, was on the phone and looked annoyed until he saw who it was, and noticed the broad smile on the face of his National Security Adviser.

He just dropped the telephone, quite literally on the floor, and left it dangling there. And he stood up and said in a tremulous voice, "Tell me he's safe, Arnie. Please just tell me he's safe."

"He's safe, sir. On board the nuclear submarine USS *Hartford*, under the command of Commander Jack Crosby. They're on their way back to the carrier, USS *Ronald Reagan*. Linus is shaken, but unharmed. He sent you his love via the satellite."

President Clarke almost collapsed with relief. He sat back in his chair and just kept saying, over and over, "Thank God . . . Thank God . . . Thank God . . . ," and he let the tears stream down his face. He was too happy to stop them, too joyful to care.

Admiral Morgan just said, gruffly, "You need me anymore, sir? We're still pretty busy on this. I was going over to the Pentagon . . ."

"No, Arnold. No, I'm fine now. You go right ahead. But could you ask Kathy to come in and see me, soon as you're on your way . . ."

"Sure, sir. Maybe catch you a little later?"

"Arnie, I sure hope so. If it hadn't been for you . . . for your belief in our ability to hit back . . . I don't think I would ever have seen Linus again . . ."

"Thank you, sir. God bless you, and Linus. I'll send Kathy right over."

The admiral left the office as brusquely as he had entered. He marched back down the corridor and said to Kathy, without breaking stride as he passed her desk, "Coffee. Car. Go see the boss."

Then he moved back into his own office and called Admiral Mulligan. It was 0445 tomorrow in the South China Sea, a quarter to four in the afternoon in Washington.

"Hi, Joe. How do we look?"

"According to Frank Hart, the SEALs should be leaving the island right now with the second and final group of crewmen, all eight boats . . . starting to take off some of the Special Forces. Their ETD Xiachuan for the second run out to the submarines is 0445, their time. No one is reporting any Chinese activity within a fifty-mile radius of the transfer zone four miles south of the beaches."

"Hey, that's great, Joe. What time do they estimate the last guys get away?"

"Frank's saying oh-five-fifty-five. Which is almost dawn."

"Hmmmmm. That puts the last transfer in daylight, right?"

"'Fraid so. But we do not really expect a Chinese attack."

"Don't you? I wouldn't put anything past those little pricks. 'Specially when they've had their noses put out of joint, as they most certainly have."

"Well, we can only keep watching, sea and air. Anything shakes loose, I'll call you . . ."

"No need, Joe. I was just coming over to see you. Get some decent coffee ready, will you? Kathy's ignoring me."

The CNO laughed as he put down the phone. And almost immediately Admiral Morgan's internal line rang.

"Outer desk to base. Coffee one minute. Car downstairs. Over and out."

The admiral hit the intercom button and snapped, "Base to outer desk. Cancel coffee. Meet me in our favorite Georgetown restaurant at nineteen-thirty. Will you marry me?"

"Outer desk to base. Lovely to the first. No to the second. I love you. Over."

The admiral gathered up his briefcase and headed out, marching down to the elevator that would take him to the underground garage where his chauffeur, Charlie, would be waiting if he valued his life, job and pension.

Kathy, meanwhile, was in the southwest corner of the West Wing, entering the Oval Office.

"Hello, sir," she said. "I'm so happy for you. Isn't it the most marvelous news?"

"The best possible," said the President, and the future Mrs. Arnold Morgan noticed that he looked about 10 years younger than he had an hour previously.

"But now I want you to do me two favors."

"Of course."

"I want you to arrange for the church across the street in Jackson Place to be open, and please inform the Secret Service that I am planning to walk over there in the next half-hour. Tell 'em to make whatever arrangements they need. Second, I would like you to come with me—I expect you remember we were together when my prayers were answered. And I would like us to walk to church together."

"Well, yessir, I do of course remember. There's a morning service at St. John's, sir. And an evening one. I'll make sure it's open in the next half-hour."

She left the office and returned to her desk. A longtime White House staffer, she knew precisely the right buttons to press. And she hit the line to the usher and requested that someone contact St. John's Episcopal Church and ensure that it was empty, open and ready to receive the President of the United States, as it had received every President since James Madison.

The next call, to the Secret Service, was more serious, because the prospect of the President walking anywhere in public is apt to hit them like an ice storm in Tahiti. A lot of people need to be alerted, since the White House grounds are swept at all times by infrared, electronic eye, audio and pressure sensors. Video cameras on the roof and all over the grounds record every movement. There is actually a full SWAT team positioned on the White House roof, machine guns drawn, every time the President enters or leaves. And that assumes he's traveling in a bulletproof car.

The mere prospect of the President, in the company of the secretary to the National Security Adviser, *walking* to church was cause for a major operation. To a Secret Service agent, the 300 yards from the north corner of the West Wing to St. John's represented something close to the Pope crossing a minefield. In fact, the President would be crossing a quiet private road, closed to all traffic and patrolled at all times by squadrons of police.

But when Kathy O'Brien announced that the President was walking to church, about 140 people went into full alert, as would be expected in a gigantic fiefdom that costs upward of a billion dollars a year to run. Guards were detailed to surround and accompany him every yard of the way, from the front door of the Earthly God to the open door of the Greater God.

They set off together at a quarter to five, walking through the corridors of the West Wing and then stepping out into the hot, sunlit 18-acre gardens, where there awaited more armed men than there were on the evacuation beach at Xiachuan.

Surrounded now by the protectors of the President, they strolled up through the lawns and across the private road into Jackson Place on the west side of Lafayette Square. And from there it was just a few yards more to the pale yellow-painted Georgian church with its six tall white columns and three-tiered tower.

The door to the empty St. John's was wide open, ready to welcome the President of the United States on a private visit. When they arrived, he ordered everyone to remain outside, while he and Kathy walked in and closed the main door behind them.

And there in the cool half-light of the 190-year-old church, "the Church of the Presidents," John Clarke humbled himself before his God, kneeling quietly next to Kathy O'Brien in the front row of the left-hand pews and silently expressing his ineradicable gratitude for the safe delivery of his only son, Linus.

His prayer was, he said, not just thanks, but a formal recognition that his "still small voice" had been heard above the tumult of a world of sins. It was, he believed, an affirmation of his faith, the faith with which he had been brought up by his Baptist family in faraway Oklahoma.

He remained kneeling for perhaps 10 minutes, and then he turned to Kathy O'Brien and asked if she was ready to accompany him back to the White House.

They both stood and walked back down the dark red carpet of the left aisle. At the door, before he opened it, John Clarke said quietly, "I am not the President of anything in here, am I?"

"No, sir. No you're not. But I am sure you are welcome, because God gets many more requests for help than He ever does expressions of thanks. And it was St. John himself who wrote the words of Our Lord, "I am the way, the truth, and the life.""

And there was a smile on the face of the Chief Executive as he walked back to the White House with a clear conscience.

0555. Monday, July 17.
On the beach. Xiachuan Dao.

As the senior officer in the evacuation, Captain Judd Crocker elected not to leave the island with the second flotilla, but rather to wait for the final boat and travel in the cold light of dawn with Lieutenant Commander Hunter and Ray Schaeffer.

And there were already orange fingers of light out over the water as the eastern sun fought its way above the horizon. They could not yet see the five Zodiacs making their way across the bay, but they could hear a distant growl of outboard engines, moving very fast over the flat calm water.

Three minutes later the SEAL drivers came charging into the beach, a new note of urgency obvious in their attitudes as they cut the motors and hauled up the engines, while the SEALs in the shallows grabbed the painters and hung on to the boats. There was no need even to spin them around away from the waves now, because the ocean was like a pond.

The lead driver came in yelling, "OKAY, SIR, LET'S GO . . . all equipment in the second boat plus three . . . seven in each of the others . . . we're outta here."

The light was having a nerve-wracking effect on everyone. Surely the Chinese could not now be unaware, somehow, that a diabolical attack had occurred on their heavily manned jail, even if the SEALs had wrecked every possible communications system. No one expected a counter attack by night, but this was different. The cloak of darkness was gone, and everyone on the beach felt very vulnerable as the light grew stronger.

The very least the Chinese Navy must do would be to send a couple of helicopters in to find out why they could not contact the jail anymore. If those choppers arrived in the next five minutes they would surely open fire on the fleeing Americans.

"COME ON, YOU GUYS . . . LET'S GO! GO! GO!"

The lead driver, veteran Petty Officer Zack Redmond, was growing more jumpy by the minute. And he was not alone. Olaf Davidson was in the water, manhandling the machine guns into the boats. Buster and Rattlesnake were up to their waists, shoving men up and over into the boats.

When it was Rick's turn he stood next to them and bent his left leg at the knee, and the two SEALs grabbed his tree-trunk shin and lifted. The world's largest jockey thus vaulted over the gunwales like Bill Shoemaker at Santa Anita.

It was a minute after 0600 when the last boat was pushed the few yards out deep enough to lower the engines. The beaches were completely deserted now, and as the five motors roared into life, all of the SEALs found themselves looking back at the tiny Chinese island on which they had fought with such superhuman courage.

The black smoke over the jail had gone, and the place looked peaceful again, an idyllic tropical beach, with water turning more turquoise blue every minute. Nonetheless, they were all ecstatic to get away from it. Only Judd Crocker looked sad as he stared at the jungle and wondered where the body of Lieutenant Commander Rothstein had been buried, and if anyone would ever know his final resting place.

The Zodiacs hurtled out into the bay, and now for the first time, the SEALs could look at the seaway between the two islands. Opposite, on the shores of Shangchuan Dao, the coastline was long and flat, with low mountains rising in the background. Xiachuan looked altogether more rugged. But the best news was the total lack of activity. Here on this bright Monday morning, there was still no sign of even a junk, far less a warship. And the U.S. Navy drivers opened the throttles and sped across the calm sea, making their course change after three miles, and then making a beeline sou'sou'west, straight toward the waiting submarine *Greenville*, in which most of them had arrived.

0620. Monday, July 17.
On board the Chinese destroyer *Xiangtan*. 112.20E
21.30N. Course zero-eight-zero. Speed 30.

Colonel Lee had held his ship at flank speed all the way from Zhanjiang, easily outpacing the much smaller frigate *Shantou*, which was currently some five miles astern.

Lee had twice checked in with his own fleet commander, Admiral Zu Jicai, and had been told that Admiral Zhang had by no means altered his mindset. In fact, he was as determined as ever that the guns, missiles and torpedoes of *Xiangtan* should open fire on the Americans at the earliest opportunity, the earlier the better.

Colonel Lee was bewildered. It was so atypical. After a lifetime in the Navy of China, he had never been told to open fire, not even when Taiwan was involved, or even Japan. This was totally out of character. China was a very old civilization and it had long ago learned that discretion was almost always the better part of valor.

Letting loose high explosive at a modern-day trading partner with whom all-out war would be a massive disaster for China was not reasonable. And the Chinese prided themselves on reason. They might cheat, lie, steal, obfuscate the truth, evade and frequently commit the sin of omission. But lack reason? Never.

And here was this great Chinese warship being ordered to march, effectively into the jaws of death, with guns blazing. In peacetime. In cold blood. In total madness, so far as Colonel Lee could tell.

He turned to his XO, Lieutenant Commander Shoudong, and murmured for the umpteenth time, "I do not understand it."

The XO did not understand it either. But now he was becoming fatalistic, ever since the last call to Fleet Headquarters. And he said resignedly, "Sir, we are probably ten miles from the edge of the search area. Does this really mean that if we pick up a submarine, we just go straight in and start firing?"

"That is precisely what it means."

"No warnings? No instructions to leave Chinese waters immediately? Not even a shot across her bow?"

"No, Guan. None of that. My orders are to open fire, straight at her, with whatever means necessary to sink her."

"My God," said the XO. "We better not miss, sir. Or she will surely obliterate us."

"Guan, she may do that even if we don't miss."

Lt. Commander Anwei Bao, the combat systems officer, returned to the bridge and caught just the end of the conversation.

"I have done as you instructed, sir. We are ready to open fire with all systems immediately . . . but there is just one thing, sir, I'd like to ask . . ."

"Please do."

"Does anyone know any background to this? Why we apparently are prepared to risk an out-and-out conflict with the United States?"

"Well, there is the matter of the submarine that blew up in Canton last night. I suppose that may be implicated. But the Americans did not blow it up. I thought we did, our own scientists."

"Well, that's the official line, but you never know."

"And what are we doing heading for the shallow waters around the two islands up ahead?"

"Now that's a real mystery. I have no idea."

"And why do they think we're going to find another American submarine due south of Xiachuan? There's no one on that island."

"I have not been told that, either. Just that we are likely to find one, and then to destroy it."

0629. Monday, July 17.
South China Sea. 112.34E 21.31N.

"Green-two-zero, sir. Submarine on the surface." Buster Townsend, leaning forward, peering through the binoculars, had USS *Greenville* in his sights. She stood about a mile farther to the south than they thought, with two American frigates from the *Ronald Reagan* CVBG about four miles beyond.

Despite the heavy protection, everyone was growing nervous about the evacuation in Chinese national waters in broad daylight.

On board the Los Angeles–class attack submarine, they literally could not wait to get under the surface.

The SEAL drivers headed straight toward it, bringing the Zodiacs expertly alongside, forward of the sail, where the crew had lowered climbing nets. Everyone in the inflatables was a highly trained SEAL who knew everything about boarding submarines in the worst possible conditions, right down to banging on the hull with their fighting knives underwater in order to be let in. The only non-SEAL in the Zodiacs was Captain Judd Crocker, and he was a submarine commanding officer. He'd manage.

Greenville's crew grabbed the first boat and as soon as it was empty hauled it up, deflated it, and sent it below. Heavy loose gear was just ditched, even the engines. The five boats were dealt with in 90 seconds flat. And the submarine accelerated rapidly away to the south, still on the surface.

The navigation officer, up on the bridge with the CO, heard the report: "Conn-ESM. Racket. X-Band. Military. Bearing two-six-zero. Approaching danger level."

Commander Tom Wheaton picked up his binoculars and looked out to the darker western horizon, but could see nothing. But from the ESM report, he knew this radar was most likely to be a Chinese warship, and it was about to come over the radar horizon. At which moment he would be caught *in flagrante*, an American submarine on the surface in Chinese national waters, his worst nightmare. He could expect no mercy. He could expect hot lead within the next 20 minutes.

Now, Commander Wheaton was not empowered to get into combat. However, he did not have sufficient water to dive the submarine, so he would have to concentrate on making his getaway on the surface. The nearest water deep enough to dive was still four miles ahead. He could be underwater in about 18 minutes, with the two frigates blocking for him.

On board the destroyer *Xiangtan*.

"Bridge-Radar. New surface contact. Track two-three-zero-one. Bearing zero-eight-zero. Range thirty-five thousand meters . . . two more surface contacts, close together. Tracks two-three-zero-two and two-three-zero-two. Bearing zero-nine-one. Same range. Indicating to weapons control."

"Radar-Captain. Good. Gimme course and speeds as soon as you can. . . . Navigator, plot their positions. I want to know if the Americans are outside the twelve-mile limit. ACTION STATIONS . . . SURFACE."

"Wheel-Captain. Steer zero-eight-three."

Seventeen tense minutes dragged by. Then, silhouetted against the morning sun, the clear shapes of the American ships were sighted, the small black square of *Greenville*'s sail to the left, and the bulkier hulls of the two frigates to the right.

"The submarine can't dive," replied Colonel Lee. "Not here. There's only just about one hundred feet under the keel . . . my orders are specific. Follow her. And then sink her. But I am opening up the line again to Fleet Headquarters, probably for the last time."

COMMANDER TOM WHEATON, IN A LONG NAVAL
career stretching right back to Annapolis, had never encountered anything quite like the situation in which he now found himself. A lifelong submariner, he'd crept around some highly dubious
waters in the service of his country, some hot, some cold. But he
had never been faced with an onrushing foreign destroyer coming
straight at him, in water insufficiently deep for him to dive, much
less to make a sharp, judicious getaway, *and* in foreign national
waters where he was not supposed to be. *Greenville*'s mission
was, after all, merely to arrange safe passage for American prisoners who had in some instances suffered Chinese torture.

Commander Wheaton considered that this had all the makings of
a small war, and he opened up his encrypted line to the captain of
Kaufman, the 4,000-ton Oliver Hazard Perry–class guided-missile
frigate from the *Ronald Reagan* CVBG.

He too was seriously concerned at the sight of an onrushing
Chinese destroyer, and understood *Greenville*'s quandary about

diving in this shallow water, about 110 feet. But the immediate aim was that the submarine should get the hell out of the way.

In the conn below, Commander Wheaton's only wish was to "get underwater, and leave the frigates to cover my ass." He was unsure of the reliability of the charts, and he normally took a relatively cautious view of driving 7,000 tons of American steel straight into an unmarked sandbank. He had no need to remind himself of one simple equation: "Mass multiplied by velocity squared equals a whole lot of inertia. When it's seven thousand tons times even ten knots, it'd knock us to pieces." But this was no time for caution.

Commander Wheaton decided to vanish, even at a low speed. Every time he looked to the west, the Chinese destroyer grew ever closer.

And the CO of the USS *Greenville* was not the only anxious man. On the bridge of *Xiangtan*, Colonel Lee was in direct communication with Admiral Zu Jicai, and the Southern Commander was sufficiently concerned to order "caution, for the moment."

He went to see Admiral Zhang again, and at the risk of irritating the all-powerful C-in-C even further, he said, simply, "*Xiangtan* is nine miles west of a surfaced American nuclear submarine. There are two American frigates close by. Do you continue to want Colonel Lee to open fire on her?"

"Immediately," replied Zhang, not even glancing up from the papers he was reading.

Admiral Zu glanced around helplessly, and just said, "Sir, you are not only my immediate superior, you have been a friend for almost all of our lives. I implore you to think very carefully before you make me order this."

"I've thought. Say no more, Jicai. Tell Colonel Lee to sink the American submarine, right here in Chinese national waters where she has no right to be. *RIGHT NOW!*"

And so the Southern Fleet Commander walked slowly back to his office and picked up the telephone again.

"Colonel Lee. My orders from the C-in-C are to sink the American submarine immediately."

And the commanding officer of *Xiangtan* replied, in deep Cantonese dialect, "Aye, sir. But I should warn you, there is an entire United States Carrier Battle Group in very close proximity. We are looking at two of her guided missile frigates at this very moment. We shall be committing suicide."

"Then you are ordered perhaps to die for your country. . . . Make no mistake, Colonel Lee . . . you are to take whatever extreme measures are necessary to put that American submarine on the floor of the South China Sea. Maximum honor to you and your crew."

And so Colonel Lee walked back to his high chair in the ops room and ordered *Xiangtan*'s 157-millimeter Russian-built guns into action on Track 2301.

"Fire at will," he said. "And God help us all." And the first of a salvo of 10 shells screamed in toward the *Greenville*.

It was 0641 when the biggest gun on the Chinese destroyer opened fire. The first shell went right by.

"Over. Down four hundred. SHOOT!"

"Bracket. Up two hundred. SHOOT!"

Greenville was in the process of diving. The upper lid of the conning tower was half-shut when the third shell exploded with deafening impact right inside the sail.

Greenville shuddered, and above the casing seven more shells came whistling past, with that unmistakable *WHOOOOSH—WHOOOSH— WHOOOSH* of naval ordnance. The Americans were lucky to take only one hit, because there were three very near-misses.

Commander Wheaton knew nothing about them, but he did know that something extremely large and explosive had just gone off right above him. *"Christ!"* he thought. *"That's a goddamned shell. That bastard's shooting at us. I just hope to God the pressure hull's not breached."*

"Helm-Captain," he said, steadily. "KEEP HER GOING DOWN."

"Upper lid shut and clipped, sir. . . ."

"There's a lot of noise coming from inside the sail."

"Was that one bang or two?"

"I think only one . . . try the periscope?"

"Go ahead. . . ."

"Damn. It's not moving, sir. . . ."

"How about the radio mast . . ."

"That's not moving either. Nothing."

"Upper lid's fine, sir . . . we're not shipping water."

"Right. Shut the lower lid . . . and make your speed ten . . . steer one-eight-zero . . ."

"Sounder shows thirty feet below the keel . . ."

Commander Wheaton turned to his XO. "This is not absolutely perfect. We're just about blind. The bow sonar is all we got left and there's so much noise coming from the inside of the sail I doubt that's gonna be much good to us. Fact is we can't see, we can't use radio, and we can't hear much."

By now Judd Crocker had made his way up to the conn, and found himself in the slightly awkward position of outranking the commanding officer. This meant that if he spoke at all, he must do so with extreme care, and great courtesy. Because, IF, as the top submarine commander in the U.S. Navy, Judd issued an order, it would mean, in the myriad of complicated laws of the Silent Service, that he had assumed command, relieving Tom Wheaton of his duties.

But Judd knew the CO personally, which made it easier, and he just said, "Well, Tom, at least we're still breathing."

"Actually, sir, at most we're still breathing."

"That shell wreck all the masts?"

"Looks like it. We're blind below the surface, and I got no radio aerials—but thank God, we're not leaking. The reactor's fine and we have propulsion."

"But if we want to have a look around, we have to go all the way to the surface?"

"Yessir. 'Fraid so."

"Well, we better not do that, Tom, in case that fucking destroyer has another whack at us."

"We sure hadn't."

"I guess if push came to shove, we could just go ahead and sink the bastard," said Judd, whose proximity to the free-wheeling warriors of SPECWARCOM had plainly had a profound impact on his psyche.

Commander Wheaton smiled grimly and replied, "Well, sir, we have been fired upon, so it would be self-defense, if anyone questioned us."

"Yes, it would. But there's something damned odd about this. The frigates should have frightened the Chinks away. But they weren't frightened, they blew our sail away without even thinking about it. Didn't give a rat's ass for the frigates."

"Hmmmmm," pondered Captain Crocker. "We stick our head out of the water, they'll blow the bastard off."

"Looks that way, sir. And we can't fire at them. We're still just in Chinese territorial waters, and they have a right to want us out. Anyway, you know how damned tricky it is to fire torpedoes in water this shallow. Goddamned things will probably go deep right out of the tube and then hit the bottom.

"Fact is, we gotta get back to the carrier. But the damned racket up in the sail is making our bow sonar next to useless. We need a guide dog. And the only one we got right now is *Kaufman*."

Tom moved over to the underwater telephone and picked up the handset.

"*Kaufman*, this is *Greenville*. Execute Plan Kibbec Five. Read back. Over."

Slightly to his surprise, *Kaufman* came straight back, faintly, but only slightly distorted: "*Greenville*, this is *Kaufman*. Roger. I read back. Execute Plan Kibbec Five. Out."

Tom replaced the handset. "Beautiful. We're in business."

"Huh?" said Judd. "What's up?"

"It's a DEVGRU plan—not yet for general use, but by chance Carl Sharpe and I were working on it a few weeks back. It's just a way of getting an SSN in from the deep field, in a big hurry, without radio comms."

"Oh, right. I gottit . . . er . . . at least I think I have . . . er . . . how?"

"No sweat. *Kaufman* switches on her high-power active sonar in a certain pattern, so we know it IS *Kaufman*—Pattern Five— and we just home in on her, treat her like she's some kinda under- water lighthouse. Get underneath and stay there. Then we got full comms, through her. Got ourselves a guide dog. Better still, he's a guide dog who'll run interference for us."

Ten minutes later, Tom Wheaton had driven *Greenville* underneath *Kaufman*. And they both headed out at 12 knots. The two CO's talked easily on the UWT. The new guidance plan was in place, but Commander Sharpe was still concerned about the proximity of the Chinese destroyer. "She closed to within a mile, and then stood off, just watching, appeared to show no interest in the frigates . . . as if she was waiting for you to reappear."

"Well, we'll give 'em a damned long wait, right, Carl?"

"That's what we're gonna do. This is going to work."

And so they set off, *Reuben James*, two miles astern of *Kaufman* and a half-mile astern of *Xiangtan*, heading home to the carrier group.

Kaufman kept station above *Greenville*, and its boatload of SEALs, right underneath. The distance to the *Ronald Reagan* was some 200 miles, but Admiral Barry had the 100,000-tonner in retreat, heading further east.

If *Xiangtan* was determined to continue firing on the Americans, the carrier must be removed from harm's way. Never, as they say in the trade, lose your "mission critical"—especially if it is currently home to a private air force of 84 fighter-attack bombers and a billion gallons of fuel. The carrier makes the difference. It represents the frontline muscle of American naval power. If it really should come down to a real shooting war, or even a full-scale battle, the *Ronald Reagan* wins it, hands down, with whatever means are necessary. The U.S. Navy would regard the early loss of the "mission critical" as negligent in the extreme. Admirals commanding the CVBG are apt to take no chances. Which was why the *Ronald Reagan* was essentially on the move.

And it was wise to do so. In the CIC of *Kaufman*, the CO could see the Chinese destroyer on radar, but 10 miles astern was another contact on precisely the same course, but catching them up. It was most probably Chinese, plainly a second warship backing up whatever the destroyer's ultimate task was.

And inside the communications room of *Xiangtan* there were extraordinary exchanges taking place. Colonel Lee was far too old a commander to be certain he had sunk the *Greenville*. He had watched the shells go in, and so far as he could tell only one had hit, deep in the sail. He could not tell whether one had penetrated the pressure hull, but he thought not. If it had, he had not observed it. And he knew that *Greenville* had been in the process of diving at the very moment he had ordered his gun into action.

In his opinion, the American submarine was very much alive. They had twice picked up UWT transmissions—always a solid indicator of the presence of a submarine. But the "noisemaker" *Kaufman* was towing, designed to confuse the life out of all acoustics, was making such a buzz that passive sonar detection of *Greenville* was impossible. And active contact was at best tenuous through the swirling wake of the frigate.

Colonel Lee thought the submarine must be heading out into the open ocean, and feared that she might stay underwater for days. All he could hope was that the damage might force her to the surface. He could not get close enough to depth-charge her because of the *Kaufman*. And they were already clear of Chinese waters, where the law was no longer on his side.

As such, he opened up the line to Southern Fleet Command, and once more reported his actions to Admiral Zu Jicai. He stressed that he could not recommend further pursuit, since he was powerless under the present circumstances to take any measures against *Greenville*—"Not until she returns to the surface."

Admiral Zu asked him to remain on the line while he spoke again to the Commander-in-Chief. But when Colonel Lee next heard a voice on the line, it was not the calm, measured tones of his immediate superior. It was the raging voice of the C-in-C himself. And, as voices go, this one was (a) loud, (b) furious, and (c) owned by a man who had apparently lost it.

"HAVE YOU GONE MAD, LEE? ANSWER ME THAT!" screamed Admiral Zhang. "YOU MUST HAVE GONE MAD. THERE CAN BE NO OTHER EXCUSE FOR YOUR CONDUCT. MY ORDERS WERE CLEAR—SINK THE AMERICAN SUBMARINE. NOT GO AND PUT A DENT IN ITS HULL. SINK IT. SINK IT. THAT'S WHAT I SAID. AND YOU HAD THE MOST POWERFUL DESTROYER IN THE NAVY TO DO IT. I REPEAT, LEE—HAVE YOU GONE MAD?"

Colonel Lee kept his cool. "Sir, I do not believe I have lost my senses. But the submarine was in the process of diving when we first saw her. The only target we had was her sail, which we hit with a one-hundred-fifty-seven-millimeter shell. Also, she is guarded by two guided missile frigates."

"I DON'T CARE IF SHE'S GUARDED BY THE ENTIRE UNITED STATES NAVY," raged the C-in-C. "I ORDERED HER TO BE SUNK AND MY ORDERS WERE NOT CARRIED OUT. DO YOU UNDERSTAND THAT?"

"Yessir."

"WELL, WHY WERE THEY NOT CARRIED OUT?"

"Because it was impossible, sir. We were only able to see her for less than a minute, and we were eight miles away."

"AND WHERE IS THE SUBMARINE NOW?" he yelled.

"Under the water, sir. Following one of the frigates. I presume back to the American carrier."

"PRESUME NOTHING!" roared Zhang. "NOTHING! DO YOU UNDERSTAND ME?"

"Yessir."

And now the C-in-C spoke in more measured tones for the first time. "Colonel Lee. You are the most senior surface ship commanding officer in the Navy. Your record until today was exemplary. And because of that I am going to ignore your flagrant defiance of my orders. However, those orders still stand.

"Colonel Lee, you will continue to track the American submarine, and when she surfaces, as she surely must sometime, you will open fire and put her on the floor of the ocean for trespassing illegally in Chinese waters. IS THAT CLEAR?"

"Yessir."

"Colonel Lee. YOU WILL FOLLOW THE AMERICAN SUBMARINE TO THE ENDS OF THE EARTH IF YOU HAVE TO. BUT YOU WILL SINK HER."

"Yessir."

"And Colonel Lee, should the American frigates open fire on you in defense of their submarine, you will open fire on them, too. You outgun them, and you have excellent missiles and torpedoes.

In case you had not noticed, that's what your big destroyer is for."

"Yessir."

"TO THE ENDS OF THE EARTH, COLONEL LEE. . . . NOW GO."

And so *Xiangtan* fell in two miles astern of *Kaufman*, running at 12 knots. And there she would stay until she saw her chance to carry out the orders of the Chinese C-in-C. They were orders that might amount to committing suicide. They were orders that might have been issued by Captain Queeg. But there was no longer any doubt in Colonel Lee's mind about their validity.

Meanwhile, back in Zhanjiang, Admiral Zhang Yushu was almost beside himself. The first reports were coming in from Xiachuan Dao, and they were confirming every single one of his worst fears.

The jail had plainly come under heavy attack. Both helicopters had been destroyed. The patrol boat had been reduced to a hulk, and was sitting in shallow water on the jetty. The communications room had been obliterated. The guardroom had been leveled. The gates to the jail were blown off. The dormitory had been gutted, but with many civilian survivors, all of whom had been gassed. The entire Chinese guard force had been wiped out, at least six of them with their throats cut. And, needless to confirm, there was no sign of the American prisoners.

The team of Navy investigators who had now been on Xiachuan Dao for around an hour were quite shaken by the sheer brutality of the attack. And Admiral Zhang could hardly believe his ears as Admiral Zu Jicai read out the initial report from the island.

"But how many, Jicai?" the C-in-C kept repeating over and over. "How many were there? What kind of a force must it have taken to literally take out an entire armed garrison and free more than one hundred prisoners? How many were in that force? And where did they come from? How did they get there? How come we saw nothing?"

In his long career in the navy of China, Zhang had never faced such a terrifying list of unanswered questions. He felt as though his navy had been attacked by a phantom force, one that he could not see.

"There must have been two hundred of them, Jicai."

"I don't think so, sir. Because that would have meant more than three hundred of them escaping. And no one could have done that without a very sizeable boat. And that's what they did not have, otherwise we would have seen it."

"Well, how did they get away?"

"In the absence of a ship that could get into the jetty, and in the absence of American helicopters, I would have to say in small boats, landing craft they ran right into the shallows."

"But why did we not see them? On radar, on the overheads?"

"Because they came a long way inshore in those submarines, Yushu. And then broke cover and ran fast for the island, just the last two or three miles, I'd say. We easily could have missed them."

"But I ask again, Jicai. How many were they? And what kind of men were they? Devils?"

"No, sir. Not devils. They were American Special Forces, which is considerably worse."

"How do you know this, Jicai?"

"Because even from this initial report, it bears all of their hall-marks. Total destruction of everything that posed a threat, in particular the helicopters, the patrol boat and the communications room, from where there could be signals sent back to HQ. And of course the guards, particularly those in the towers and those patrolling the inside and outside perimeters of the jail. Classic Special Forces."

"Jicai, I do of course respect your views, and I believe you may be right. Indeed, it is hard to arrive at any other conclusion. But how did the Americans find out they were on the island?"

"That I cannot answer. Because in our vast land they could have been transported anywhere. But we know to our cost how clever the Americans are. They wear very wide smiles, but they have a tiger's teeth. And they are completely ruthless if they are sufficiently riled."

"You think the capture of that submarine crew was sufficient to rile them so badly that they would undertake an operation like this?"

"Yushu, I'm not at all sure they did not blow up *Seawolf* in Canton. So my answer is, yes. They plainly were sufficiently riled to go to extreme lengths to get that crew back. And perhaps to even more extreme lengths to make certain we did not spend much time on their precious submarine."

"But, Jicai, the sequence of events of the last twelve hours means that I shall almost certainly be asked to resign and court-martialed for gross incompetence."

"That, Yushu, is the downside of high command. And it may happen. However, you have many friends in very high places, and most of them would be unwilling to force you to fall on your sword, particularly since the events were entirely unpredictable. And everyone knows you have taken all reasonable care to ensure that the operation to copy the submarine was conducted in strictest secrecy. I do not think they will allow you to be disgraced.

"Because in the end it was the Americans who stepped beyond the bounds of reasonable behavior. No one could have predicted they would have reacted with measures as desperate as this. Bombing, mayhem, murder, destruction . . . it's not in their character, and I will forever wonder what prompted them to such extremities.

"I do not think you will be blamed. But I am afraid we have to alert our government about the current events. And that, I'm afraid, is a task you will have to mastermind, sending the ill tidings up through the chain of command."

"Who do you imagine knows already?"

"Sir, I am certain news of the two disasters, the submarine and the jail, is no longer strictly private. However, I do think we have to ensure that the Chief of the Naval Staff, Admiral Sang Ye in Beijing, is informed. And probably at the same time the Chief of the PLA, Qiao Jiyung.

"In both those instances I am happy to make the contacts, since both catastrophes occurred in areas of my command. However, I think it would be politically prudent for you to personally talk to the political commissar, and then for you to speak formally to the general secretary of the Communist Party."

"Since he also chairs the Military Affairs Commission, perhaps I should speak to him first?"

"I think not. The political commissar will not thank you for keeping him out, and he would appreciate some well-thought political views from us. At this moment, Yushu, you need friends."

"Perhaps my weakness is always that I lack your prudence, Jicai?"

"Yushu, you took a major step when you elected to pick a very serious fight with the U.S.A. I know you did it for the very best of reasons. So does everyone else. We all understand the significance of a great submarine fleet. But adventures like stealing an American SSN and its crew must always be carried out at great risk.

"You embarked on the adventure driven purely by your concern for your country and your concern to arm it against its enemies in the best possible way. However, that is only one part of your task. The other is always to ensure that we do not take on an opponent when the odds are stacked against us. And in this case, every one of your advisers and your very few superiors would have agreed with your actions. Indeed, most of them did agree.

"I repeat, no one could have predicted an American reaction of this unusual severity. And I say again, I do not understand it."

"Also, remember the diplomatic exchanges, Jicai. There was no suggestion that the United States was even concerned. And all the while they must have been planning this ruthless reprisal. I could not have known."

"No, Yushu. You could not have known."

"And now my only wish is to save my career. And I may not be very good at that, since I have never had to think such thoughts before . . ."

"Then I must ask you again: Do you really want Colonel Lee to pursue the American submarine to the ends of the earth and then sink it?"

"Jicai, I believe that changes the world for me. If at the end of it all we sink an American nuclear boat in revenge for what they have done, I can make out a good case for the courage and decisiveness of my Navy. I cannot end the mission with a whimper. We must save face and issue a warning, an international warning, that we will not be trifled with."

"Ah, Yushu. *'Real power comes from the barrel of a gun.'* The words of the great Mao, eh?"

"Exactly so."

"Let us hope the Americans have not read them. For it would surely be even more shocking if they sank the *Xiangtan.*"

Back out on the ocean, the bizarre convoy began to swing to the east as *Kaufman* increased speed to stay above *Greenville*. The SSN was stepping up her speed two knots at a time, checking her sail constantly, for fear it might rip right off.

On the plus side, she was not leaking, although she sounded like a floating steel strip mill. On the minus side, the Chinese destroyer showed no signs whatsoever of giving up the chase. A little over a mile and a half behind, she now steamed along steadily, making an easy 16 knots through the water, just as *Greenville* was doing. She made no attempt to establish contact with either of the American frigates. She just stayed right where she was, watching, waiting, tracking.

In *Greenville*, Commander Wheaton, clattering along now at 17 knots, decided to go for another speed increase, since there appeared to be nothing wrong with either the reactor or the turbines.

"Make your speed nineteen," he said. The battered submarine surged forward, and the only discernible result in the control room was an even greater racket coming from inside the shattered sail. But she kept going.

Up on the surface the American operators in the frigates were unable to pick up any radio contact from the Chinese, but every time they looked back over the stern, there was *Xiangtan* running through the fading wake of the frigate *Kaufman*. The unnerving presence of the big Chinese destroyer seemed to increase as the day wore on, because they ran eastward for hour after hour, and nothing changed. Where *Kaufman* went, *Xiangtan* went, and by early afternoon the Americans were beginning to wonder if they should do something to discourage this strange game of follow the leader, particularly since the *Shantou* had now caught up and was steaming along 200 yards off *Xiangtan*'s starboard quarter.

Commander Carl Sharpe opened up his encrypted line to the Flag at midday, informing Admiral Barry that the destroyer from

Zhanjiang, which had summarily opened fire on *Greenville* some-time before 0700 that morning, had now been tracking the sub-merged and damaged submarine for the best part of five hours. It was also in the company of a Chinese antisubmarine frigate.

He added that he had no idea what the plans of either Chinese captain were, but they had made no attempt to fire on either of the American frigates. "They seem, sir," said Commander Sharpe, "to have an exclusive interest in the submarine, and a total disregard for our surface ships."

Admiral Barry asked if the *Kaufman's* CO had any recommen-dations. But the frigate captain said he could not come up with anything more constructive than perhaps firing a shot or two across the *Xiangtan's* bows. But this seemed extravagant, and Admiral Barry told him just to proceed back toward the battle group, but to keep him posted, on the hour, as to the precise move-ments of the Chinese warship. "Remember, you are not authorized to shoot, Commander, except in self-defense. That's straight from Washington. She's a big ship, and we'd have to sink her to disable her, and I'm not sure Washington would be crazy about that."

Commander Sharpe returned to the bridge and ordered the helmsman to hold course and make their best speed back toward the carrier, which was of course only the best speed *Greenville* could make, rattling along underneath with virtually no sonar. However, Commander Wheaton had now wound her speed up to 27 knots and they were clattering along extremely smoothly, though you would never have known it, judging by the shrieks of tortured steel from the sail.

Two miles astern, still following with bland, impassive determi-nation, were *Xiangtan* and *Shantou*, pitching through the rising ocean swell, as apparently innocent as a couple of tourist ferries, but with menace in their gun turrets.

The *Ronald Reagan* was now positioned eight hours away to the east, and for every one of those hours the Chinese warships kept a constant vigil on the American frigates and her unseen underwater colleague *Greenville*. Every hour Commander Wheaton checked in on the UWT to check if they still had company, and the answer was always the same: "They're still there, two miles astern, same speed."

It was five o'clock in the evening when Commander Sharpe again contacted the giant aircraft carrier, which still steamed 200 miles east in company with her battle group.

He knew both *Cheyenne* and *Hartford* had transferred their big cargoes of SEALs and former prisoners to the *Ronald Reagan*, but he did not yet know how *Greenville* was ever going to conduct a similar operation, since the destroyer seemed determined to follow them until she was able to open fire again on the American submarine she had already hit and almost crippled with a sizeable shell.

Commander Sharpe was now convinced they should put the god-damned destroyer on the bottom and have done with it. And he relayed these thoughts to the distant Admiral Barry in forceful terms.

But the battle group commander had been told this had not been authorized. His instinct was to avoid a confrontation with China if possible. But right now, with *Greenville* damaged, he opened up the line to CINCPAC in San Diego to report.

Again there was great caution in the American camp, and CINC-PAC emphasized no shooting unless fired upon. However, they did believe that the heavily gunned *Xiangtan* was showing an obdurate interest in the submarine, and they developed a new plan . . . to send two more ships back to join *Kaufman* and *Reuben James*, surround *Xiangtan*, and try to ride her off—Navyspeak for forcing the destroyer away, under the IRPC rules governing international waters.

Admiral Barry detailed the frigate *Simpson* to head back and resume station close aboard *Xiangtan*, which was of course by far the most menacing of the two Chinese ships. He also ordered the big 9,000-ton Ticonderoga-class guided missile cruiser *Vella Gulf*, under the command of Captain Chuck Freeburg, to join them and to take overall charge of the operation.

And two hours later, the four American warships moved into position for a complicated maneuver that carried with it the danger of a collision. However, the veteran commanding officer of *Vella Gulf* knew precisely what he was doing, and he ordered *Kaufman* and *Simpson* to make a wide sweep and then come in fast, with *Simpson* spearing in on *Xiangtan*'s starboard quarter, and *Kaufman* coming in at a right angle straight at her starboard bow, with full right of way.

Under the laws of navigation, as laid down in the International Regulations for the Prevention of Collisions at Sea (IRPC), the ship that can see a red portside navigation light coming in on her starboard side *must give way.*

They even have a poem for it:

> *If to starboard red appear,*
> *It is your duty to keep clear.*

In instances like the one now unfolding in the China Seas, it was not much more than a very grown-up game of chicken. Chuck Freeburg had *Simpson* blocking the Chinese captain's escape route on her starboard quarter, while *Kaufman* came straight at her bow on the same side.

Right in front, off *Xiangtan*'s port bow, angled in on course zero-seven-five, would be the massive bulk of the *Vella Gulf*, which would prevent her swerving away and still somehow holding her easterly course. Which would leave *Xiangtan* just one option: a hard left turn, forcing her right away. Captain Freeburg had *Reuben James* in prime position making four knots right on the American cruiser's starboard quarter, ready to run in and force the Chinese destroyer around in a half-circle.

All of the above were slick, operable, time-honored navy tactics in such circumstances. But all of it was entirely dependent on the Chinese captain's willingness to obey the rules.

Thirty years previously, Great Britain's Royal Navy found itself in a total "bugger's muddle" when trying to force Iceland to allow British trawlers in their fishing grounds. To Iceland, this was economic life or death. Their patrol craft, completely outgunned by RN frigates, used their hulls instead of guns, smashing into Royal Navy warships, simply refusing to alter course.

In the end, the Navy had to turn away, to avoid serious damage to expensive warships a long way from home. It proved what every navy CO knows; if you want to win a fight at sea, you'd better be prepared to sink your opponent, otherwise you have a very sporting chance of losing.

It was a little after 1900 when Captain Freeburg's particular game of chicken began. All four of the American ships were in position, and *Kaufman* made its run-in, driving forward from a quarter-mile out, straight into the precise same square of water where *Xiangtan* was headed, from her starboard side.

On the bridge of the destroyer Colonel Lee assessed the situation: "*Are they going to ram us? We're badly boxed in. . . . I can't turn to starboard because of the second American ship. . . . The port side is my only chance. . . but if I turn, they will force me right around. . . . I can't drive through the cruiser . . . and the fourth American ship will have me under the same starboard rule . . . what now? They're going to turn me right around.*"

Colonel Lee made his decision. There was, he knew, a get-out clause that applied to the "burdened" ship, in this case, *Kaufman*: If collision is inevitable, you must alter course.

The get-out clause meant, of course, that the entire rule did not work, not if a particular CO decided he was not going to be ridden off. And Colonel Lee, who this day had been on the wrong end of a tongue-lashing from the C-in-C himself, was a lot more afraid of Zhang, who plainly did not care if he and all his crew perished, than he ever was of the USS *Kaufman*.

He said quietly, "Maintain your course and speed."

Which put Commander Carl Sharpe in a difficult spot, as he drove his frigate straight toward Colonel Lee's much bigger destroyer.

"They're not going, sir!"

"He's holding course . . ."

"Jesus, we'll slam right into him . . . sir . . . sir, we have to bear off . . . and it's gotta be to starboard . . ."

"HARD RIGHT TO ZERO-NINE-ZERO!"

On *Xiangtan*'s bridge they could only watch as the knife-edged bow of the American frigate came arrowing in toward their hull . . . and then fractionally began to turn away. They all watched through the bridge windows as *Kaufman* slewed right around from a southerly course to an easterly, fetching up right alongside the *Xiangtan* with a grinding of steel as the two hulls slammed into each other, and then locked.

Sailors on deck looked right into each other's eyes, two sets of men, all trying to do the same job as best they could. Two sets of men from either side of the planet Earth. Two sets of men from different worlds.

On *Kaufman's* bridge, Commander Sharpe could scarcely believe what had happened. The Chinese CO had simply held course, nerve and helm. And now *Xiangtan* was pulling away again, passing *Vella Gulf* and moving right on toward the submarine she so obviously still sought.

Captain Freeburg ordered the cruiser hard to port, flank speed, his 86,000-horsepower gas turbine engines driving her back level with the Chinese destroyer, into a position out off her starboard beam. The other American frigates also closed in, more or less ignoring *Shantou.*

There was, however, one shining fact emerging here: nothing was going to stop the *Xiangtan,* short of sinking her. And Captain Freeburg was not about to allow her to break free without demonstrating once more that the U.S. Navy meant business. And he ordered his big five-inch forward-mounted gun into action.

"TWO SHOTS ACROSS HER BOW . . . NOW."

The Mk 45 shells, programmed for much greater distances, exploded out of the barrel aimed loosely at the airspace in front of *Xiangtan.* They whistled across her bow, 40 feet above the foredeck. For a split second Captain Freeburg thought the Chinese would return fire, and he said quickly to his XO, "If she shoots, sink her."

But Colonel Lee had no intention of deviating from his allotted task, which was to sink the submarine. *"To the ends of the earth."* The words of Admiral Zhang refused to leave his mind, and he ignored the obvious warning shots and pressed on forward into the waters where he knew the damaged *Greenville* must still be lurking beneath the surface. The sonar might be inoperable, but the underwater telephone was decisive, and the Chinese knew what they were hearing.

Captain Freeburg immediately accessed the Flag and spoke directly to Admiral Barry. "Right now, sir. We have a stalemate out here. We tried to ride her off, in fact *Kaufman* crashed right into *Xiangtan*, just a sideswipe, a lotta metal grinding, but only minor damage. But that Chinese ship refused to be intimidated. She never altered course by one inch, just kept going forward on her easterly bearing, right through the middle of all four of us.

"I put two warning shots across her bows, which she most certainly saw, but offered no response, just kept on her course, easterly, possibly picking up *Greenville* on the UWT. Sir, I am forced to conclude that this destroyer is either under the command of an absolute fanatic, or her CO is under orders from an absolute fanatic. Either way, I don't like it. In my view, sir, you should let me sink the sonofabitch before he sinks one of us. It would only be tit-for-tat, since she's already put a shell into *Greenville*."

Admiral Barry was inclined to agree with all of that, because he did not want this obsessive Chinese destroyer to suddenly open fire and cause serious damage to one of the Battle Group ships, which she plainly could. But he considered that he was not yet empowered to start sinking heavy-duty Chinese warships, and he told Captain Freeburg to form a threatening "escort" around the two Chinese intruders while he contacted CINCPAC.

At this point they were beginning to run out of ideas. CINCPAC opened a line up to Admiral Mulligan, who did not want to be a party to a real big-ship shooting war against China, and his orders were still not to sink either destroyer or frigate unless they opened fire first, now in international waters.

The solution, when it came, was relatively simple, dependent only on *Greenville*'s ability to continue submerged at speed: just keep heading home right across the Pacific. "The two Chinese ships cannot refuel," said Joe Mulligan. "And sooner rather than later, one of 'em is going to run out of gas. We can keep going all the way to San Diego if we so wish."

Admiral Barry quickly grasped the sense of that, and announced that he would steam the carrier another 600 miles east, by which time at least one of the Chinese ships would have to be considering turning around. The range of the frigate was only 2,700 miles at 18 knots, and she'd been traveling a lot faster than that for several hours.

At this moment, in the gathering darkness, they were almost 200 miles offshore, and the two Chinese ships had already made a fast 120 miles before that. The range of *Shantou* at high speed was probably much nearer 1,800, maybe less, which meant 900 miles out and 900 back. And with 320 already under her belt, she could not have more than 1,480 miles in her fuel tanks.

And so Admiral Barry ordered the entire Battle Group to continue heading east for another 30 hours at 20 knots, 600 miles, every one of which would drain the Chinese frigate's fuel supply. The admiral had shrewdly kept one of his tankers well to the east.

He doubted whether the destroyer had much more than 3,000 miles at these speeds, even if she'd started with full tanks. The issue was, would the Chinese high command be willing to risk their newest destroyer, all alone, way out in the Pacific, within striking range of an angry U.S. Navy CVBG?

"I wouldn't, given the current climate between China and the U.S.," was the considered opinion of the admiral. And with that, both Captain Freeburg and Commander Carl Sharpe agreed.

And so they all headed east for the next day and a half, running fast, draining the fuel out of the Chinese ships. Hour after hour they charged through the Pacific, driving the ships forward, knowing the carrier and her escorts were way out in front.

Somehow *Greenville* kept going right underneath *Kaufman*'s keel, still rattling along underwater in a thoroughly alarming way. But her turbines never faltered and she ran smoothly at 27 knots, her reactor running sweetly. God knows what she must have sounded like in the sonar room of the pursuing Chinese destroyer, but the ability of the 7,000-tonner to take a hit and keep going was a mighty testimony to the engineers at Newport News Shipbuilding in Virginia.

Down in the crew quarters, the SEALs had done their best to rejoin the human race, removing the camouflage paint, trying to wash off the grime, the blood and the sweat, removing their bandanas, trying to look again like trained U.S. Navy personnel, rather than hired killers and demolition men.

Several of the younger members of *Greenville*'s crew were quite anxious to talk to the hit squad that had freed their fellow submariners. But in the hours following a tense and dangerous mission it is unusual for the participants to have anything much to say, except to each other. Men who have killed ruthlessly in the service of their country often need time to adjust, to regain inner peace, reexamining their respective role in the operation. And the first place they tend to turn is to each other, to other participants who will understand the pressures, in the face of which they had all brought home the bacon.

The great saving grace about an operation like Xiachuan Dao was that the Chinese would most certainly have killed them had they not struck first. Nonetheless, all of the key SEALs in Operation Nighthawk were very much within themselves as the men of the USS *Greenville* attempted to get them home.

Most of the SEALs had been privately scared when the shell had ripped into the submarine's casing. And the journey had been, from their point of view, somewhat worrying—locked in a damaged underwater ship, running through the dark and endless depths of foreign waters where the seas of China finally wash into the immense Pacific.

None of them knew much about submarines, and there's something forbidding about being deep underwater if you are not used to it. Plainly one major leak, far less a torpedo, could wipe out the entire ship, condemning them to the endless black silence of the deep. And the SEALs' iron discipline and amazing skills could not save them from that.

The fact that *Greenville* was obviously hit and hurt made matters considerably more tense, and tired as they were, it was difficult for anyone to sleep for long. Lt. Commander Rick Hunter had been in long conversations with Judd Crocker and was more or less approaching the point where he understood the massive safety systems in a nuclear submarine. He now understood that *Xiangtan* might open fire on them again, should they go to the surface, and that generally speaking it was a whole lot better to stay deep and comfortable. *Greenville*'s nuclear reactor would give them all the warmth, air and power they could need.

Buster Townsend had completed his first mission, two missions really, since he was active in the recon. He would never look at the world in quite the same way again, having gazed into the jaws of death on several occasions since he had first dropped into the water four days ago, right on Lieutenant Commander Bennett's shoulder.

And now he sipped coffee in companionable quiet with his colleagues. The young SEAL from the bayous who had twice made the journey to Xiachuan Dao, who had marched across the island hauling the heavy gear, logged the guard movements in the jail and dodged the machine-gun fire to blow off the main cell door, was suddenly incapable of conversation.

Next to him sat his lifetime buddy, Rattlesnake Davies, who had cold-bloodedly knifed the Chinese guard who threatened the entire mission. Rattlesnake too sipped coffee, saying nothing.

Petty Officer Steve Whipple, the iron man who had carried 80 pounds of high explosive through the jungle, who had gunned down the Chinese guards on the hill and blown up the communication center, was talking, but only to his pal Catfish Jones.

Petty Officer Jones, another iron man who had carried the big machine gun, plus all of his other equipment, had also blown up the headquarters of the camp commandant, Commander Li. But at this time he talked only of baseball, wondering aloud how Steve could possibly waste his time in support of a team such as the Chicago White Sox.

"Jesus, you Atlanta Braves guys are getting goddamned pleased with yourselves," muttered Steve. "But we'll be back, maybe not this season, but next . . ."

"In your dreams."

It was an unconscious attempt to return to something near normality after the mayhem and the death, the bombs, the guns and the knives. They made it seem like routine. But it never was.

Up in the wardroom, Lt. Paul Merloni was making a valiant attempt to act normally, with his customary edge of black humor. But wit came unusually difficult today for the New Yorker, who had shot down three of the Chinese outside guard patrol and then cut down the guard in the interrogation room, probably saving the life of Linus Clarke.

Paul was talking to Lt. Dan Conway, who was never effusive but now, in the grim aftermath of the operation, deep below the surface of the Pacific, was absorbed only with thoughts of getting out of here alive. Dan too had faced death, in the thick of the fighting in the jail, and more so when he rushed the entrance of the dormitory block hurling his grenades at the Commander Li's armed guards.

In the other corner sat Lt. Commander Rusty Bennett, looking surprisingly presentable, wearing a spare pair of Navy trousers and shirt, on the basis that he could not walk around covered in the blood of the watchtower guards. He was glad to be out of those clothes, and was already being treated as something of a celebrity by the young officers in the submarine. He had asked for special permission to bring Chief McCarthy into the wardroom, and now the two men who had scaled the towers and made the entire mission possible sat eating chicken sandwiches and trying not to think about what might have happened if their luck had run out high above the prison complex.

What each of them knew was that this mission was not yet over. They knew they were in a submarine that could not, for the moment, go to the surface. They also knew they had been hit by a Chinese destroyer that was still out there, still trying to get at them. And they listened with both ears for any shred of information which might illuminate the situation.

It was becoming clear that they were on a long, 600-mile ride out into the Pacific, and that the officers of the submarine were fervently hoping the *Xiangtan* would give up and leave. The SEALs were of the opinion that they had fought quite enough battles for one weekend, and they would deeply appreciate getting back to the aircraft carrier without being caught in the middle of another one.

"Right now I'm overexploded," said Paul Merloni.

Meanwhile, out in the *Xiangtan*, Colonel Lee was under-exploded, and the conundrum that faced him was growing more pressing by the hour. At this stage, 400 miles east of the hunting ground off Xiachuan Dao, they were driving through pitch-black, rainy seas in the small hours of Tuesday morning, July 18.

They were in the northern waters of the 200-mile-wide Luzon Strait, which separates the south coast of Taiwan from the Philippines. In an area strewn with shoals and tiny islands, they were in steeply shelving waters that were sometimes 4,000 feet deep, sometimes 6,000. Right now the lead American frigate, *Kaufman*, was heading for the Bashi Channel, which leads steadily through the shoals and out into some really bottomless water, three miles deep.

Shantou had already expressed concern about her fuel situation, and Colonel Lee realized that even the vast tanks of *Xiangtan* could not last forever, especially at these high speeds. Four hundred miles from now he would have to consider turning back. Even Admiral Zhang in his current state of mind must know he could not run fast for more than three or four days.

Also, if *Shantou* turned back, he would be in a very exposed position, in massively deep water. If the Americans decided to sink him way out here in these desolate acres of the Pacific, no one would ever really know what had happened. He and his crew could end up on the bottom, a mile deeper than the *Titanic*, and it had taken over a half century to find her.

It seemed to Colonel Lee that the sooner he made his move the better, because the farther they went the more the advantage swung toward the Americans. The trouble was that he could not work out quite what to do. Neither could any of the officers who sailed with him. The task presented by the plainly deranged Admiral Zhang was an order formed by a madman.

Here he was, hundreds of miles from either help or a Chinese base, surrounded by three American guided missile frigates and a monstrous American cruiser, and he was supposed to (a) find the damaged American submarine they were all protecting and (b) attack it, in the face of the superpower's armed escort. Was this crazy, or what?

And how to conduct his attack? He could scarcely use depth charges, because the submarine was plainly right underneath the frigate *Kaufman*. Mortar charges were a kind of lunatic possibility, but the mortars carried by *Xiangtan* were only the old FQF 2500s, which had a range of 1,200 meters. Therefore, from his current position, astern of the *Kaufman*, which was making 27 knots, he would somehow have to come in a mile closer and throw the mortars forward straight over the American frigate, which would then watch them plop into the water out ahead.

At that point Lee and his crew probably would have about one minute to live, maximum, before the shuddering power of *Vella Gulf*'s big Harpoon guided missiles slammed them all into oblivion. Also the chances of one of the mortar charges actually hitting *Greenville*, and exploding, were, by Colonel Lee's reckoning, remote.

The gun was no good, because the submarine was still under the water. Helicopters were no good because the Americans would blow them out of the sky in about two minutes. Which left only torpedoes. If Colonel Lee was going to put *Greenville* on the bottom, he would have to launch two of their Yu-2 active/passive homing weapons, and he assessed the chances of success at only fifty-fifty. The torpedoes could not go in passive because of the noisemaker off the stern of *Kaufman*.

They would have to use active homing, and they still might not be fast enough. However, he could program them with a 50-foot ceiling, which meant they would not go for anything up to 50 feet below the surface. Right below that, they should find the USS *Greenville*.

And the chances of the Americans NOT knowing the torpedoes were on their way in? Zero, was Colonel Lee's guess.

And so they all thundered on east, *Shantou* running out of fuel fast. By midafternoon her captain had made his decision, and he contacted *Xiangtan* to announce he would have to turn back. "I am, sir, reaching the point of no return. If I run for another hour at this speed I may not get back at all."

Colonel Lee, now almost 700 miles away from the coast of his homeland, decided that he also must make his move. He informed *Shantou* he would run for another 100 miles and then he, too, would try to turn back, but he had a private mission to complete for Admiral Zhang before he did so. He could see no point in *Shantou* remaining on station to go down with him.

At 1630 the Americans saw the Chinese frigate turn away and began to head back toward the west. But they noted that *Xiangtan* kept right on coming, all on her own, matching them for speed. She was a big ship to be showing such singleminded hot pursuit, and the four American surface commanders wished as one that she would get the hell away, and go follow the goddamned frigate home for a nice bowl of rice.

Kaufman's sonar room got on the underwater telephone and informed Tom Wheaton that one of the Chinese warships had turned back.

"The little one, I guess?"

"Aye, sir. The destroyer's still there, coupla miles astern."

The conversation was short, but Colonel Lee's men picked it up and were grateful for it, since it confirmed that their quarry was still very much within striking range.

And now Colonel Lee ordered an increase in speed, winding *Xiangtan* up to 30 knots. And as he did so, Captain Freeburg began a wide swing way out to her port side, settling in a position eight miles off the Chinese beam, the precise range he would need for an accurate launch of his McDonnell Douglas Harpoon surface-to-surface missiles with their big, ship-killing 227-kilogram warheads. Those things fire high, right out of the big stern-mounted quad launchers, then tip over and lose height before leveling off and screaming in at wavetop height at almost 900 knots, active-radar homing, just about unstoppable. Someone fires those babies at you, you need sharp eyes, a life jacket and a prayer book. And while Chuck Freeburg had no intention of beginning anything, under his present orders, one false move and the Chinaman was history.

Kaufman had her eyes glued on the destroyer and noticed the increase in speed. They had an open line from the ops room direct to *Vella Gulf*, where Chuck Freeburg was preparing his Harpoon missiles for launch, if necessary.

It was 1645 when the Chinese commanding officer decided that at roughly a mile he was close enough.

Not that he knew precisely where *Greenville* was. Only the general area, under *Kaufman*. And even that was sheer guesswork. And to act on that guesswork amounted to his own death warrant.

All he could do was to fire his torpedoes into that area on the outside chance they would find *Greenville*.

"Left standard rudder . . . steer zero-eight-zero. STAND BY ONE AND TWO TUBES."

"Steady on zero-eight-zero, sir."

Colonel Lee hesitated for one split second, preparing to join his God. Then he snapped the death-or-glory command. "FIRE ONE."

"Number one tube fired."

"FIRE TWO."

"Number two tube fired."

Just two small clouds of smoke were all that betrayed Colonel Lee's actions as the two torpedoes blasted out of the tubes, 50 yards over the water, and then dropped with a heavy splash below the surface, searching, searching, searching for the USS *Greenville*.

Kaufman spotted the smoke. The control room snapped out the information to the cruiser: "The Chinese destroyer has fired two torpedoes from his starboard side."

Simultaneously they hit the underwater telephone to *Greenville* right underneath the keel, and the submarine's ops room was, if anything, a split second ahead

"We just picked 'em up. Active homers . . . ping interval fifteen hundred meters . . . I'm going on to thirty knots . . . full pattern active and passive decoys launched."

Judd Crocker, in *Greenville*'s conn with Tom Wheaton, said, "What's that, Tommy? Thirty-five knots. They got five on us . . . range fifteen hundred . . . that's a five-hundred-yard gain every three minutes . . . gonna take 'em nine minutes to catch us . . . right?"

"Correct, sir. But we got those Emerson Mark Two decoys out there . . . Christ they're good, light-years in front of those old Chinese torpedoes . . . have faith . . . we may not outrun 'em, but we'll definitely outsmart 'em."

Greenville surged forward in the water, pursued now by Colonel Lee's comparatively primitive weapons, which were already being completely confused by the decoys. Every time the torpedo's homing sonar pinged, the Emerson decoy pinged it right back, announcing to the iron Chinese brain, *Here I am, a darned great American submarine . . . come right in and hit me . . . over here . . . way, way over here.*"

And *Greenville* had four of them in the water, which quadrupled the confusion factor.

Over in *Vella Gulf*, Captain Freeburg had drawn a bead on *Xiangtan* a long time ago. And now he seized the moment. "Prepare to launch Harpoons One and Two . . ."

"Launchers One and Two ready."

"FIRE ONE AND TWO."

The roar of the aft launch from the two fire-belching missiles was deafening, and the crew members watched them shriek skywards, higher and higher, before turning down at 800 feet to complete their deadly business.

Captain Freeburg, still positioned directly off *Xiangtan*'s port beam, ordered both his five-inch guns, fore and aft, to sink the Chinese destroyer. And the shells arrived before the missiles, slamming into the superstructure of the ship, blasting havoc into the ops room, the bridge, the comms room and the helicopter flight deck.

Colonel Lee ordered retaliatory fire, but he was too late. Both Harpoon missiles crashed into the portside of the *Xiangtan* and exploded with shattering force. The massive *K-E-R-R-R-R-B-A-A-M!* literally blew the Chinese destroyer apart in a massive fireball, black smoke rising in a mushroom cloud 100 feet high into the rainy skies. The ship vanished, leaving only traces of its sudden death and an ever-increasing oil-slick, which spread thinly over the waters of the western Pacific.

Captain Freeburg and his team stood for a while, watching the smoke-cloaked aftermath of the gigantic destruction they had wrought. And there was not a man among them who was not conscious of some misgivings over the loss of hundreds of lives.

"I guess they'da done it to us, sir?" said a lieutenant junior grade, a little sheepishly.

"Guess they would at that, Jack. Besides, they probably shoulda thought about all that before they decided to capture a crippled American submarine on the high seas, in international waters, against every kind of maritime law. Wasn't real smart, right?"

"Nossir."

Meanwhile, back on *Greenville*, Judd Crocker and Tom Wheaton watched the Emerson decoys do their work. The little computer screens showed the incoming torpedoes pass harmlessly by, one a hundred yards to port, the other even further to starboard. Neither of them found a target, never even exploded.

Commander Wheaton accessed the UWT once more, heard the news, and announced he was coming to the surface to secure the damage to his sail, "because this sucker's making a racket which is telling me she ain't real happy."

In the next 10 minutes, Admiral Barry detailed *Reuben James* to pick up any survivors, and set a rendezvous for the carrier to make the transfers from the submarine. After that they were heading directly to Pearl, where, for some reason, there was to be a Presidential welcome for the U.S. Navy SEALs and the rescued crew of the USS *Seawolf*.

Midday. Friday, July 21.
The Oval Office.

PRESIDENT JOHN CLARKE WAS, FOR THE FIRST TIME in a six-year association with Admiral Arnold Morgan, profoundly irritated with the man. In fact, he was rapidly being drawn to the conclusion that the fire-eating admiral was growing too big for his boots.

Two hours previously he had issued a presidential memorandum outlining his plans to go to Hawaii early the next week to meet the aircraft carrier *Ronald Reagan*, which was bringing home his son. And almost by return of interoffice communication he had received a reply from Admiral Morgan that had only just stopped short of saying, "Don't be a prick."

The actual wording had been, "Not a terribly good idea, sir. In fact, if you stop to give it serious strategic thought, a very bad idea. I'll be along momentarily to explain precisely why."

The President was not used to being patronized. But more important, he knew that this was an argument he was certain to lose because Morgan did not write memorandums like that unless his logic was flawless. However, the President badly wanted to go to meet Linus, and he was damned if this bombastic admiral was going to stop him.

As he waited, in a dark and rather petulant mood, he was giving no thought whatsoever to the fact that Linus lived in the protection of the giant American carrier instead of a Chinese jail as the result of the determination, aggression and intelligence of one man: Arnold Morgan.

No, President Clarke had rather forgotten that. He thought only of the injustice of the situation, that he, the most powerful leader in the free world, was being warned against going to meet his own son, *his only son, for God's sake,* by some kind of half-assed military red tape. And he was not having that. Nossir. Arnold Morgan could take his rulebook and insert it in the place where the sun does not shine. He, President Clarke, was going to meet his boy in Hawaii, and that was that.

The door was opened and the admiral was shown in, breezily remarking, "Hello, sir. Hey, you look kinda gloomy. What's up?"

"Arnold, I thought your little note was insensitive in the extreme, given that you above all others understand how the capture and possible torture of my son affected me these last couple of weeks."

"Note, sir? What do you mean?"

"Hawaii, Arnold. Going to Hawaii."

"Oh that, sir. Right. Just forget all about that. You can do more or less anything you want, sir. But you can't go to Hawaii."

"Arnold. Might I ask why not? And who might take it upon themselves to stop me?"

"Sir, I'm just trying to stop you from committing suicide. Politically."

"Then perhaps you had better explain yourself."

"Sure. The main issue is USS *Seawolf* . . . as you know, we just lost it under highly mysterious, but not too sinister circumstances.

Nuclear accident, after collision in the South China Sea, okay? Now, until this moment, the media have taken only a passing interest, because there has not been drastic loss of life, and accidents can happen. Also, they cannot find out much, because when they ask us, we say we're still awaiting full report from velly solly Chinese pricks. And in Canton and Beijing they will be told nothing."

"Which means it's all gone fairly quiet. The media have not been told anything about the crew, or the crew's return, but they presume there will be a navy statement when they arrive back in San Diego. In the meantime, we're playing down any kind of drama. Just an accident. Chinese tried to help. But there was a fault in the reactor core.

"Just a valve. We're secretly pleased it did not happen here. And the Chinese have very gallantly apologized for any part they may have inadvertently played. Not much harm done.

"Now, sir. We know the facts are very, very different from that, correct? We actually blew *Seawolf* to bits, causing a huge nuclear accident in Canton. We then damn nearly went to war with China over your son, Linus. Because, sir, I assure you, we would never have gone that far unless he had been on board. We blew up a jail on a Chinese island, killed up to one hundred Chinese military personnel, and blew up two other ships, one of them the biggest destroyer in the Chinese Navy. We blew up two helicopters, and took this country to a naval standoff out on the edge of the South China Sea. A real, shooting, missile-firing standoff. And in the very first case, we were spying on them with a major American nuclear boat in deepest Chinese national waters.

"That, sir, is without doubt the biggest single military story since Schwarzkopf clobbered the towelheads in the Gulf."

"I still do not see what that has to do with my going to meet my son."

"Because, sir, if you go, you will inadvertently take two hundred American media people with you, all of whom will have guessed that Linus either was or may have been on *Seawolf*. They're gonna want statements, photo opportunities, and God knows what else. And you will have led them right into the middle of the biggest story any of them could imagine . . . right into the middle of sixty returning U.S. Navy SEALs, and one-hundred-plus returning former captives of the Chinese, all of whom witnessed a full-blooded military battle between the U.S.A. and China, with many dead. Make no mistake. This was a small, secret, classified war."

"Well, I guess we can't keep the lid on it forever."

"Sir, we most certainly can. Because the Chinese do not want it publicized any more than we do. For them, it looks like the most terrible loss of face. For us, it looks like reckless military adventurism, bullying on a global scale. Also, we don't know our own casualties yet. But more important, sir, much more important . . . you as Commander-in-Chief are going to have to explain the loss of a billion-dollar submarine—a billion dollars to build, plus another billion on research and development. Taxpayers' money. Is this the most incompetent navy and the most dubious administration in the entire history of this country? That's what they'll ask.

"And you, sir, are attempting to take two hundred of the Fourth Estate's finest, right into the one place on this earth where they can nail that story right down. Sailors talk. You can try and shut 'em up, but it only takes one with a few beers on board, and you're looking at a prairie fire.

"If you don't go to Hawaii, none of them will go either, because they don't even know the carrier's calling at Pearl. But if you do go, you will find yourself in a storm of controversy. And the left-wing press will kill you—especially if there's American dead."

"But Arnold, Linus will expect me to be there. And after all he's gone through . . . just imagine how bad he'll feel."

"Probably not as bad as if he was still in the slammer on Xiachuan Dao."

"Arnold, with the greatest respect, I do not think you are hearing me."

"Sir, if you still wish to make that point, you are most certainly not hearing me . . . in which case I will have to be blunt. Mr. President, if this little lot somehow gets into the media, it could bring down your administration. It would just be a matter of time before someone asked, *Did this President actually go to war in secret with the People's Republic of China in order to save his son's ass?*

"Sir, I cannot let you do this. You cannot go to Pearl to meet the carrier. And if you attempt to do so, the carrier will be diverted and head straight back to the U.S.A. I cannot let you do this to yourself. Do you really want to be up there on the goddamned television explaining how we managed to LOSE a nine-thousand-ton nuclear submarine . . . sir, please . . . I promised you I'd get him back . . . now you have to promise me you'll let us handle the aftermath. Remember, sir. I did it for you."

The President stood and nodded gravely. "I understand, Arnold. Truly I do. And I am grateful to you. And I would like to ask you one favor."

"Sure."

"Will you go and spend the next twenty minutes trying to think of a way for me to go and meet my boy? With no harm done. Not like you just explained."

The National Security Adviser smiled. "Okay, sir. Gimme a little time. I'll be back in thirty . . . but don't hold your breath."

"Thanks, Arnie. I'd appreciate it."

Admiral Morgan walked back to his office slowly, which was rare since he normally hit a pace containing the inertia of an aircraft carrier. He always looked as if he might walk straight through any door he approached with a splintering of wood and wrenching of hinges. But this was a slow walk, and he executed it with his head down, lost in thought.

"Am I seeing things," he muttered, *"or is this President losing his grip? Jesus Christ, I just told him the facts of life in words of one syllable, and he did not quite get it. That's not like him at all. This Linus crap has affected him. No doubt of that. As it might affect any father, faced with the terror of his son's torture on the other side of the world. But we got him out of that, and he ought to be through it. At least, he ought to be if he wants to stay on in that office.*

"Right now he's too preoccupied with that boy to be any good to anyone. . . . Christ, he must see the danger of taking the Washington press corps to Pearl, which is what would happen, whether he likes it or not. He answers to the people, and that

means the press . . . it ain't great, because they're about as loyal to this nation as the fucking Chinese. But that's show business, Johnny-baby, and you gotta live with 'em."

He rounded the corner to his office, and entered the outer area, where Kathy was on the telephone. "Come on in, soon as you're through," he said, and continued walking slowly to his desk.

Three minutes later, she came in and closed the door behind her. "Don't tell me," she said. "He wants you to go to Hawaii with him, while I stay here and look after the store."

"Wrong. On both counts. He ain't going anywhere near Hawaii, and neither are we. Which has left one surly little Oklahoman in the Oval Office."

"You didn't tell him he couldn't go, did you? He is the President."

"Yes, I did tell him. And I told him that if he wanted to go on being President, he better see sense over this particular issue."

"This, Arnold, is a Linus issue. And if you'd told me where you were going I'd have told you to keep quiet. He's developing an obsession over that boy. I would not be surprised if he converts to Catholicism as a result of the safe delivery of Linus from death."

"I know. You told me all about that church business."

"Arnie, you know what I think . . . just from talking to him . . . when he heard there was a possibility of torture, he fixed in his mind a picture of sweet freckle-faced Linus as a little boy back home in Oklahoma. And whenever he though of torture—red-hot pokers up your butt or whatever—he thought of the desecration of that little boy. There's a psychologist's name for it—kind of worst-case-scenario in terms of the psyche. And I think he still has that picture in his mind, which is clouding his judgment on all matters. All he wants is to put his arms around his little boy."

"Kathy, I don't know if that's right. But it sure does fit . . . that's what I'm hearing from him. Even after I laid on him the calamitous consequences of going to Pearl, he still just asked me to try to find a way to make it possible for him to see Linus again, the minute they dock in Hawaii . . . and I'm not going to be able to do that . . .and he's gonna be real disappointed."

He and Kathy had lunch together, sharing one medium-sized

tuna fish sandwich, which caused the boss to wonder if she was expecting a kitten for lunch. But he ate it in a couple of bites, and gulped down a glass of mineral water and prepared to talk again to the President.

"Two things are now for certain in this uncertain place," he growled. "The Chief ain't gonna like what I'm telling him, and tonight we are going to find some proper food . . . steak magnifico, with fries and spinach . . . and wine from the great vineyards of Bordeaux, left bank of the Gironde . . . Pauillac, home of the snorto de luxe."

Kathy wanted to tell him it was Friday and that she was supposed to be having fish, as she always had since childhood, but she was laughing too much to speak coherently, and just shook her head as the President's NSA strode purposefully back to the Oval Office.

"Sir," he told the boss, "you cannot go. It's too public, too dangerous, we're too vulnerable, and you'd end up getting the sack or being impeached, and the Democrats would be back in power . . . the most I can offer you is to fly a half-dozen of *Seawolf*'s officers in direct from Hawaii on some pretense. Also, maybe the top SEALs, all to San Diego. Then maybe Linus and one or two significant other personnel could fly on to Washington, and we can pick him up and deliver him wherever in secret. That's the most. Hawaii is out, out, out. Mr. President, you're staying in, in, in."

Even President Clarke was obliged to chuckle. "Are you sure you're not overreacting to all this, Arnie? I just want to meet his ship, like any other dad."

"What you are not, sir, is any other dad. The U.S. made mistakes on this. Do you really want all of that to come out? Don't answer. You don't. Trust me. I'm leaving you with just one thought. This afternoon I'm bringing Who Flung Dung in for a chat. By seventeen-hundred the recent events that took place in the China Sea NEVER HAPPENED. Both our governments will agree for different but equally subversive reasons, all to do with total embarrassment."

And he stood, preparing to leave, saying very simply, "You want me to get Linus home, by air, in secret, as fast as possible?"

"Arnold, thank you. I'd be more grateful than you'll ever know."

1530. Friday, July 21.
Office of the CNO. The Pentagon.

"Joe, I'm telling you, we have a real problem here. The President's lost the plot."

"What do you mean, he's lost the plot? Come on, Arnie, this is the best President the military has ever had."

"That may be so. But right now, he's a goddamned time bomb. The only thing in his mind is his son Linus. He actually wanted to go to Hawaii and meet the kid, complete with the omnipotent Washington press corps. All two hundred of them, all asking every sailor in Pearl Harbor precisely what happened in the South China Sea."

Admiral Mulligan sucked in his breath. "Jesus Christ, Arnie, are you kidding?"

"Kidding! Yeah, right. Just a little joke to give us both heart attacks. Joe, if the full length and breadth of this whole scenario ever got out, that we actually started a shooting war with China to save the ass of the President's son, there'd be a change in administration, and we'd all be out of here in disgrace. And that includes the President."

"Does he understand that?"

"Barely. I've tried to tell him that his only chance is secrecy. But he doesn't care. He only wants to see his son as soon as possible."

"And do you think secrecy is possible?"

"Not total secrecy. But we don't want total secrecy. We have to come clean about the loss of the submarine, and how it happened, and who, if anyone, was to blame. That's gotta be hard, regular U.S. Navy routine. But we do not want anything released about its mission, nor the actual . . . er . . . demise of the ship."

"How about the SEALs and the release of the prisoners?"

"Nothing. We cannot admit there ever were any prisoners, certainly not that we effectively went to war over them without telling anybody."

"Think we'd have done it if Linus hadn't been there?"

"Nah. Not a chance. We'd have tried to negotiate them out, failed, and then had to threaten massive economic retribution. Which may have worked, over time, maybe, six months."

"You really think we could keep this whole thing secret?"

"For one reason only . . . the Chinese also want it kept secret."

"You know that?"

"Absolutely. I had Who Flung Dung on the phone an hour ago . . . for once we're in step."

"WHO FLUNG WHAT?"

"Oh, that's just my nickname for Ambassador Ling Guofeng . . . slippery little prick, like all the rest of 'em. But smart. He knows what a disaster this would be if it got out. His government is more worried than we are. There's a press clampdown in Beijing and Canton."

"What worries them so much?"

"Well, not that they kidnapped the submarine and its crew in international waters. They'd just lie and lie about that. Much more, that they were unable to hold on to the hundred-man crew, that their jail was stormed and breached, that they lost a patrol ship and two hugely expensive helicopters, not to mention a destroyer plus some three hundred naval personnel. The navy C-in-C, according to the ambassador, may not survive it. To the Chinese it all represents the most awful loss of face. In fact, it represents total incompetence. Let's face it, old pal, they think they're tough and militarily proficient. We made 'em look like fucking children."

"Guess so, Arnie . . . but what you're telling me is that both the governments of the U.S.A. and China wish nothing more to be learned about this confrontation beyond the loss of the submarine, in an accident, and the safe return home of the crew with maximum goodwill on both sides."

"You gottit, CNO. And that's fine with me, just so long as the little pricks understand that NO ONE fucks around with our navy. NO ONE. And should anyone try anything on, they will live to regret it."

"Guess our old friend Admiral Zhang Yushu is feeling kinda sorry for himself right now?"

"Hope so. Cheeky fucker."

"Which I guess brings us to the next real problem. How, Arnie, does the Navy deal with the total loss of the top submarine in the fleet?"

"In the regular way. There was an accident in the South China Sea. Something in the reactor room, and this loss of power caused some kind of collision with a close-by destroyer. That much is already known. The Chinese answered a call for help, towed *Seawolf* back into Canton, and while they were helping to get the submarine going again, there was a further problem, and the reactor failed completely. The Chinese deeply regret any part they may have had in the final damage to the submarine, and we express our gratitude for their attempts to help us out. That's all there is. That's all the press are getting. From either side of the Pacific."

"Arnie, can this be kept quiet indefinitely?"

"Probably. Since the two involved governments have no wish to say anything whatsoever."

"And what about the guys? Someone may eventually talk."

"If he does, it will be dismissed out of hand as the rantings of a lunatic."

"And how about the President? Does he go along with this?"

"The President's out of it for the moment. All he wants is to cruise through the last couple of years of his second term . . . and to see his beloved son again as soon as possible."

"Which leaves us to organize a Navy Board of Inquiry, right?"

"That's it, Joe. It'll happen in San Diego, under the auspices of CINCPAC. Makes sense. CINCPAC is Captain Crocker's Commander-in-Chief. He's the guy who decides what happens downstream of the inquiry."

"I just hope it doesn't get messy . . . but I know it's unavoidable."

"You can say that again. The U.S. Navy simply cannot lose a billion-dollar SSN and not have an official and formal explanation to both the government and the taxpayer."

"Jesus. You mean the Board of Inquiry hearings have to be public?"

"Hell, no. They'll be held *in camera*, with a lot of witnesses. But the findings will be made public. The Board's report will have to be published, with its recommendations."

"And that's where life could get a little tough . . . if they start recommending the severest reprimands, or even censures, of the senior officers of the ship."

"Might not even stop there, either," replied Admiral Morgan.

"Huh?"

"In a case such as this, they could actually recommend the court-martial of the CO or his XO, or even both."

"A court-martial? Hell, Arnie, I wouldn't think so. We don't court-martial for carelessness. Only the Brits do that, and even then they usually find the captain not guilty. It's been years since the Navy court-martialed anyone for anything that was not actually criminal."

"Maybe, Joe. Maybe. But there is nothing ordinary about this case, and I'm interested to hear whether anyone decides to draw a firm line separating a genuine but inexcusable mistake from gross negligence. This is a very, very big loss . . . it's beyond imagination that a captain with firm orders not to get detected proceeded to do so, two or perhaps even three times, and then crashed into a Chinese destroyer . . . I mean, Jesus . . . it sounds like the boat was being driven by some kind of nut. . . . Joe, I would not be surprised to see a recommendation for a special court-martial. Unless they got some real classy alibi."

"Well, I hope they don't feel the need to go that far . . . because that's likely to muddy up the waters real bad. As it is, that Board of Inquiry is going to be told their brief, and indeed their powers, are restricted to those actions that led up to the submarine's loss of propulsion in the South China Sea. They are not empowered to ask any questions beyond the moment when the Chinese moved in to assist them. Otherwise we'll end up with a public report, which details the whole gruesome saga. Which no one needs."

"Hell, no. We gotta avoid that, Joe. In fact, I think for the purpose of this inquiry we'll have a Navy lawyer from the Pentagon sitting in at all times, to make sure our guidelines are strictly followed."

"I don't think we can avoid that, Arnie. But this might mean that the senior officers of the submarine may feel they have to be legally represented. Some of them might. I wonder whether the captain himself might be advised to do so."

"Well, I think he would, Joe. And this will almost certainly mean the President will insist Linus has some hotshot attorney in his corner. I don't have a problem with that. In fact, I think it's better we advise the President that's what ought to happen. In Linus's interests."

"Of course, we don't even know whether Linus was personally involved in this debacle."

"No. We don't. But I somehow doubt Judd Crocker achieved it all on his own."

0900. Thursday, July 27.
The Oval Office.

"Arnie, do I have the power to stop this?"

"Yessir. But you'd have to do it publicly. You'd have to say, *Look here, guys, I'm the goddamned Commander-in-Chief of the United States Armed Forces and I hereby order you not to inquire formally into the loss of USS* Seawolf. *Do not come up with any conclusions or recommendations. Just forget about the whole thing.*"

"Well, I plainly cannot do that."

"Not if you like working here."

"What I meant was, can I just ask you to express on my behalf a general disapproval of putting these brave men through some kind of a trial? Might my disapproval not be enough?"

"Nossir. It would not. The Navy is obliged to inquire into the loss of any warship. We cannot just put it down as bad luck and write the ship off. No one would put up with it. Least of all the Senate Armed Forces Committee. We cannot be held unaccountable for our actions. Not least because such an attitude would be held over our heads forever . . . *What do you need? Another five billion? And you don't even have to explain where it goes?*"

"Well, Arnie, I really do not want any criticism or blame attached to anyone over this."

"Sir, you might make that view known. It worked for the Brits after the Falklands War back in 1982. They found it politically convenient to avoid any courts-martial, which there probably should have been . . . they lost seven ships, for Christ's sake. But there was no action beyond regular Boards of Inquiry. But I do not think your admirals would ever approve of a presidential restriction being put upon the men inquiring into a very serious disaster that cost the Navy a coupla billion dollars."

"How about the other tack, Admiral? How about I threaten not to approve the massive increase in shipbuilding budgets unless they do what I say over this inquiry?"

"Sir, if anyone other than my loyal self ever heard you say that, proceedings would begin to have you removed from this office. Remember, sir, it's Linus. His presence, right in the thick of this mess, makes you an interested party . . . interested to see your son exonerated from whatever blame there may be."

"Arnold, I am interested. I do not want Linus in disgrace. And I'm not having it. You heard my threat. Do not ignore it. Though I shall deny ever having said it."

"Sir, I am going to pretend I never heard any of the last few sentences you have uttered."

"That may or may not be a wise move on your part. It could cost your beloved Navy a couple of aircraft carriers."

"Then so be it, sir. The budget veto is your privilege. But I could not recommend you use it as a blackmail weapon to save Linus's reputation."

The President stood up and walked to the end of his office and back. And then he asked a question that had plainly been on his mind: "Have you seen the preliminary reports from *Seawolf*?"

"Nossir."

"Are they in? Have the admirals read them?"

"I do believe so, sir."

"Do you have any idea what they contain?"

"Nossir. Except there was a mighty problem right before the collision in the South China Sea."

"Do you have details?"

"Nossir."

"Could I demand to see the reports?"

"Yessir."

"Would they acquiesce?"

"To the parent of one of the officers? I doubt it."

"No, Arnold. To their Commander-in-Chief."

"Possibly, sir. But they have one weapon that will always finish you. Any one of them could just say, '*This is tantamount to corruption. I resign from the Board and I shall have no hesitation in making my reasons public. Crooked President.*'

"Knowing them, sir, they might all do it. You are contemplating very dangerous ground. But right now I have no reason to believe Linus is in any danger. Take a worst-case situation . . . let's say he made some kind of mistake, maybe compounding another. That's not life-threatening. Maybe a reprimand or a letter of censure. Maybe nothing. Just a warning. It's part and parcel of command in the U.S. Navy."

"Arnold. I do not want my son to be reprimanded publicly. Do you understand me?"

"Yessir."

"Can you and I save him from that? With the combined powers of persuasion that we have?"

"Nossir. The Navy will not tolerate interference in a case as serious as this. Long after you're gone, they'll still have to answer to Congress."

"Then we'll just have to see about that. Thank you, NSA. That's all."

0930. Monday, September 11.
United States Navy Base. San Diego, California.

The Board of Inquiry was charged with investigating "the circumstances surrounding the accident to USS *Seawolf* some time before 0600 (local) on Wednesday, July 5, 2006, in the South China Sea." It was convened in the main conference room under the Chairmanship of Admiral Archie Cameron, Commander-in-Chief of the Pacific Fleet.

A tall, graying man of 55, Admiral Cameron was a former Fifth Fleet Commander. In the 1990s he had served for several years as commanding officer of the state-of-the-art guided missile cruiser USS *Ticonderoga*, and was regarded as a potential CNO when Joe Mulligan retired.

Seated to his right was the Commander of the Seventh Fleet, Vice Admiral Albie Peterson. To his left sat Rear Admiral Freddie Curran, Commander Submarine Force Pacific Fleet (COMSUB-PAC). Flown in from New London was the newly promoted Trident commander, Captain Mike Krause. The final member of the five-man board was Captain Henry Bonilla, commanding officer of *Seawolf*'s sister ship, USS *Jimmy Carter*.

At the end of the long mahogany table sat Lt. Commander Edward Kirk, the Pentagon's attorney, whose task it was to restrict the inquiry to those matters relevant to the effective seizure of the American submarine by the Chinese. Not, understandably, the aftermath. Everyone was given to understand that when Lieutenant Commander Kirk spoke on a point of order, his words were to be heeded at all times. Those orders came from Admiral Mulligan in person.

And the CNO had serious reasons for ensuring that the inquiry did not somehow get out of hand. For the month previous to the opening session, he and Admiral Morgan had endured bruising hours with the President's personal advisers, all of whom were attempting to arrange the fairest possible treatment for Lt. Commander Linus Clarke.

The CNO had argued for a week that the preliminary reports were private to the United States Navy, and that no one beyond CINCPAC should have access to their contents, certainly not the parent of one of the significant officers. Certainly not the father of the man who might very well have had the conn of the submarine on that fateful morning.

But the President's men had come out fighting, arguing that as Commander-in-Chief of the United States Armed Forces he had the right to see any documents he so wished. For five days the rights and wrongs of the Presidential position had been debated, and finally it was agreed that the deadlock should go to immediate arbitration, and the decision of the Chairman of the Joint Chiefs, General Tim Scannell, would be final.

General Scannell took only a half-hour to rule against the President, on the grounds that it would compromise him unforgivably throughout the investigation. It would be, he said, "just plain wrong for the President to be seen trying to gain any advantage whatsoever for Lieutenant Commander Clarke. Certainly he cannot be seen attempting to obtain a preview of the case, and then acting on it, against the interests of other serving officers."

Nonetheless, the President had secured one advantage for his son, a most unusual advantage in a U.S. Navy Board of Inquiry. He had gained permission for Linus to have one of the best lawyers in the country sitting with him throughout the entire evidence. The attorney was the urbane and learned Philip Myerscough, who was not permitted to make any statement whatsoever, but was permitted to question witnesses. Admiral Mulligan made it clear that he would not tolerate any civilian cross-examining witnesses, as they might in a regular court of law. However, Mr. Myerscough would be allowed to "probe and clarify" certain points of evidence. But he would answer at all times to Admiral Cameron and, if necessary, to Lieutenant Commander Kirk.

Judd Crocker's father, the 66-year-old Admiral Nathaniel Crocker, himself a former destroyer commander, had flown to the West Coast to meet with his son and visit his daughter-in-law. And for the past few weeks he had taken a keen academic interest in the forthcoming case. The moment it was agreed that Lieutenant Commander Clarke would be permitted an attorney in his corner, he insisted that *Seawolf*'s CO should also have one.

He appointed an old friend with whom he had attended the Naval Academy in Annapolis back in 1960—Art Mangone, who had lasted only six years in dark blue before leaving to take a belated law degree at UCLA. Art liked the law better than he liked submarines, and had been practicing in La Jolla, the coastal suburb of San Diego, since 1976. The investigation of USS *Seawolf* would grant him a chance to combine knowledge acquired in both his careers.

"The only thing I know about Mangone as a lawyer is that he plays golf to a five handicap," said the admiral. "But I trust him, he's a gentleman, and he's free."

"Spoken like a true Boston Yankee," observed Judd.

And now the scene was set. Captain Crocker and his attorney, plus Lieutenant Commander Clarke and his, would sit in the courtroom throughout all of the evidence.

And now Admiral Cameron called the Board of Inquiry to order, read out the formalities, and requested the first witness to enter the room and swear to tell the truth.

The routine examination of each witness would be undertaken by the vastly experienced ex-Polaris commander Rear Admiral Curran. At the conclusion of his questioning, other members of the board would ask their questions and then the two attorneys would be permitted to elaborate on certain points should Admiral Cameron deem it relevant.

After the regular establishment of identity and career, Lt. Andrew Warren, *Seawolf*'s Officer of the Deck, turned to face Admiral Curran directly.

"Lieutenant Warren," he said. "Will you tell us where you were between the hours of oh-four hundred and oh-eight hundred on the morning of July fifth this year?"

"Yessir. I was on duty in the submarine *Seawolf* in the South China Sea. I served as Officer of the Deck."

"And did your duties take you to various different stations in the submarine?"

"Yessir."

"And did you spend some time in the control room?"

"Yessir."

"And were you able to see who had the conn at all times?"

"Yessir. Whenever I was in there."

"And would you mind telling the board who did have the conn during your watch?"

"Yessir. For a short while, maybe a half-hour when I first came on duty, Captain Crocker had the ship. Then he went to his bunk, and Lieutenant Commander Clarke took over. I was in the conn at the watch change."

"And how would you describe the period of time while Commander Clarke had the ship?"

"Fine, at first, just like always. But then something terrible happened."

"Would you describe that?"

"Yessir. At around oh-five-thirty, our sonar picked up a Chinese destroyer coming toward us at flank speed."

"Lieutenant Commander Clarke had the conn, correct?"

"Yessir. And then the destroyer slowed right down. We were twenty-four hundred yards off her starboard beam. I had the conn while Linus Clarke used the periscope. He ordered me to keep the ship straight and level, which I did."

"And then?"

"Lieutenant Commander Clarke was going in closer. He was after some close-up shots of the extra-large housing for the towed array, which he could see on the stern."

"Did he say he was going in closer?"

"Yessir."

"And did you reply?"

"Yessir. I said, 'Steady, sir, we don't know how long that towed array is.'"

"Do you normally issue that kind of advice to your Executive Officer?"

"Nossir. In this case I meant it as some kind of a warning. In good faith, sir."

"And did Lieutenant Commander Clarke reply?"

"Yessir."

"And what did he say to you?"

"He said, 'Don't worry, Andy.' Then he said he would not go in closer than a mile. I remember he said the towed array 'won't be that long, will it?' And he mentioned that it would be angled down in the water, not straight out like a submarine."

"And what happened then?"

"Well, by now Master Chief Brad Stockton was in the control room, and he spoke up suddenly. He said he thought the CO should be informed we were 'groping around the ass of a six-thousand-ton destroyer.' I remember his words very well."

"And was he issuing those words to Lieutenant Commander

Clarke in an informative way, because he thought the XO did not know what he was actually doing?"

"Oh, nossir. He was telling the XO to inform the CO of our actions."

"And did the lieutenant commander heed that warning?"

"Nossir. He said there was no need to alert the CO. He was just going to take the destroyer's stern a mile off and take some pictures."

"And did the Master Chief reply?"

"Yessir, he said again that in his opinion the CO should definitely be informed because this was a critical part of our mission."

"And did Lieutenant Commander Clarke heed that second warning?"

"Nossir. He did not. He said in his judgment, he was fine. And then he ordered the course change to cross the destroyer's stern."

"You still had the conn?"

"Yessir. He ordered me to steer right standard rudder, course zero-nine-zero at eight knots."

"And did you do so?"

"Yessir."

"And what happened then?"

"Sir, I thought we had made it, but there was a sudden slowing down in power. We were still at PD, and I could feel there was a slight alteration in trim, stern-down just fractionally. The regular beat of the machinery was just different, and we were slowing down, definitely not completing our crossing of the destroyer's stern."

"Were you able to ascertain what had happened, Lieutenant?"

"I KNEW what had happened, sir. We've had enough talk about the length of the new Chinese towed arrays."

"And then what happened?"

"Captain Crocker came charging into the conn."

"No longer asleep?"

"Nossir. Wide awake, and not real pleased with Lieutenant Commander Clarke."

"Did he realize what had happened?"

"Nossir. Not immediately. He kinda snapped, 'What's going on,

XO?' Then he grabbed the periscope and took a very quick look before it washed under the water because of our stern-down trim."

"How long was he able to look?"

"I'd say about three seconds. No longer."

"And was that long enough?"

"Definitely long enough for the CO, sir."

"How do you know?"

"Sir, he solved the problem right away. He said the destroyer was only five hundred yards away. Not the mile Lieutenant Commander Clarke had stated. He said the XO had turned the periscope handle the wrong way, right onto low power, which made it look like a mile when it was nothing like that."

"And did the XO reply?"

"Yessir, he did. He said, 'Oh my God,' twice. And then he said he was extremely sorry."

At this point Myerscough sprang to his feet and said that he objected to this line of hearsay questioning involving his client.

Admiral Archie Cameron was furious. He ordered, "SILENCE." And then he said quietly, "Mr. Myerscough, if you attempt to interrupt these military proceedings one more time, I'll have you escorted out of the room, and right off the station, by navy guards. You may speak when I say you can speak, and at no other time. Do you understand me?"

It was a while since Myerscough had been spoken to in quite those terms. But he was not about to tangle with this admiral, and he did not think he would be much thanked by the President for being evicted in the first hour of the proceedings.

And so he just nodded formally, apologized and sat down. The admiral then added, "I do not consider the sworn testimony of a lieutenant in the United States Navy, and second officer of the deck at the time, to be giving us hearsay when he recounts a conversation that took place within five feet of where he was standing. . . . Please continue, Admiral Curran."

"Lieutenant, was it your impression that Lieutenant Commander Clarke agreed with the CO's assessment of his error?"

"Yessir. Very definitely. He was really upset. Very apologetic."

"Did you, the officer with the conn, agree with the CO's assessment?"

"Absolutely, sir. No doubt in my mind. The difference between five hundred yards and one mile through a periscope is unmistakable."

"Quite so," replied Admiral Curran, a lifelong submariner himself. And with that, he said he had no further questions for *Seawolf's* Officer of the Deck, though his colleagues might wish to question him further.

Admiral Cameron conferred with his colleagues very briefly, and they were in agreement that this was as far as the investigation should go—to the point where the submarine became disabled. No further.

"Very well," said Admiral Cameron. "The attending lawyers may now ask questions of the witness. But I do stress, this is not some kangaroo civilian court. This is a United States Navy Board of Inquiry. And I will not tolerate theatrics or aggression toward one of my trusted submarine officers."

"I have no questions, sir," said Art Mangone.

"I have a few," said Philip Myerscough, rising to his feet on behalf of the President of the United States. "First, I would like to ask whether three seconds is a sufficient amount of time to make a judgment call of this dimension?"

"Plenty, sir. We are all trained to make the fastest possible observations through the periscope. Seven seconds is routine maximum in hostile waters. Captain Crocker is renowned for his grasp of the surface picture. He's the best, sir. The best I ever saw."

"That was rather more than I asked for, Lieutenant," said Mr. Myerscough, not quite interrupting, but almost. "Perhaps you could restrict your answers to my precise question, rather than adding on a character reference for your CO."

"Absolutely, sir. No problem right there. I just thought you'd like to know, sir. . . . he's the best."

Philip Myerscough visibly flinched. But he recovered and then said, with civilian inexactitude, "So you believe that short space of time would be fine to make such a judgment?"

"Oh sure, sir. Three seconds concentration, for a man trained like Captain Crocker . . . no problem. He probably could've done it in one second."

Admirals Cameron and Curran could hardly contain their thin smiles at the obvious discomfort of a city lawyer trying to deal with navy precision.

"Lieutenant," said Mr. Myerscough. "You stated that you thought Lieutenant Commander Clarke was plainly upset and apologetic. Could you have been mistaken in that assumption?"

"Nossir."

"On what do you base that assumption?"

"It's not an assumption, sir. It's a fact. He was upset and apologetic. I heard him saying, 'Oh my God,' and I heard him say, 'I'm extremely sorry.'"

"Are you quite sure of that? Because Lieutenant Commander Clarke has a very different recollection."

"He was probably too upset to think straight right then, sir. Anyone would have been. You make a mistake like that. Sir, I even recall what Captain Crocker said after the XO said how sorry he was."

"I have not asked you to recount that."

"Nossir. But I'm real happy to tell you. He said, 'So am I, Linus. So am I.'"

"No further questions." Mr. Myerscough shook his head in some exasperation, as if unable to cope with the ingenuous, no-lies, no-bullshit mind-set of a Navy officer accustomed to telling the truth to all higher authority. Lieutenant Warren, like everyone else, had it ingrained in him since first he entered Annapolis and was told, "The only thing they'll throw you out for is lying. So don't even consider telling one. They'll forgive damn near anything, except for a lie. That's death in the Naval Academy."

"Call Master Chief Brad Stockton. . . ."

Recovered now from the battering he had taken in Xiachuan Dao, the Master Chief entered the room and walked purposefully to the front, saluted the admirals and swore to tell the truth.

Admiral Curran walked him through the first exchanges and then concentrated on the significant points.

"And when did you first realize that Lieutenant Commander Clarke was intending to conduct a maneuver with which you were personally uncomfortable?"

"Just as soon as he said he was intending to cross the stern of that destroyer, sir."

"And what was your own judgment?"

"Sir, I knew we were uncertain about the length of the Chinese towed array. And I did tell him that, just as a kind of warning."

"But what did he say?"

"He said he had no intention of coming in closer than a mile, which would be plenty of clearance."

"Did you know that he was seeing the destroyer a mile off?"

"Nossir. I did not look through the periscope. I assumed he was certain of at least that fact—like we were a mile clear of the Chinese warship."

"And was the clearance distance the biggest thing on your mind?"

"No sir. It was not."

"What was?"

"That we were not informing the CO of our actions. I thought that was really wrong."

"And did you inform Lieutenant Commander Clarke of your concerns?"

"Yessir. Twice. I told him that since we were groping around the backside of a six-thousand-ton destroyer in Chinese waters the captain ought to be informed."

"And did he heed this warning from the Chief of the Boat?"

"Nossir. He did not. He said there was no need. He said the destroyer was not transmitting on anything and he was just going in closer for pictures."

"And what then?"

"Well, sir. I was being overruled by our Executive Officer. I had no choice but to accept his order. But I did say again, I still thought the CO should be told what we were doing."

"And was that final advice accepted?"

"Nossir. It was not. Lieutenant Commander Clarke proceeded

to order the boat across the stern of the destroyer at one mile distance. At least that's what he believed."

"And did you believe that distance."

"Yessir. You expect your XO to be able to handle the periscope accurately."

"But in hindsight, you now believe he was not doing that."

"Obviously not, sir. And when the CO finally arrived, that much became very apparent."

"You mean you accept Captain Crocker's version of what had gone wrong—low power on the periscope, which made the destroyer seem much farther away than it really was?"

"No question, sir. I heard the lieutenant commander apologize. That's what happened."

"That's all, Master Chief," replied Admiral Curran. "Admiral Cameron may wish to say more."

"I don't think so," replied the chairman. "The evidence of the Chief of the Boat and the evidence of the Officer of the Deck are identical. Mr. Mangone? Mr. Myerscough?"

"Nothing further from me," said Art Mangone.

And once more Philip Myerscough stood up and attempted to cast Linus Clarke in a somewhat better light than that of error-prone number two on a nuclear submarine.

"Mr. Stockton," he said, as if trying to distance himself entirely from the military. "You stated that you were certain that Lieutenant Commander Clarke had mistakenly placed the periscope on low power, which subsequently increased the apparent distance between *Seawolf* and the Chinese destroyer?"

"Yessir. I did. And I am."

"What proof is there? What proof do you have? Is this not a mere speculation?"

"Well, sir, our commanding officer looked right through the periscope within moments of the error and stated that the *Xiangtan* was five hundred yards away."

"But what proof is there that it was not Mr. Crocker who was mistaken and that Linus Clarke was correct all along?"

"I guess because we then wrapped our screw around the towed

array, which was a lot nearer than Lieutenant Commander Clarke believed."

"But how do you know it was not a mile long—and that Lieutenant Commander Clarke made no mistake?"

"Well, I don't know that for certain, sir, but I never have heard that the Chinese own a mile-long towed array. No one in the United States Navy has ever even suggested such a thing. Longest I heard was one thousand yards."

"But with respect, Mr. Stockton, the fact that you never heard of such a thing does not preclude it from existing?"

"Nossir. I guess not."

"Then it would be foolish to discount the possibility?"

"Nossir. It would be foolish to include it. Captain Crocker saw the submarine with his own eyes five hundred yards off our port beam."

"For three seconds, I believe. Not very long."

"Sir, in our trade, assessing the surface picture, three seconds is long. Like three hours to a normal untrained person."

Philip Myerscough chuckled a deep sardonic chuckle. "But Mr. Stockton," he said, "no one else saw it, did they, because the submarine was trimmed stern down and the periscope was under the water?"

"No one saw it right then. But we came to the surface a very few minutes later. And the destroyer was still five hundred yards away."

"And who had the periscope then?"

"The commanding officer, sir."

"Anyone else?"

"Yessir."

Philip Myerscough looked temporarily uncomfortable. "And who was that?" he asked.

"Me, sir. The CO handed over the periscope for me to look at the long wire on our screw. You could see it, about fifteen feet across, a huge tangle."

At this point Mangone arose, and requested just one question at this juncture.

Admiral Cameron said, "Please proceed." And with some annoyance, Myerscough sat down.

"Master Chief," said Mangone, "when you looked through that periscope on the surface, within a very few minutes of the accident, how far was the destroyer from *Seawolf*?"

"Five hundred yards or so, sir."

"Thank you, Master Chief. Just checking. No further questions."

Philip Myerscough stood again. "Mr. Stockton, how long have you served with Captain Crocker?"

"Oh, we've done maybe six tours of duty together."

"Would it be fair to say you admire him greatly?"

"Yessir. The best I ever sailed with."

"And would you say you are completely loyal to him? As your CO?"

"Yessir. I am."

"Perhaps too loyal?"

"Nossir."

"Perhaps more loyal to Captain Crocker than you might be to the absolute truth?"

"THAT'S ENOUGH!!" Admiral Cameron was on his feet. "I have already explained to you, Mr. Myerscough, that I will not have my men examined as if they were in a civilian court. Perhaps I should spell it out further. Men like Brad Stockton hold this Navy together. He is not an ordinary man. He is a man of vast integrity, holding a position of quite awesome responsibility. Not for money, not for cheap glory, but for the sense of achieving a massively important task. Every day. In harm's way. Protecting this nation. *I will not have him treated like the kind of criminal you deal with in your chosen way of life.*"

And then he softened a little. "Mr. Myerscough, you will treat my men with total respect, or I will not hesitate to have you escorted from this Board of Inquiry. IS THAT QUITE CLEAR?"

Admiral Cameron, however, was too late. The question had been asked, though not answered. And it was in the record. The seed of doubt had been sown, that Brad Stockton would support anything Judd Crocker said.

And Philip Myerscough knew it. He just said, "With respect, sir." And resumed his seat.

The next witness to be called was Lieutenant Commander Clarke himself. And for the first time he moved away from his lawyer's side, standing now in front of the admirals.

The formalities were dispensed with, and the President's son swore to tell the truth.

There were no discrepancies in the basic points of evidence. The times and facts were not in dispute. What was in dispute was how far away that destroyer was when Linus Clarke drove *Seawolf* over the towed array.

And if Linus had been apologizing in the conn on the morning of July 5, he very definitely was not doing so now. He stood back and argued with Admiral Freddie Curran that he had been correct, that there was a mile between the ships. It was not, could not have been his fault. He would never make such an elementary error with the periscope.

In his opinion, the Chinese towed array must have been a mile long. There was no other explanation, and it could not be proved one way or another. So far as Linus was concerned, it was his word against Judd Crocker's and that was all.

The Board of Inquiry listened carefully to the deadlock, and then invited Mangone to ask any further questions, if he so wished.

The California attorney came straight to the point. "Two important members of the submarine's crew, the Officer of the Deck and the Chief of the Boat, have both sworn they heard you apologize to the CO for committing the fundamental error of having the periscope on low power. Do you now deny that was so?"

"No sir. I did apologize. I was completely intimidated by Captain Crocker, sir. He looked as if he was going to strike me. He was out of control."

"Were you normally afraid of Judd Crocker?"

"A little. He's a very physical person. And he can be quite threatening."

"Mr. Clarke, I did anticipate that you may wish to develop that line, and I took the trouble to comb through his naval record. Would it surprise you to know that no one else in all of his career has ever suggested for one split second that Judd Crocker had ever threatened anyone, or even growled at anyone, far less actually struck anyone? Does it surprise you to learn that?"

"Yessir. He almost knocked me flying trying to get to the periscope."

"Since you had virtually wrecked his ship, he might have been excused a little haste, don't you think?"

"Not that much, sir."

"Lieutenant Commander Clarke, do you know what he wrote about you in his personal log of the incident, written on the carrier on the way home?"

"No sir."

"Let me read it to you. *'Poor Linus Clarke. Never was I so sorry for a young officer. It was a devastating mistake to make. But he will have many years to reflect upon it. At the time I was so angry, and I am just grateful that I kept it all in check. Never even raised my voice, because it would not have done any good. Linus Clarke was sufficiently distraught without my adding to it. There were many times I enjoyed serving with him.'"*

Mangone looked up. "Does that sound much like the raging bull you describe?"

"Well, no, sir. But he'd had time to think about his image by then."

"So he may have done. But he still doesn't sound much like a raging bull to me. No further questions."

The final witness of the day was Captain Judd Crocker, and his tenure in front of the admirals would be short, because of the four principal crew in the conn at the time of the disaster, he was there the least amount of time, arriving only after the mistake had been made.

The only disputed issue upon which he had to pronounce was the distance he saw through the periscope between the two ships, and he confirmed to Admiral Freddie Curran that it was indeed 500 yards. No doubts. "And," he added, "it was still five hundred yards when we got to the surface and checked again a few minutes later."

Admiral Curran concluded by saying, "Yes, Captain Crocker. I think that is all very clear to the board now."

Which left the coast clear for Philip Myerscough's final attack. He rose to his feet and said, "Captain Crocker, I believe this patrol had an element of a disaster to it right from the start?"

Judd looked puzzled, and said nothing.

"I mean, Captain, that you were under strict orders not to be detected under any circumstances. Is that correct?"

"I am not at liberty to mention any details of a classified operation in Far Eastern waters."

"But Captain Crocker, it is, I believe, general knowledge that your submarine was detected by the Chinese three times?"

"Sir, you could only have learned such fantasies from Lieutenant Commander Clarke, and he is no more empowered to speak of them than I am."

"Are they fantasies, Captain?"

"I have nothing to say on that, counselor. Our mission was highly classified."

"Very well. Perhaps I may conclude by saying there were mistakes made by the commanding officer of USS *Seawolf* throughout the voyage. And possibly he made another when the distance had to be judged between the destroyer and the submarine."

Philip Myerscough knew well enough that he must have incurred the immediate wrath of Admiral Cameron, and he sat down swiftly.

But the senior admiral was measured. "I am not entirely surprised that things may have been said to you which ought not to have been said. But such things happen in incidents like these when lives and careers are threatened. For the record, I would like to confirm that the United States Navy has no formal proof that *Seawolf* was ever detected before she caught the towed array. But we do have proof that her very difficult mission was accomplished under the command of Captain Crocker, who was not of course in the conn when the accident happened."

The chairman then thanked everyone for the frank and honest way in which the evidence had been presented, and confirmed that the board would continue in session for the rest of the week, examining further aspects of the loss. And that the findings would be made public on October 9, as previously stated.

1130. Tuesday, September 26.
The Oval Office.

President Clarke was as angry with the United States Navy as he had ever been. In his hand he held the report from the Board of Inquiry investigating the loss of *Seawolf*, and the news it contained was not good.

The admirals, conscious of a growing unrest in the media and the public about the precise circumstances of the submarine's demise, were considering the possibility of a Special Court-Martial charging both the captain and the executive officer with gross negligence.

In the past four days there had been a succession of stories leaked about the loss of *Seawolf*, and the media was beginning to get warm. The admirals felt that a court-martial would clear the air and put everyone off the scent of what had really happened in the South China Sea, especially since the President's son was involved. Nothing, surely, could be worse than that.

And so the admirals, including Mulligan and Cameron, had agreed upon this course of action. The court-martial would almost certainly find both men not guilty, but to have staged it, and put two of their own through the humiliation, would hopefully absolve the Navy from further blame.

The trouble now was that the President was not having it. He stood before Admiral Morgan and said categorically, "No one is going to court-martial my son. Not while I sit in this chair as Commander-in-Chief of the Armed Forces."

"But, sir, I don't see that we have any choice. We have to deflect the media from the real story, which would have this administration thrown out. You would be in disgrace, sir. Going to war with China, to save Linus. Even you, sir, could not get away with that."

"Okay. I accept that. But look here, Arnie, I've read this report, and I don't think anything of this Crocker guy. Jesus, I'm a lawyer, and there's not one shred of corroboration to back his claim that

Linus made a mistake. Nothing, 'cept stuff that happened after the fact. I mean, give me a break. There was three seconds on the periscope. And you guys want to hang my own son on that? Nossir. That's not going to happen."

"Mr. President, the Navy is going to court-martial either Linus, or both him and Judd, for the loss of the ship. After all, he was driving the damned thing."

"So he may have been. But this Crocker guy should have been there. He's the captain. And his evidence is flawed against my boy. Linus has always been truthful, ever since he was little . . . and this Crocker character is trying to turn him into a liar. And that's what I'm not having.

"Admiral Morgan, I want that captain court-martialed. But I'm not having Linus there with him. He's the CO. Let him take the blame. It's just his word against the truthful word of my boy. I'll even have Linus stand witness for him. But I'm not having that boy facing a Navy court-martial, which would ultimately bring a much greater disgrace upon him than it would for a normal person."

"Sir, I will make your wishes known to the respective admirals, and we'll just have to see how the cards fall. But I do know everyone is very concerned about how much press this thing is beginning to attract."

"All right. But don't come back with a lot of crap. I just want to be told that Linus is not going to be facing a U.S. Navy court-martial. Not after all that boy's gone through."

0900. Wednesday, September 27.
The Oval Office.

Morgan paused before the door of the Oval Office, then entered.

"Sir, you're not going to like this," he said to the President. "The Navy is to convene a Special Court Martial charging both Captain Crocker and Lt. Commander Linus Clark with gross negligence in the loss of the submarine *Seawolf*. Sir, they feel they have no choice in the current climate, and I agree with them."

"GODDAMNIT, ARNIE! Can I overrule, strike Linus off the charge?"

"Yessir. As C-in-C you may do as you wish. But I am told you will then receive the instant resignations of your chief of naval operations, Admiral Joe Mulligan, and that of the commander of the Pacific Fleet, Admiral Archie Cameron."

"THEN TELL 'EM TO GET THE HELL OUT AND I'LL APPOINT A COUPLE OF GUYS WHO WILL HELP ME OUT HERE . . . MAYBE APPRECIATE SOME OF THE STUFF I'VE DONE FOR THE NAVY."

"Is that your last word, sir?"

"It sure as hell is. I need a new CNO and a new CINCPAC, right? Please start things moving, and announce nothing about the court-martial."

"Very well, sir. But we have to hurry. They intend the court-martial to sit on Friday morning, while the evidence is fresh."

"They can sit whenever the hell they like. But the only man they'll be trying is Captain Judd Crocker. I want him charged with being absent from his place of duty in the face of the enemy. China, right. That's an enemy."

Arnold Morgan left without another word. And within 30 minutes the two resignations were in. It took another five hours to make new appointments, and both men were given to understand that if the navy wanted its massive budget for the next two years to be approved by the President, they would acquiesce to his wishes in the court-martial of Judd Crocker.

Admiral Dick Greening, flying in from Pearl to replace Archie Cameron, had no feelings about the trial, and felt that the probable letter of censure to a captain who had lost his submarine could not possibly be worth such a total disruption.

The appointment of a new CNO was more difficult, but in the end they appointed Admiral Alan Dickson, Commander-in-Chief of the Atlantic Fleet. His views, too, were ambivalent on the subject of Judd Crocker's court-martial. He was not, however, appraised of the President's wish that the captain should be found guilty, and the entire matter closed at that point.

Admiral Morgan requested a delay until Monday for the trial of Judd Crocker, which was granted. And he spent much of the weekend trying to reason with the President. But there was no reasoning. He did not wish Linus Clarke even to attend the hearing, and he sent him home to the ranch in Oklahoma.

Which meant that on Monday morning, in the same room where the Board of Inquiry had sat, Captain Judd Crocker faced the court-martial alone. Only his father was there, waiting outside for the verdict. And for three hours, the former commanding officer pleaded his case, explaining the circumstances, trying to explain his XO's mistake.

But there was no pleading here. The Navy wanted a conviction, to get everyone off the hook. The President wanted a conviction, to get his son off the hook. This was a trial that was lost before it was held.

At 1625 on the afternoon of Monday, October 2, Captain Judd Crocker was found guilty of gross negligence, effectively "on grounds that he had been absent from his place of duty in the face of the enemy." He was relieved of command and issued a letter of the severest censure, with a recommendation that he leave the service forthwith.

1400. Tuesday, October 3.
Office of the National Security Adviser.

Admiral Morgan had just proposed to Kathy O'Brien. "Thought I'd get that absolute formality out of the way before I go along and tell the Chief I've resigned," he said.

"Well, yes. I will marry you. But this is all a little sudden. I presume it's about Judd Crocker's court-martial?"

"Not quite. It's just that I can no longer give my loyalty to a man like President Clarke. This whole thing has been riddled with dishonesty and corruption. Nothing's ever been straight, right from the start. And I cannot put up with it. I'm outta here, though he will not know that for a couple of days.

"I've been in the United States Navy almost all of my life, and I have never known such a series of totally shocking events. Losing Joe

Mulligan? Archie Cameron? Disgracing our best submarine CO? All for this little shit Linus Clarke? No, Kathy, I'm not having it. I'm out."

Then the admiral was gone, on his way to the Oval Office, taking with him his letter of resignation, effective Friday.

The President was stunned at his decision to quit on him.

The two men talked for an hour, John Clarke trying to persuade Arnold Morgan not to leave the ship. But there was no changing the mind of the National Security Adviser. He simply felt he could not offer this President the kind of loyalty he needed.

They shared a pot of coffee, and just as they were preparing to shake hands, there was a tap on the door, and a thoroughly distraught Kathy O'Brien came in slowly, a white handkerchief pressed to her face.

"Sir," she blurted out, "Captain Crocker has shot himself. He's dead."

President Clarke went white. His hand was clasped across his mouth as if trying to stop himself from crying out.

Admiral Morgan steeled himself and put his arm around Kathy, guiding her out of the room. Just before he walked out through the doorway, he turned and said, "Corruption, sir, when you're dealing with men of honor, sometimes carries a very high price."

EPILOGUE

THEY BROUGHT JUDD CROCKER'S BODY HOME BY military aircraft, landing at Cape Cod's sprawling Otis Air Force Base. His heartbroken family arranged a small private funeral on the outskirts of Osterville, just for relatives and the small contingent from Washington—the President, Admiral Morgan and Kathy, and Admiral Joe Mulligan. However, Lt. Commander Rick Hunter flew in with Brad Stockton on a military jet from San Diego, and they flanked Nicole and the two little girls throughout the proceedings.

The service was conducted by the local pastor, and they laid Judd Crocker to rest near the grave of his grandfather in the hillside cemetery. The President himself looked as if every one of his worst dreams had just happened.

Here, in this village by Nantucket Sound, he faced for the first time the consequences of his actions. The entire place was in mourning for a native son who had died by his own hand. Down at the Wianno Yacht Club, where Captain Crocker had learned to sail as a boy, the flag of the United States flew at half-staff.

It was the same in the center of the town, outside the country store, where the town flag was also at half-staff. Shops all along Main Street were closed for the funeral, and a huge crowd was gathered on the sidewalks all the way down to the cemetery.

There had been just enough in the newspapers and on television for everyone to know there had been something highly suspicious about the court-martial. No one believed that Judd Crocker could possibly have been solely responsible for the loss of the *Seawolf*.

And now the President seemed to be in shock at the outpouring of hometown grief. The worst news he heard was that Admiral Nathaniel Crocker had told the *Cape Cod Times* that he would devote the next five years to writing a book about the loss of the submarine, and his son's part in the disaster. He had, he revealed, been promised total cooperation by many of Judd's crew.

In the event, the final word, perhaps, went to Admiral Crocker, who waited for the President after the service.

Judd's father walked up to him, and he did not offer his hand. He just said softly, "I wonder, sir, whose son has the greater honor, yours or mine?"

ACKNOWLEDGMENTS

F OR MY FOURTH MILITARY NOVEL, MY PRINCIPAL
adviser was again Admiral Sir John "Sandy" Woodward, who
was thus obliged to steer me through the dangerous waters of the
China seas in a large nuclear submarine.

Where I wanted to go was often impossible. "Depth, man,
depth, for heaven's sake watch your depth!" Will I ever forget his
admonishments as he paced the office glaring at the charts? While
I tried to grapple with the subtleties of English prose, he mostly
talked to me as if I were a petty officer third class wrestling with
the conn.

But the admiral and I have sailed difficult literary waters before,
and somehow we made our way around the course. I am deeply
indebted to him for his insights, incomparable knowledge of the
operation of a submarine, and, in this case, his knowledge of
nuclear physics. He's pretty good on the construction of a plot
too—radar-alert to the weak, the unlikely, and, to quote him again,
"the grotesquely impossible."

The highlight of writing one of these novels is, for me, the moment the admiral concludes months and months of scheming, criticizing, and checking with a curt nod and the words, "That'll do." I am sure his commanders in the 1982 Falklands War saw that decisive finality many times.

It's reassuring, of course, to have an ex–Battle Group commander, and the Royal Navy's former Flag Officer Submarines, in your corner. But no one ever said it was supposed to be easy.

For this book I also required expert guidance from officers who had commanded Special Forces. For obvious reasons, none of them ought to be named. However, I am profoundly grateful for their advice and insights into a large-scale assault action.

I thank also Anne Reiley for her eagle-eyed appraisal of certain Washington landmarks. And also my friend Ray McDwyer of Cavan, Ireland, for providing me with a haven on the south side of Dublin City, where I annually carry out the lonely task of writing a 400-page novel.

Patrick Robinson